THE
DEVIL'S
DICTIONARY

Last Tango in Cyberspace

The Future Is Faster Than You Think: How Converging Technologies Are Transforming Business, Industries, and Our Lives (with Peter H. Diamandis)

The Art of Impossible: A Peak Performance Primer

Stealing Fire: How Silicon Valley, the Navy SEALs, and Maverick Scientists Are Revolutionizing the Way We Live and Work (with Jamie Wheal)

Tomorrowland: Our Journey from Science Fiction to Science Fact

Bold: How to Go Big, Create Wealth, and Impact the World (with Peter H. Diamandis)

The Rise of Superman: Decoding the Science of Ultimate Human Performance

Abundance: The Future Is Better Than You Think (with Peter H. Diamandis)

A Small Furry Prayer: Dog Rescue and the Meaning of Life

West of Jesus: Surfing, Science, and the Origins of Belief

The Angle Quickest for Flight

THE
DEVIL'S
DICTIONARY

STEVEN
KOTLER

ST. MARTIN'S PRESS
NEW YORK

First published in the United States by St. Martin's Press, an imprint of St. Martin's Publishing Group

THE DEVIL'S DICTIONARY. Copyright © 2021 by Steven Kotler. All rights reserved. Printed in the United States of America. For information, address St. Martin's Publishing Group, 120 Broadway, New York, NY 10271.

www.stmartins.com

Library of Congress Cataloging-in-Publication Data

Names: Kotler, Steven, 1967- author.
Title: The devil's dictionary / Steven Kotler.
Description: First Edition. | New York : St. Martin's Press, 2021.
Identifiers: LCCN 2021027554 | ISBN 9781250202093 (hardcover) |
    ISBN 9781250202109 (ebook)
Subjects: GSAFD: Science fiction.
Classification: LCC PS3611.O749295 D48 2021 | DDC 813/.6—dc23
LC record available at https://lccn.loc.gov/2021027554

Our books may be purchased in bulk for promotional, educational, or business use. Please contact your local bookseller or the Macmillan Corporate and Premium Sales Department at 1-800-221-7945, extension 5442, or by email at MacmillanSpecialMarkets@macmillan.com.

First Edition: 2021

10 9 8 7 6 5 4 3 2 1

FOR THE FURRY ONES, THE
DEPARTED, THE RANCHO
DE CHIHUAHUA CREW—
STILL MISSING ALL OF YOU

ARE WE?

WE ARE.

ARE WE?

WE ARE.

THE WAITING.

—Green Day

PART I

PRE-INCIDENT, FOUR MONTHS AGO,
LONDON

People," says Ramen, like they're some kind of disease.

He jabs the air with his chopsticks, pointing at something behind Lion's left shoulder.

Ramen is ancient, Asian, and given to blaring Billy Idol out of the cheap speakers duct-taped to the top of his decrepit food cart. He wears an old chef's coat over a dirty T-shirt, the sleeves pushed back, revealing arms flecked with burns and scars. Still, there's truth in his advertising: Ramen makes ramen. "Best in London," according to the sign, even if you have to sit in the cold rain, under a cheap plastic awning, on the rotting edge of Chinatown, to enjoy it.

Rotting—that is definitely the right word.

Whatever else Chinatown has been, it isn't that anymore. The place stinks of basic needs gone horribly wrong. The streets are crowded, loud and plastered with living screen billboards, their ceaseless motion lending the air a kind of liquid shimmer. The whole mad crush gives Lion a headache. Still, he knows, if you need to score a drug like Evo, Chinatown is definitely the spot.

"People," repeats Ramen, jabbing the air again.

This time, Lion takes the hint. Despite a mouthful of spicy glass noodles, he sets down his spoon, pushes back from the counter, and spins around to look at the street behind him.

It's a blur of bodies. And it's London: so always this relentless drizzle.

Lion glances right and left, but sees only a parade of cheap plastic raincoats, ratty umbrellas, and living screen billboards. Then he spots them. It's their stillness that gives them away, an anti-pattern set against this tide of motion. On the sidewalk, about fifteen paces to his left, two Chinese men stand frozen in the rain, staring straight at him.

Both are young, both wear black clothes, but that's where the resemblance ends. One has hair angled into five tall spikes, each dyed a Chernobyl yellow. The other looks like he's just out of boarding school: black sneakers, black satin jacket, black Buddy Holly glasses, and a face like a ten-year-old.

But, you know, the kind of ten-year-old who carries a gun.

Before Lion can react, the universe does it for him. The same instant he catches sight of the duo, a momentary hush falls across Chinatown. It's a cosmic timing thing, one of those impossible possibles: a hundred conversations silenced at once. The only sound is the music blaring from the speakers and an old whore giggling from the edge of a nearby alley.

"In the midnight hour," sings Billy Idol, "she cried more, more, more."

The whore says, "Baby, ain't nobody giving blow jobs for bitcoin these days. That's so 2020."

The guy with five spikes for hair whispers to the baby-faced guy with Buddy Holly glasses, leaves his spot on the sidewalk, and saunters toward the food cart. He looks high on something fast. There's a shiver in his step and a hard twitch to his eyes.

Lion slides a hand inside his jacket, finds the holster, and slips his fingers through the cold metal rings of his death punch. It's the very first weapon he's ever had to carry. But since the Splinter—which is a word Lion has come to despise—he's just trying to be careful.

His death punch is the newer model, stainless nano-steel flex rings, better hydraulics, more precise delivery. Penelope gave it to Lion before he left. The older version, she'd said, you hit the trigger, the electric pistons came out so hard they could kill. This newer one, the one Lion is gripping, it's just supposed to maim.

Rain drizzles off the plastic awning, pooling in the street. Sidestepping the puddle, Five Spikes crosses to stand near Ramen, between the back of the food cart and the corner of the building, his motorcycle boot resting on the edge of a grease bucket.

Ramen is famine thin, like the weight just never came back. His eyes are tired, his bones frail, and other than the word *people,* which Ramen just said twice, Lion's never heard him say a thing. But Ramen doesn't like anyone this close to him. He sets down the chopsticks, picks up a large knife, and starts sharpening the blade against the cold blue light of a laser-grinder.

Five Spikes smiles at the threat, leans in closer, and says something guttural. The language sounds like one of those newer poly-tribe dialects, the mashed-up lingo that pervades the street. This particular vernacular could be West Coast American hip-hop slang crossed with something Asian, but Five Spikes is speaking too softly for Lion to make out the words.

Ramen says something back, then sets down the knife and picks up his chopsticks. Tension fades from the scene. The twitch that Lion's feeling, maybe that's just street paranoia. Maybe this has nothing to do with him.

Lion relaxes his grip on the death punch, slides his bowl back in front of him, and goes heads-down into the soup. But before he can shovel a slice of tofu into his mouth, Ramen's chopsticks poke the air again, this time near his chest.

Lion looks up to find both Ramen and Five Spikes glaring at him.

Five Spikes says a few words, Ramen translates. "He say, you em-tracker."

Lion feels a rush of adrenaline.

After the Splinter, he needed to vanish. So Penelope asked Sir Richard for a serious favor, and Lion emptied his bank account to pay for the scrubbing. His name, his image, his early history as an investigative journalist, his middle history as one of the world's first em-trackers, his more recent history at the center of the Sietch Tabr controversy—one of the bigger drug scandals turned cultural uprisings in recent blah-blah-blah—all of it supposedly AI-erased from the net.

Lion tries to stay calm, covering his surprise with a spoonful of noodles to the mouth, chewing slowly. "Tell him I'm eating," he says eventually, eyes flat.

Five Spikes snarls a response. This time the dialect registers. East Asian poly-tribe, what the kids call Six Nation Speak. Lion knows the lingo, every good em-tracker does, but wanting to see how this plays out, he waits for Ramen to translate.

"He say, Go home, Lion Zorn. No more here. He say, London not safe for em-tracker."

"Tell me about it," says Lion, sliding his hand back inside his jacket.

But before he can jam his fingers back inside the grip of the death punch, Five Spikes catches sight of something in the distance. His eyes go wide. Then he makes a hard slashing motion with his hand, darts sideways, and disappears. Buddy Holly glasses must have done the same. By the time Lion spins around to look, they've both vanished into the rain.

He glances up and down the street, seeing thug life in every direction. The menacing business of pleasure. Tourists searching for a very different kind of vacation, the dealers who service them, the street vendors who take a cut to look the other way, the tired, the lonely, but none of them interested in him.

Yet, when he turns back to the counter, Ramen is interested. He's standing directly in front of Lion, not smiling.

"Rebel, rebel," he says, "you finish noodles, you no come back."

Lion nods, slurping one final gulp of soup into his mouth. He's not angry. No one needs his kind of trouble, least of all an ancient man wearing a plastic name tag that reads *Ramen,* serving ramen in Chinatown.

Lion sets down his spoon and pushes back from his stool. Just as he's about to walk away, he feels a chopstick poke in the shoulder and turns around.

"You want Evolution?" says Ramen.

Lion blinks. He'd asked three days ago, like he was told to, but Ramen hadn't said a word. He'd come back every day since, and Ramen hadn't said anything then, either. Now he says, "Evo-loo-shun," giving the syllables a different twist.

The accent, plus it's been a little while since Lion's heard anyone use the drug's full name. It takes him a second. Then he gets it. Evo, short for Evolution, short for the first clue he's actually found.

"That would be helpful," he says, trying to sound casual.

Ramen points his chopsticks toward the giggling whore.

"You want evolution, you go ask Sharijee."

"Sharijee?"

"Sharijee," repeats Ramen, with a gap-toothed grin. "Sharijee all the evolution you can handle."

I AM THE SINGULARITY

come here on boat, now I own boat."

The billboard is driving Lion crazy. It's another living screen, an advertisement for one of those info-marketers turned self-help gurus, Chang Zee, who seems to have self-helped himself to damn near every piece of real estate in this part of London. Like seven different billboards in sight.

But this is where Sharijee wanted to meet: in the rain, beside the "Chang Zee billboard," at 11:37 P.M. She was very precise. There's a holographic clock tower in the courtyard to his left, the ghost projection reading 11:58.

So now Lion's cold, wet, and precisely annoyed.

All seven Chang Zee billboards shift again. They must be synched. And Zee's version of self-help must involve biohacking. The screens alternate between scenes of Zee's wealth and fame and scenes of his ongoing transformation. A yacht somewhere tropical and Zee, shirtless, surrounded by bikini-clad women. Cut to Zee onstage, in a flowy white shirt, tribal jewelry, a cashmere scarf, leading a packed crowd of nearly five thousand through his Zen-Christ Tantra Turbo-Boost Executive World Beater Retreat. Cut to a sliver of nano-mesh floating in a blue gel, viewed through an electron microscope, then sucked up into the needle tip of a syringe and injected into Chang Zee's carotid artery.

"I don't believe in the Singularity," says Zee to the camera. "I am the Singularity."

"Fuck this," says Lion, starting to walk away. The thought of Kendra and Ibrahim stops him.

He can't help wondering: Are they already dead?

YOU TRIP EVOLUTION?

Lion used to be a journalist, but that was a lifetime ago. Now he's an empathy tracker, an em-tracker for short.

Em-tracking is a talent—though they once called it a "syndrome"—tied to a recent genetic mutation. It appeared in the early twenty-first century, in a thin slice of the population, usually in their late teens, often as the result of an emotionally charged inciting incident. A few months after the incident, the brains of em-trackers show significant rewiring: acute perceptual sensitivity, rapid pattern recognition, hyper-mirror-neuron activity. It's a long list of changes with one major result: a wildly expanded sense of empathy.

Em-trackers feel for all people, of course, but they also feel for plants, animals, and ecosystems. Their empathy is more than individual, it's cultural. They can feel how cultures collide and blend, the mash-up of minds and memes, the winners and losers and whatever truth remains. In Lion's case, he's like a cultural prediction engine—a lie detector for potential possible futures.

It's a useful skill in today's competitive business market.

About three months before Lion came to Chinatown to find Ramen, Kendra and Ibrahim went to San Francisco to find him. They showed up at Lion's door, wanting to hire him for his empathic abilities.

"You're both em-trackers," Lion had responded. "Why do you need my help?"

"Sietch Tabr" was Ibrahim's answer.

"Fuck that," said Lion, starting to shut the door.

Ibrahim, a preppy in a tartan plaid turban, wedged a bright green penny loafer into the jamb. "You've got expertise . . ."

Kendra finished his sentence: "We've got a serious problem."

Sietch Tabr is what sent Lion into hiding in the first place. Technically, it's a novel psychopharmaceutical that produces the same kind of hyper-empathy found in em-trackers. Neurologically, the drug alters everything from thalamic sensory gating to foundational reward chemistry, obliterating all traces of in-group/out-group bias, while greatly increasing a user's ability to detect nonverbal social cues—which is why Sietch Tabr hit the market as a treatment for autism.

But that wasn't the issue.

The issue was that Sietch Tabr has serious psychedelic side effects. While drugs like LSD and MDMA can produce a hive-mind sensation, Sietch Tabr does the same; only the merger crosses species lines, allowing humans and animals to become one. Take the drug while hanging out with your golden retriever, you trip golden retriever. Take the drug with elephants, you trip elephant.

Sietch Tabr alters emotions, but it also changes pheromones. Animals scent humans as friend, not foe. Take the drug with tigers, you not only trip tiger, but the tigers treat you as kin. Scientists describe it as "artificially induced bidirectional cross-species empathy," but Lion dubbed it "empathy for all."

That was the description that stuck.

Five years ago, Sir Richard, the billionaire tycoon who owned the company that brought Sietch Tabr to market, hired Lion to em-track a crime scene. That's how it started. It ended with Lion going rogue and going public. He revived his old reporter's skills to write one final article, telling the world the truth about Sietch Tabr.

So much for good intentions.

Sir Richard made bank, for sure, but Sietch Tabr became a street drug of epic proportions. Like acid in the 1960s, MDMA in the 1990s, and DMT in the 2010s, one giant consciousness-raising clusterfuck.

Lion's fault? Maybe, maybe not. But he was definitely the one who told the world about Sietch Tabr, and it was definitely his little article that kicked off that clusterfuck. Lion wanted nothing to do with the mess. That was why he paid a fortune for the scrubbing and spent two years in hiding and wasn't exactly excited to find Kendra and Ibrahim at his door.

"I have expertise in what, exactly?"

"Have you heard of Evo?" asked Kendra. "They're calling it the next step."

"It's a psychedelic," clarified Ibrahim. "Remember ibogaine?"

"West African," said Lion, digging through the memory banks. "You trip for like twenty-four hours and have some kind of whole life review. What about it?"

"Evo is ibogaine in the same way that Sietch Tabr is MDMA."

"Sietch Tabr is like MDMA times a thousand."

"And that's not even the problem," said Ibrahim.

Lion chewed on this for a moment. Sietch Tabr produced the Splinter, the great fracturing of the poly-tribes, or so sayeth the hype machine.

Maybe. Maybe not.

Humans are a social animal, but it's a double-edged sword. The very thing that binds us together is what drives us apart. The neurochemicals that create the emotions of love, friendship, and fidelity are exclusionary by design. It's never just us. It's always us versus them.

Sietch Tabr is a glaring example. The drug creates cross-species empathy. It bonds humans to animals, but it's a bridge that divides.

Humans who bond with animals versus humans who don't bond with animals or humans who bond with *this* animal versus humans who bond with *that* animal. And plants. And ecosystems. Us versus them becomes us versus them versus them versus them. The Splinter.

But if Evo's anything like that . . .

Lion refocused. "How does it work?"

"No one knows," says Kendra. "But what it does?" She looked up and down the street. "That's a story better told inside."

He let them in.

They sat in the kitchen. Lion drank coffee, Ibrahim drank tea, Kendra drank water and filled in the details.

"Ibogaine gives you a whole life review," she said. "With Evo, you get a whole species review. The trip starts at the beginning of evolution and plays the tape forward. Different people experience different developmental paths. One arc goes from bacteria, viruses, and protozoa into insects, dinosaurs, and birds. Another goes small mammals, large mammals, humans."

"You trip evolution?"

Ibrahim nodded.

"No shit," said Lion. "I mean, with our abilities, you fire up those circuits . . . I mean, no shit. When can I try some?"

"That's the other part of the problem," said Kendra. "We did."

"We were in London," explained Ibrahim. "Remember Raj?"

Lion shakes his head.

"You met him at that UCLA conference. Em-trackers helping the CIA break up a sex trafficking ring—that was his talk."

"Barely," said Lion, recalling a skinny Indian in a skinny suit, not sure if he's remembering right. "Raj gave you Evo?"

"Sort of," said Ibrahim. "All he knew was that you tripped evolution, and that people were throwing Evo parties near Chinatown. He'd been invited to one, but with his fat government contract and no idea if Evo showed up on drug screens, he didn't want to chance it."

"But you did."

Kendra nodded, grinding her heel into the floor.

"How was it?"

"That's the thing," explained Ibrahim. "Everyone else seemed to trip. But Kendra and me, we dropped into . . ."

"K-hole hell," said Kendra, "mixed with electroshock therapy."

"About sums it up," agreed Ibrahim. "Like a twenty-four-hour fuzz-out. Nothing. No self. Just this lonely feeling of being trapped somewhere and tormented by electricity. This buzzing in the head, the brain. Like someone was going synapse by synapse with a stun gun. And afterward . . ."

"Afterward," sighed Kendra, giving her heel one final grind, "we couldn't em-track for shit."

"How is that even possible?"

"It came back," Kendra explained. "A month before anything changed, six before I was a little close to normal."

"Close to normal is as far as we've come," said Ibrahim. "I've got the involuntary stuff. The automatic reactions. Show me a leather jacket and I still get weepy. But I couldn't begin to tell you anything else."

Lion nodded. Em-trackers have powerful involuntary responses to eco-cruelty. The reactions are different in different people. The sight of a logging truck can send some em-trackers into hysterics. Ibrahim got weepy around leather. For Lion, his allergy was to taxidermy. Put him in the room with dead animal heads and he'd just start puking.

"We've been blunted," continued Kendra.

"Mate," said Ibrahim, "this is where you come in. We need you to em-track Evo. We can pay you." He laid a thick envelope on the table. "It's not a charity thing."

"We'd do it, but we can't," added Kendra. "Plus, aren't fucked-up psychedelics kind of your thing?"

Not anymore, thought Lion.

Then again, he was broke—so he took the job.

And it wasn't much of a job, at least not for the first few weeks. All Lion learned was that there was little to learn. Evo was less a drug than the rumor of a drug. As far as he could tell, the psychedelic had showed up five times, with long gaps between appearances. There were a pair of Evo parties in Seattle a couple years back, then nothing for six months. After that the drug resurfaced in Tokyo and São Paulo simultaneously, sticking around for a month in each place, then vanishing again. Finally, a few months ago, it arrived in London, this time staying for six weeks, which was when Ibrahim and Kendra attended that party. Afterward, Evo vanished for good, Ibrahim and Kendra showed up at Lion's door, and he took the job.

Two weeks later, the job went sideways.

Both Kendra and Ibrahim disappeared. Their phones dead, social media inactive, and no one, not at any of the virtual gatherings, had heard from them. Lion backtracked Kendra to an apartment in Dublin, but she'd paid the year in advance, and her roommate hadn't seen her in months. Ibrahim lived in a top-floor walk-up attached to a mosque in Liverpool. Lion bribed the super, had him look inside. No one home was all he learned.

Afterward, he got nervous. While Lion barely knew Kendra, he had history with Ibrahim. So he spent another month tracking down Raj, who didn't know much more than that address in Chinatown, the spot where they were throwing the party. And a name: Ramen.

"Ramen?" Lion asked.

"He's a Chinatown fixture," said Raj before hanging up. "You'll know him when you see him."

"Know him how?"

"He wears a name tag that says *Ramen*."

So Lion traded some of Ibrahim's cash for a plane ticket to London, spent three days trying to find Ramen, and another three trying to get him to talk. Then Ramen told Lion about Sharijee, and Sharijee told Lion to wait beneath this damn billboard.

So here he is in the rain, still waiting.

Above him, the billboard starts to repeat itself: "I come here on boat—now I own boat."

This is when Lion feels them more than sees them. It's an em-tracker's hunch, a kind of cellular awareness, a felt-sense of another, and tinged with menace.

It takes him only a second to spot the threat. It's the same Chinese duo, Five Spikes and Buddy Holly. They're half-hidden across the street, tucked behind yet another Chang Zee billboard. Buddy Holly looks cold, wet, and determined. Five Spikes holds a stun baton in his left hand.

They're both staring straight at Lion.

EXPENSIVE KINK

Lion thinks about fighting. Apparently his brain doesn't like the odds, because the next second he's fleeing. Full speed and in the rain, his boots slapping wet pavement.

He sprints down the block and around the corner, but the street Lion finds himself on is quiet residential. It's too empty to do much good. He needs crowds. He needs people. He needs a map. Instead, he darts halfway down the block and tucks in beside a minivan, risking a backward glance.

They're still chasing him. Buddy Holly is about fifty yards back, passing beneath a streetlamp in front of a brownstone. Five Spikes is about ten feet ahead of his companion, stalking the middle of the road. In less than thirty seconds, they're going to reach Lion's hiding spot behind the minivan.

He whirls around, checking out nearby houses. But all the driveways lead to chain-link fences and locked doors. Other than garbage cans—nope, there really is no place to hide.

Lion breaks cover and dashes down the street, passing shuttered storefronts at full speed. In his peripheral, he sees a pizza delivery robot, like a squat coffin with wheels, red running lights and some kind of glitch in the circuits. As he speeds by, it bangs its nose into a brick wall, repeatedly.

Reaching the end of the block, Lion rounds the corner and runs straight into heavy traffic. Three lanes of busy. He brakes hard and hop steps, waiting for an autonomous taxi to pass. His legs twitch with adrenaline. He tries to slow his breathing, then glances back.

"Fuck."

Five Spikes is faster than expected, and closing fast.

Spinning toward the street, Lion finds the taxi gone, but there's a double-decker bus bearing down. Yet the thought of that stun baton . . .

Lion leaps from the curb before he can think twice. Dropping into full video game mode, he catches sights in snatches: the dirty steel grille of the bus; a burka-clad woman, wide-eyed, sitting in the front seat of the upper deck; a pothole in the street to his left, filled with rotten, foamy runoff.

Lion jukes past the bus, but a black slick on the road nearly costs him his footing. Twisting to avoid it, he stumbles into the next lane. The screech of brakes, horns blaring. He regains his balance just in time to see a baby-blue Volvo screaming toward him.

Lion plants his left foot with a grunt, then springs right, launching himself across the final lane and into the path of a well-dressed man riding a Vespa scooter. Volvo back draft blasts the back of his neck. Lion swerves right, nearly clipping the Vespa's front tire as he leaps for the sidewalk.

"Ya numpty wankstain!" shouts the driver in his wake.

Lion slows to a jog, his heart still pounding, but the driver's words still echo in his brain. "Ya numpty wankstain" is the kind of thing Penelope tends to say, especially when angry. Being Scottish, being Lion's sometime girlfriend, Penelope is frequently angry.

Not the right time for nostalgia, thinks Lion, glancing around to get his bearings. North and south offer rotting industrial or quiet residential. Neither are what he needs. There's an old man walking a pair of pugs to the east, and a bakery doing a brisk business in scones to the west.

Lion chooses west, heading toward the bakery. He weaves into the crowd, slipping between a pair of couples out for a late-night snack, then comes out the other side at a trot. Passing a row of closed shops, he gets halfway down the block before noticing a tiny, dark alley, half-hidden behind a Dumpster, running between two oversize warehouses.

Hard to spot if you didn't know it was there.

Lion glances back but doesn't see his pursuers. He sprints into the alley. It's two feet wide and stinks of garbage. When he reaches the other side, he takes a sharp right and pulls up short.

Did he just run in a circle?

In front of him sits that same damn Chang Zee billboard, this time showing the billionaire paragliding above the Serengeti, a herd of zebras grazing calmly below. And beneath the billboard, stepping out of a cab and straightening her platinum blond wig: Sharijee.

"Sharijee!" shouts Lion, nearly pushing her back into the cab.

The taxi belongs to one of those holdout London cabbies, an actual human driving an actual car.

"Please drive," says Lion, sliding inside.

"Spot of trouble?" asks Sharijee, drawing out the s into a slight hiss.

"Spot of trouble," he says, breathing hard.

The cab slips into traffic. The driver catches Lion's eye in the rearview mirror. "Where to, mate?"

He doesn't have a clue.

Sharijee glances over at him, clucks her tongue, and makes a decision. "Head north," she says.

The cab drives down the street. Lion slides to his left, giving himself a clear view of the rearview mirror. Then he slips down in the seat, hoping to watch the reflection of the street in the mirror while staying out of sight.

In the mirror, Five Spikes dashes into the center of the road, an arc of electricity hissing at the tip of his stun baton.

Lion slides down further, trying to be inconspicuous about it.

"Baby," says Sharijee, glancing over at him, "this kind of kink, on the Sharijee menu, this kind of kink gets expensive."

The cab turns a corner and Lion straightens up. "Like I said, I'm just looking for information."

"No, baby, you're looking for information about Evo. That's expensive kink."

Lion reaches toward his pocket. Sharijee reaches for her own, raising a well-plucked eyebrow. She's probably not much older than him, maybe late thirties, but she's been street-aged and looks fifty. Definitely poly-tribe. Balinese bone structure, Lebanese skin tone, Mexican ladyboy clothes, yet wearing expensive Tyko retinal projection AR glasses while working a beat in Chinatown—which might make her batshit crazy, but definitely makes her strapped.

"Just getting my wallet," says Lion.

His wallet is black synth-rubber, and packed with American hundreds, which, in his experience, has always been the international currency of all things batshit crazy. He lays three bills on the seat between them.

Sharijee shakes her head.

He lays out another hundred. "Just want to talk, nothing more."

"Take us to Wood Green," Sharijee tells the cabbie. "Not the dodgy side, the posh side, or close to the posh side."

"Wood Green?" snorts the driver. "That's North London. Ain't been nothing posh there since the Krauts bombed the place."

"We call them Germans now," says Sharijee.

"Wasn't my point."

"Baby, we wish your golden chariot to take us to a nasty pub on a nasty street with a nasty name. It's called Defenestration." She plucks another hundred out of Lion's wallet. "But we're tipping well."

"Holy crap," says Lion. "Defenestration?"

"You know it?" asks Sharijee.

"Worse," he says. "I know the owner."

YEH BOUNCE

Defenestration is a long, narrow room, spray-painted matte black, and lit only by a holo-projection on the back wall: a three-dimensional slow-motion parade of men and women getting thrown out of windows.

Another sign of Two Tone's dark sense of humor.

Defenestration is literally the act of throwing someone out a window. It was once a standard practice in Europe, or standard enough to merit its own word. Now it's a Rasta-biker bar in North London, owned by a Jamaican guy who made a killing selling meth to speed-metal bands, invested in crypto, and turned his bitcoin into real estate, or so the story goes.

Freddy "Two Tone" Sarrows runs the joint. He's tall, bald, and jet-black—his skin so dark it almost looks purple. But that wasn't how he got his nickname. They called him Two Tone because someone gouged out his left eye in a fight, and he replaced it with one of those early syn-bio fashion hacks, a proto-cat's eye, from back before they got the genetics right. Now one eye is lazy and feline, the other light brown. Two Tone.

On an earlier trip to London, Lion had met Two Tone backstage at a death reggae dreadstep show, back when Peter Tosh meets Slipknot was still a thing. Two Tone told Lion that the after-party was being held at his new club, Defenestration.

"We got us a trade," he'd said proudly. "I get high-quality public relations for my new establishment. The band gets high-quality party favors, plus full beef security."

"Full beef?"

Two Tone smiled, flashing gold teeth. "'Cause, cuz, Two Tone ain't opposed to smackin' a bitch up."

"Good to know," said Lion.

"By bitch, I ain't being, whatchamacallit, misogynist. Don't have to have a pussy to be a bitch, just gotta be a pussy." Two Tone flashed more gold teeth. "Anyway, gonna be full riot. You should, most def, be there."

Lion had passed on the party, but Two Tone was hard to forget. It was also hard to forget Defenestration, and how Two Tone had laughed a little too hard when he asked for an explanation of the name.

"How we do around here," Two Tone explained. "If you screw up, we kite you out a fifth-story window. Smash bones into muscles at high speeds—yeh bounce. Seventh story, splat like a watermelon. But fifth story, the skin holds, yeh bounce."

Now, almost a decade later, walking into Defenestration, Lion experiences a dark mirror déjà vu—the experience of an experience he didn't want to experience the first time around.

And he's not liking it much.

The room is dark and the music loud. Heavy dreadstep thumps out of hidden speakers. He doesn't see Two Tone. He doesn't see Chinese gangsters. Then again, in the gloom, it's nearly impossible to see anything.

Sharijee's AR glasses must have a night-vision setting. On six-inch platforms, she glides through the crowd without bashing into anyone. They cross to a dimly lit back corner, taking a seat at a heavily scarred wooden table.

Once they're settled, Lion asks, "Why are we here?"

"You ain't the only one who knows the owner," says Sharijee.

"You know Two Tone?"

"Sharijee, baby, Sharijee gets around. I'm a high-mileage hookup.

What you give up in youth, I make up for . . ."—licking her lips—"in expertise."

A waitress appears out of the darkness. Lion orders a stout. Sharijee orders a screaming orgasm.

After the waitress leaves, Sharijee says, "Don't you love those words? *Screaming orgasm*. So rare. Like an extinct species."

"Evo," says Lion, changing the subject.

"No one can get that shit, baby. It showed up for a couple of parties. Then it was ghost."

"So why'd Ramen tell me to talk to you?"

"I was at one of the parties. Weird party, dark vibes." She places her hand on his thigh. "You know, for a couple more of those hundred-dollar bills, Sharijee could give *you* a screaming orgasm."

Lion thinks for a moment. He needs information. Yet Sharijee seems hardwired for the hard sell. He could em-track his way out of the situation but using his skills in this way always leaves him feeling a little lonely. Then again, Kendra and Ibrahim are missing and he was just chased through London by the Wu-Tang Clan—so that settles it.

He looks at Sharijee and takes a breath, giving his pattern recognition system a moment to dial in the right frequency. "Don't sell yourself short," he says eventually. "A Sharijee orgasm—I'd be howling like a wolf at the moon."

She gives him a look of mild surprise.

He continues, "Pride in one's work—that's never a bad thing."

"I've not heard it put that way before."

Lion smiles. Whenever people find out he's an em-tracker, they always ask what it feels like—"being an em-tracker"—because they think it's like ESP. But there's nothing extrasensory about his talent. Lion thinks it's more like an allergy, a hypersensitivity to emotional cues and where they lead, coupled to an expanded sense of empathy. In most of us, we have to work past our sense of self to find another, but Lion's sense of self already includes the other, so that expanded sense of empathy—if he takes the time to dial in the frequency—he finds it automatically.

"I travel a lot," Lion continues. "For work. I meet all kinds of people. You know what's rare in this world? Stupid people. They're out there, but not in the numbers that most believe. But you know what is out there, what is everywhere? People who speak different languages. Even if they speak the same language, they speak different languages—know what I mean?"

Sharijee nods slowly.

"But," he continues, "if you can figure out what language someone speaks, and talk to them about something they truly care about, pretty quickly you figure out everybody's smart about something. Taking pride in one's work, that's never a bad thing."

Sharijee smiles, lifts her hand off Lion's lap, and sets it back on the table.

He holds her gaze for another second. "Please tell me about that party."

"It was a weekend thing," says Sharijee.

"Weekend?"

"There were about twelve girls. We all got hired to work the room. They paid cash, up front. It didn't seem so bad at first."

"This was in Chinatown?"

"Near Chinatown. A warehouse. It looked abandoned from the outside, but it was swanky inside. No windows, but done up proper. Holo-candelabras, velvet couches, an uptown crowd."

"What kind of uptown?"

"Couple of em-trackers, sprinkle of poly-tribe, and a bunch of Asian moneymen. Mostly, though, it was London straights out for a dark-side joyride. And everyone took the ride." She taps her nose. "We all got two squirts."

"Evo's a nasal spray?"

Sharijee shrugs. "I saw a couple people popping pills, but that could have been anything. Everyone else got the spray."

"What happened?"

"The moneymen split. The bastards locked the doors behind them.

We ripped the place apart trying to get out. Found video cameras in the walls. Old-school stuff. Film. Nothing digital. Right around the time we were going for the fire axes, Evo—the drug—kicked in like a rocket. Took the fight right out of us. I parked my ass on a couch for a day and dreamed of slime, worms, and fish."

Lion thinks for a second. "You had phones. Before the drugs kicked in, why didn't you call for help?"

"Our phones were confiscated at the door. Like a coat check. They got dumped in a Faraday. Everybody got a ticket."

"The trip lasted all day?"

"Just about. When I came down, it was nighttime again. My head hurt, like something had fried it, but I was sitting on the same couch. The em-trackers were gone, the girls, the straights, all accounted for. But the doors were open, so we split. Like I said, weird party."

Lion pulls out his phone, showing Sharijee a photo of Kendra and Ibrahim. "Were these the em-trackers?"

"No." She shakes her head. "Four Thor-types. Nordic. Swedish, maybe. I only talked to one of them for a second."

The waitress arrives with their drinks, Lion's stout, Sharijee's screaming orgasm, and a couple of shots of bourbon.

"The shots are from the owner," she says, pointing toward the bar.

Lion glances up and sees Two Tone leaning against a stool, wearing a tight black T-shirt and a pair of living snakeskin pants that seem to undulate on their own. He's holding a shot of bourbon in his hand.

"To your health, Lion Zorn," he says, lifting the glass.

"Two Tone," says Lion, lifting his shot, "your health as well."

"My health," says Two Tone, walking over to their table, shooing the waitress away with a flick of his fingers, "ain't the question."

"The question?"

"'Cause, cuz . . ."—smiling that same gold-toothed grin—"I heard you're hunting Evo."

"Shhh," says Sharijee, lifting a finger to her lips. "Maybe we can find a place more discreet?" She points at Lion. "Might be better for his health."

Two Tone drinks the shot, sets his glass on the bar, and starts to walk away. Lion ignores the bad feeling in his gut and follows him into the gloom. Sharijee brings up the rear.

They snake through the bar, threading behind the holo-projection, then stepping past a thick black curtain. Lion finds himself in a long, dim hallway. Two Tone walks halfway down, stops at a closed door, enters an eleven-digit code in a keypad, waits for a click, then steps inside. Lion follows, with Sharijee crowding behind.

The room is pitch-black.

"Baby," says Sharijee, closing the door and clicking the dead bolt, "will you please turn on a light."

"Alexa," says Two Tone, "lights."

The lights snap on. Lion blinks, seeing a much fancier office than expected: tall brick walls, sleek furniture, and serious tech gear. It looks like Two Tone's got a small server farm running a stacked holo-monitor display worthy of a three-letter agency. Then he notices two Chinese men standing across the room from him. One has hair the color of nuclear waste. The other wears Buddy Holly glasses and is pointing a rifle directly at him.

"You should have go home, Lion Zorn," says Buddy Holly. "We tell Ramen tell you, go home. Chinatown not safe for em-tracker."

Then he pulls the trigger.

Something blasts into the right side of Lion's chest, hard enough to make him grunt. He looks down, expecting to find a bullet hole. Instead, he sees a tranquilizer dart.

"What the . . . ?"

"Good night, baby," says Sharijee.

"Smack a bitch up," says Two Tone.

Lion crumples, unconscious, to the floor.

ion wakes to a grim nightmare.

He's tied to a four-poster bed, faceup and spread-eagled. The room is filled with blinding bright light. His shoulders have been propped up onto pillows, so he's half sitting, yet completely immobilized. His hands and feet are locked into place with professional flexsteel restraints, his head sandwiched into a surgical vise and his eyes winched open, lids held up by some kind of metal contraption that glimmers in his peripheral.

Lion twists against the restraints, trying to kick free.

Nothing budges.

Off to his right side, a man's voice mutters, "He awake," in heavily accented English.

Lion tries to spin toward the sound, but he's pinned.

To his left, he hears footsteps, followed by the click of a switch. A motor starts to run, like an old movie camera. The lights dim, and Lion can see again, which is when the rest of the room comes into view.

"Fuck me," he says.

Lion knows where he is. Worse, he knows what's going to happen next.

Em-trackers have *inciting incidents*, which are the emotionally charged events that bring on their talent. But em-trackers also have *confirming incidents*, which are when those automatic responses to eco-cruelty first arise.

Lion's *inciting incident* took place on a job in Jamaica, but that assignment morphed into something bigger and he left Jamaica and took his first trip to London. He was supposed to be there to facilitate a meeting between a couple of British airline executives and a handful of Rasta elders.

That conversation didn't go as planned.

The meeting was held in the Tartan Suite at Claridge's Hotel, in the heart of London's Mayfair district. Lion walked into the room and found himself inside the textbook definition of "overkill."

The suite was palatial, the walls covered in tartan green plaid wallpaper and dead animal heads. Deer, antelope, moose, red fox, Iberian lynx, three different Siberian tigers, a pair of Scottish wildcats, and in a distant corner, a family of puffins, arranged in a panorama.

Lion took one look around and started puking. Involuntary projectile vomiting, textbook em-tracker *confirming incident.*

This time, as soon as Lion recognizes the same tartan plaid wallpaper, he tries to slam his eyes shut. But they're wedged open, the lids locked into place. Then he sees a deer head, a ten-point buck mounted on an oval of polished mahogany, those sad doe eyes staring straight at him.

Lion tastes bile. His throat constricts as he tries to stifle the response. To his left, a man wearing doctor's scrubs and a mask steps into view. He has a pair of Buddy Holly glasses pushed high on his forehead and an ancient movie camera pressed to his right eye. Lion can make out the words Bolex H-11, in silver Helvetica printed across the side.

But that's all he has time to see.

An instant later, puke fires out of him.

Lion's head rocks forward and his neck stretches taut. He writhes against the restraints. In the strain, the metal prongs that hold open his eyes rip into his skin. A second later, the spasm subsides and Lion gasps for breath.

It's an awkward inhale, and it brings his lunch back into his throat.

He chokes, tries to cough, desperate to clear his windpipe. But his head is vise locked. He can't move, he can't breathe. His chest sears, his eyes start to roll back in their sockets. The second before his vision vanishes, Buddy Holly sets down the camera, reaches out a hand, and pinches his cheeks, right below the upper jawbone.

His mouth snaps open.

Two gloved fingers ram between his teeth, then down his throat. Buddy Holly swipes the vomit out of his mouth, clearing his airway.

Lion gasps a few times, but there's no relief. His eyes are still propped open. When his vision clears, the first thing he sees is a dead moose.

The sight brings on another spasm.

This time it goes on for too long and he starts to lose consciousness. The second before his world goes black, he feels his jaws snap open. Two fingers ram down his throat and clear his airway, once again.

PART II

POST-INCIDENT, FOUR DAYS AGO,
LOS ANGELES

Lion glances out the window of his Los Angeles hotel room. It's been about four months since his torture by taxidermy—what's he's come to call the Incident—and winter has arrived. Now it's February and forty degrees outside. Yet it's not much warmer inside.

Lion could turn up the heat, but the cold keeps him focused.

Trying to avoid hypothermia, he's bundled himself into a black hooded sweatshirt, black jeans, and a black watch cap. The cap is pulled low, but it doesn't hide the damage. The cuts over his eyes, where the metal prongs ripped into his lids, have healed, but there's a jagged scar below each eyebrow, like a child's drawing of a sideways lightning bolt.

The scars make him look angry.

He turns his attention back to the wall of his hotel room, where he's taped up an old-fashioned murder board. Arranged in concentric circles are three rings of photos and press clippings. Each clipping tells a different Evo story. Lion's been staring at them for hours, trying to em-track his way to a clue.

The debris from his effort litters the bed: a pack of rolling papers, a pouch of organic rolling tobacco, and a half ounce of marijuana— Sour Dictator Booty, according to the name on the label.

Em-trackers use marijuana to augment their talents. Certain strains cause the brain to release anandamide and dopamine. The former decreases anxiety, the latter increases pattern recognition. Add in the heightened focus that comes from nicotine and you have a potent combination for empathy tracking.

But not this time. No matter what he does, Lion can't seem to em-track his way to a clue.

He blames the weed.

For em-tracking, Lion's preferred strain is Ghost Trainwreck #69. Unfortunately, he placed his marijuana order through his recently acquired JOBZ, and their selection menu didn't offer much variety.

The JOBZ also sits on the bed, to the left of the rolling papers. It resembles an ancient iPhone, one from the era when Steve Jobs was still running that show—which is why it's called a JOBZ.

But it's not a phone, or not exactly.

A next-generation anonymizer, the JOBZ scrambles signal origins and disguises voices, essentially keeping the user off everyone's radar. Definitely illegal and ridiculously expensive, but it was the best Penelope could do, given the time frame and the circumstances.

As a bonus, the JOBZ comes with a built-in delivery service, which is how Lion ordered his weed. By dialing a number preprogrammed into contacts and uttering an ever-changing phrase buried in the settings folder, he unlocked an encrypted interface to a dark web drone delivery service. His marijuana arrived twenty minutes later, the package winch-lowered to avoid human contact, tucked inside a Faraday pouch.

That was a few weeks back. Since then, Lion has spent most days staring at his murder board, frustrated, unable to em-track, unable to solve the puzzle.

Still staring at his murder board, Lion notices a photo of Sealand 4. It must have been taken post-Splinter, after the former seasteading colony became a Sietch Tabr commune site. The image shows a top-down view of the northern edge of the original floating spur and the first seven colony rings. In the center, Lion can make out the preparatory stages of a freediving ritual, organized around the bright blue waters of the colony's main lagoon. There are three dozen participants and five servers, each carrying a tray containing silver straws and small piles of Sietch Tabr, already cut into easy-to-snort lines.

But it's not the five servers who catch his eye. It's the half image of a sixth, just at the edge of the photo, holding a dozen bottles of nasal spray in a wicker basket—a possible first sighting of Evo.

Lion studies the photo for a moment, then slides left to look at another, but a mirror on the wall grabs his attention. His scars still give him pause. Another chilly reminder of the Incident.

He shivers at the sight of them. The shivers seem to be a new addition to his growing list of startle responses, a supposedly "worse in em-trackers" PTSD reaction that he'd once written off as trauma hype.

That was then.

Lion moves on to a clipping about an Evo party in Seattle. It's from The Leary, a psychedelic fanboy site devoted to the scene, or really to the celebs who made the scene.

Reading off the names, Lion recognizes a few. Three catch his attention. Two men and a woman. All are multi-corns, the new plural of unicorn, or the latest crop of tech billionaires to crop up.

There's something familiar about the names. As he's stretching his brain to make the connection, his JOBZ begins to vibrate.

Lion glances down at the screen and sees a text slide into view.

Lorenzo, his best friend, seeking contact.

Ignoring the text, Lion turns back to the wall to study a photograph of the Burning Man riots, later known as the Thunderdome massacre, taken in the moments before the hackers gained full control of the flamethrowers. There were rumors that Evo was involved, but they remain unconfirmed.

He turns his attention to an article entitled "Mega-Linkages: An Ecological Idea Whose Time Has Come." It's about a series of panel discussions held at the Long Now Foundation in San Francisco. None of the panels were about Evo, but according to the article, the drug was mentioned repeatedly throughout the series.

Skimming the story, Lion finds nothing of interest for eight paragraphs.

In the ninth, he spots the same names, his three tech billionaires, all participants in a seminar about the Pacific Rim Mega-Linkage. Instead of writing out the words, the author used the acronym PRML, also noting that it's pronounced "primal."

Data bit finds data bit—Lion's seen this acronym before.

Grabbing the JOBZ, he clicks into his texts. He finds Penelope's screen and doesn't need to scroll any further. The text he wants is the last one she sent, which was also the first one she sent, arriving not long after that well-pierced messenger who initially dropped off the JOBZ.

Just nine words: "Sir Richard called in that favor—heading to PRML."

That's why he recognized the acronym.

On the bed, the JOBZ starts to vibrate again.

It's another missive from Lorenzo, another request for contact. Since the Incident, they've come in like clockwork.

"All right, Mom," says Lion, "I'll be right there."

Threat Level Orange

Lion slides on his brand-new pair of wire-rimmed Tyko AR glasses, the John Lennon model, with blue sapphire lenses and a few necessary customizations. It was his first purchase, after the JOBZ arrived, but delivery was delayed because he'd back-channeled his way into all sorts of XLR protection ware and paid extra for the "supposedly" uncrackable silencer uplink.

The mods took a while to install.

As a result, Lion's still not fully acquainted with the anonymizer. It takes him nine tries to link the JOBZ to his AR glasses. Try number seven is a total dud. Try eight takes him to a corporate espionage menu, sort of like Amazon for industrial spies. Try nine is the charm. It opens a Skype knock-off portal, a drop-down menu of peripheral devices, and his full contact list, which, he notices, have each been assigned a threat level.

Lorenzo is threat level orange.

Lion knows the JOBZ works off a cloud-based AI, and sure, doing social media scans to assign threat levels to the people on his contact list isn't—or isn't anymore—rocket science. Yet it reeks of stolen defense tech—and it doesn't take an em-tracker to know that can't be good.

Still, with the delayed delivery of his AR glasses, Lion hasn't had a conversation with anyone for a long time. How bad could threat level orange actually be?

Better than being alone with his thoughts, he decides.

Lion taps an ant-shaped button on the right arm, activates the microphone, and says, "Call Lorenzo."

A translucent image of Lorenzo pops into view. Not an avatar, rather a 3-D holo-rendering: his friend, in all his oversize glory, playing a gig somewhere, wearing a straw cowboy hat, brown Carhartts, and his ever-present aviator shades.

Lion recognizes the photo.

It's a wide shot of Hank Mudd and the K-Holes, taken long before the band got famous. Lorenzo's playing a pair of congas center stage. Hank's playing guitar to his left. The rest of the band is a blur in the back.

Suddenly the image resolves into the actual Lorenzo, wearing a black denim work shirt, a straw cowboy hat, and those same aviator shades. He's in his early sixties, with sandy blond hair and heavy jowls. The background is grayed out, which means Lorenzo's probably in a vehicle of some kind, as heavy motion in the holo-rendering tends to induce nausea in the viewer.

"If you've got 'em by the balls," says Lorenzo, by way of greeting, "their hearts and minds will follow."

When on tour, Lorenzo likes to limit most of his communication to quotes from the movie *Apocalypse Now,* which, he maintains, was once a very viable form of conversation.

But, as Lion points out, "That doesn't sound like *Apocalypse Now*."

"It's not," replies Lorenzo. "I'm on an *Apocalypse* fast. Since the Incident, until we find those fuckers, I'm strictly *All the President's Men*."

Lion smiles. *All the President's Men* is ancient reporter porn—a 1970s film about two journalists who take down a rotten president. Then he notices the grayed-out background again. "Where are you?"

"São Paulo. We're being driven around in armored cars, which Hank keeps bitching about."

"You can't smoke in the car?"

"Nope. Plus, we're a cow-punk band in an armored car—the whole thing clashes with his image." Lorenzo takes off his glasses and squints at Lion. "And where are you? The JOBZ scrambles the visual. All I get is your face floating in a sea of fuzz. Like little insects on speed."

"Still in Los Angeles. The same spot: Beverly Laurel Motor Hotel redux, the remodel above the place that used to be Swingers."

"I thought you were outta there."

"To where? Nobody takes cash, and these glasses burned through most of my crypto. Also, the hotel's psycho about privacy. Just say the word *selfie* and they throw you out."

"I can transfer more cheddar."

"You've transferred enough already." He touches his glasses. "You paid for my shades, my JOBZ, this hotel room, and there's still a little scratch left in the account. Plus, remember Sharijee?"

"Bitch-dot-com, who set you up."

"In London, she told me she was a *high-mileage hookup*. Turns out, it's not just a cute phrase. It's an actual service. Remember that Uber autonomous prostitution scandal in Dallas?"

"The robo-taxi brothel ring?"

"The feds never shut it down. Couldn't. When they backtracked the app code, it led to a distributed autonomous organization. All run by an AI somewhere, through, like, six layers of blockchain. When the feds took the Dallas fleet offline, the AI snuck out a backdoor and took the company global. Robo-taxi brothels on five continents.

High-Mileage Hookups. And get this, the Sharijee menu—that's a real thing, too. She wasn't talking about herself in the third person. There's an actual Sharijee menu. I accessed it through the JOBZ."

"Stolen defense tech," snorts Lorenzo, shaking his head.

"I was thinking the same thing. But that stolen tech let me book a high-mileage hookup with Sharijee—not cheap, either."

"Isn't Sharijee in London?"

"I sent a proxy. Two proxies. Remember those Angela Davis clones, Kali and Shiva?"

"You sent the Black Power twins to meet Sharijee?"

"They're the only people I know in London right now. Plus, the twins got a thing for guns. I was hoping one of them might shoot Sharijee."

Lorenzo raises an eyebrow.

"Didn't happen," says Lion. "But I sent them with 411 to trade."

"What kind of 411?"

"That the cops found Two Tone in a garbage can."

"Didn't know that happened."

"Two months ago."

"Did you learn anything in return?"

"I learned that it was Five Spikes who hired Sharijee, which doesn't help much. But he paid her in Zen-Christ tokens. That could help."

"That's a cryptocurrency?"

"The net name for one. The real name is Soul Ripple M5. It got dubbed 'Zen-Christ' because Chang Zee was one of its creators."

"'I come here on boat, now I own boat'—that Chang Zee?"

"Besides the boat, Zee owns a lot of billboards and his own cryptocurrency."

"So the assholes who tortured you paid off the hooker who set you up in spiritual influencer bitcoin?"

Lion shrugs. "Doesn't make sense to me, either, but until I figure out why Kendra and Ibrahim vanished—"

"Kendra and Ibrahim aren't the only ones," says Lorenzo.

This catches Lion's attention.

"It's why I texted. Gonzales ran down your hunch. You were right: Ichika Adel was at one of the first Evo parties. But it wasn't the one in Tokyo. It was Seattle. And that's the same Ichika Adel, right?"

"The giggle girl. Yeah, that's her."

"That giggle freaks me out."

Lion knows the giggle is actually birdsong, or birdsong with a Japanese accent. The giggle girls started out as a group of Japanese em-trackers, but they all had an epigenetic variation of the original em-tracker genetic mutation. Once triggered, the mutation unlocked new empathic talents. Sietch Tabr was the trigger. The result: The giggle girls came back from their psychedelic trip talking to birds.

"It was Instagram?" asks Lorenzo. "What, like, fifty-seven million followers in ten minutes. But I saw something on *Troll Week* or *This Week in Troll,* one of those Hate-Tube shows. The world landed on her."

"Hard," agrees Lion. "Until the translation algorithms confirmed the language was actual birdsong. That ended the trolling."

"It also started the Splinter."

Lion knows the giggle girls were the first of many poly-tribes to radically self-identify with an animal, with Sietch Tabr being the technical cause of that self-identification. He also knows that without his article, the whole mess might have been avoided.

"In the beginning," says Lion, "the press called them fetishists. Bird fetishists."

"And fish petters."

"That was just the seasteading crowd, with their freediving rituals. Giggle girls started out as bird fetishists."

"No one calls them that anymore."

Lion nods. Once scientists saw their brain scans, the media replaced the fetishist idea with a more accurate descriptor: tribal obsessions. The ultimate in-group/out-group divide. It showed up differently in different poly-tribes, but the fracture lines were always the same: us versus them versus them verses them, ad infinitum.

The Splinter.

"Ichika Adel took Evo at a party in Seattle?" asks Lion.

"That's what Gonzales said."

"You trust him?"

"It's Gonzales. If you've got hard dollars, he's got hard data."

"You're the famous rock star on tour. I'm the broke em-tracker in hiding."

"I misspoke. I've got hard dollars, you've got shit."

"You've got that right."

"But check this out," continues Lorenzo. "Two weeks after that party, Ichika disappeared. Just like Kendra and Ibrahim. And I mean gone. Zero net presence for over a year. And this is Ichika Adel we're talking about, so a couple of the gossip sites put a paparazz-bounty on her."

"A bounty?"

"For anything more than a three-second video. So far no one's claimed it."

"This was in Seattle?"

"Last sighting at her hotel. I don't know which one, but you still appear to be in Sherlock mode, so it shouldn't be too hard to dig up."

"Yeah," says Lion, walking over to the murder board to look at the clipping about the mega-linkage speaker series. "Can you ask Gonzales to run a few more names for me?"

"Is this about Ichika?"

"Just another hunch," says Lion, texting Lorenzo the names of those three tech billionaires. "They're multi-corns who have something to do with the Pacific Rim Mega-Linkage."

"The one Sir Richard built?"

"That's the one. But the mega-linkage is also Penelope's last known whereabouts."

"I thought she was just paying back Sir Richard for the scrubbing."

"She is paying him back—by doing something at the Pacific Rim Mega-Linkage. But I haven't heard from her since."

"This is Penelope we're talking about."

"Yeah," says Lion. "But she's not usually this quiet."

"I know you two have a thing," says Lorenzo, "but . . . it's an on-again, off-again thing, right?"

"You think she met someone," says Lion. "I thought about it. And you're not wrong: Penelope and I are definitely in one of those off-again phases. But where? PRML is a protected wildland. No humans allowed, except in the viewing zones."

The gray-out ends. Lion can see through the window of Lorenzo's armored car. It's parked at the back entrance of an old stadium, a marquee in the distance advertising *Hank Mudd and the K-Holes* in blinking lights. Except, Lion notices, there's some kind of problem with the letter *K*. The upper right fork is dark, making it look like the letter *A*.

Hank Mudd and the A-Holes.

"Gotta jet," says Lorenzo. "But I'll get Gonzales those names. And Lion, go outside or something. Get a meal. Talk to an actual human. Might be the AR, but seriously, man, you look like shit."

THE VINCE VAUGHN MEMORIAL DINER

Lion sips his coffee and glances at his backpack, perched on the red vinyl seat to his left. The upper compartment is zippered shut, but he sees the pale blue glow of the JOBZ, visible through the fabric.

He resists the urge to check the device's settings again. Lion has done it twice already, but the distortion field is brand-new tech and tricky to program. Supposedly the field extends four feet in every direction, making facial recognition impossible, at least according to Penelope.

Lion hopes she's right. He's seated next to a window. If she's wrong, image recognition satellites now work down to the centimeter range, and the newer lenses see right through glass.

He glances at the glow in his backpack.

Well, at least the JOBZ is switched on.

"Black bean burger," says his waitress, sliding a plate in front of him. "Vegan Cajun, with jalapeño fries."

She's dressed in roller derby chic: tall, striped socks and tattoos. There's a black bra strap visible beneath a hot pink tank top, with the words *Vince Vaughn Memorial Diner* printed across her chest.

"Thank you," he says, grabbing a fry.

Lion's hotel is above a restaurant that used to be called Swingers, which got famous because of a movie of the same name, which was also the film that launched Vince Vaughn's acting career. After Vaughn's untimely demise, maybe at his star-studded funeral, possibly during the celeb-heavy wake, Vaughn's friends decided a tribute was in order. They purchased Swingers, changing nothing but the name: the Vince Vaughn Memorial Diner.

"Can I get you anything else?"

Munching on the fry, Lion decides a conversation with an actual human might not be a bad idea.

"Is this the only diner?" he asks, pointing at the logo on her tank top. "I heard something about an Owen Wilson Memorial, over on Pico."

"It's a chain now," says the waitress. "Who knew dead celebs and breakfast pancakes would go global?"

"Global?"

"The J-Lo Memorial Diner, in Jalisco. The George Clooney, in Rome."

"George . . ." Lion realizes he has absolutely nothing to add to that. Instead, he says, "Can I get another cup of coffee?"

"Yup. And if we were in Jalisco, I could offer you the J-Lo-fat coconut creamer with that."

"Black is fine."

L ion eats while rereading the press clipping about the mega-linkage speaker series, once again pausing when he sees the names of those three tech billionaires. Two men and a woman. The men's names mean nothing to him, but the woman's name—Susan Jackson—rings a bell. Lion thinks Penelope mentioned something about her being one of Sir Richard's partners, maybe a co-investor in PRML.

He picks up a fry and keeps reading.

There's nothing more about Susan Jackson until the bottom of the story, where, almost as an aside, the article mentions that all three of the tech billionaires tried Evo, and all three reported remarkably similar experiences.

Didn't Ibrahim mention this, too?

Lion thinks back to their conversation in London. What did Ibrahim say? You don't just trip evolution, you trip the same version of evolution that everyone else trips—like watching the same movie.

But how is that possible?

A ripple flows across the fabric of Lion's backpack. It's the JOBZ, vibrating inside the pocket.

Slipping it out, he sees a text from Carlos slide onto the screen. "Finally," he says.

Lion swallows a last slosh of coffee, flags down the waitress, and pays for his meal. He leaves in a hurry. The night is starless, the sidewalk deserted. In the street, two autonomous taxis drive past, perfectly side by side, both of their cabs completely empty.

At the corner, waiting for the light to change, Lion feels a prickle run across his spine, like he's being watched. He looks around: deserted streets, shuttered shops, but no humans in sight. In the distance, he sees the fading twinkle of the lidar sensors perched atop those autonomous taxis.

Then it clicks.

Those lidar sensors are Big Brother on wheels. They see in the dark, see in the distance, and see everything in sight, gathering over a million bits of data a second, including the suspicious look on Lion's face as he watches the autonomous taxis drive into the distance.

The light changes. Lion steps off the curb, trying to shrug off the paranoia.

"Get a grip, Zorn," he says softly.

He makes it across the street without incident, but finds himself still checking out dark corners, looking for anyone looking for him. The sidewalk to his left is empty, but a reflection in a window to his right grabs his attention.

Not the reflection, the color of the reflection: Chernobyl yellow.

Aiming for casual, Lion stops walking, lifts up a boot, slowly retying the laces while staring at the image. He didn't imagine it. There's a spike of Chernobyl yellow reflected in the window.

Lion whirls around, expecting to find Five Spikes standing across the street. Instead, he sees a yellow-crested cockatoo with feathers the same color as Five Spike's hair, staring at him from a pet shop window.

"Seriously?"

Lion scowls and starts across the intersection. Two steps later, he looks back at the cockatoo.

"Fuck you and your yellow feathers."

Still scowling, Lion hikes on. Like his exaggerated startle responses, these extra doses of paranoia are screwing with his mood, his em-tracking abilities, and—thinking about Penelope—his on-again, off-again relationship.

Still, that text from Carlos might mean progress. And progress might mean a clue as to why he was tortured or what actually happened to Kendra and Ibrahim.

The thought of his friends makes him wince.

Lion doesn't really know Kendra very well, but history bonds him to Ibrahim. They were both part of the first wave of em-trackers, back when psychologists were still calling it "hyper-empathic response syndrome," in the same way the military once termed PTSD "shell shock." They'd met at one of the first virtual meetups and tried to grab a meal whenever Lion was in London. Once, they'd taken a trip to the Galápagos Islands together because they both wanted to hang out with the animals that had once hung out with Darwin. Ibrahim wore his lime-green penny loafers the whole time.

Lion misses the preppy bastard.

Trying to feel hopeful, he angles toward a three-story Spanish colonial that once housed an old film studio, then a CrossFit gym, and is now home to Silver Screen Gizmos, a vintage movie camera rental house. It was also, as Lion learned, the only place left in the world that still rents a Bolex H-11 camera.

The make and model are seared into his memory. Since the Incident, if Lion closes his eyes, the first thing he sees is Buddy Holly, with a Bolex H-11 in hand, leaning in for a close-up.

After the Incident, Lion put his old journalism skills to use. It took a while, but he eventually tracked the camera to this rental house, then learned that Carlos Jones, one of the repair clerks, happened to be the nephew of Balthazar Jones, a high-end jeweler Lion knows from New York.

This was his first big break.

So Lion left London and came to L.A. to see if Carlos could help him backtrack the Bolex H-11. A week later, the JOBZ arrived. Penelope sent it so they could talk discreetly, and long distance.

But they never did talk.

Instead, he got the JOBZ switched on and immediately found that text from Penelope waiting for him. It was the one telling him that Sir Richard had called in that favor and she was heading to PRML.

Lion didn't think much of it at the time. He was building his murder board, feeling frustrated and twitchy. Then, as now, he couldn't em-track for shit. Big surprise. Then, as now, he blamed the weed.

But Lion knows the truth: Rage blocks empathy.

He glances back at the cockatoo. "Sorry, buddy. What can I tell you? Rage blocks empathy."

Leaving the street, Lion walks down a long dark alley. The three-story stucco wall of Silver Screen Gizmos is on one side, while a row of tall bushes hides a two-story brick wall on the other. The alley dumps him into a mostly empty parking lot, with the awning-covered entrance to the rental house coming into view to his left.

Walking inside, Lion climbs three flights of stairs and finds another door at the top. Unlike the first, this one is locked. He pushes a buzzer and waits. A few seconds later, there's a soft click and the door swings open.

Lion steps into a long hallway lined with vintage movie cameras behind thick plates of glass. The Eumig 8mm, the Leica M9-P, the Bauer 88B, all on tripods, spot-lit from above.

He walks past the display and pushes through a frosted glass door marked *Rentals*, seeing an old movie poster for Jim Jarmusch's *Ghost Dog: The Way of the Samurai* directly across from him. The small print at the bottom reads: "Live by the code. Die by the code."

A long gunmetal counter sits to the right of the poster. There's a tall man standing behind it, staring at a laptop. He's maybe thirty, dark-skinned, wiry, with a thin mustache and baggy skater clothes.

"Carlos," says Lion. "I got your text."

The man looks up. "Yo-yo, Lion Zorn."

"Tell me you got somewhere."

"I got somewhere," replies Carlos. "But I had outside assistance. Balthazar says to say hello. He also says he hasn't learned anything about Evo yet, but he's still on the case."

"You talked to him?" asks Lion.

"Last night. He helped me fill in a couple missing pieces."

"What did you learn?"

"Plenty," says Carlos. "The Bolex H-11 rental—it was paid for through a triple crypto exchange. That's why it was so hard to track.

Bitcoin classic into Ethereum into this token I've never heard of—Zen something."

"Zen-Christ," says Lion, feeling a tingle on his scalp.

"Sounds right. So, yeah, Zen whatever, the crypto was used to rent the H-11, the one you saw in London."

Clicking a few keys on the laptop, Carlos spins it around to show Lion a spreadsheet. He taps a fingernail on an entry halfway down the page. "According to the logs, the H-11 is ghost tech. The two times we sent the camera to London—only times we've rented it this decade."

"So you can track the transactions?"

"No, which is creeptastic. Other than the payment and the delivery address in London, there's not even a name on the order. But that doesn't make sense. It's a smart contract. So how'd they manage to get around the automatic encoding of the blockchain?"

Lion remembers what Sharijee said about Five Spikes being able to track crypto transactions. Could Five Spikes also alter them?

"But check it," continues Carlos, leaning conspiratorially across the counter. "There's a seventh camera, which we never owned."

"Only six were made."

"The seventh was different. Actually, the sixth, the one you saw in London, was like the beta version. But the seventh was the finished product. Like the others, it captures both thermal and regular images, but flick a switch and it becomes a retinal camera. Click, click, click. You can use that bad boy to take pictures of the back of someone's eye."

Lion flashes on Buddy Holly, leaning in for the close-up. "Why would you need that?"

"I wondered myself. I asked Balthazar. He said maybe the retinal camera was beside the point. Maybe it was about the thermal imaging, early spyware, so you could see live bodies. Or maybe a medical experiment. But these cameras are from the late 1970s, so it's anyone's guess."

"Who owned this seventh one?"

"Tech Museum in Seattle, or they used to. It was in storage—until it got stolen."

"Seattle," says Lion.

"Does that mean something to you?"

Seattle is where Ichika Adel disappeared, thinks Lion, and that might mean something. But he keeps that thought to himself, instead asking, "How come you know this?"

"Four months after the camera was stolen, the police found it after some kind of all-night drug party. Again, this was up in Seattle. Balthazar helped me get my hands on the report."

"Did it say what kind of drug? Was it Evo?"

Carlos shakes his head. "Doesn't say. But the camera, after the cops found it, there was some kind of mix-up. Instead of checking it into evidence, someone decided it was one of ours and drop-shipped it back."

"Because you're the only ones who rent Bolex H-11s?"

Carlos nods. "Big online presence. But apparently no one had ever tried to return a camera we didn't own before. Screwed up the system. They had to call in tech support, which is how I heard about it."

"What happened to the camera?"

"We shipped it back to the Tech Museum in Seattle."

"Do you have a date?" asks Lion. "For when you sent it back?"

Carlos walks over to the laptop and taps a few keys. "It didn't get checked in the normal way, because it never belonged to us." He taps a few more. "Yeah, here we go. It arrived three years ago, March 22. We shipped it back a week later."

The timeline fit. The first of the Seattle Evo parties was held on the second week of March, three years ago. The Bolex H-11 could have been used at the party where Ichika tried the drug, just before she vanished. The Zen-Christ currency links the Seattle party and the London party to Buddy Holly and Five Spikes, which might also link them to Kendra and Ibrahim.

"This helps?" asks Carlos.

"Yeah, man, it really does."

"What are you going to do?"

The movie camera points to Seattle. Ichika Adel's disappearance points to Seattle. It's the first decent lead Lion has had in a while. But the fewer people who know this, the better.

"Dunno," he says. "I need to think about it. But I appreciate the hard work. And tell your uncle thanks for trying."

"Sorry it took so long. Hope you got to chill at the beach or something."

"Or something," says Lion, heading out the door.

NOW NOT SEE YOU

Lion takes the steps three at a time.

He gets halfway down the staircase then pauses, realizing his problems aren't entirely solved. He still has to get to Seattle, and that's not going to be easy.

Lion doesn't want to risk being caught on-camera. Neither can he carry the JOBZ through any major transportation hub. With all the security, they'd find the device and he'd go to jail, probably for a while. Then Lion remembers the autonomous taxis gliding through that intersection.

That might work, he thinks, if he could use someone else's phone to order the car.

Descending the last flight of stairs, he pushes through the door and steps outside. In the parking lot, directly across from him, there's an ancient Honda Gold Wing parked by the curb. The windshield is tall and curved and catches his reflection. Lion sees his own face in profile, and behind him, emerging from the bushes to his left, a slash of Chernobyl yellow.

Spinning around, he half expects another yellow-crested cockatoo optical illusion.

But it's not an illusion.

It's Five Spikes. Flesh and blood.

There's no running this time. Lion is pinned down. There's a building behind him, a motorcycle blocking his getaway lane, and Five Spikes directly in front of him, approaching fast.

Lion closes the gap between them with two quick steps. Packing four months of fury into a sidekick, he aims for Five Spikes's rib cage. A soft target, Penelope once called it.

But you have to hit the ribs to hurt the ribs.

Five Spikes has skills. He slips sideways and blocks the kick, spinning Lion around and exposing his flank. Before Lion can right himself, a fist jabs into his side and staggers him backward. His ankles hit the curb, and he sprawls onto his ass.

Lion looks up to see Five Spikes standing a few feet away from him, a sad look on his face.

"Fuck you," says Lion, planting his foot on the concrete and trying to push to his feet.

But before he can stand, Five Spikes pulls a stun baton from his back pocket and telescopes it outward, a sizzle of electricity hissing at its tip.

Lion sits back down.

Five Spikes takes another step toward him, bends over, and uses his non-stun baton hand to grab Lion's backpack. Lion attempts to grab it back, but Five Spikes pulls the pack free with one hand and swings the stun baton with the other, the tip slicing past Lion's nose.

"No move," he snarls.

"I don't speak Chinese," says Lion.

Five Spikes shakes his head, lifts the pack, and examines the exterior. When he spots the pale blue glow of the JOBZ, he collapses the baton on his thigh, and drops it back into his pocket. Then he unzips the backpack, pulls out the device, then sets the pack at Lion's feet.

Hitting a few buttons, Five Spikes swipes right, then kneels down to show Lion the screen. It's the password box for the distortion field. Five Spikes uses the home button to tap in an override code, which pulls up the distortion field's landing page. With his finger, he brings up a drop-down menu in the upper left-hand corner.

Lion hadn't noticed it before.

Five Spikes clicks open the menu, which appears to be a list of low-light refractor settings, whatever that means.

He selects *myopic,* then passes the JOBZ back to Lion.

"Now it work," says Five Spikes. "Now not see you."

Then he stands back up and walks quickly away, leaving Lion sitting on his ass in the alley.

OPEN LOOPS

Lion rides the adrenaline out of the alley and back to his hotel room. He takes a long shower, puts an ice pack on his ribs, and climbs into bed.

But there's no sleep to be had. Images of Five Spikes keep jolting him awake.

An hour later, Lion gives up, gets up, rolls a Rasta-sized joint, and smokes most of it while standing on a micro-terrace outside his hotel room's third-story window.

The weed does its job.

Now calm, Lion comes back inside and picks up the JOBZ. Was Five Spikes telling the truth? Does he still trust the device to keep him safe? And what was up with that sad look on Five Spikes's face? Like he was resigned to his fate.

Back in London, the first thing Buddy Holly said was: "Go home, Lion Zorn." After the Incident, Lion decided Buddy Holly had been toying with him, but considering Five Spikes's sad look, maybe that was a genuine warning. Maybe neither Buddy Holly nor Five Spikes actually wanted to hurt him—that would explain the look.

Did not explain the torture.

Fuck no, it didn't.

But if the look was genuine, then Five Spikes was telling the truth, and Lion could trust the JOBZ. Anyway, it was the distortion field, not the signal scrambler that had been screwed up.

And on and on . . .

Eventually, Lion grabs AR glasses and calls Lorenzo. He reaches him post-concert, in a hotel room, on the outskirts of São Paulo. Lion walks his friend through the evening—Carlos and the stolen Bolex H-11, Five Spikes and the maybe attack. Then he changes the subject, asking if Gonzales learned anything about the three tech billionaires, especially Susan Jackson.

Lorenzo takes off his aviator glasses to squint at Lion. "You sure you want to talk about this now?"

"Yeah, man, we're making progress."

"If bruised ribs are progress."

"It's my fault. I started the fight."

"Yup, and you tied yourself to that bed at the Claridge's."

"Fair point, but I did start this fight."

"Fine," says Lorenzo, giving up on the debate. "So, yeah, Gonzales learned something. All three of your tech billionaires are Tompkinsites, whatever the hell that means."

"Tompkinsites?"

"Yeah."

"Devotees of Doug Tompkins."

"The guy who made crazy money in fashion?"

"Back in the 1980s. In the nineties, he spent most of it buying up land in Chile. Millions of acres. He tried to create a countrywide nature preserve, one of the first attempts at a mega-linkage. He was way ahead of his time. We're talking long before they started teaching grade school kids about Michael Soulé."

"Michael who?"

"Seriously?"

"I play congas in a cow-punk band."

"Siri, who is Michael Soulé?"

The holo-rendering of Lorenzo dissolves into a tropical beach, complete with palm trees, booming surf, and a Polynesian woman standing center screen. "Brah," she says, shaking her head sadly. "The animals, the fish, the birds. Going, going, gone. Lonely now, brah. Lonely everywhere."

"Sorry," says Lion. "Siri, turn off pidgin mode, go back to normal."

The image shifts to the same woman, now dressed in a lab coat, standing in a lecture hall. "Michael Soulé is the godfather of conservation biology. A professor of environmental studies at the University of California, Santa Cruz, Soulé pioneered the idea of rewilding by applying the principles of island biogeography to . . ."

"Bio-geo what?" says Lorenzo.

"Island biogeography is the study of populations on islands," replies Siri.

"This is taking too long," snaps Lion. "Siri, never mind."

"*Nevermind* is an album by the American grunge band Nirvana, from the . . ."

"Siri," says Lion, "off."

The lecture hall dissolves back into a holo-rendering of Lorenzo.

Lion continues the explanation. "Michael Soulé was obsessed with the root causes of extinction. Overharvesting, deforestation, habitat fragmentation, introduction of exotic predators—essentially the story of the modern world. He came up with mega-linkages as a solution."

"The Pacific Rim," says Lorenzo.

"Exactly."

"Sir Richard owns what now, like, most of Northern Cali and a big chunk of Oregon?"

"Pretty much, between him and his partners. They're rewilding everything beside the weed and grape farms. And those have been replanted, interspecies pastures, mandatory migration corridors, or they have to provide tunnels."

"I heard about that," says Lorenzo. "The Heavenly Bypass. I heard Sir Richard got the ski area to build like four runs underground."

"Three, I think, but I haven't talked to him."

"Not even to ask about Penelope?"

"Sir Richard and I didn't leave things on great terms. The Splinter made it worse."

"That was a while ago."

"Yeah," says Lion, "but once the riots started, when I really had to vanish, I let Penelope negotiate for the scrubbing, and never got back in touch."

"Where was I during all this?"

"You were getting famous."

"Heard something about that, too," says Lorenzo, sliding a cigarette out of a pack and lighting up.

"Cow-punk revival." Lion snorts. "Who the hell saw that coming?"

"You got famous, too," says Lorenzo.

"I got notorious," says Lion. "And that's not nearly as much fun."

"You still get recognized?"

"Not often. If they're hard-core animal rights people, it happens. A bunch of my early articles appeared in print. The scrubbing erased everything digital. But some stuff, it's still on paper."

"Forget the myths the media created about the White House. The truth is, these aren't very bright guys, and things got out of hand."

"Now I have no idea what you're talking about."

"I'm quoting *All the President's Men*. Out of solidarity, remember?"

"I remember," says Lion.

"What are you gonna do?"

"I'm going to smoke the rest of my joint, ice my ribs, and go to sleep. When I wake up, I'm going to text you an address. I need you to order me an Uber autonomous. Get a car with a bed, something built for distance. I have to go to Seattle."

"Seattle?"

"Between the early Evo parties, Ichika Adel going missing, the cops who found the Bolex H-11, and the Tech Museum where it got stolen, someone in Seattle knows something."

"It'd be faster going aerial. Uber's new flying car fleet, the Ehang 185s, they're pretty sweet."

"Huge stretches of no-fly between here and there. Plus, the recharging stops are all at Sky Hubs. Those places are seriously TSA-d out. I'd get spotted. Even if Five Spikes didn't want to attack me tonight—I still got tortured. Until I find the asshole who's behind that . . . ," Lion smiles, "my friend Lorenzo thinks I should be careful."

"You got that right," says Lorenzo. "One sleeper car, coming up."

"Do we know anyone who knows anything about crypto? I need to figure out what's up with that Zen-Christ currency."

"Who was that creepy guy who works for Sir Richard? With the white suits and no socks—the hacker from Croatia?"

"Jenka," says Lion. "He's from Moldova."

"He'd know."

"I'm trying pretty hard never to see him again," says Lion, stifling a yawn. "But you're right, Jenka would know."

"He might also know where Penelope's at."

"Open loops," says Lion, suddenly bone-tired. "Too many open loops."

"You'll close them."

"Yeah," says Lion. "Believe that."

PART III

The sleeper car is a yellow stretch Vette, a 1976 Corvette with its once nearly nonexistent back seat elongated into a slender bed, adding an additional six feet of center mass to the vehicle and making it look like a banana on steroids. But the Vette has excellent aero-dynamics, clocking 150 miles per hour in the autonomous lane and turning the 1,200 miles between L.A. and Seattle into an eight-hour journey, minus recharging stops and bathroom breaks.

The map on the screen on the center console shows their location as Highway 5, approaching the Washington border. Lion remembers almost nothing about Oregon, having slept through most of the state. He does recall waking up at a charging stop near Eugene, buying two bean pies from a well-dressed black man in a dark suit and bow tie, working out of a Last Call Food Truck in the parking lot. Lion must have fallen back asleep after eating the pies, because he recollects little else until they were already north of Portland, where the traffic started to thin and the Vette could begin to accelerate.

"Hey, Siri," says Lion, to the console screen.

The screen doesn't change. It still shows a map of Highway 5, snaking through the Pacific Northwest, a bright red dot indicating their location.

"Hey, Siri," Lion says again.

The screen goes black. Lion sees the pulsating lines that mean voice recognition.

"My name is Rod," says an overly masculine voice, the lines forming vibrant diamonds. "I'll be your digital assistant."

"As in Rodney?"

"As in Hot."

Lion starts to laugh, but winces instead, his ribs still hurting from the attack. "When did you get a sense of humor?"

"Each vehicle in the Chevrolet autonomous line comes equipped with a TensorFlow version 17.5 digital assistant. There are seven different personality settings."

"Which one are you?"

"Greaser mode comes preset on all stretch Vettes."

"Greaser mode?"

"The term is archaic slang, derogatory ironic, originally referring to a motor vehicle mechanic."

"Okay, Hot Rod, what can you tell me about Ichika Adel?"

The screen stays blank, the voice-recognition feature failing to do its job.

Lion tries again. "Hey, Hot Rod?"

The lines reappear.

"How may I help you?" says the same overly masculine voice.

Lion realizes that asking about Ichika is going to bring up too much stuff he already knows. Her em-tracker background, the giggle girl controversy. None of it will be useful. But the name of the hotel where Ichika disappeared—once he gets to Seattle—that could be useful.

"Hey, Hot Rod, where was the last public appearance of Ichika Adel?"

"Fourteen months ago, net influencer and giggle girl founder Ichika Adel was seen entering the Braveheart Hotel in downtown Seattle. But there is breaking news on the topic of Ichika Adel's last public appearance. Would you like me to continue?"

"Yes."

"The *Hollywood Vanity Reporter* has obtained a 'vanity exclusive,' a seven-second video of Ichika Adel at an Anti-Nagel encampment, on the side of Seattle's iconic Space Needle. Would you like me to play the clip?"

Lion remembers reading about the Anti-Nagels. Thomas Nagel was a twentieth-century philosopher who wrote a famous essay about how human beings could never understand the mind of a bat. Nagel's issue, if Lion's memory holds, was about *umwelts*, or the world as perceived through the senses. Bats are blind, winged creatures that primarily navigate via auditory cues; humans are sighted, terrestrial animals that steer primarily via vision. Different umwelts, different realities, and, according to Nagel, no way to bridge that gap.

The Anti-Nagels started out as a group of em-tracking rock climbers who took Sietch Tabr in a mountain cave somewhere and ended up communing with bats. Thus the name. Lion also recalls that the Anti-Nagels made some enemies during the early days of the Splinter. Once the Humans First riots began, the group hid in high places, building encampments under bridges and off the sides of buildings, using drones to deliver supplies and, as far as he knew, never coming down.

"Play the clip," says Lion.

The video starts out over the city of Seattle, shot from somewhere up high, maybe a drone, heading in the direction of the Space Needle. The camera is focused on a collection of nano-steel-reinforced skynets supporting a vast collection of pup tents, all hanging from climbing ropes tied to the sides of the structure, about five hundred feet above the ground. Then the camera swoops in closer, zooming in on a pup tent, showing a woman's face, partially hidden behind a rain flap.

Closer still.

The image is grainy, but now Lion can see Ichika Adel in profile, her unmistakable pink dreadlocks, looking at something off-camera. She shivers slightly, then steps backward and closes the tent flap behind her. Two seconds later, a long rifle barrel protrudes from the flap, aiming in the direction of the camera. The muzzle jumps and a tiny puff of blue smoke floats out of the barrel. Then the video ends.

Now he definitely knows where to find Ichika Adel.

Yet this creates another problem. The Anti-Nagels live five hundred feet off the ground, and as the rifle shot attests, are well armed and ferociously private. So finding a way to talk to Ichika won't be easy.

But there's something else about the video that bothers Lion.

"Play it again," he says.

Lion watches in silence, then asks Hot Rod to freeze the video on Ichika's face.

"Play it forward."

He sees her shiver again. There's something PTSD-twitchy familiar in the way it wracks her body. It looks like the same kind of amplified startle response common to severely traumatized em-trackers, the same response he's been dealing with since his first encounter with Five Spikes and Buddy Holly.

"Play it again."

REMODELED

On the outskirts of Seattle, Lion grabs his notebook and decides to make a list of all the things he doesn't know. What happened to Kendra and Ibrahim remains the biggest mystery, but finally there's a flicker of hope. If Ichika is still alive and hiding out, his friends might be as well.

Could Kendra and Ibrahim be secreted away with the Anti-Nagels?

Lion thinks about the Anti-Nagels' fondness for facial tattoos and Ibrahim's bright green penny loafers and decides it's unlikely. But if things got desperate? Lion can't completely rule out the possibility.

What about Ichika's shiver? It looks a lot like his shiver.

Was she tortured, too?

Lion woke up the morning after the Incident in a king-size bed in a mini-suite at Claridge's. But there was no tartan plaid wallpaper on the walls, and there were no dead animal heads nor Chinese gangsters in sight. They did leave him a pair of oversized sunglasses to hide the cuts above his eyes.

Lion wore the sunglasses out of the room, took the elevator to the lobby, and inquired at the front desk about the Tartan Suite. The clerk looked at him as if he was crazy, but an elderly bellman overheard the question.

"Remodeled," he'd said, "like fifteen years ago."

That was the moment Lion abandoned the idea of going to the police. What would he tell them? He was kidnapped, tortured with taxidermy, and woke up in a hotel room that no longer exists? They'd think he was nuts. Or on drugs. Plus, going to the police would require filling out a report, and this would put his name and face back into the database. After two years in hiding, Lion didn't want to pop back up on anyone's radar.

He shakes off the memory.

What he really wants to know is if Ichika had a similar experience. Or if she knows what happened to Kendra and Ibrahim. Or for that matter, what the hell is going on with Five Spikes and Buddy Holly?

In his notebook, he underlines *hell* twice, for emphasis.

He also writes *Braveheart,* deciding the hotel where Ichika disappeared raises another question: Why there?

Lion was kidnapped in the back office of a seedy nightclub in a bad neighborhood, where they routinely shoot out the CCTV cameras. The Braveheart is in the middle of downtown Seattle. It's way more public. And there are way more cameras. The Zen-Christ tokens are another open loop. And the Bolex H-11.

The questions keep coming.

Lion rubs his temples, feeling the edge of a headache beginning to poke its way into consciousness. Either residual PTSD effects or too many questions.

He decides to start where Ichika's story starts, at the Braveheart Hotel. Afterward, he'll move on to the Tech Museum, where that fabled seventh Bolex H-11 was stolen. Along the way, maybe he'll figure out how to get into the Anti-Nagel encampment, or, at least, how to get a message to Ichika.

"Hey, Hot Rod," he says, "redirect from the Tech Museum. I want to go to the Braveheart Hotel instead."

AN OIL-AND-WATER SITUATION

The stretch Vette cuts across two lanes of freeway traffic and slices onto an exit ramp. Still reclining on the bed, Lion gets his first view of Seattle through the upper edge of the windshield. It's a maze of tall buildings against a dark sky spilling fat drops of cold rain.

Traffic crawls.

Lion's ribs hurt and he's restless. A button on the side console collapses the bed back into a seat.

Once upright, Lion digs out the Sour Dictator Booty. Perfect pain relief. Plus, the marijuana will fire up his em-tracking abilities, maybe help him answer a few of his questions.

He rolls a spliff, but before he can light it, the Vette pulls into a parking spot in front of a slender high-rise coated in shiny black metal. Silver letters reading *The Braveheart* run down the side of the building. Below them, there's a long awning made from black silk, with some kind of shiny water-repellent coating, and a tall black doorman, with some kind of shiny coating of his own.

Swanky is Lion's first thought.

With its grunge history, Seattle isn't typically swanky. And with her pink dreadlocks and deep poly-tribe roots, Ichika Adel is seriously anti-swank. It's an oil-and-water situation.

So what was she doing here?

Lion manages to slide out of the car without jarring his ribs, but a glance at the doorman persuades him to smoke his spliff down the street. A few steps in the rain changes his mind.

Lion tucks the joint back into his pocket and starts toward the hotel, aiming for the main entrance: a pair of smooth black metal doors with no discernible way to open them.

The doorman doesn't move.

"Welcome to the Braveheart," says a disembodied woman's voice. There must be throw-speakers hidden somewhere. It sounds like the building itself is talking to him.

The doors slide open.

Lion strides past the doorman, who still hasn't moved. Then he gets it: Robo-doorman—he only comes to life only when needed to help with the luggage.

Lion walks into a dimly lit lobby. The walls are also coated in shiny black steel, the interior dominated by a freestanding fireplace designed to resemble a giant iron heart. There's a fire burning in the center of the heart and a basset hound asleep on a rug in the corner.

"Good afternoon," says another disembodied woman's voice, this one from Lion's left.

Lion spins and sees a tall blond woman: pale skin, hazel eyes, and frighteningly attractive. She's wearing a shimmering white one-piece jumpsuit, skintight, scoop-necked, with living screens built into the sleeves. The screens display an underwater scene: schools of puffer fish swimming in and out of view.

Up until this moment, Lion's plan had been to snap into reporter mode and inquire about Ichika Adel's disappearance. But this woman looks custom-designed to deflect questions.

"Checking in," he says instead.

"Right this way."

She leads him around the fireplace and into a hidden alcove, housing a small check-in counter. Walking behind the counter, the woman touches something out of sight and a holo-screen rises into view.

"Name?" she asks.

"I don't have a reservation."

"I'll need a credit card and an ID."

"I'd like to pay cash."

"I'm sorry, sir." Her eyes are flat. "We no longer take cash."

He thinks about this for a moment.

"You're Lion Zorn," she says suddenly.

Lion backs up, taking two fast steps away from the counter. It's an automatic response. Even with the scrubbing, in certain communities, he still gets recognized. Unfortunately, after the Splinter, in certain communities, they don't like him much.

"I'm not," he says.

"Thank you," she says, her gaze softening.

"You've got the wrong guy."

"Sietch Tabr," she says, pulling on the edge of the jumpsuit's scoop neck, revealing a dolphin tattoo beneath her clavicle. With her other hand, she tugs the fabric in the other direction, showing him a second tattoo. "I'm a fish petter," she says with a smile.

"No one calls you that anymore."

"You changed my life."

"I'm sure you changed your own life."

"I have a manager's override. I can take cash."

"You're sure?"

"You changed my life."

Lion smiles. "I have no idea what you're talking about."

THere Are RumOrs

The Braveheart's room key is supposed to download onto Lion's phone, but he threw his phone away months ago and now only has the JOBZ. Trying to figure out how to get the hotel's key onto his anonymizer with the receptionist watching defeats the purpose of having an anonymizer.

"I lost my phone," says Lion. "Any chance I can get a digital key?"

She has to go into the back to print it.

The basset hound gets up from the rug and wanders over to the counter. Lion crouches down to say hello, trading an ear rub and a back scratch for two licks to the nose.

"Mr. Zorn?"

He stands up. The woman is back at the counter, still frighteningly attractive, but her cold tone is gone.

"Just Lion," he says. "Everybody calls me Lion."

"Your digital key, Lion." She slides a rectangle of white plastic across the counter. "If you follow me, I'll show you to your room."

She steps around the desk and starts walking. Lion gives the hound a final scratch and trails her across the lobby, through a door, and into a narrow corridor. Behind another door, they traverse another hallway, turn two corners, and finally arrive at a row of elevators.

"This place is a maze," Lion says.

"Nooks and crannies," explains the receptionist, stepping into the elevator. "Lots of dark spots to get into a little bit of trouble."

"Intentional?"

"The guests seem to enjoy it," she says, pushing the button for the eighth floor. "It's romantic. People get drunk and fool around in the corners. But there are cameras everywhere and the owner likes to . . ."—she makes air quotes with her fingers—"'review' the footage."

Lion laughs, concluding this woman is more friend than foe. He decides to take a chance and ask about Ichika's disappearance.

"We're not supposed to talk about it. And I wasn't here then . . . but there were rumors."

Lion stays silent.

"Double-D," says the woman, "this is Miriam, manager's override, pause car."

The elevator stops quickly. The cessation of motion lurches Lion forward. The woman reaches out a hand and catches him before he hits the wall. Her palm lingers on his chest.

"Sorry," she says. "Double-D has fast reflexes."

"Double-D?"

"The AI that runs the hotel. The servers are housed inside these two huge cones. They look like boobs."

Her hand hasn't left his chest. "Why have we stopped?"

"Privacy," she says, using her other hand to point around the elevator. "After Ichika disappeared, the paparazzi put micro-cams everywhere. We sweep regularly, but you can't be too careful. The elevator is signal-insulated."

"Why isn't there a hotel security camera in here?"

"There is, but the manager's code turns it off."

"Your name is Miriam?"

She nods.

"What can you tell me about Ichika's disappearance?"

"You mean rescue."

Lion raises an eyebrow.

"At least that's what we think. Double-D got hacked, so the feeds were down. But there was a mix-up when they installed the security system and the roof never got wired. There was an off-network camera pointed at an emergency exit. It caught a guy with a gun in a ski mask coming through the door, and then, like, ten minutes later, going out. Ichika was following him."

"You're sure she was following him?"

"There's no sound, but just before he goes through the door, it looks like he tells her to wait. Then he disappears and comes back fifteen seconds later. She could have fled. She didn't. The last image shows her following him out the door and onto the roof."

"How'd they get off the roof?"

"No one knows."

"The ten minutes between when the guy in the ski mask came in the door and when he left with Ichika—what happened then?"

"Something bad in room 1107. We think Ichika was held hostage. Chandra, in housekeeping, found restraints all around the bed. There was also a head vise, the kind used in brain surgery, and these eyelid things . . ."

Lion shudders at the memory. "Metal prongs that hold open the eyes?"

"I don't know if they were metal, but that sounds right."

"How hard is it to hack Double-D?"

"Harder than hard. Threefish encryption, 372-bit length, passwords mutate daily, and she reads biometrics."

"What happened to the restraints?"

"The cops took them. Apparently, they kept that detail from the press, trying to smoke out the people who did this."

"But that never happened."

"No. Besides the restraints, the video, and a fancy business card, there was nothing to go on."

"Business card?"

"Yeah. Chandra found it, too. The card was made from metal, laser-etched with a couple of Chinese characters and a weird web address. A string of numbers that ended in dot-onion. Dot-com, dot-net, sure. But dot-onion?" She shrugs. "I think the cops still have it."

"It's a dark web address," says Lion, "that's what dot-onion means."

It was Jenka, the Moldovan hacker, who first taught Lion about the dark web. Jenka, with his white suits and no socks. Jenka, whom Lion perpetually wants to punch in the mouth. Jenka—enough with the Jenka. Lion refocuses. "Anybody ever figure out the Chinese characters?"

"I don't know if anybody tried. Chandra might know. I can ask her when she gets on shift"—glancing at an expensive watch—"in two hours."

"You're a fish petter," says Lion, an idea for how to get in touch with Ichika forming in his head.

Miriam takes a micro-step closer to him and smiles. "No one calls us that anymore."

"Do you have contact with the Anti-Nagels?"

"Bird fetishists and fish petters, they don't tend to enjoy one another's company." She taps her fingernails on his chest. "But everybody seems to enjoy my company. And I've got a friend who's got a friend."

"Can your friend of a friend get a message to the Anti-Nagel colony at the Space Needle?"

"Tension," she says, as if that explained it.

"At the Space Needle?"

"When the Anti-Nagels took over, they were smart about it. They took a bunch of homeless war veterans up there with them. Seattle's overflowing with people with no place to sleep, so no one wanted to throw them out. The city council decided to let them be. But two weeks from now, when the whole privatization thing kicks off, that's a different story."

"Privatization?"

"Don't you know? Seattle decided to become the first city to privatize neighborhoods. City can't afford the upkeep. So welcome to the Amazon Zone. There's a Starbucks Zone. I think the Space Needle is in the Microsoft Zone."

"No shit," says Lion.

"The city wants the Anti-Nagels out of the Needle before the switchover. That caused a fuss. Then a giant Humans First contingent showed up and made it worse. I can't stand those fuckers."

"Humans First?"

"Yeah."

"Nobody can stand those fuckers."

Miriam nods. "There have been huge protests at the Needle for a couple weeks now. Everybody thinks there's going to be a riot. Paparazz-bounty for anyone who captures the first punch. As I said, tension."

"Some world," says Lion.

"Yup," she says, taking another micro-step toward him. "So can I show you to your room now, or would you prefer to fool around in the elevator?"

L ion has a strict "no sex with groupies" policy. The vibe is never right. One way or another, it feels like the person he goes to bed with actually wants to be in bed with someone else. Plus, there's Penelope, and their on-again, off-again relationship. Lion likes to be logical in these situations.

Logic dictates these situations don't come along every day.

Logic wins.

He pushes the button for the eighth floor. They spend forty minutes rolling around on high-thread-count sheets before Miriam has to go back to work. While getting dressed, she glances at an employee tracker app on her phone and lets him know that Chandra clocked in early.

At Lion's request, Miriam texts Chandra and arranges for him to meet her at the second-floor housekeeping station in thirty minutes. Then Lion tries to make a plan to meet Miriam in the hotel bar after she gets off work, but there's a management seminar across town and she doesn't know when she'll be back. Instead, he admits to having a JOBZ, they trade numbers, and Miriam gives him an awkward "Just text me" on her way out the door.

Then the door opens again, and she pokes her head back inside the room. "That message for Ichika, if I talk to my friend, what do you want it to say?"

"Buddy Holly glasses. We need to talk. Lion Zorn."

Miriam furrows her brow. "Buddy Holly glasses. We need to talk?"

"Ichika will understand."

"That's it?"

"Also give her my number so she can get in touch."

"Fish petter out," says Miriam, winking at him and closing the door.

Lion takes a shower, gets dressed, pockets the JOBZ, and heads down the hall to the elevator. He's got five minutes until he's supposed to meet Chandra.

He pushes the button and waits. Before the elevator arrives, the

JOBZ starts to vibrate in his pocket. As he's pulling it out, a text from Miriam slides onto the screen. "I talked to my friend. He delivered your message. I'll let you know if I hear anything back."

That was fast, thinks Lion.

SUICIDE GIRLS

The housekeeping station sits at the end of a long hallway. Lion opens the door and sees a rectangular laundry room lined with concrete floors and brick walls. One wall is packed with washers and dryers; the other has a long chrome table pushed up against it. Three humanoid robots stand at the table, their backs to Lion. Two robots fold bath towels. The third is completely lifeless, arms dangling, head hanging down.

In the middle of the room, a middle-aged black woman with a copper-colored Afro sits behind an old metal desk, filling in numbers on a spreadsheet.

"Excuse me," says Lion. "Are you Chandra?"

The woman doesn't look up.

Lion walks a few steps into the room and repeats himself.

She keeps working.

"I'm Lion," he tries again. "I'm supposed to meet Chandra here."

Finally the woman lifts her gaze and points at the lifeless robot. "That's Chandra."

Lion takes a step toward the robot, then looks back at the woman. "You're messing with me."

"I am," says the woman. "Teasing the Yankees is a long tradition in my family."

Lion laughs.

"I'm Chandra. You must be Lion."

"Nice to meet you."

"Miriam said you wanted to see the business card I found in room 1107."

"I thought the cops had it."

Chandra's phone sits on the desk. She picks it up, clicks an icon, then scrolls through a series of images before selecting one. Holding the screen out, Chandra shows him a photograph of a metal card etched with Chinese characters.

"I wanted to sell the photo. Thought, with Ichika missing, the press would pay. But then I heard about the police wanting to keep the details out of the press. I was in 1107 and saw that head vise. Whatever happened to Ichika was the devil's work." She crosses herself. "After seeing that, I wanted the police to catch Satan much more than I wanted pictures of dead white men on green paper—no offense."

"None taken."

Lion looks at the photo, pointing at the Chinese characters. "Any idea what they say?"

"I'm mostly a spareribs woman. I don't speak no moo shu pork."

"I had to ask."

"I wasn't finished. My auntie grew up outside of Hangzhou. She says it says, 'Suicide Girls.'" Chandra taps a fingernail on the screen. "At least these two characters say that."

Swiping the image away, she shows him another. It's the other side of the same business card, the web address ending in dot-onion. Chandra taps her nail on the bottom right corner.

Lion sees a trio of Chinese characters, fainter than the others.

"According to auntie, these say, 'Place your bets.'"

"Suicide Girls—place your bets?"

"Yup."

"Sounds like French poetry to me."

"Uh-huh," says Chandra. "But auntie's an old old-school feminist. She says the Suicide Girls were a burlesque dance troupe from the early days of the internet. Punk rock gals with tattoos and piercings trying to broaden our definition of beauty. She called them 'third wave wom-en's lib.' Said they mostly faded from sight in the West, but popped up in China around the time of the Splinter."

"Do you mind if I take a picture of those pictures?"

"I'll text 'em to you."

Lion gives her the number for the JOBZ. Once her text arrives, he double-checks the images to make sure he can read the web address and both sets of Chinese characters. Satisfied, he turns back to Chan-dra. "Is there anything else you remember about 1107?"

"Ichika was tortured, I won't forget that."

"You sound certain."

"Someone was tortured. There was blood on the sheets." Then she looks Lion square in the eye. "You get tortured, too?"

His eyes pop wide. "How'd you know?"

"I saw the head vise," she explains. "The metal prongs used to hold open the eyes. I also saw the video. Right before Ichika goes through the door and onto the roof, you can see that her eyelids are bleeding." She points at Lion's face. "Bleeding in the same place you've got those lightning bolt scars."

"Not my favorite memory."

"Ichika's a famous em-tracker. Miriam says you are, too. Was it because of that?"

"I don't know."

"Humans First," she says. "Sounds like their kind of cracker red-neck Nazi bullshit. No offense."

"None taken, and you're right, it does sound like their kind of cracker redneck Nazi bullshit. But I still don't know."

"You find out," says Chandra. "And when you do find out—you be sure to handle that business."

"Shoot first, ask questions later."

"Amen."

Lion leaves the housekeeping station and heads back to his room. Walking inside, he notices the decor is telltale Braveheart: four walls of shiny black metal. He's amazed he didn't notice before. Beside the black metal platform bed and a black metal desk, there's nothing else in the room.

Lion crosses to the desk, slides out a chair, and sits down. He pulls out the JOBZ and clicks open their custom-designed Tor Browser. A quick search brings up a map of downtown Seattle. The Tech Museum that houses the seventh Bolex H-11 sits about a mile from the Braveheart, in the same part of town as the Space Needle.

Business hours are listed beside the map. The museum stays open late two nights a week, with tonight being one of those nights.

A glance at the window tells him the rain has stopped.

Lion changes into a thick black hoodie, lined with Sherpa fleece, the word *Faction* printed across the chest. He grabs his black down puffy, the JOBZ, and the joint he rolled earlier. Then he remembers what Miriam said about tension at the Space Needle and digs the death punch out of his backpack.

Sliding his fingers into the flex-steel rings, Lion extends his arm and presses the trigger. Five steel pistons punch outward, like tiny supersonic fists. A second later they retract, disappearing back into metal slots atop the knuckles.

Fully charged and ready to rock.

Lion slips the weapon into his pocket and heads out the door. The lobby is empty. There's no sign of Miriam. But as he exits the hotel, the robo-doorman stands his solitary watch.

Outside, he's greeted by a sky that's two shades darker now, and an icy chill in the air. Lion pulls on his watch cap, flips the hood of his sweatshirt over his head and, when he's halfway down the block, lights the spliff.

A couple of women across the street glance at him as he exhales. They have tribal face tattoos and dyed black hair. The tattoos are classic Anti-Nagel style, and the black dye jobs could make them raven fetishists or bat fetishists. But neither seems particularly interested in him.

He walks down the block and around the next corner, spotting a long glass skybridge stretched between buildings, some eighty feet above the ground. A sign reads: WASHINGTON STATE CONVENTION CENTER. Dangling beneath the bridge, there's a giant web of climbing ropes supporting an array of skynets and pup tents. It's another Anti-Nagel colony, though it looks completely deserted.

But not everything's deserted.

Across the street, Lion sees those same two women with the face tattoos—even closer than before.

His pulse quickens.

Pot paranoia or is something weird going on?

Lion can't decide, but picks up his pace all the same. Catching sight of the Space Needle between buildings, he aims in that direction, passing a brand-new street sign thanking him for visiting the Amazon Zone, and another, not five feet in front of it, welcoming him to the Microsoft Zone.

Another half block and a sneak peek in the side mirror of an old Chevy tells him the women have closed the distance again. Lion doesn't know what to do. He doesn't feel like running, but death-punching these ladies in their face tats doesn't seem like the better option.

There's a Starbucks two storefronts up. Lion tucks the half-smoked joint into his pocket, strides inside, and buys a triple-shot Americano while watching the door.

Nothing happens.

He pays for his coffee, still watching.

Still nothing.

Lion walks back to the doors and sneaks a glance through the glass. But there's no one in sight. The street is empty.

So pot paranoia after all.

"Get a grip, Zorn," he says, heading out the door.

Lion aims in the direction of the Space Needle. A few steps later, his JOBZ starts to vibrate in his pocket. Pulling it out, he sees a text from Lorenzo.

"Big news," it reads. An exploding skull emoji appears next, then more text. "Remember the three tech billionaires you asked about? One found dead at PRML last week. Covered in snakebites. Cause of death: inland taipan venom." Then another exploding skull. The text ends with: "Onstage soon, will call later."

Inland taipans are the deadliest snake in the world, but they are found only in Australia. Lion slides the JOBZ away, trying to figure out how someone could get attacked by an Australian snake in America.

Exotic pet accident?

Yet the text said the billionaire was covered in snakebites—so what, like, one really pissed off exotic pet or a bunch of them?

Maybe an exotic pet store accident?

But there's no way it's legal to sell inland taipan snakes in America, except to zoos.

Illegal exotic pet store accident?

Lion decides to park this line of inquiry until he has more information. He takes a sip of his coffee and starts down the street. Two steps later, those same pair of tattooed women step out of a doorway, not five feet ahead of him. One has neon purple lipstick and a large black square inked over her right eye. The other has traditional Polynesian ink covering the left side of her face.

"You're Lion Zorn," says the woman with the square-eye tattoo.

"Seriously?" he says.

"You really are Lion Zorn," she repeats, closing the distance between them.

More groupies?

"Fucking took you long enough," says the Polynesian-inked woman. "I'm freezing."

She doesn't sound like a groupie.

"Are you stalking me?" asks Lion, sliding his hand into his pocket.

"Absolutely," says Square-Eye, taking a step closer and reaching for his arm. "You're coming with us."

"I am?" asks Lion, yanking the death punch out of his pocket.

The woman with the Polynesian ink glances at the weapon and starts laughing, her face tattoos scrunching into a kind of geometric death mask. Then she lifts up her right hand and points a Glock 39 at his chest.

"Classic mistake," says Square-Eye. "You brought a death punch to a gunfight."

"Ichika wants to see you," says the Polynesian-inked woman.

Lion takes a sip of coffee and stares at the Glock for a couple of seconds, then slides the death punch back into his pocket.

"Put the gun away," he says. "I want to see Ichika, too."

Love Your Species

After realizing that Lion wants to meet Ichika as much as Ichika wants to meet Lion, the two Anti-Nagel women calm down. Jannah, with the Polynesian ink, puts the gun away and tells him she has a car nearby to take them to the meeting. Cathy, with the square-eye tattoo, apologizes for stalking him.

Jannah's car is a retro-electric Miata, what the kids call a "mini-mini," and more like a sleek golf cart than an automobile. They cram inside. Jannah spins the wheel, guns the engine, and rockets into traffic.

The mini-mini has some get-up-and-go.

Slicing between an oversized SUV and an undersized Toyota, Jannah nearly clips a bus. She glances over at Lion and shrugs. "Force of habit."

"Force of habit."

"Force of habit?"

"I learned to drive in Lagos."

"Slow down," demands Cathy.

Jannah smiles at her in the rearview, then jams her foot on the accelerator. Lion slams back into his seat, then gets tossed around as they bob and weave for a few blocks. Finally he asks, "Where are we going?"

"Near the Space Needle" is all either will say.

Lion doesn't push it. With Jannah's lead foot on the gas, they should be near the Space Needle in under five minutes. But as they draw closer, the sidewalks grow increasingly crowded, then overcrowded, then people start spilling into the street, slowing their progress to a crawl.

"Are all these protesters?" asks Lion.

Jannah shakes her head. "Not just protesters. Tourists, cops, undercovers from all the three-letter agencies, every panhandler for fifty miles and . . ."—pointing at three bedraggled men with face tattoos sitting on a dumpster—"our people."

Around the next corner, the crowd overtakes the street completely, and the mini-mini grinds to a halt.

Bodies begin to press up against their car.

Lion eyes them warily. "Let's park and walk."

"Not into crowds?" asks Jannah.

"Or heights."

"Really?"

"Both scare the shit out of me."

Jannah gives him a strange look, then lays on her horn and scatters the crowd. She makes a sharp right into a 7-Eleven parking lot and pulls into a spot. Lion gets out of the car, wondering about her look. He doesn't wonder for long. A rising tide of battle chants catches his attention.

"Humans First!" shouts the Humans First contingent. "Love your species!"

"Empathy for all!" is the poly-tribe reply.

"Love your species" is more redneck cracker Nazi bullshit. It's an updated version of the white power classic, "Love your race." Yet the chant of "empathy for all" hits even harder. "Empathy for All" is the title of the article Lion wrote about Sietch Tabr, the one that told the world about the psychedelic. Even after the scrubbing, the phrase stuck around—first as underground graffiti; next as a poly-tribe rallying cry; and finally, as just another protest chant.

As an em-tracker, Lion probably should have seen that one coming.

"Tension," he says, surveying the scene.

"It's been like this for two weeks," says Cathy, stepping out of the car to stand beside him.

"And worse every day," adds Jannah, walking over to join them.

"What now?" asks Lion.

Jannah points to her right. "We're this way," she says, speeding off into the crowd.

Humans First

Jannah walks like she drives, weaving between bodies at high speeds. Lion has to jog to keep up.

Down the block and around a corner, and the Space Needle comes into view.

The sight pulls him up short.

The Needle is constructed from three massive steel girders shaped like a gigantic hourglass. Tip to tail, the entire structure measures 605 feet. At the base, the girders start out in a wide tripod stance, then come together 400 feet above the ground to form a tightly corseted waist, before spreading wide apart again, creating the four-pronged cradle that supports the observation deck up top.

"It was designed to look like a flying saucer," says Cathy, pointing at the observation deck.

But that's not where Lion is looking.

Beneath the deck, there's a massive web of ropes supporting a miniature village. There must be a hundred skynets housing over two hundred pup tents. Lion has seen photos, but those were taken in the early days, when the initial cadre of thirteen Anti-Nagels first occupied the Space Needle. Now that occupation has grown into a colony.

"That looks like it could hold three hundred people," says Lion, pointing at the platform.

"Three hundred and twenty-seven," says Cathy, "as of last night."

"We count heads," explains Jannah. "We think the structure can hold four hundred people, but no one wants to find out."

"There are that many Anti-Nagels in the colony?"

"There are that many Anti-Nagels in Seattle. Once the protesters showed up, Ichika thought we'd all be safer together . . ."—Jannah points at the encampment—"up there."

"That's why the Washington State colony was deserted."

Cathy nods.

Lion looks at the crowd. "Do you also count protesters? Any idea how many there are?"

"Maybe a couple thousand," says Jannah. "But the Space Needle is a big tourist attraction. Once the Anti-Nagels arrived, it got bigger. Add in the cops, the undercover feds, and the people visiting the museums nearby—maybe five thousand at any one time."

"Humans first," chants the crowd. "Love your species!"

"Empathy for all," comes the reply.

Jannah angles them past the Needle, avoiding the protest barricades and the cops in riot gear. They wind through the crowd, ending up near a giant curved metal blob. The Museum of Pop Culture, a sign tells them, and the newly added Museum of Technology. This must be the Tech Museum that houses the seventh Bolex H-11.

"*Maybe later*," thinks Lion.

Jannah climbs onto a concrete bench and motions Lion up. Once he's beside her, she points toward the Space Needle, leans in close, and raises her voice over the chanting. "The group closest to the Needle—they're mostly cops and the professional protest types."

"Are you giving me a tour?" asks Lion.

Jannah nods. "Next ring out is your standard poly-tribe contingent and the cross-race crowd."

"The switchers," clarifies Cathy, stepping up on the bench.

Lion sees Asian girls with blackface makeup and surgically enhanced buttocks interspersed with black girls with yellowface makeup and surgically altered eyelids.

"The final ring," Jannah says, pointing to a skinhead with a swastika tattoo, "is the Pacific Northwest arm of the Humans First movement."

"You mean the pencil dicks," clarifies Cathy.

"Exactly," says Jannah.

Humans First began as a protest movement in the early days of the Splinter, after Congress passed the Michael Soulé Restoration Act. Technically, the act significantly increased livestock grazing fees in an attempt to charge ranchers for the environmental damage they were actually causing. The fees went to a buy-back program, in which the government bought back ranchland from the ranchers being driven out of business by the higher fees. The land was then connected to nearby national parks via a long series of migration corridors, creating a not-yet-completed string of three continent-wide mega-linkages, with the Pacific Rim being one example. The ranchers got pissed. And vocal. When their message reached the evangelical arm of the Aryan Brotherhood—who feel that taking land away from people and giving it to animals is a sin against God—the Humans First movement was born.

"When am I meeting Ichika?" asks Lion.

"As soon as it gets dark."

"Here?"

Jannah shakes her head. "Someplace safer."

"Where?"

"That's the part you're not going to like."

Lion gives her a look.

"Remember when you said you're afraid of crowds and heights?"

"Yeah."

"It's like that," she says, "only worse."

FUCK BaLtimore

Jannah doesn't explain. Instead, she points into the distance, jumps off the bench, and weaves into the crowd. Lion glances at Cathy, but she's already hopped down and followed Jannah into the crush.

He starts after them, but doesn't make it very far, immediately getting clipped by a drunken Midwestern woman in an *I Eat Animals* sweatshirt. She scowls at him, then stomps away.

Lion pushes onward, trying to keep Jannah and Cathy in sight, but the crowd is starting to get to him. Everywhere he looks, all he sees are angry faces shouting angry slogans.

"Dominion! Dominion! Dominion over the beasts!"

Lion recognizes this chant as well. It's an Old Testament quote, from the book of Genesis, 1:26. "Then God said, "'Let us make man in Our image, according to Our likeness; let them have dominion over the fish of the sea, over the birds of the air, and over the cattle, over all the earth and over every creeping thing that creeps on the earth.'"

The battle chants grow louder. The air smells of weed and sweat. Lion's left foot clanks off an empty beer can, his right foot does the same. People are getting fucked up, he thinks, shouldering through the mess.

A shoving match breaks out to his left, so Lion cuts right, still attempting to keep Jannah and Cathy in sight. It was the wrong move at the wrong time. The moment he takes his eye off the crowd, he's smacked in the head by a bearded Indian man carrying a large cardboard sign reading: NEXT STOP: NOWHERE.

"Nope," says Lion, pulling to a halt.

"You are lost?" asks the man.

"Nope," repeats Lion.

"I was lost once."

"Nope," he says again.

The man squints at Lion, recognition in his eyes. "You're that empathy guy," he says, "You're Lion . . ."

"Nope," says Lion, slicing back into the crowd.

He makes it two steps before realizing Jannah and Cathy have vanished. He looks around, but neither of his companions are anywhere in sight. What Lion does spot is a small cleft between a falafel stand and a souvenir shop, about twenty feet to his left, that is somehow completely free of people.

Screw it, thinks Lion. As long as Jannah's no longer pointing a gun at him, he has zero desire to play bumper cars with a Humans First riot waiting to happen.

Weaving toward the cleft, Lion steps inside and breaks free of the crowd. He takes a deep breath, digs the joint out of his pocket and lights up. Turning his head to exhale, he sees a barrel-chested man in a bright orange Cleveland Browns sweatshirt holding a ten-year-old boy by the shoulders.

"Son," says the man, "only two rules in this life: Fuck Pittsburgh. Unless Pittsburgh is playing Baltimore. Then fuck Baltimore. Never forget these rules."

Five minutes later, Lion is still standing in that cleft and staring out at the crowd, maybe a little higher than expected. The man and his son are gone, leaving the space directly in front of him empty.

Five minutes after that, a woman with a square-eye tattoo appears in that space.

It takes Lion a second, then he smiles.

"Cathy," he says, "it's nice to see you."

"Fuck you, Zorn," says Jannah, appearing beside Cathy, her facial tattoos once again scrunched into that geometric death mask. "We're on a schedule."

"You're on a schedule," he says, lifting up the mostly smoked joint. "I'm on Sour Dictator Booty."

She gives him another death-mask look.

"When you do that with your face," he says, "it's kind of scary."

Cathy grabs Lion's left arm, Jannah grabs his right, and they both tug him into the crowd.

Protocol

It takes another ten minutes, but they work their way away from the Space Needle and into a quieter, industrial part of the city. The sidewalks empty out, and the battle chants fade into the distance.

Jannah leads them down a slender alley between buildings, stopping at a side door in an aluminum-clad warehouse. She knocks twice. A few seconds later, the door opens and a flashlight snaps on, revealing a middle-aged Mexican man in a guayabera shirt, an arcing line of ravens in flight tattooed across his face, and a stairway behind him.

"Enter," he says.

Once they're all inside, the man shuts the door and snaps the flashlight off. There's a hard clank—the sound of a bullet being chambered.

"What do you call a group of ravens?" asks the man.

"An unkindness," replies Cathy.

"A what?"

"An unkindness of ravens."

"Frank," says Jannah, "stop being a drama queen."

"Protocol," mutters Frank, turning the flashlight back on and heading up the stairs.

Pretty Big Bug Zapper

Five flights up, Lion steps through another door and onto the roof. A cold wind slaps him across the face.

"Keep moving," says Jannah.

Frank leads them through a maze of ductwork, finally stopping before a door cut into the side of a shipping container. He tugs it open and disappears inside. Cathy and Jannah push Lion after him.

The container is forty feet long and twenty wide. Lit by a single overhead bulb, the room is empty except for a large lump under a blue tarp and a wooden table holding a laptop and some kind of remote-control device.

Crossing to the laptop, Frank hits a key. "Stand back from the walls."

A quick blue hiss of electricity rushes up all four sides of the container, then flickers out.

"Pretty big bug zapper," says Lion.

"It's an anonymizer," explains Frank, pointing toward the ceiling. "Anything looking down from above sees a serious heat signature, but can't pinpoint location or motion for the next five minutes. Then the signature dissipates, and we have to charge it again."

"Stolen defense tech," says Lion.

"Not stolen," scolds Jannah. "The military is filled with good men and women who love animals and care about the environment. You, of all people, should know that."

"You really should stop doing that with your face."

Frank hits a few more keys and a large panel in the ceiling recedes, exposing an inky rectangle of night sky. Jannah crosses to the tarp and slides it halfway off the lump. There's a black duffel bag beneath. Unzipping the bag, she reaches inside, pulls out a climbing harness, and holds it up.

"You know how to put this on?"

Lion eyes it warily. "I took rock climbing lessons once. But, I told you, I don't like heights."

"Just a precaution," she says, tossing him the harness.

Lion steps into the leg loops while Jannah digs back into the duffel, pulling out two long coils of black rope and an assortment of carabiners. Dropping the ropes on the floor, she grabs the edge of the tarp and pulls it the rest of the way off the lump.

"Not gonna happen," says Lion, when he sees what's beneath.

"It's the only way up."

"Why can't Ichika come down?"

"She'll tell you once you're up."

"Not gonna happen," he repeats.

Beneath the tarp sits a heavy-lifting drone. It's a chubby quadcopter: four large rotor blades attached to a squat central body. Clamped to the underside are two long chains of webbing that come together in a single locking carabiner.

"You'll be fine," says Jannah.

Frank ties a figure-eight knot at the end of one rope, and then clips it into the carabiner dangling from the drone. He does the same with the other end of the rope, then tries to attach it to Lion's harness.

Lion steps backward.

"It's like riding a bike," says Frank, grabbing his harness, yanking him close, and clipping the carabiner to his belay loop. "Except there's no pedaling and you're five hundred feet in the air."

"I mean it," says Lion, suddenly very sober. "No fucking way."

"Way," says Cathy from behind him.

Lion spins around. Cathy's pointing a Glock 39 at his chest.

"I'm really starting to hate bird fetishists."

Jannah crosses to him, double-checks his harness, then lifts the hood of his sweatshirt over his head. "It gets cold on the way up."

Frank picks up the controller and hits a button. The drone whirs to life, rising from its cradle to hover a few feet off the ground. He hits another button and the vehicle lifts through the gap in the ceiling. The ropes pull taut.

Lion feels like he's sitting on a swing.

Jannah taps the center of his forehead with two fingers. "If you keep your eyes closed, it's over in less than three minutes."

Frank hits a button on the remote.

Lion closes his eyes and feels himself rise into the cold grip of the empty sky.

O ver in less than three minutes—that's so much bullshit.

The flight lasts three minutes and twenty-five seconds. Lion knows for certain because focusing on his breathing and counting out slow five-second inhales and slow ten-second exhales are how he survives. When he reaches the last breath of that final ten count, he feels rapid deceleration, followed by a couple of yo-yo bounces as the drone slows to a hover.

"Look at me," shouts a male voice. "Do not look down."

Lion opens his eyes and sees a bearded man in a trucker's cap ten feet in front of him, standing at the end of a fifty-foot skybridge constructed from yellow climbing webbing. The bridge has been cantilevered off the colony's main platform, like a plank off a floating pirate ship.

Then, of course, Lion looks down.

The lights of the city and the mash of the crowd some five hundred feet below. Immediately, a rush of adrenaline washes over him. The ghost trace of a single drop of sweat runs down his spine.

"Look at me!" shouts the man again.

Lion does as he's told. The man has tribal ink striping the left side of his face, and a sleek tactical shotgun strapped to his back. He lifts two fingers, points at his eyes, and says, "Keep it right here."

Lion nods.

"Now swing," says the man, motioning with his other hand.

"You got to be . . ."

But there's no other way.

Forcing himself to lock onto the man's eyes, Lion slides his grip up the ropes and pumps his legs with the same kick-coast-kick rhythm he once used on playground swings. It takes five nauseating back-and-forth rocks until he's got enough heave-ho for the man to grab his legs and halt his motion.

With a practiced tug, the man yanks him out of the sky and onto the platform. Steadying Lion with one hand, he unclips the carabiner and drops the rope on the floor. Above him, Lion hears a soft whir as the drone starts to reel in the rope. He glances up just as the carabiner disappears into the vehicle's cargo hold.

"In here," calls the man.

Lion looks down to see that his companion has crossed the sky-bridge and is stepping through a tent flap at its other end. Once again, Lion notices the tactical shotgun strapped across his back.

Fancy, he thinks, wondering where the Anti-Nagels are getting their designer artillery.

"Zorn!" shouts Jannah. "Get the fuck out of the way."

Spinning around, Lion sees Jannah arcing through the sky, the soles of her boots heading straight at his head. He ducks and springs backward into the railing. Jannah flies past and lands in a smooth crouch a few feet away. She stands up, unclips the ropes from her harness, and walks toward the tent flap.

"We're this way," she says, stepping into the next room.

He follows her inside, finding himself on a slightly larger platform than the first, empty except for a blue trash barrel in its center. Beside the barrel sit the same three bedraggled men Lion saw perched on a dumpster a couple of hours ago. "Our people," Jannah had called them.

The men are arranged in a circle on the floor, each holding a small plastic cup. On the ground to their left, there's an open bottle of Wild Turkey inside a brown paper bag. Two of the men sport ravens-in-flight tattoos, not quite Frank's design, but close. The third has a solitary dolphin leaping out of his left eye.

Dolphin-Eye looks at Jannah. "Spare change?"

Jannah ignores the request, steps out of her harness, and tosses it into the trash barrel. She walks across the platform and disappears through another tent flap, calling "Zorn! Keep up," as she goes.

The next structure is much larger than the first, and more of a room than a platform. The walls are made of thick plastic sheeting, stretched taut, with windows cut through them. A pair of bird feeders hang in each window. Lion sees a small flock of yellow-throated warblers clustered around one, and a trio of Steller's jays crowding another. Farther in, a group of raven-faced men stand in a semicircle, two of them with parrots on their shoulders. On the floor beyond them, five women share a bowl of chips and guac with a trio of pigeons. One of the women glances at Lion, taps a closed fist to her heart, then slides to her left to expose the back wall of the room.

"Empathy for All!" is spray-painted in large block letters.

So they know who I am, thinks Lion.

Jannah appears beside him, holding a cup of tea.

"Drink this," she says, pointing at his right hand. "It'll help."

Glancing at his fingers, Lion notices he's shaking.

He takes the tea, tries a sip, and realizes it's whiskey.

"Thank you."

Jannah nods, gesturing around the room. "At this end of the colony, most of the residents are bird fetishists, but we're cross-species friendly. There are also fish petters, ghost dogs, a bear tribe down from British Columbia, and the cacklers, visiting from Harar."

"Cacklers?"

"A cackle. It's what you call a pack of hyenas. They guard Ichika."

"Where's Harar?"

"Ethiopia."

"I've never met a hyena," says Lion.

"Focus, Zorn," says Jannah. "You need to know where you are." She points toward the skybridge. "You just came in from the Western Sky Dock. The room we're in is the Western Murder Hall."

"Murder Hall?"

"Murder of crows," she says. "There's also an Eastern Murder Hall on the other side of the colony. In the center are the living quarters, alongside the temple."

"Is this another tour?"

"It's my job. Somebody needs to show the new arrivals around. This place is tricky enough during the day, but at night?" She shrugs. "If you take a wrong turn up here, it's a long way down."

Jannah leads him out of the Western Murder Hall and into a small corridor that wraps the outer edge of the colony. Halfway down, Lion sees a larger window housing a pair of bird feeders. A tall woman in a long white robe stands between them, pouring birdseed from a cloth sack into the feeding trays.

She ignores Lion, going silently about her work.

He passes her. The hallway forks. Lion pauses, realizing that Jannah's disappeared from sight. As he's wondering which way to go, she reappears in the distance, down the right corridor.

"Zorn," she calls, irritation seeping into her voice. "We're on a schedule."

"You keep saying that."

"Like, ten minutes ago—we were supposed to meet Ichika in the temple."

She marches off.

They leave the service corridor and enter an even skinnier platform, really just planks of wood supported by cradles of yellow webbing that snake around the exterior of the colony. Jannah hikes for another sixty feet, then stops at a gray wool blanket, hung perpendicular to the corridor. She pulls it aside, revealing another skybridge, longer than the first, but no wider. It runs down the middle of the encampment. One side faces outward, just wide sky and the ocean in the distance. The other faces inward, toward the main living quarters, where a couple of hundred people and a sea of pup tents are spread across a platform about half the size of a football field.

"Zorn," calls Jannah again, disappearing through the blanket.

Fifty feet ahead, he pushes aside the wool and realizes the skybridge curves left, runs for another twenty feet, then ends at a small wooden platform with nothing beyond it but open space.

Or almost.

About forty feet away, on the other side of the abyss, sits another landing platform. In between, a long climbing rope dangles in the center of the chasm, with a single locking carabiner at its end.

Walking to the edge of the skybridge, Jannah lifts a long wooden pole from a white plastic cradle. There's a large metal hook at its tip. She spears the hook into the abyss, snags the rope, and pulls it over.

"Ready?" she asks, turning to face Lion.

"Ready for what?" he says, coming up beside her.

Jannah grabs his climbing harness and tugs him close. "Want to make out?" she whispers.

"You really are a groupie."

Lion hears a click at his waist. He looks down to see she's attached the rope to his harness via the locking carabiner.

"That's the temple," says Jannah, pointing at the platform on the other side of the abyss. "You've got to swing."

The landing is nothing more than a five-foot wooden platform. Miss it and there's four hundred feet of open air to fall through as you consider your error.

Lion glares at Jannah. "What is *wrong* with you people?"

"It started with a drug called Sietch Tabr and an article entitled . . ."

"Don't remind me," says Lion, backing up and preparing to launch himself into the sky.

"Hold on," says Jannah, stepping in front of him. "Abbas," she calls across the chasm.

A tall Ethiopian man steps onto the other platform, his face tattooed with black-on-black hyena markings, another of those fancy tactical shotguns strapped across his back. He squats in a catcher's stance and spreads his arms wide.

Jannah faces Lion, taps two fingers against his forehead, and slides to one side. "Now swing."

"I definitely hate bird fetishists."

Down on the street, Lion hears the Humans First contingent shouting: "Dominion, dominion, dominion over the beasts!"

"Yeah," she says, glancing at the restless crowd far below, "we get that a lot."

GIGGLE GIRL GONE WILD

Lion, Jannah, and Abbas stand in the shadows at the rear of the temple. The room stretches out before them, thick with incense and candles. The walls are made from white tubing and decorated with mash-ups of religious iconography. One displays a large painting: A trio of Egyptian gods are holding hands with major figures from Norse mythology beside a six-foot Star of David with the elephant-headed Hindu god Ganesh trumpeting through its center, and Krishna, Shiva, and Vishnu performing an Inuit Bladder Dance to the left. The other wall has been entirely covered in Islamic tile, ornamented by a thirty-foot cross supporting an emaciated Jesus with, Lion now sees, real bald eagles perched on the crucifixion nails.

He turns his attention to the central pulpit, where Ichika Adel stands alone on a raised dais, in some kind of a trance, wearing a hot pink vinyl jumpsuit that matches the color of her long pink dreadlocks. She appears to be in singsong conversation with a pair of small brown birds that bop in time on a driftwood perch to her left. The dialogue is a mix of whistles, chirps, and tweets, the sounds flying out of Ichika's mouth with such speed that the results exactly mimic the high-pitched crescendo of a giggling Japanese teenager.

Lion's never seen Ichika in person before. Up close, she's a great aristocratic beauty. Japanese and French on her mother's side, Jewish and African American on her father's, the results are race-free exotica—which explains her popularity with the switcher crowd below. Lion had always assumed she was younger than him, but now, seeing the light dusting of crow's-feet running off her eyes, he realizes she's older. Yet it's the crazy mix of birdsong pouring out of her mouth that he can't get past.

"Hermit thrushes," says Jannah, pointing at the birds perched beside Ichika. "They're the only bird to sing harmonic scales. Major, minor, and pentatonic."

"It's . . ." He has no words to describe the sound.

"I know," she whispers. "I've heard it called everything from 'the one true song' to 'giggle girl gone wild.'"

The temple's acoustics catch Jannah's whisper, amplifying her words into a cascading echo. In her trance, Ichika doesn't stop singing, but a dozen Ethiopian men emerge from the shadows behind the pulpit. Like Abbas, their faces have been hyena-inked and each carries a tactical shotgun slung across their back. None are smiling.

"Shhh," scolds Abbas. "To stop the song will anger the gods."

The temple's acoustics bounce his words toward Ichika. This time, the echo yanks her out of her trance. Twelve hyena-faced men snap their shotguns horizontal, barrels aimed toward the three of them.

"Mother," says Jannah, dropping to one knee, "we meant no disrespect."

Ichika looks at the hermit thrushes, opens her mouth, and chirps twice. Immediately, the birds fly off into the rafters. Then Ichika turns to face them, focusing her gaze on Lion.

"Yoho, Lion Zorn," she says, with a friendly wave. "Up jump the boogie to the bang-bang. Howzit, brah? Come to kibitz with an alte makhsheyfe?"

The language is some kind of Six Nation Speak. Lion hasn't heard this dialect before, but he recognizes most of the phrases. *Yoho* is Japanese slang for "Hey, how are you?" while the boogie bit, he believes, is early hip-hop. *Howzit, brah,* is Polynesian, and the final phrase sounds like Yiddish, which makes sense considering Ichika's origins, but mashed up with everything else?

"Not sure I got all that," says Lion, "but it's nice to meet you, too."

Leaving Jannah in the temple, Ichika leads Lion and Abbas through a wooden trapdoor cut through the floor of the pulpit. They climb down a tall iron ladder and into a Japanese tea garden. The room is thick with trees, shrubs, and flowers. The floor is coated in a dense layer of topsoil; the walls are made from cardboard and covered in ivy.

Ichika seats Lion at a small table in the middle of the garden, then disappears into the foliage. Abbas follows her into the greenery. She comes back alone, carrying a simple black teapot and two small white cups. Setting them on the table, Ichika sits down across from him.

A gray parrot flies out of a tree and lands on her shoulder.

"Kon'nichiwa, bitches!" squawks the parrot.

"2 Chainz," says Ichika, "where are your manners?"

"Aaargggt," shrieks the parrot, "I'm so high I can talk to rain."

Lion laughs.

Ichika gives 2 Chainz a stern look.

"Back to reality," says 2 Chainz. "Oops, there goes gravity."

Ichika taps a finger to her lips.

2 Chainz squawks, "No more music by the suckas," then flies away.

Ichika smiles, then pours tea. Afterward, she cradles her cup between her palms and asks Lion about the note he sent.

He's been thinking about his answer. Lion doesn't know Ichika at all and has no idea what really happened to her at the Braveheart. Could she be working with Five Spikes and Buddy Holly? The lightning bolt scars beneath her eyebrows tell a different story, but he can't be certain.

Still, Lion didn't come all this way to beat around the bush.

He tells her the story, starting with the disappearance of his friends, Ibrahim and Kendra, and continuing through his most recent discovery, the business card with the words *Suicide Girls, place your bets,* printed in Chinese.

"Mishpocha," she says afterward, "drink your tea, it'll get cold."

"My Yiddish is terrible."

"No worries, bruddah," she says, laughing, "I speak da kine." She switches to English. "I'm also fluent in Japanese, Amharic, Spanglish, Swahili, and seven bird languages." Ichika twirls a solitary dreadlock between her fingers. "How did you know I was involved?"

"I saw the video," Lion explains. "The drone shot from the sky. Right before that happens, you shiver. I've got the same shiver. It made me wonder, did we get them in the same place?"

Ichika bows her head. Lion drinks tea. 2 Chainz sails down from a tree, lands on the table, and pecks at his now empty cup.

Ichika lifts her head again and looks at Lion. "2 Chainz thinks you need more tea."

As she refills his cup, battle chants echo in the distance, maybe louder than before.

"Do you know why we were tortured?" asks Lion.

Ichika lifts a finger to the scar on her left eye, yet remains silent.

"What about Ibrahim and Kendra—do you know what happened to them?"

Ichika shakes her head.

Switching tactics, Lion tries, "Why'd I take the drone elevator up here? You could have come down."

"You're afraid of heights," she says softly. "I'm afraid of the ground."

"How'd you know I was afraid of heights?"

Ichika points at 2 Chainz. "My friends watched you on the way up."

The parrot ruffles his feathers and squawks, "She got a big booty. So I call her Big Booty."

"Who are the Suicide Girls?" asks Lion, in a final attempt to get the conversation on track.

"I don't have all the answers."

"Lady," he says, exasperated, "I don't have *any* answers."

"Family, religion, tradition," replies Ichika. "In China, these are very serious things. Virginity as well, especially among Christians. Three years before the Splinter, there was a fad, a sickness, I don't know what to call it. Men would seduce Chinese Christian girls and deflower them.

After the act, these same men would use the girl's faith against them, building up their guilt so much they would kill themselves. Those are the Suicide Girls."

"That's . . ."

Once again there are no words.

"Yes," she says. "It's unspeakable."

"This is still happening?"

"On the business card, that dark web address—it's an advertisement for a betting site. The procedure is almost the same. Ten girls are chosen, seduced, and deflowered. Then the site opens for business. People wager on which girl will kill herself first. The entire thing is documented, via stolen satellite feeds, hacked autonomous car lidar image capture, and anything posted on social media."

"Dominion," Lion says quietly.

"Yes, my sentiments exactly."

"The guy with Buddy Holly glasses," says Lion. "What can you tell me about him?"

"I'm not certain who he is," says Ichika, "but I think he works for someone very powerful. A daimyo."

"Daimyo?"

Ichika calls out in Japanese. Abbas must still be in the room because Lion hears his voice emerge from somewhere back in the greenery.

"Shifta," he calls back. "Shogun."

"Shogun," agrees Ichika, turning to Lion. "A warlord."

"Shogun," says Lion. "That word I know."

"The shogun is using the betting site to raise funds."

"Funds for what?"

"Abbas is very good with computers. Over the past year, he's been trying to follow the trail. We believe the money is being funneled through a half-dozen shell corporations to pay for two projects: the Devil's Dictionary and Pandora II. I don't know if these are separate or related. But there's also a trail that leads straight to a New York . . ."

Battle chants surge from below.

"A New York what?" asks Lion. Then he realizes those aren't chants. Those are screams.

Lion jumps to his feet, looking for a window or another way to look down.

"Humans First got their wish," says Ichika, still cradling her teacup. "The riot has begun."

"Is there a . . ." But before Lion can finish that sentence, Abbas runs out of the foliage.

"Mother," he shouts, "we must go!"

Before anyone can move, a fireball rips through the floor, not ten feet from the table, then explodes through the ceiling. The entire colony swings wildly. A support cable snaps, and the left side of the garden drops down seven feet, flinging Lion sideways through the air. He smashes face-first into a tree, the branches catching his limbs and arresting his motion.

Between the leaves, Lion sees Ichika and Abbas holding on to a different tree about fifteen feet above him and, beyond them, there's a gaping hole in what was once the ceiling. Through the hole, he sees the night sky and Cathy, dangling from a long rope beneath a heavy lifting drone, her square-eye tattoo open wide.

Another missile streaks through the night. The drone explodes in a fireball, the flames searing through the rope in an instant. Cathy screams and drops into the darkness.

A third explosion rocks the colony. Ichika, Abbas, and the left side of the garden disappear behind a curtain of flame. The shock wave blows Lion out of the tree and into an ivy-covered wall. He smashes into it, then bounces to the ground in a heap, his right arm now hanging at a wrong angle.

Lion grimaces, blinks against the pain, and forces himself to roll onto his side so he can look around. He's wedged into a crevice, staring at a chunk of bare wall. The explosion ripped away the ivy and there's a single line of graffiti visible beneath.

Empathy for All, is spray-painted, wild style, on the cardboard.

With the room tilted at a 45-degree angle, Lion is gravity-pinned between floor and wall, covered in dirt and debris, not sure that he can use his right arm. Above him, he sees only smoke and flames. In front of him, the now uptilted floor rises like a wall, exposing rows of white plastic tubing that run upward like a ladder. The tubes were once covered in topsoil, but the plastic beneath has caught fire and is starting to melt, mixing with the soil and flowing toward him like a burning white river.

The tubing directly in front of Lion has yet to catch fire.

He reaches out and tugs on the plastic. It feels solid enough to hold his weight.

He looks up—maybe twelve feet to the top.

Lion takes a breath, grits his teeth, and uses the rung to pull himself to his feet. Once standing, he reaches up and grabs a plastic tube two feet above him, then pulls himself upward again, starting to climb one-handed. The entire structure sways like a rope ladder, but it holds. Still gritting his teeth against the pain, Lion grabs the next rung, yanks himself upward, resets his feet, and repeats the process.

And again.

Finally he pulls his head over the top and gets his first look around. The view is awful in every direction.

Half of the garden is gone, just an open hole facing empty space. The other half is listing seven feet to one side, and almost completely on fire.

Below him, things look just as bad. Down on the street, there's a full-scale riot. Lion hears the pop-pop-pop of gunshots and spots a dozen different fires and just about as many melees.

There's a whooshing sound above him, growing louder. Whipping toward the noise, Lion sees a meteor of burning plastic heading straight for him.

He ducks. His bad arm bangs into the edge of the floor, but his good arm wraps the upper tube, halting his fall with a painful bounce.

Directly in front of Lion floats the ghostly silhouette of a hoverbike.

Is the pain making him hallucinate?

He blinks—but the bike remains.

It looks like an oversized racing motorcycle supported by four circular rotors, two in front, two in back, their whirling fan blades providing the lift. The machine's exterior is completely covered in shiny metal tiles, mirror-polished and assembled in a crazy angle pastiche that glimmers in the moonlight. The driver wears all white: a white motorcycle helmet, a white leather jumpsuit, and white riding boots. The visor snaps up and, even in the chaos, Lion does a double take.

"Jenka?" he shouts. "What the . . ."

"Quick," says Jenka, patting the seat behind him. "You must jump!"

There's a five-foot gap between Lion and the motorcycle, and a five-hundred-foot fall below.

"I will drop down and hold steady," shouts Jenka. "Like cowboy on horse in Western. You must land on saddle."

"Fuck," says Lion.

Jenka swoops into position.

Placing one foot on the swaying edge of the garden, Lion keeps his eyes pinned on the motorcycle below. He rocks forward, preparing to spring over the side.

"Now!" shouts Jenka.

Lion leaps over the wall, twisting his body midair so he's centered above the motorcycle seat, ready to wrap his arms and legs around the machine on impact.

As he jumps, Jenka drops the bike down a few feet to cushion his fall.

Lion's boots catch the foot pegs. The sure-grip rubber latches onto his soles and holds firm. He ass-crashes into the seat, snaps his knees together, and whips his good arm around Jenka, snugging himself tight.

The bike bounces under his weight, but steadies. Jenka revs the throttle and rockets them through a rain of burning ash and into the night.

Lion groans with the motion, then glances back over his shoulder.

A third of the colony has vanished, another third is on fire. A fleet of heavy lifting drones with long ropes dangling from their undercarriages are soaring into the blaze, then soaring out again, with four or five people daisy-chained beneath. A flying fire engine, like a grain silo surrounded by giant fans, blasts water out of a dozen independently rotating cannons. Each douse a different part of the Needle, creating billowing clouds of white smoke.

Another wave of pain runs down Lion's arm. He grits his teeth, looks away from the colony, and rests his head on the back of Jenka's jacket. He closes his eyes and starts counting breaths.

Five-second inhales, ten-second exhales.

A mile away from the chaos, Jenka touches a button on the dash and a compartment near his feet pops open. He lifts out an extra motorcycle helmet and passes it over his shoulder. Pinching the bike between his legs, Lion uses his good arm to take the helmet and slide it on. Jenka taps a finger on the side of his own helmet, showing him a small red button.

Jenka pushes the button. Lion does the same.

A second later, he hears a thick Moldovan accent coming through a speaker in the helmet. "What can I tell you," says Jenka, "stealth flying motorcycle test drive. I was in neighborhood."

"You saved my life," says Lion.

"Dah," replies Jenka dryly. "Now you owe me sex favor."

"Probably true."

"You have sister? Maybe she owe me sex favor, too?"

"Fucking Jenka," says Lion, shaking his head.

"Dah, fucking Jenka is what we are talking about."

Lion laughs, then winces. "Where are we going?"

"PRML," says Jenka, banking right into the clouds and leaving the burning colony in the rearview.

"I need a hospital. My arm's dislocated."

"We land over there," he says, pointing at a park in the distance. "I fix arm."

"You're not fixing my arm."

"No worry, I learn on internet. Then we go to PRML."

"I need a hospital."

"PRML," says Jenka. "You will want to first be there."

"Why?"

"Penelope. PRML was last place anyone saw Penelope alive."

PART IV

PRESENT TENSE,
THE PACIFIC RIM MEGA-LINKAGE

THE BLACK COAL OF MY MOLDOVAN HEART

The next few hours are hazy. Lion remembers a parrot named 2 Chainz and a flying motorcycle covered in mirrors. He remembers landing someplace with trees. He remembers a ray gun: thin, silver, and aerodynamic.

A ray gun?

Then he puts it together.

Jenka landed in the park, popped a hatch, and extracted a silver injection gun—that was the ray gun. It must have been loaded with some heavy-duty painkiller. A memory of Jenka injecting him is hard to find, but the shoulder of his good arm hurts from where the needle went in, and the shoulder of his bad arm no longer hurts from being dislocated.

Thankfully, Lion has zero recollection of Jenka fixing his arm.

He also has no memory of leaving the park. Yet they must have left, because Lion is stretched out on a cot in the back corner of a storage room. The ceiling is bare wooden planks, thick with cobwebs.

Where the hell is he?

Lion sits up and sets his feet on the floor. He sees a wall lined with metal bookshelves overflowing with office supplies and medical equipment. Coffee cans, cardiac-arrest paddles, and an ancient confocal microscope. There's a dirty window behind the shelves, and beside it, an old wooden rack holding seven pairs of skis and a cluster of ski poles.

Looking in the other direction, Lion sees another wall, mostly dominated by a glass-fronted gun cabinet. Five injection guns occupy the left side of the cabinet. Three are rifles, for shooting tranquilizer darts. The other two are of the handheld variety, similar to the ray gun that Jenka used on Lion. On a shelf toward the cabinet's bottom, there's a line of small glass vials filled with liquids.

Lion tries to stand—which goes better than expected. A quick body scan reveals his arm isn't ready to throw baseballs, but he can move it without much pain. There's bruising down his right leg and his head hurts, but in that distant way that means painkillers are on the job.

Walking over to the cabinet, Lion reads the labels off the glass vials. Telazol, ketamine, carfentanil. That explains the blank spot where his memory used to be. They're all potent animal tranquilizers.

Behind him, a floorboard creaks.

Lion spins around to find Jenka standing in an open doorway, still wearing his all-white motorcycle gear. With his helmet off, Lion sees Jenka hasn't changed his hairstyle. It's a bleached white pompadour, making him look a little like a pale, skinny Elvis.

"Welcome to PRML," says Jenka, with zero warmth in his tone.

"Thank you for saving my life."

"It was not my first choice."

"So you're still pissed?"

When Lion told the world about Sietch Tabr, he did so at Jenka's considerable expense. To say they have unfinished business, that would be putting it mildly.

"I am undecided," says Jenka.

"You lost a lot of money because of me."

"Dah," says Jenka. "Old news. How is arm?"

"You didn't learn that on the internet."

"No, in war. I was medic."

"I didn't know you were in a war."

"You could fill dump truck with metric tons of shit you do not know."

"So you are still pissed."

"Sir Richard made the money back," says Jenka, taking a step forward and revealing more of the doorway behind him. Through it, Lion sees a small research laboratory: a mass spectrometer, an industrial glass sterilizer, and a woman in a red ski suit peering through an electron microscope while absently feeding apple slices to a Siberian husky near her feet.

"You wanted change," says Lion. "That happened."

"No. *You* wanted change. *I* wanted revolution. These are not same thing."

"The Splinter wasn't enough? Humans First just blew up an Anti-Nagel colony."

"Dah," says Jenka. "But is still wait-and-see game."

"Wait and see what?"

"If underdog win."

"Which underdog?"

Jenka snorts. "This is lesson I learned from you. The über-underdog: plants, animals, ecosystems. Empathy for all—or don't you remember."

"I remember."

"Wait here," says Jenka, spinning around to walk out of the room. Through the doorway, Lion watches the woman feed another apple slice to the husky. Jenka returns ten seconds later, carrying a small black box, ornate and etched with dragons.

Lion's seen this box before. "Ghost Trainwreck #69, I presume?"

"The weed will help with arm," says Jenka, opening the lid and revealing a row of twelve joints inside stoppered test tubes. He shuts the lid again and passes the box to Lion. "You must go on porch to smoke."

"Tell me about Penelope."

Jenka points at a coatrack in the corner. "You should put on parka to go on porch."

Jenka takes a step toward the door, then stops and turns around again. "Know this, Lion Zorn. The dragon box is gift from Sir Richard. From me, box is not gift. From me, you only get the black coal of my Moldovan heart."

"Thanks for saving my life," says Lion.

"You are welcome," says Jenka, walking out the door.

I Have an Allergy

Lion starts toward the coatrack, but before making it halfway across the room, he notices his backpack sitting under the cot.

Lion's pretty sure he left it in his hotel room at the Braveheart.

Dragging the pack out from under the bed, he unzips the main compartment, seeing his black down puffy wadded up beside the JOBZ, his toiletries stuffed into their stuff sack, the death punch, and a paperback copy of Frank Herbert's *Dune,* which he carries everywhere for luck.

Lion grabs his down puffy and a couple of test tubes from the dragon box, then walks into the lab, trying to sling the coat around his shoulders. He stops walking near the husky because the slinging isn't going well. The coat keeps slipping off his shoulders before he can grab it with his good hand and finish the job.

The woman in the ski suit notices, slides off her stool, steps around the dog, and walks over. She's in her late thirties, with blue eyes and brown hair, worn straight and long, and skin weathered from a life spent outdoors.

"Let me," she says, lifting the jacket onto Lion's shoulders and sliding in front of him to zip it closed. "I'm Lizzy."

"Lion."

"I know."

Over her shoulder, he notices mountains through a window.

"Where am I?"

"Genoa, Nevada."

"That doesn't help."

"Just outside the southeastern gate of the Pacific Rim Mega-Linkage." She points toward the door. "If you went out that door and up the mountain, you'd be at the bottom of the Heavenly Valley ski area. If you kept going for a little while longer, you'd hit Lake Tahoe."

"Lake Tahoe," says Lion, doing a rough calculation in his head. It was early evening when he met Ichika in Seattle. It's daylight now, and he's in Nevada. "How long was I out?"

"A while," she says, walking back to the counter. "Go talk to Jenka. I've got to get you to the main gate before three-thirty and . . ."

"And what?"

"Your arm. I was planning on snowmobiling you over, but with the sling, you'll have to ride one-handed."

"I'll be okay."

"You're sure? It's only fifteen minutes by snowmobile. Part of it will be bumpy, but the bike has sure-grip seats."

"I won't bounce off?"

"No. But it might not feel so great. The other option is the truck, but the roads are bad, and with all the new snow, it could take a while."

"What's a while?"

"An hour. Longer if they haven't plowed."

Lion wants to find Penelope. He wants to find a warlord. He doesn't have time for a long drive. Then he remembers the Ghost Trainwreck.

"I've got weed for pain," he says. "I'd rather get there fast."

"Good," says Lizzy, pointing at an array of jars stacked on the far end of the counter. "Before I can go home tonight, I have to catalog all these samples."

Lion glances at the jars, noticing they contain decapitated snake heads, floating in formaldehyde. The sight of dead animals brings bile to his throat.

He looks away quickly.

Seeing his reaction, Lizzy covers the samples with her jacket. "Sorry."

"I have an allergy."

"My sister's an em-tracker," she says. "You don't have to explain."

Once his breathing steadies, he looks over at Lizzy again, then points at the samples beneath her jacket. "Were those inland taipan heads?"

She nods.

"What's an Australian snake doing in the Sierra Nevada mountains?"

"Go talk to Jenka."

IS NOt NEW PrOBLEm

Walking onto the porch, Lion is greeted by blue skies and snow-covered mountains. It's about twenty-five degrees, but there's no wind and the sun is out. He removes a test tube from his pocket, uncorks it, and slides out a joint, thinking, despite the circumstances, it's a hell of a view.

Jenka stands at the edge of the porch, smoking a thin black cigarette. Beyond him, a pair of electric snowmobiles and the stealth flying motorcycle sit beside one another in a small snow-covered field.

"Who am I meeting at the front gate?" asks Lion.

Jenka, lost in thought, doesn't hear him.

Lion repeats the question.

"At gate," says Jenka, snapping out of his daydream, "you are meeting no one. In office, you meet Sir Richard. The office has holo-chat. Sir Richard is in Cambodia."

"What happened to Penelope?"

"I know little more than you."

"I don't know anything."

"Dah," says Jenka, taking a drag on his cigarette. "Is not new problem."

Lion hits the joint, exhales, and says, "Sir Richard told Penelope that something went wrong in PRML."

"Dah," says Jenka again, stabbing out his cigarette in an ashtray. "Do you know Heavenly Bypass?"

"The underground tunnel with ski runs built over it?"

"Two tunnels. One is a local habitat corridor. The second is a regional corridor, over three hundred meters across. Wide enough to accommodate migrating—what is word?"

"Moose?"

"Megafauna," replies Jenka. "That is word. That is moose, bear, wolf, mountain lion—"

"I know what megafauna means," Lion interrupts. "What does this have to do with Penelope?"

"There is a bar for skiers near the entrance to the main tunnel. Ten days ago, that bar was last place anyone saw Penelope."

"Ten days?"

"According to bartender, Penelope had a drink, asked a couple of questions, then left to go to look for something in park. She went on skis, took equipment, sampling jars."

"Ten days is a long time."

"This is field biology research station. People in park for weeks at a time is business as usual. But there are rules. People go in pairs, with strict check-ins. Unless there's storm, every twenty-four hours. Penelope went alone, without partner, did not sign out equipment. Then there was a storm."

"She never checked in?"

"Under sunny skies, communication is shaky. In storm?" He shrugs. "When she didn't check in, Sir Richard tried radio, tried phone, tried satellite thermal."

"The satellites couldn't find her? How long were they overhead?"

"The first time, not long. The second time, a day later, much longer. They found other park rangers, moose, bear, wolf, mountain lion, but not Penelope. That was when Sir Richard sent a search party into park and asked me to find you. I found you. The search party did not find Penelope."

"How did you find me?"

"You are like song," says Jenka. "Band on run."

"My one-man band."

"It's not true."

He thinks for a moment. "Lorenzo. You called Lorenzo."

Jenka shakes his head no.

"Why would Lorenzo give me up?" asks Lion, suddenly puzzled. "Especially to you, no offense."

"Calling is not my bag. Computers are my bag."

"You hacked Lorenzo's computer?"

"Is ugly word, hack. I ask question. Computer answer question."

"You should be in jail."

"Dah," agrees Jenka. "But does not change fact. My computer says Lorenzo's smartphone is in Brazil. So why, I ask, does his phone request an Uber ride from Vince Vaughn Memorial Diner in Los Angeles to Braveheart Hotel in Seattle? Perhaps because you are stupid, you did not know that every Uber autonomous has camera in car."

"But you were at the Space Needle."

"At Braveheart, I am told the famous Lion Zorn is meeting the famous Ichika Adel at the famous Anti-Nagel colony."

"Miriam gave me up?"

"Perhaps, because you are stupid, you did not know that Sir Richard owns Braveheart Hotel. No offense."

"Sir Richard owns the Braveheart?" But Lion's not even surprised.

"I decide to party crash meeting with Ichika," continues Jenka. "But Humans First riot got in way. I arrived right after guy with spiky hair shot Stinger missile into colony. Fine American craftsmanship, that Stinger missile."

This catches Lion's attention. "A guy with spiky hair fired a Stinger?"

Before Jenka answers, the door to the research station bangs open and Lizzy strides onto the porch. She has Lion's backpack in one hand and a snowmobile helmet in the other. "I got a text from Sir Richard," she says, passing Lion the helmet and backpack. "We have to go."

He takes the helmet but is still staring at Jenka. "A spiky-haired guy shot a Stinger missile?"

"I will see you in office," says Jenka. "There's Wi-Fi in visitors' center. Ask internet. The spiky hair missile video went viral."

Lizzy starts toward the snowmobiles. Lion taps out his joint, slides on the backpack and helmet, then follows her into the yard.

He stops near the hoverbike and glances back at Jenka. "What about the snakes?" he calls. "I saw the sample jars. The billionaire who got killed by an inland taipan snakebite—that's what Penelope was investigating, right?"

"Not taipan," yells Jenka.

"What?"

"Lizzy!" shouts Jenka. "Permission granted."

Lizzy stops walking, looks at Jenka, and points at Lion. "You want me to tell him?"

"Dah. But he is idiot, so do not expect him to understand."

syn-Bio CHImera

Standing beside an electric snowmobile, Lizzy takes off her glove and presses her thumb against a red starter button. Lion sees the blue flicker of a fingerprint scanner, then hears a soft click as the machine kicks to life. Lizzy straddles the sled as Lion climbs on behind. As he does, he feels the sure-grip seat mold around his thighs, snugging him tight.

"Tell me about the snakes," he says.

"Hold on," replies Lizzy.

She revs the throttle and starts off into the trees. Lion wraps his good arm around her waist and leans into the turns. The electric engine is almost completely silent, but the roar of the snow being hurled backward by the treads discourages further conversation.

Lion looks at the scenery, thinking it looks cold. Ten days in the mountains is a long time, especially during a storm. Penelope can handle herself in almost any situation, but alone in a winter storm in the mountains?

Banking left, Lizzy passes through a tight copse of trees, over a hill, and onto a snow-covered fire road. Without turning around, she calls, "How's your arm?"

"Pretty good."

"No pain?"

"Ghost Trainwreck on the job."

"Good," she says, slapping his thigh. "Here comes the fun."

Running hot down a smooth fire road, they slice through a small valley before Lizzy cuts right into the forest, following a long ridgeline up the mountain. Granite boulders dot the scenery like ancient sentinels. Pine trees, their boughs heavy with snow, watch them as they pass.

Lizzy tops a rise, eases off the throttle, and calls back to him: "They're not snakes, or not entirely."

"What are they?"

"Syn-bio chimera. A genetic hybrid: icefish and snakes—plural. Both inland taipan and black mamba."

"Black mamba?"

"Most aggressive snake on Earth. Someone found the genes that produce the aggression and spliced them into the genes of the deadliest snake on earth."

"The taipan."

"And that's just what we've figured out so far," says Lizzy, swinging the snowmobile around to face a steep rise that leads to the mountain's crest. Way too steep, in Lion's estimation, for a snowmobile carrying two passengers.

"The icefish genes," he asks, "is that why the snakes can survive in the winter?"

"Antifreeze proteins in their blood."

"Is that even possible?"

"It is now," she says, patting his thigh again. "Hang on."

"You're not . . ."

"If we go around, it'll add twenty minutes."

Lion stares up the steep slope. "It can't be as bad as getting blown out of the sky."

"That's the spirit."

Lizzy rockets up the ridge. The bike chews up the slope and pops over the top without a problem. The crest is smooth and flat. The view is pine forests to the west, the whole of the Carson Valley to the east. They ride into the forests, following the ridgeline for a few minutes before Lizzy cuts back down the mountain, through a grove of pine trees and onto another fire road.

Lion sees a parking lot and a few buildings in the distance.

It takes five minutes to close that gap.

Lizzy stops at the edge of the parking lot. She kills the engine, climbs off the machine, and takes off her helmet. "You okay?"

He nods.

She leads him past a row of pickup trucks, down a short sidewalk, and to the main doors of a log cabin chalet. Lion pauses at the entrance.

Lizzy notices.

"Places like this," he says, pointing at the chalet, "sometimes come with deer heads."

"Taxidermy free. You're safe."

They push through the entrance and into a standard visitors' center, minus most of the visitors. There's an empty welcome desk, adorned with a pile of brochures and a small holographic sign that reads: PACIFIC RIM MEGA-LINKAGE, SOUTHEASTERN GATE. To his left, a small gift shop sits beside the front doors of a movie theater.

Lizzy passes him a ticket and points at the theater. "For the three-thirty show."

"I thought I was meeting Sir Richard."

"Afterward. Jenka will grab you at the exit and take you to the meeting."

"Afterward?"

"The movie theater is the only way into the park."

"Why?"

"Bio-sniffers in the theater," explains Lizzy. "The park is a protected ecosystem. If you're carrying pathogens, we'll know." Then she puts on her helmet, lifts up the visor, and says, "It was nice to meet you, Lion Zorn."

"Thanks for the ride."

"You're welcome. And Sietch Tabr—you changed a lot of lives. Just wanted you to know."

"It wasn't me."

"Yeah," she says with a smile, "but thanks all the same."

TWO LEGS, NOT FOUR

Lion looks around the visitors' center. It's empty except for an elderly woman in the gift shop and a few tourists on the other side of the room.

He finds a quiet corner, unslings his backpack, and pulls out the JOBZ. It takes thirty seconds for the device to power up. After the welcome screen appears, Lion opens the Tor Browser, types: "Humans First + Space Needle riot" into the search bar, and clicks the first video that pops up. A familiar scene snaps into view: the Needle. The crowd. Tension.

"Love your species!" screams a throng of protesters.

"Empathy for all!" comes screaming back.

Lion pauses the video to scan the image. It appears to be from a few moments before the riot began. He sees a couple of shoving matches and a Humans Firster about to throw a Molotov cocktail into the crowd.

He lets the video play, noticing that when the Molotov cocktail blows up, nearly the entire Humans First contingent starts throwing punches, like the explosion was some kind of signal.

A moment later, a flaming projectile screams through the frame.

The Stinger missile?

Lion rewinds, tracking the origin of the flame. The projectile emerges from the upper corner of the image.

He peers closely until he sees it: a slash of Chernobyl yellow.

Lion puts his thumb and forefinger on the screen and widens out the picture. Now the image is clear as day. Five Spikes is standing where Lion had stood, in that gap between the falafel shop and the souvenir stand, patiently staring into the crowd.

Lion plays the video forward.

Five Spikes turns around, squats down, and lifts a black tube off the ground, then stands up again and steadies the tube against his shoulder. It's a compact rocket launcher.

Five Spikes looks out at the crowd, watches and waits.

Something about the scene bothers Lion. It's an em-tracker thing. An emotional fault line that emerges from . . .

Lion pauses again, stares at the image, but can't find the connection. Instead, he gives up and hits play. A few seconds later, the Molotov cocktail sails into view. He tracks the bottle as it comes in for a landing, seeing a fireball explosion near the feet of a large man with raven tattoos. Flaming gasoline splashes outward and Raven Tats jumps sideways to avoid it, slamming into a middle-aged woman wearing a "Two Legs, Not Four" T-shirt. The woman bashes into her boyfriend, who retaliates by punching Raven Tats in the face.

It's the proverbial first blow—the start of the riot.

In the next instant, Five Spikes steadies the missile launcher, drops to one knee, and sights down the viewfinder. He aims skyward, at something outside the frame, and pulls the trigger.

The missile fires into the night.

There's an off-camera explosion and a rain of fire. People run in every direction.

Five Spikes loads another missile, aims, and fires.

Total chaos erupts. There's the pop-pop-pop of gunfire and a chorus of screams. Two more explosions rock the middle of the crowd and a trash can sails straight up into the air. The frame jerks upward to catch a third explosion. It's the heavy-lifting drone blowing up, and Cathy, with the square-eye tattoo, screaming and falling from the sky.

"Fuck," says Lion.

The image shifts back to the riot.

He hits pause so he can reorient to the scene. It takes a moment for him to find Five Spikes.

Lion plays the video.

In the next second, Five Spikes tosses the rocket launcher behind him and spins around to face the camera. Before he can take another step, a bullet hits him right between the eyes. It blows a hole clear through his head.

That's the end of the video.

To Lion's right, the main doors to the theater swing open. A woman's voice comes over the PA system.

"Three P.M. show," she says. "Please take your seats."

Demographic winter

It's an old-fashioned movie theater. There's a projector in the back, a screen in front, and seats in the middle. Lion sits in the middle of the middle. A few rows behind him, a pair of bird watchers are discussing upper canopy ornithology. In front of him, there are a trio of European backpackers and a handful of solitary graduate students. Other than that, the room is empty.

So where are the bio-sniffers?

It takes Lion a second to realize the sniffers have been disguised as stereo speakers and embedded into each seatback. According to Lizzy, they're hunting deadly pathogens, but can also detect more subtle human odors. Knowing Sir Richard—no way the sniffers are just protecting the park.

For sure, Sir Richard is gathering bio-intel about each visitor, especially those tidbits that can be later used for advertising and marketing purposes. Six months from now, when one of those bird watchers receives a mysterious text about a new company making an all-natural eco-friendly antiperspirant designed specifically for their genetic phenotype—well, this is why.

The theater darkens and the movie begins. White text appears on a black screen, reading: "Plants and animals need room to roam." The image shifts to an overview of the Earth. A silky woman's voice begins the narration: "How much room to roam? That's the question that launched Michael Soulé's career."

The film goes on to review Soulé's founding of the field of conservation biology and his discovery of the field's central insight: Ecosystems are complex machines made from interconnected organic parts. "Like any machine," says the woman, "once the parts begin to fail, the entire machine collapses."

The screen shows bleached coral reefs, dying forests, lonely animals searching for nonexistent mates. "'Demographic winter is the term used to described this collapse. It refers to our current biodiversity crisis, the Sixth Great Extinction, where species die-off rates are a thousand times greater than normal. At this rate, without drastic change, fifty percent of all the plants, animals, and insects will vanish before the start of the twenty-second century. Yet Soulé envisioned a solution: the mega-linkage. Continent-wide stretches of wilderness providing plants and animals with the room to roam. Ladies and gentleman, there is real change on the horizon. Welcome to the Pacific Rim Mega-Linkage."

A Sir Richard highlight reel comes next: his advertising background, his founding of the Arctic Corporation, and of course, his jet-black mane and fabulous white teeth. The fortune he made off Sietch Tabr is treated as "accidental good luck," while his decision to use the profits to establish the Pacific Rim Mega-Linkage is explained as "The only right thing to do at the time."

A map on the screen shows PRML in its current form. It's a collection of twentieth-century national parks, mostly in Northern California and Oregon, connected by migration corridors such as the Heavenly Bypass, to produce one massive unbroken wilderness. A mega-linkage.

"Mega-linkages are a life raft for life," continues the voice. "Research has repeatedly shown they are the very best way to preserve biodiversity while battling climate change. . . ."

Lion feels his pocket buzz. It's the JOBZ on the job.

He slips out the device and sees a text from Lorenzo: "Nothing's riding on this except the First Amendment of the Constitution, freedom of the press, and maybe the future of the country. Not that any of that matters. But if you guys fuck up again, I'm going to get mad."

Lion recognizes the quote. It's another one from *All the President's Men,* spoken by Ben Bradlee, the executive editor of *The Washington Post*, the moment after he learns that the Watergate scandal goes all the way to the White House. It's a moment of deep, sad resignation.

Data bit finds data bit.

Lion realizes what was bugging him a few minutes ago, when he was watching the video of the Space Needle riot—the emotion he felt but could not name. He closes out texts, pulls up the Tor Browser, and finds the riot video again. Muting the sound, he fast-forwards until he reaches the moment Five Spike fires the first missile. The last time Lion watched the video, his attention had been focused on the Molotov cocktail and the start of the riot. This time, Lion plays it while watching the expression on Five Spikes's face.

He sees it then: resignation. It's the exact same look of sad resignation Lion saw on Five Spikes's face in that alley in Los Angeles.

Lion plays the video yet can't find anything to explain the look. He rewinds to thirty seconds before missile launch and plays it again.

That's when he notices: As Five Spikes bends down to pick the rocket launcher off the ground, behind him, there's a glimmer that doesn't belong. It's a pinprick of light in the crease between the souvenir shop and the food kiosk, in the darkest corner of the cleft.

Fumbling around, Lion tries to figure out how to get the JOBZ to enhance the photo. Then he recalls how Five Spikes showed him the hidden drop-down menu. Running the cursor along the upper edge of the screen, Lion finds the menu and pulls up a grid matrix, dividing the image into eight squares.

Tapping his finger on the square that contains Five Spikes and the mysterious glimmer expands the image to fit the screen. A "fill shadows" tab doesn't do much, but the pixel reversal feature, which turns light to dark and vice versa, uncovers a telling detail.

Actually, two telling details.

First, behind Five Spikes, the shadow of a human figure can just be made out. Lion sees the faint outline of a heavyset woman's face. She looks a little like an enforcer for a roller derby squad—short hair, dyed white, and a hard set to her jaw. But Lion's not really looking at her face. It's her hand that has his attention.

She's holding a gun and it's pointed at Five Spikes—that's the source of the glimmer.

That also explains the sad look of resignation on Five Spikes's face. He didn't want to attack the colony; this woman forced him to attack the colony. The look might also clarify why Five Spikes helped Lion in Los Angeles, but it still doesn't clear up why he was tortured in the first place. Was Five Spikes being forced to torture him? Is Buddy Holly doing the forcing? If Ichika was right, then Buddy Holly and Five Spikes are working for a warlord. Is the warlord behind all of this?

That, at least, makes sense.

But what does any of this have to do with a deranged betting site, a drug called Evo, or the disappearance of Ibrahim and Kendra?

Lion doesn't know.

Yet, as the movie ends, he feels a familiar buzz. It's what he used to feel as a reporter, on the front end of a story, when the puzzle pieces started to slot together.

Lion hears Ichika's voice in his head. "Shogun," she says, "warlord."

I'm coming for you, he thinks, tick-tock.

Never Drive a Car When You're Dead

Jenka meets Lion in a courtyard just outside the exit to the theater. He's traded the white motorcycle leathers for a white snowsuit and white snow boots. The color of his outfit, Lion notices, still matches the dye job of his pompadour.

The courtyard is a large rectangle constructed from blocks of black stone. The only decoration is a circular firepit in the center, where an all-weather robot with a tank-tread lower half and a humanoid upper half distributes free mugs of hot chocolate.

A light snow falls.

Jenka points at the other end of the courtyard, where the eight-foot walls that surround the space are bracketed by a pair of enormous granite boulders. "Past boulders is southeastern gate into PRML," he explains. "Gate serves day visitors, scientists, and backpackers, but is hard to get permit, so not many backpackers."

"What about skiers?"

"They enter farther up mountain, or on California side."

"I skied here," says Lion, "back when I used to compete."

"Dah," says Jenka.

"Dah?"

"When Penelope went missing, because you are skier, is reason Sir Richard thought you might be useful. I disagree. But I did not get vote."

"How much money did you lose because of me?" says Lion, start-ing toward the exit. "Millions? I'll bet it was millions."

He gets halfway across the courtyard before Jenka calls after him. "We are not that way."

Lion backtracks to Jenka, who leads him over to a section of black wall and places his right hand against the stone.

Hidden palm reader, perhaps?

But instead of the blue flicker of a laser scanner, Lion sees the stone quiver, then start to liquify. A jet-black human hand extends out of the wall itself. It's animatronic, made of some kind of shape-shifting poly-rubber. Jenka reaches out and grasps the hand, then executes a complicated shake: standard business clench into closed fist bump, knuckle to knuckle; then top of fist against bottom of fist; then a back-handed soul slide into a knuckles-forward fist bump. Afterward, the hand recedes into the wall, and a recessed door slides open.

"'Never trust a man in a blue trench coat,'" says a woman's voice.

"'Never drive a car when you're dead,'" replies Jenka, stepping through the door.

"Those are Tom Waits's lyrics," says Lion, a fact he knows because the K-Holes do the occasional cover.

Jenka nods. "Best American lyricist. Gets right to point: Never drive a car when dead."

"Why is the door quoting Tom Waits?"

"We take turns. It's Tom Waits, when I choose password. When Sir Richard's turn, hip-hop. Last week: 'Get up, get down,' is question. Answer: 'My Uzi weighs a ton.' What kind of answer is answer? I do not understand American hip-hop."

"And the handshake?"

"Also changes weekly."

"Heavy security."

"Dah," says Jenka. "Not everyone believes plants and animals should have room to roam."

He leads Lion through the door and into a long hallway, then down two flights of stairs. They come out in a massive subterranean garage. Two electric snowcats are parked to their left, beside a dozen electric snowmobiles. Beyond them, the garage opens into an underground cavern housing a bus-sized silver tube with a giant drill bit on one end and the words *The Boring Company* printed on the side.

Lion points toward the machine. "Is that for digging tunnels?"

"Dah. Elon Musk loaned Sir Richard four electric boring machines for Heavenly Bypass."

"What did Sir Richard have to loan Musk in return?"

"How do you say . . . firstborn son."

They cross the garage, passing through a steel door and down another hallway, then up another flight of stairs and through a final door. Lion finds himself in an all-white room, empty except for a single wooden bench in its center.

"This is what?" he asks.

"Is holo-chat," says Jenka, sitting on the bench.

"It's a room."

"Bigger unit." He taps the bench to his right. "Sit."

Lion sits. The lights dim, a pedestal rises out of the floor, and a panel opens in one of the walls. A holo-projector slides out from behind the panel. A beam of blue light pours out of the lens, followed by the ghostly image of a four-foot-tall bullet-shaped robot.

"That's R2-D2," says Lion.

"Sir Richard is *Star Wars* fan."

The holo-R2-D2 whistles, chirps, and slides into the room. The robot stops a few feet later and projects a beam of light that's identical to the beam of light being projected by the projector. It's a hologram of a hologram. The second hologram crystallizes and Lion sees Sir Richard, standing maybe a foot high, wearing jeans and a denim work shirt, his telltale mane of black hair hanging to his shoulders.

Sir Richard turns to face Lion, bows slightly, then straightens up. "Imagine," he says in his crisp British accent, "the first animal that did not have to eat other animals."

"What?"

"Soon," continues Sir Richard, "we will be able to engineer vegetarian carnivores. Grass-nibbling mountain lions, leaf-eating tigers. So, Lion Zorn, if 'empathy for all' is our starting point, are we not morally obligated to make animals that don't eat other animals?"

"Nice to see you, too," says Lion dryly.

"Hello, sport."

"I see you're still pontificating without provocation."

"Old habits," says Sir Richard. "Sorry I couldn't be there to greet you. Project in Cambodia seems to be melting—"

"Should I be worried about Penelope?"

Sir Richard isn't used to being interrupted. He raises an eyebrow.

"Penelope," says Lion again. "Jenka says you dragged me here because she went missing. Should I be worried?"

"We don't know, but we have reason to suspect she's still alive. When Penelope left, she was carrying a tracker."

"If she was dead," explains Jenka, "with tracker, we'd find body."

"We think she turned it off," says Sir Richard. "She left the bar and entered the Bypass, and that was the last signal we got."

"Why would she turn off her tracker?"

"We don't know."

"Why'd you send her into the park in the first place?"

"I didn't send her. She volunteered."

Lion doesn't need to check the text messages on his phone to know that someone's lying. Either Penelope lied to him about getting a message from Sir Richard, or Sir Richard's lying to him now.

"Why?"

"You were told about the snakes?"

"I was told they're man-made," says Lion. "But I didn't think we had the technology to make full multispecies chimeras."

"We don't," explains Sir Richard. "But someone does."

"So someone has figured out how to make hybrids." He thinks for a second. "But why release them in the park?"

"That's what Penelope wanted to find out."

"Why did she want to know?"

"Susan Jackson."

This catches Lion's attention.

"Susan was one of my partners, a co-investor in PRML, a brilliant neuro-geneticist turned entrepreneur. Her company makes the bioreactors for almost all of the world's cultured beef. It's actually one of the main reasons PRML exists. With her tech, lab-grown beef could scale up to compete with hoof-grown beef. It helped push ranchers out of business, and we were able to buy up their land."

"Was?" asks Lion. Then he remembers the text Lorenzo sent. "Susan Jackson—she was the first person who got killed by the snakes."

"The second. We lost a ski patroller first."

"You kept that quiet."

"We told people she died in an avalanche. But we found a dozen snakebites on her legs. This was before we found the snakes. We kept it quiet until we could figure out what was going on. When Susan died, Penelope heard and wanted to investigate."

"Snakes? How many are there?"

"We've trapped seven."

"Jenka told me Penelope disappeared after visiting a bar."

Sir Richard nods. "The ice bar."

"Did she talk to anyone there?"

"The bartender."

"Did you talk to her?"

"She won't talk to us."

"You understand," says Jenka. "We're an equal opportunity employer."

"She's a Rilkean," explains Richard. "Because of . . ."

"Me," says Lion, finishing the sentence. "Because of me, the Rilkeans hate you."

"Dah," says Jenka, "but you, Lion Zorn, are hero to Rilkeans."

The Rilkeans were one of the first poly-tribes. They started out as an international hacker collective with a shared interest in animal rights, deep ecology, consciousness hacking, and the writings of the nineteenth-century poet Rainer Maria Rilke—thus the name. The poet's admonishment to "live the questions" jibed with the Rilkeans' experimentalist approach to life. Both poet and poly-tribe felt that empathy was the very best way to live those questions. Rilke called empathy his "greatest feeling, my world feeling, the indescribably swift, deep, timeless moments of this godlike in-seeing."

For similar reasons, a Rilkean chemist created Sietch Tabr as an empathy-expanding psychedelic to be used in their private rituals. Then, Sir Richard found a way to commercialize their ritual, peddling the drug as a potential treatment for autism. Next, Jenka tried to sneak the formula for Sietch Tabr out the back door and use it to jump-start a revolution. Finally, Lion wrote his article, "Empathy for All," and told the world the truth. Thus the Splinter.

The Rilkeans don't especially like Sir Richard for this reason.

Penelope, his on-again, off-again girlfriend, is a Rilkean.

The bartender who won't talk to Sir Richard is a Rilkean.

"If I'm the one asking the bartender the questions," says Lion, "you think I'll have better luck getting some answers."

"Dah," says Jenka. "Perhaps not quite as dumb as you look."

SKIING IS MY BAG

The holo-chat ends. Lion stands up, slowly following Jenka out into the corridor. He feels pretty banged up. The whirlwind of the past week—the colony attack, Penelope's disappearance, his reentry into Sir Richard's orbit—has taken a toll.

"I'm knackered," says Lion.

"Is late," agrees Jenka, starting down the hallway. "Park will wait until tomorrow."

Lion is still worried about Penelope, but he's too exhausted to do anything about it now. Plus, Sir Richard's explanation of her disappearance makes sense. His on-again, off-again girlfriend has a severe allergy to surveillance, even when it's for her own good. Would she ditch her tracker just on principle?

Maybe.

"Where am I sleeping?" asks Lion, hoping it's not that cot in the storage room.

"There is hotel for you," explains Jenka. "Near ski resort. Driver will take you now. Lizzy will get you in morning. She will be guide into Heavenly Bypass."

"The Rilkean bartender works tomorrow?"

"It has been arranged."

Lion wonders how that conversation went, but he's too tired to give it much thought. Instead, he sleepwalks after Jenka until they're back in the subterranean garage, where the tunneling machine is still parked. A rush of cold air reminds him that he's going skiing in the morning.

"I'll need gear," says Lion.

Jenka looks at him.

"If I'm going into the Bypass," he explains, "I'll need ski gear."

"Is already at hotel."

"My boots?"

"You print ski boots. There is sizing kit in room. Hotel has 3-D printer."

It's been a few years since Lion's skied, though he doubts this will matter. Skiing is what Lion used to do with his parents, back when they were still a family. After they stopped being a family, skiing is what Lion would do to hide from that fact. Lion has done a lot of skiing.

"You are smiling," says Jenka.

"Dah," replies Lion.

"Dah?"

"Skiing is my bag."

But this reminds him that computers are Jenka's bag—and this gives him an idea. "I'll talk to the bartender on one condition."

"You are capitalist," says Jenka. "Capitalist always have condition."

"I need you to backtrack a website."

Lion digs out the JOBZ and pulls up the text from Chandra: the photograph of the business card advertising the Suicide Girls' betting site. He shows Jenka the image.

"Dot-onion," says Jenka. "Is dark web."

"I didn't say it would be easy."

"I didn't say it would be hard."

"I'll take anything you can find about the site," says Lion, "especially the name of whoever set it up. I also think the profits are being funneled into two projects: the Devil's Dictionary and Pandora II. Anything about either would also be useful."

Jenka taps the card. "Chinese characters."

"They say 'Suicide Girls.'" He flips over the card. "This side says, 'Place your bets.'"

"This means?"

"It's a long story."

"And if I leave you at Space Needle, is shorter story, no."

"Fair point."

Lion tells him the story. He starts with the appearance of Evo and the disappearance of Kendra and Ibrahim and continues through his torture by taxidermy and the rain of fire that ended his meeting with Ichika.

"Someone is hunting em-trackers," says Jenka afterward.

"You think?"

"With Evo as bait—it is how I would do it." Jenka thinks for a moment. "You said Susan Jackson was at early Evo party?"

Lion nods. "The party was on Sealand 4, the seasteading colony. There's a photo online."

"I will find photo."

"And you'll find out about the Suicide Girls?"

"Is sick fuck, this warlord."

"Yeah."

"I will find Suicide Girls," says Jenka, "but I do not think I will like what I find."

THE PERFECT BAIT

Lion's hotel is a retro-chic Swiss chalet nestled between high-end condos and some kind of Soviet-bloc-looking parking structure. Lizzy drops him out front.

He drags himself inside and manages to check in without incident. The clerk points him toward the elevators. He remembers nothing about the trip to his room, only realizing he's made it inside once he spies the requisite ski-town decor: a faux Navajo blanket on one wall, a faux Ansel Adams print on the other.

But the bed looks big and comfortable.

Babying his bad arm, Lion fumbles through his rituals. He plugs in the JOBZ to charge, brushes his teeth, and starts to undress for bed. As he's removing his sling, he remembers he has to ski tomorrow.

For that, full use of all his appendages seems important.

Taking a deep breath, Lion exhales and gingerly straightens his arm. It feels better than expected. He flexes his elbow out a few times, surprised to discover that most of the pain is gone.

Not bad, he thinks.

Lion finishes getting undressed, turns off the light, and crawls into bed. He should be asleep in seconds.

But he's not asleep; he's thinking about Penelope. His on-again, off-again girlfriend is no longer in the Bypass, maybe not in PRML itself, of this he's fairly pretty certain. In Lion's experience, vanishing without a trace—that's just Penelope being Penelope.

"Shit."

He'd forgotten to print his ski boots.

Snapping on the light, Lion finds the sizing kit behind the couch, beside a pair of poles, a helmet, and a small backpack filled with long underwear, pants, goggles, a beacon, a shovel, and a probe. There's also a pair of Faction skis, his favorite brand.

Why is he not surprised to discover Sir Richard managed to unearth his favorite brand of skis?

Better not to think about it, Lion decides.

He takes a closer look at the sizing kit. It appears to be nothing more than a pair of tall black rubber boots with a touchscreen built into one toe. A small instruction card tells Lion to step into the boots, click the red power button beside the touchscreen, and let the built-in sensors do the rest.

He steps into the boots and clicks the power button. A miniature air compressor hidden in each heel whirs to life. The walls of the boot expand around his feet and lower legs.

The display lights up: "Hold still. Scanning in progress."

The expansion stops and there's a flicker of a white light inside the boots. Less than a minute later, the flicker stops and the boots deflate, the air rushing back out of the heels.

Following the instructions on the display, Lion enters his height, weight, and skiing ability, and, having no idea what it means, selects "nostalgia" from a boot-style menu. He finishes with the five-letter code for the hotel's 3-D printer. The screen tells him his boots will be ready by morning.

A moment later, he's back in bed, but sleep feels even further away. Whenever he gets close to nodding off, he sees a flash of the burning colony, Cathy plunging to her death, or his own wild leap onto the back of Jenka's flying motorcycle.

But something else is bothering him.

Getting out of bed, Lion walks over to the window. It's still snowing. There's a small porch on the other side of the glass. He could bundle up and step outside for a smoke. Weed might calm him down.

But he doesn't have the energy to get dressed.

Then it clicks—what's actually bugging him—what Jenka had said: Someone's hunting the em-trackers.

Not that this was news to him. Yet he'd been assuming that someone was hunting specific em-trackers: Kendra, Ibrahim, Ichika Adel, Lion Zorn. But if someone was hunting em-trackers in general, then Jenka's right: A drug that makes you trip evolution, a drug like Evo, it's the perfect bait.

But why hunt em-trackers?

Companies now hired em-trackers to assess a product's cultural viability in the same way that companies once hired cool hunters to assess a product's market fit. Em-trackers are also useful at the front end of relationships—business, personal, interspecies, etc.—as an emotional matchmaker of sorts. But neither of these things explains why someone would bother hunting them. The only thing that an em-tracker has that's worth having is hidden inside their heads. The wiring diagram of an em-tracker's brain—their connectome map—that's where the real value lies. If you had that map, you'd have the secret to their empathic superpowers. This idea, at least, makes sense.

Lion crawls back in bed. This time, he's asleep before his head hits the pillow.

OLD SCHOOL

Lion wakes at first light and climbs out of bed. His arm feels stiff, but a little stretching takes care of that. He gets dressed, once again not surprised to discover that all the clothing Sir Richard acquired for him fits perfectly. He finishes by tugging on his black watch cap, grabs his wallet and the JOBZ, and heads out the door.

Breakfast is a buffet in the lobby. He piles a plate with avocado toast and vegan sausage, then grabs a bowl of oatmeal and a side of raisins and nuts. He finds a seat beside a window.

A waiter brings him coffee.

The view is of the eastern side of the Sierra Nevada mountains, a jagged parade of peaks rising up from a glacier-carved valley. Everything is blanketed in white. "Ten inches of powder," according to a notice beside the check-in counter.

It'll be a good day on the hill, even under the circumstances.

But the circumstances dictate that he has work to do.

Lion pulls out the JOBZ, brings up the Tor Browser, and then hesitates. *Tor* is short for "the onion router," which refers to the way information moves through the dark web. Encrypted data is sent through nodes known as onion routers. Each node must peel away a single layer to discover the message's destination, the next layer of the onion. The sender remains anonymous because each node knows only what came immediately before and what comes immediately afterward, making back-tracing complicated, though not impossible. The JOBZ adds more encryption to the onion, but considering what Sharijee said about Buddy Holly being able to back-trace the crypto, Lion's still nervous entering "Pandora II" into the search bar.

He glances around the room. No one's paying any attention to him. He hits return.

Lion learns that a carpet company sells a product called Pandora II. They also sell Pandora, Pandora I, and Pandora III. All are slightly different shades of the same neon blue shag. There's also a bunch of references to the film *Avatar,* where Pandora is the name of the lush alien world at the center of that movie. Lion recalls that the skin color of the inhabitants of that world is a bright neon blue—which explains the color of that shag.

Doesn't explain anything about why that warlord cares about Pandora.

Lion turns back to the browser, deleting his first query from the search bar and entering "Devil's Dictionary."

"More coffee?"

Lion glances up to see a waitress standing beside him. She's maybe twenty-two, possibly Japanese, but she's had epicanthic surgery, so her eyes read blue and Nordic. Her living screen T-shirt displays classic Switcher messaging: swirling gene codes followed by the phrase *We Are Everyone*.

"I'd love some more coffee," says Lion.

"Ten inches of pow-pow," she says, looking out the window as she pours.

"Pow-pow," says Lion with a laugh. "Way to kick it old school. That's what we called fresh snow when I was a kid."

She stops pouring to look at him. "And that was back when? The Late Cretaceous?"

"Geology humor," says Lion, "funny."

"More like amateur rock hound," she explains. "Welcome to Nevada. Geology is in our blood. Everybody in the state has a great-granddaddy who came for the gold rush."

Lion points at her shirt. "Doesn't 'We Are Everyone' mean that everyone everywhere has a great-granddaddy who came for the gold rush?"

"Ah," she says, heading toward another table, "genetics humor, funny."

Lion takes a sip of coffee and glances back at the JOBZ.

According to the search result he's looking at, *The Devil's Dictionary* is a satirical dictionary written by a Civil War soldier and journalist named Ambrose Bierce. It took Bierce three decades to compile the entire volume, publishing sections as installments in magazines and newspapers along the way.

A second link brings up sample entries.

"Air, *n*. A nutritious substance supplied by a bountiful Providence for the fattening of the poor."

Lion smiles.

"Advice, *n*. The smallest current coin."

He laughs, but the sound catches in his throat. The first time he met Kendra, she was wearing a T-shirt that read: "Don't ask me for advice. I still think punching stupid people in the face is the right idea." He hopes she's still alive. He hopes Ibrahim's still alive. He tries to refocus.

Why would a warlord be interested in the Devil's Dictionary?

Before Lion has time to consider that question, a text from Lizzy slides onto the screen. "Be there in twenty."

He's going to need fuel to ski. Lion puts the JOBZ away and focuses on eating. Another two pieces of toast, all of his oatmeal, and the vegan sausage. He asks his waitress for a check and for directions to wherever he's supposed to pick up his 3-D-printed ski boots.

"Ski shop," she says, passing him the bill. "Across the lobby and down the hall. You can't miss it."

"Thanks," he says, signing the food to his room, tipping well, and standing up to leave.

"Have fun shredding the sick gnar."

"Old school," says Lion, "you have yourself a great day."

A Certain Vibe

Back in his room, Lion fills his pack with gear, shoulders his skis, grabs his poles, and leaves his shoes. Carrying everything down to the lobby in his socks, he sets the gear on a rack beside the front door and makes his way to the ski shop.

"Hanson rear-entry Spyders," says the clerk, setting his boots on the counter. "That's old, old school."

Lion gawks.

The boots are fire-engine red with two black buckles, a black spider on the toe, and the word *Spyder* printed along the side. He can't believe what he's seeing—they're the same boots he wore as a kid. But even back then, they were hand-me-downs.

"Are these the original design?" asks Lion.

"Just the cosmetics. Everything else is new. Air-fill liners that adjust to your foot, warming coils in the toepiece and ankle, and electromagnets in the heel plate that match your bindings."

Lion pangs with nostalgia. "How could you possibly know?"

"Did you read the small print?"

"When?"

"When you entered your information in the sizing kit."

"I didn't see any small print."

"It was on the flip side of the instruction card. You selected 'nostalgia' from the style menu."

Lion sort of remembers doing this.

"If you select nostalgia," continues the clerk, "the AI does a social media scan. It finds pictures of you in your old ski boots."

"That's . . . intimate."

"Familiarity," explains the clerk. "If you haven't skied in a while, it helps."

"The familiar look of the boots—makes sense. It tricks your subconscious and makes you feel more comfortable."

The clerk nods. "You'll ski better. But I've only seen one other pair of Hanson Spyders before."

"They were hand-me-downs from when I was a kid," explains Lion. "I think they belonged to a friend of my dad's originally."

"Have you skied since then?"

"Used to compete."

"I wonder if we've got a glitch."

"Why?"

"Usually the AI finds the most recent pair of boots you wore, not the earliest pair."

Lion realizes this is because the scrubbing erased most of the images of him online. But his mom definitely went through a Facebook phase. Maybe she posted one of his old ski photos. Maybe the scrubbers missed it. But he tells none of this to the clerk.

Instead, he sits down on a bench to try on the boots. Unlike the originals, the new ones fit perfectly.

Lion looks up at the clerk. "Do I need to sign anything?"

"For the boots?"

He nods.

"Retinal scanners," says the clerk, pointing at a dome camera in the ceiling. "The one over the check-in counter scanned you when you arrived. This one matched your eyes when you first requested your boots. If your eyes don't match your request . . ."—he points toward a back room—"the robo-stocker can't grab your boots."

"Didn't I sign a check in the restaurant?"

"Yeah," says the clerk, "but you didn't have to."

"Familiarity," says Lion when it clicks. "The old-school check, like the old-school boots."

"It creates a certain vibe."

"Yeah, it does," says Lion, still staring at the boots.

"Welcome to the Old School Inn," says the clerk.

"What?" asks Lion, confused.

"The Old School Inn?"

"The name of this hotel is the Old School Inn?"

"There's, like, a gigantic sign out front."

"I got dropped right there. I guess I didn't see it."

"The nostalgia setting on the 3-D printer—didn't you think that was a little weird?"

"I was tired," he says, heading toward the door.

Lion clunks through the lobby in his new boots, grabs his skis and poles from the rack, and walks outside. The crisp scent of winter punches him square in the face. Like a tidal wave of time, an even more powerful sense of nostalgia washes over him.

It stops him dead in his tracks.

Nostalgia is particularly acute in em-trackers. When most of us hear a familiar song on the radio, the brain replays the original memory, matches it to the new memory, and rewards the match with neuro-chemistry. The good feeling at the heart of nostalgia—that's dopamine. In em-trackers, this is exactly where their talents come into play. The end result is that Lion feels nostalgia and doesn't just flash back on childhood memories of skiing. He also feels all the cultural mood shifts that combined to make those memories even possible.

Standing in that driveway, Lion experiences the lucky exuberance of the 10th Mountain Division, having defied the odds and survived World War II, building the foundations of the ski industry in the late 1940s. He feels the conservative churn of the 1950s cold war machine that birthed both the chemical and aerospace industries, which, in turn, created the flexible plastic needed to modernize ski boots. Then the iconoclastic 1960s inspired the hot dog ski movement of the 1970s, which begat the need for that ultimate showman's ski boot: the Hanson Spyder.

Of course, Lion doesn't know these exact facts. What he does know is how they felt at the time. He can feel how the past stitches itself to-gether to become the present, and it's this memory of cultural mood shifts that allows em-trackers to unveil the future.

Then it hits him: All of this was intentional.

Sir Richard's penchant for knowing everything about everyone would also include knowing that em-trackers have an acute reaction to nostalgia. And the clerk was right. Now that he's standing in front of the hotel, he can see for himself: That damn sign is gigantic.

Suddenly Lion knows why he's staying at the Old School Inn. Sir Richard is priming his em-tracking skills, ensuring he gets the very best out of Lion Zorn.

That is just so Sir Richard. Lion isn't even pissed.

Lizzy arrives five minutes later.

Still lost in thought, Lion loads his gear into the back of her truck, then climbs into the passenger seat and stares out the window. As they turn out of the parking lot, he glances back at the parking structure. It looks even more Soviet-bloc in the daylight.

"You're quiet this morning," says Lizzy.

"Nostalgia," says Lion.

"If you say so."

Lion glances at her.

"Round here," she says, "we call that Sir Richard's way of fucking with people."

intraspecies transportation network

"Growing up," says Lizzy, "I wanted to be Michael Soulé."

They're riding a chairlift, a few runs into their day, heading toward the Milky Way Bowl, near the top of Heavenly Valley. Lizzy has one of those newer electromagnetically sealed splitboards. It's a snowboard most of the time, but a button on her phone unseals the electromagnets and transforms it into a pair of fat skis.

"What happened?" asks Lion.

"Changed my mind and decided I wanted to be Elena Hight."

"The snowboarder?"

"She kicks ass," says Lizzy. "But then I discovered rock climbing, and rock climbing got me into snakes."

"Because that happens."

"Happened to me. I bumped into a rattlesnake sixty feet off the ground, in the middle of a crack climb. Everything sort of slowed down. I saw the snake, and instead of freaking out—I don't know, the snake looked terrified, and not of me. A second later, he crawled out of the crack and up my arm, wrapped around my neck, and hung out there while I finished the climb."

"So you're an em-tracker, too?"

"I know, right?" she says. "That's exactly what I thought. And I told you my sister is one, so it would make sense. But no, I'm not."

"I've never had that experience with a snake. Dogs, wolves, coyotes, birds, and once, a Galápagos penguin."

"Really?"

"Swear to Zeus. But a rattlesnake? If you're not an em-tracker?"

"Only thing I can figure, a hawk grabbed the snake. If the snake bit the hawk mid-flight, I can see the poor guy getting dropped into a crack. He was trapped until I came along."

"So you're a snake elevator?"

"Intraspecies Transportation Network is the technical term. It's my calling."

"What is your calling?"

"I'm a mutt. Undergraduate double major: herpetology and genetics. My PhD is in complex systems, focusing on the health of large-scale ecosystems. But snakes are my first love."

A gust of wind rocks the chairlift. Normally, skiing makes Lion forget his fear of heights. Now he puts down the safety bar.

"When you were a kid," she asks, "what did you want to be?"

"A pro skier, my Candide Thovex phase. Also a scientist, which started with dinosaurs, went into astronomy, then died in physics."

"Physics is cool."

"I know. But I suck at math. So I decided on rock star. Sadly, I'm worse at guitar than math. But I was good at writing lyrics, which made me think poet. Then I got to college and had seven majors."

"Didn't become a poet?"

"Freshman year, I got obsessed with William James. He got me out of poetry and into psychology and philosophy—majors one and two—which got me into drugs."

"That's a major?"

"Psychopharmacology."

"How long did that last?"

"A semester. But all the cool problems were in consciousness studies, which lasted two weeks. Whole department was full of nutcases."

"Next?

"Slight left into neuroscience, which almost took. But once I figured out what neuroscientists were doing to animals in the name of neuroscience, it was ecology, which lasted six weeks, and journalism, which happened accidentally, but reminded me of poetry. That stuck."

"Journalism reminded you of poetry?" she asks. "'Cause why? They both use words?"

"Yup," says Lion, "that's it exactly."

The lift crests a small rise and the upper terminal comes into view. Lion raises the safety bar. Lizzy pulls out a pair of telescoping poles from her backpack, extends them to the length of normal ski poles, and wiggles to the edge of the seat, preparing to unload.

Lion does the same.

They push away from the lift, sliding onto a cat track. Lizzy keeps her splitboard split as they wrap around the mountain on a high traverse, fresh snow rising like white smoke from their tails.

Lizzy slows to a stop near a granite boulder. She puts her poles away, reactivates the magnets with her phone, and snaps her snowboard together.

"See that tree line," she says, pointing down the mountain. "That's just above Killebrew Canyon. Stop before you get to the rollover."

Then Lizzy hops her board into the air and uses the gravity assist to accelerate into the run. Lion watches her speed away, then pushes off to her left, feeling the glide of the snow as the slope starts to steepen. He spots a little feature: a rock, maybe a tree stump, covered in snow and twenty feet ahead. It forms a perfect ramp, which gives Lion his first air time of the season. The feeling of flight rekindles an entirely different kind of nostalgia. The thing that skiing awakens. Animal memory, he's heard it called, a deeper primal freedom.

Lion lands in a puff of white, shoots down a tight gully, and spots the tree line. Lizzy bounces into view to his left, giant plumes of snow trailing behind her like geisha fans. They ride side by side for four turns, then hockey stop in tandem between two pines. Lizzy whoops. Lion roars.

"Did you just roar?"

"Happens," he says, smiling.

"Is that why they call you Lion?"

"No, but maybe it should be."

Lizzy points down the mountain. "It's going to get steep by the broken pine. Drop in there. It's a pencil chute between rocks. Cut hard left at the bottom."

"Where do we come out?"

"Near the top of Mott Canyon. That's where the ice bar is, and the main entrance to the Bypass."

"Anything else?"

She gestures toward the broken pine. "When you drop in, there's a cliff to your right side, so, you know, don't miss the turn."

Lizzy glides into the run. Lion is about to follow when he spots something hovering about fifty feet to his left, beside the upper branches of a ponderosa pine. It looks like someone tried to cross a raven with a drone. It looks more bird than machine, but it hovers more machine than bird. And it seems to be hovering quietly, holding its position.

"Lizzy . . . ," but she's already gone.

Doesn't make sense, he thinks. Most ski areas have banned drone overflights for safety reasons, and the whole of the Pacific Rim Mega-Linkage is a no-fly zone.

So what is it doing here?

Down below, Lizzy carves past the broken pine and drops into the chute. Lion doesn't want to lose her. He pushes off, casting one final glance toward the sky.

The raven-drone has vanished, only his uneasiness remains.

THE END OF MAN

Lizzy waits for Lion at the bottom of the chute.

But she doesn't wait for long.

As soon he appears, she pushes off, slicing fresh tracks through a grove of pine trees, then across a small gully and onto the well-groomed snow of an intermediate slope. They ride forward for a hundred yards, then cut hard right and down a final rise. The ice bar comes into sight.

It's an appropriate nickname. The entire building has been constructed from huge blocks of ice, glimmering in the sunlight—like a cubist painting of an igloo.

Drawing closer, Lion notices it's not actually the whole of the building that he's looking at. Only the entranceway is visible. The real show must be underground. What he thought was the bar itself is just a tunnel rising out of the earth like the gaping mouth of some gargantuan frozen serpent.

Lion and Lizzy stop about thirty feet away from the opening, click out of their bindings and slot their gear into a wooden rack. They head inside, feeling the temperature drop as they go. The walls are translucent cubes of ice, lit from below and glowing a misty purple. Some kind of sure-grip coating on the floor keeps them from slipping.

Ten steps into the ice cave, Lion realizes they're at the top of a spiral ramp that curls downward. The ramp's transluscent walls glow a foggy red. They complete two laps before a tall door made from dark metal comes into view. *The End of Man* is written across it in hoarfrost.

"The End of Man?" asks Lion. "Do people come here to drink or die young?"

"No humans allowed inside the mega-linkage," explains Lizzy. "It's animals only. Get it? The End of Man?"

"Sounds like Sir Richard is pontificating without provocation again."

Lizzy smirks, removes her glove, and presses her palm against the surface of the door. The metal quivers, then liquifies. A black animatronic hand extends outward. Grasping it, Lizzy executes the same complicated handshake that Jenka used yesterday, ending in an identical soul slide into fist bump.

The greeting concludes, the door opens.

Lion sees another ice tunnel, this one with dry ice smoke seeping from translucent blue walls.

"If it's all right with you," says Lizzy, "I'm going to duck into the kitchen while you talk to Alejandra."

"Alejandra's the bartender?"

"Your conversation will go better if I'm not there."

"Is that another Rilkean thing? She doesn't like you because you work for Sir Richard?"

"No," says Lizzy, hesitating slightly. "It's a 'we got drunk and ended up where drunk people end up' kind of thing. But we left things awkward. And, Lion, seriously, you gotta keep that to yourself."

"You dated the bartender. Who cares? Who hasn't dated the bartender?"

"Company rules. Sir Richard doesn't care if his employees screw around, but he wants the incentives right. You can't fondle anyone above or below your pay grade. Keeps people at the bottom from trying to fuck their way up; keeps people at the top from abusing their power."

"You're a scientist and she's a bartender."

"Yup," says Lizzy. "The power dynamics are off, at least according to Sir Richard logic. I could get fired if anyone found out."

"That sounds like Sir Richard logic. I'll bet you my lunch money he introduced the idea with one of his long speeches."

"A ninety-minute mandatory. The entire history of sexuality in the workplace. Bet you didn't know that the ancient Egyptians used crocodile dung as a contraceptive."

"Did not."

"Mixed it with fermented dough and inserted it into the hoo-ha. The oldest recorded spermicide."

Lizzy leads him down the blue tunnel and around a corner, then stops beside a side door. "I'll slip out here. Cookie and Axel are in the kitchen. I'm gonna hang with them. When you finish with Alejandra, come find me. Axel makes a mean elk stew—cultured elk, grown from stem cells, no animals harmed, etcetera. You'll want the extra calories for the Bypass."

"See ya when I see ya," says Lion.

He makes his way down the rest of the tunnel, pushes through a final door, and into the bar itself.

"Holy crap."

The End of Man is a giant ice cave. Thirty-foot walls of misty blue ice, solid ice floors. There are ice stalactites hanging from the ceilings and ice stalagmites rising from the ground, each as big around as a tree trunk. One side of the room is dominated by a glowing purple ice bar lined with blocky ice benches. Behind the bar are bottles of expensive booze sitting in neat lines on ice shelves. The other side of the room is filled with low tables and long couches, all turned toward a two-story viewing window—a long rectangular sheet of translucent ice that peers into the Heavenly Bypass.

If Lion didn't know better, he'd never know he was underground.

The window reveals a ski slope in bright daylight. The light must be a holo-projection. The terrain is a high mountain alpine scene that appears to mimic the real high mountain alpine scene above it, the landscape known as Mott Canyon.

The real Mott Canyon is now a major wildlife corridor, providing plants and animals with room to roam. But before it was a migration corridor, it was Heavenly Valley's most difficult offering: a horseshoe canyon chockablock with cliff bands, oversized boulders and steep lines. Skiers died in there with alarming regularity. Lion remembers the stories.

"We're closed," says a woman's voice.

Lion spins from the window to find a pretty copper-skinned woman standing behind the bar, restocking bottles, her legs visible through the ice. She's wearing ice skates, tube socks, fishnet stockings, a white tennis skirt, and a huge white down parka with the hood up.

Lion says, "I'm here to see Alejandra."

"Take off your helmet."

"What?"

"Your ski helmet."

"This usually goes better," says Lion, taking off his helmet, "if you're shoving bills in my G-string."

"Well, hot damn," says Alejandra. "You really are Lion Zorn. When Jenka called, I thought he was bullshitting. I figured no way. Had to be Jenka being still hella-pissed because I wouldn't tell him about Penelope."

"Jenka says you won't talk to him because you're a Rilkean and he works for Arctic."

"Yeah, I'm sure he did say that. Did you remind him that I also work for Arctic? I didn't tell Jenka about Penelope because Jenka's an asshole, not because I'm a Rilkean. We forgave Sir Richard years ago. He paid for the Bypass—that was penance enough. Why else would I work here?"

"Money?"

"Easy to make money," she says, taking off her hood. "I'm here for the animals. I'm here because of the mega-linkage—it's about time, right? Plus, there's another reason I didn't talk to Jenka."

Lion raises an eyebrow.

"Penelope asked me not to. That lady is rad. When she swears in Scottish: 'Tongue-ma-fart-box, ya bloody wankstain.' Totally cracks me up."

"Yup," says Lion with a smile, "I am familiar with her vocabulary."

"Want some coffee?"

"Love some coffee."

Alejandra pours two mugs, set them on the bar, and takes a faux bear rug from a cupboard. She skates around to Lion, spreads the rug across the ice bench, then sits down atop it, crossing her legs at the ankles.

Lion joins her, then takes a sip of coffee. Alejandra doesn't offer cream or sugar, but he doesn't want any. Lion likes his drinks with one ingredient. Coffee. Whiskey. Water. No frills. No double-whip mocha-light-caramel whatever. His is a Zen purist's approach to beverage choice paralysis.

"So why'd Penelope ask you not to talk to Jenka?"

"She wasn't specific. She said don't talk to anyone except a guy named Lion Zorn. I said no way, not that Lion Zorn. She said yes way, that Lion Zorn."

"Penelope knew I'd come here?"

"She said there was a pretty good chance. She also said you'd be very happy to compensate me for—you know—all my effort."

"Did she happen to quote—you know—a price?"

"Nope," says Alejandra. "But she did say you are very generous. I take cash, crypto, weed, or Tesla-Verizon minutes—my freakin' data bill is off the charts."

"Did she give you a message?"

"Benjamins," she says. "Dead presidents, scratch, coin, ducats, cheddar, cash money, ya feel me?"

Lion takes out his wallet and lays a hundred-dollar bill on the counter.

"All I got," he says. "Did Penelope also tell you I was broke?"

She slides the bill back. "Seriously? You're Lion Zorn. Like, I'd ever actually take your money."

Alejandra pops off the bench and skates into the cave, hollering over her shoulder, "Be right back with your message, Lion Zorn."

SOMETHING MISSING

The message is actually a sealed envelope containing two folded-up pieces of paper. Lion unfolds the pages and sees the familiar whorl of Penelope's handwriting. He recognizes the high-crossed *T*s and the extra curl in the middle of her *K,* as if someone had drawn a circle where the crossbars meet.

The first page contains three hastily written sentences, each of them exceptionally short. The second page looks like she took her time. He starts with the first page.

The first line says: "Ask A about Zhong."

The second line reads: "Not venom."

The third: "Something missing."

Lion has no idea what any of this means. Yet the second page is even more confusing. It's filled with quotes by William James. When Penelope and Lion had first transitioned from the "friends with benefits" stage to the "whatever the hell comes next" stage, it happened because of a conversation about their shared love for William James.

For Lion, his obsession with William James coincided with the onset of his em-tracking talent. That experience was intense and confusing, like a whole new universe of feeling opened up inside of him. When these novel emotions showed up, as Lion was one of the world's first em-trackers, there was no one else he could ask. Instead, as a way to understand what was going on with himself, he turned to books about psychology. Not knowing where to start, Lion decided to begin where the field began, with Harvard professor William James, and his 1890 opus, *The Principles of Psychology*, the very first textbook on the subject.

Like so many before him, Lion read James and fell in love.

Penelope's love came from her Scottish mother. James had delivered his most famous series of lectures, which later became the book, *The Varieties of Religious Experience*, in Scotland, at the University of Edinburgh. Nearly a hundred years later, Penelope's mother was a librarian at the same school, which was where her interest in James emerged. She passed this on to her daughter, which is why Penelope left Lion a note full of William James's quotes.

But what do they mean?

The first quote is from *Varieties* and is one of James's more famous lines: "Religion, in short, is a monumental chapter in the history of human egotism."

Except, he notices, that's not actually what Penelope wrote. The words are all there and in the correct order, but she omitted the first two letters of *monumental* and the final *l*.

Instead of *monumental*, she'd written *numenta*.

He reads the line again: "Religion, in short, is a numenta chapter in the history of human egotism."

Nope—still doesn't mean anything to him.

The next quote is equally familiar: "A sense of humor is just common sense dancing." Yet equally mutilated. Instead of the final word, *dancing*, Penelope had written *ancing*.

Lion reads his way down the rest of the page. There are six more quotes from James, each of them altered in some way.

What the hell was Penelope trying to tell him?

"Do I pay you to sit?" hollers a man's voice from somewhere back in the cave.

"Shit," says Alejandra, popping off the seat and shouting back, "Q, this is the guy Jenka wanted me to talk to."

Q walks into the bar. He's a gruff older man in a plaid wool shirt, faded jeans, and battered work boots. Crossing to stand in front of them, Q puts his hands on his hips and growls, "Jenka doesn't have a bar to run. Jenka doesn't have to deal with the lunch rush on a powder day. Jenka doesn't have to wash my balls on a Saturday night."

Alejandra says, "Q, meet Lion. Lion, meet Q."

"Yeah, whatever," says the man.

"Boss," says Alejandra, gesturing around the room, "it's done already. The bar's set up."

"This place is gonna be a fucking zoo," he says.

"We're ready," responds Alejandra. "I knew about this meeting yesterday. This morning, I saw the weather report, I came in early. All that's left: I got to see X in the kitchen to grab the stew. So chill, your balls are washed."

"Tell that to my wife," he says, then turning to Lion, "Nice to meet you."

"The pleasure was all mine," says Lion.

"Hmmph," snorts Q, before stomping back into the cave.

"His name is Q?" Lion asks after Q's gone.

"Yeah. Short for Quigley. Everybody calls him Q. He calls that 'name discrimination,' so now he calls everyone by the first letter of their first name. He's Q. I'm A. Cookie and Axel, in the kitchen, are C and X."

"Penelope's note," says Lion, rattling the pages. "I'm supposed to ask A about Zhong. If you're A, do you know what that means?"

"Professor Zhong." Alejandra nods. "Yeah, she asked me about him, too. He was this creepy professor I had in college."

"Like he wanted to sleep with his students creepy?"

"No, his class was creepy: The Philosophy of Technology and Genetics."

"Where was this?"

"UC Santa Cruz. I took the course thinking Zhong would be like every other retread hippie professor there—anti-genetic manipulation."

"He wasn't?"

"Zhong thought humans have a moral obligation to take control of their genetic destiny. And he didn't just want to build better humans. He wanted to build better animals, better plants—like, create a new man-made Eden."

Lion flashes on Sir Richard's question from yesterday: "Now that we can create animals, are we morally obligated to create animals that don't eat other animals?" Is Sir Richard involved with Professor Zhong? Is that what Penelope was trying to tell him?

He glances at the note, then back at Alejandra. "Did Zhong ever say, 'Not venom'? Or use the words 'something missing'?"

Alejandra thinks for a moment. "'Not venom'—I don't know what that means. But the second one, yeah. Zhong liked to say that the main lesson of genetics is that there *is* something missing, something God forgot and, as humans, we are morally obligated to clean up God's mess."

"That is creepy."

"See what I mean?"

Lion reexamines the second page of the message, the mutilated quotes. "Did Zhong ever mention William James?"

"Who's that?"

"A famous psychologist."

"I don't think so."

"Did Penelope ask you anything else?"

"She asked me if I had ever read Zhong's PhD thesis. But I hadn't. And she asked me to give you the envelope and not to talk to anyone else."

"Did she say where she was going?"

"Widowmaker."

"That's a run?"

"Yeah. In the Bypass. Sick gnar. Like a twenty-foot cliff at the bottom. Penelope said she wanted to check out the cliff."

"That's odd," says Lion.

"What?"

"Penelope can't ski, or not very well. Why would she—"

"A!" screams Q from the other room. "Get the goddamn stew. Open the goddamn front door. A fucking zoo—or did you forget that part?"

She looks at Lion. "Come on, I'll walk you out."

"Actually, I'm supposed to go to the kitchen for some goddamn stew."

"You know where it is?"

"Uh-huh. Back up the blue tunnel and through the side door."

"Great. Tell X that Q wants him to open the front door and bring me some stew. If you do that, you can keep your hundred dollars, and we'll call it even."

THE EGO-THRILL OF PROCREATION

Lion leaves the bar, hikes up the red ice ramp, and heads through the side door. He finds himself in a large restaurant kitchen, with stainless-steel appliances and black rubber mats laid over an ice floor. Lizzy sits at a small table in the corner, chatting with Axel, a tall

German man, while Cookie, a short African American woman, chops vegetables at a prep counter.

Lion says hello and delivers Alejandra's message to Axel.

"Stew him," says Lizzy, talking to Axel, but pointing at Lion.

Axel walks over to an enormous metal pot on the stove and uses a ladle to fill a bowl. After passing the bowl to Lion, he lifts the pot off the stove and hauls it out of the kitchen.

"Spoon," says Lizzy, pointing to a silverware tray.

Lion grabs a spoon and joins her at the table.

"Lion," says Lizzy, "meet Cookie," nodding at the African American woman still chopping vegetables.

Cookie glances up, nods once, then goes back to chopping. Lion notices she's wearing a white headband with red letters, reading: *Animals Are People, Too.*

Lion tries the stew.

Lizzy asks, "Did you learn anything about Penelope?"

"Maybe," he says between bites. "She left me a message, but it's pretty confusing. I did learn that we have to go check out a run called Widowmaker. There's a cliff at the—"

"Bottom."

He gives her a puzzled look.

"There's a cliff at the bottom of Widowmaker."

"Uh-huh," says Lion, thinking about something else. "You studied genetics, right?"

"Undergrad."

"Ever hear of a professor named Zhong? He taught at UC Santa Cruz."

"My alma mater."

"You and Alejandra went to the same school?"

"I'm older. I was there seven years before her."

"Did you study with Zhong?"

"The genetic marketing guy?"

"Genetics, yeah, but I don't know anything about the marketing part."

"All I know is there was a Santa Cruz professor named Zhong who wrote a book called *Genetic Marketing*. It's about how to sell things to certain genetic phenotypes. For example, people with the VMAT2 gene tend to be more spiritual than others. If a company knows this, they could tweak their messaging accordingly. Shit like that."

"Ever read it?"

"No. And I never took his class. Zhong wasn't teaching at Santa Cruz when I was there. He didn't get there until after I graduated."

"But you've heard of him?"

"Only about what happened. Santa Cruz is an 'empathy for all, vegan or die' kind of place. The book caused an uproar. After he published it, the whole university flipped out. Zhong got fired or maybe resigned. Either way, he was outta there."

"Do you know where he went?"

"He was Chinese—from China, Chinese. I heard he went home, but that was years ago. I have no idea where he is now."

Lion finishes his stew and carries his bowl across the kitchen, looking for the sink. Then he realizes: there is no sink. Instead, there's a humanoid robo-dishwasher, sitting lifeless in the back corner of the room.

"Just set it there," calls Cookie, pointing to a counter beside the robo-dishwasher. "We'll get it later."

"I can wash it."

"That's why we have Elon."

"Elon?"

"The robo-dishwasher," explains Cookie, "when the shit works. Batteries are fried again. Whole back side of the kitchen's burnt out."

"We're all solar up here," explains Lizzy. "We run on Tesla-Verizon Powerwall batteries."

"Tesla-Verizon HQ is what, like, an hour from here," snaps Cookie.

"You'd think they could fix a battery. Elon Musk can put people on Mars, but he can't fix a robo-dishwasher. What do they do up on Mars? Wash dishes by hand? It's not like you can just hire a Mexican up there."

"Cookie's not a fan," explains Lizzy.

"Of Mexicans?"

"Of Elon Musk."

"Musk has what? Like, eight children," snarls Cookie. "And he calls himself an environmentalist. Overpopulation drives extinction, everybody knows that. Shit makes me crazy. How many animals and plants have to die because guys like Musk need the ego-thrill of procreation."

"Ah," says Lion, suddenly getting it. "You're a Rilkean."

"Bet your ass I'm a Rilkean," she says. "And you're Lion Zorn."

Something in her tone tells him to be careful.

"Nope," says Lion. "But there's a resemblance."

"Fuck that guy, too," replies Cookie, glaring at him.

"Thanks for the stew," says Lizzy, grabbing Lion's hand and tugging him out of the kitchen.

THEY HATE ME, TOO

Outside the kitchen, there's a throng of customers waiting in the blue ice tunnel, and a larger throng waiting outside the front door.

The zoo has definitely arrived.

Lizzy and Lion wade through the crowd and into the sunlight, making their way over to the rack where their gear is stowed. Lion retrieves his skis. Lizzy grabs her snowboard. They aim for a people-free zone about twenty feet away, stopping beneath the snowy boughs of a grandfather pine.

"Does that happen a lot?" asks Lizzy.

"That I get recognized?"

"I recognized you. No, I mean . . . like Cookie."

"Meaning they hate me on sight? Yeah, it happens. Not like it used to, but I understand her anger."

"I don't. The Rilkeans are mad at you because you told the world about Sietch Tabr?"

"It's complicated," says Lion. "Muad'Dib, the leader of the Rilkeans—"

"The chemist, the guy who created Sietch Tabr?"

"His real name's Luther," says Lion. "Everybody just calls him Muad'Dib—after the lead character in *Dune*. He wanted to use Sietch Tabr to bring change to society. But his plan was slow change."

"What does slow change mean?"

"Muad'Dib figured if huge swatches of society suddenly started taking a drug that produces extreme cross-species empathy, it would be too destabilizing. And there'd be a backlash. But by surrounding the experience with quasi-religious ritual—which is what traditional cultures have always done with psychedelics—the Rilkeans wanted to give people a way to anchor the experience. Done that way, Sietch Tabr would bring slow change to society, without all the mess."

"By backlash," asks Lizzy, "you mean the Humans First movement."

"They hate me, too."

"Because you caused the Splinter?"

"That really wasn't my fault."

"I know," she says, smiling. "Does anyone like you?"

"Well, definitely not anyone who's a parent. I got their kids into drugs. They really hate me." Lion clicks into his skis. "Let's go check out the Bypass."

Lizzy steps onto her snowboard, the electromagnets locking her boots into place with a thunk. They push off, gliding across a long stretch of cat track before dropping down a well-groomed slope.

A hundred yards later, Lizzy stops at a metal gate in a steel fence. She types a code into a keypad, opens the gate, and ushers Lion inside. Following him through, she closes the gate, then points toward a cluster of pines. "We're heading that way."

"I still need to check out the cliff on Widowmaker."

"Check out?" asks Lizzy. "Meaning you want to jump off it, or check out, meaning you want to inspect it up close."

"I'm not sure."

"There's a DANGER—CLIFF sign. If you want to inspect it, head past the sign through the trees and cut back into the run. You'll wrap in below the drop. If you want to jump off it, well—go get 'em, tiger. Also, angle left when you jump. The landing's better."

A raven soars across the sky above them. It reminds Lion of the raven-drone he saw earlier.

"Does anyone ever use research drones in PRML?"

"It's too unsafe. Over the mountain, the drone could crash into a skier. Over the Bypass, they're worried about screwing up bird migration patterns and nesting behavior."

"So if I saw a drone earlier?"

"Earlier when?"

"Before we went to the End of Man. Right above that pencil chute."

"It shouldn't have been there."

Something's not right, thinks Lion. He glances back toward the sky, but the raven has vanished.

"You ready to go?" asks Lizzy. "The entrance to the Bypass is on the other side of those trees."

"Ready."

Lizzy drops into the run, darting between pines. She carves a hard left turn, sending up a plume of fresh snow. Lion slides in behind her. Two hundred yards beyond the pines, he spots another gated fence, twice the size of the first, featuring a black metal door.

Lizzy rides up to the door, removes her gloves, and presses her palm against it. The metal shimmers and liquefies, and another animatronic hand extends outward. Grasping the hand, Lizzy executes the same complicated handshake that Jenka used yesterday.

The door opens inward.

On the other side, Lion sees an entrance tunnel covered in snow.

It's about as big around as a school bus, dropping down into the earth at a steep angle, and artificially lit from above. If Lion didn't know better, he'd assume that was sunlight streaming down. But everything, including the sun and the snow, has been made by humans—no real nature required.

Lizzy drops first, whooshing down the tunnel and stopping at the bottom, where their feeder corridor appears to connect to the bulk of the Heavenly Bypass.

Lion follows her down.

"It's freaking huge," he says, stopping beside Lizzy and looking around the Bypass.

The terrain is about ten times larger than the entrance tunnel, complete with trees, rocks, cliffs, and alarmingly steep runs. As far as Lion can tell, it's a perfect copy of the ski area above them.

"How'd Sir Richard build it so fast?" asks Lion.

"Sir Richard told the press that the Bypass mimics the terrain of Mott Canyon."

"It doesn't?"

"Mott Canyon is huge. Sir Richard built three runs. And these three? He hasn't been exactly truthful about their progress. Widowmaker is done. So is a run called the Y. But the third run? Right now, it's just a huge hole in the ground."

"It skis well. We blazed down the tunnel."

"The whole place is like that, but be careful. It's steeper than it looks. You can get going fast in a hurry."

"My kind of place," says Lion. Then it dawns on him. "If it's so small, why can't we find Penelope?"

"We don't know," explains Lizzy. "The electronic gate shows Penelope entering the Bypass. Her tracker was shut off inside and we haven't found it anywhere. That's what we know. According to the system, she never left. Maybe she went missing in here, maybe in the ski area, maybe in PRML itself. There have been two satellite overflights." She shrugs.

"I heard about the overflights," said Lion. "But why here? Penelope was investigating the snakes. Aren't the snakes in the park? So why'd she come into the Bypass?"

"Susan Jackson," explains Lizzy. "She didn't die in PRML itself." She points into the Bypass. "She died in here. Down there, below the cliff on Widowmaker, that's where we found her body."

WIDOWMAKER

Widowmaker is a thousand-foot gully dotted with snow-covered boulders, towering rocky cliffs, and slender pines. Lion and Lizzy are perched at the top, on the edge of a five-foot cornice, peering down the belly of the chute.

"It's wider and calmer up here," explains Lizzy, "steeper and more exciting down below."

Lion follows her gaze. The slope falls away at increasingly dizzy angles, until it vanishes from sight over a ridge far below. No question about it, a bad fall anywhere along the way would bounce you straight to the bottom. As there's a cliff at the bottom of Widowmaker—well, that explains the name.

Glancing away from the main slope, Lion examines the outer edges of the run, where dense clusters of trees are surrounded by blue sky. The optics are amazing. Whatever projection software Sir Richard is using to create this illusion, it's working. The sky, the sun, the snow—you'd never know you were in a tunnel, two hundred feet underground.

"Do you have a plan?" asks Lizzy.

Lion thinks about it a moment. "Where'd they find Susan Jackson's body?"

"See that ridge?" says Lizzy, gesturing down the center of the chute. "You can't tell from here, but the cliff is about a hundred feet below that ridge. Susan's body was about a hundred feet beneath the cliff, or about two hundred below the last thing you can see."

"Here's the plan," says Lion. "You ride the line that people normally ride. Penelope wasn't a great skier. She wouldn't have done anything fancy, especially on something this steep. If you let the run dictate your route, that's probably the same route Penelope took." Lion points to his right, at a small patch of flat snow tucked between two massive boulders. "I'm gonna head into the boulder zone and watch you on the way down. Maybe I'll learn something."

"Where do you want to meet up?"

"The spot where they found Susan's body."

"Works for me," says Lizzy. "But remember, about fifty feet below that ridge is the DANGER: CLIFF sign. It's the point of no return. Once you're below, it's a waterfall. Everything funnels straight over the drop."

"Copy that."

"Be careful in there," says Lizzy, nodding toward his observation post. "It's sneaky steep. You can get going crazy fast, get caught by the waterfall, and end up hucking that cliff whether you like it or not."

"Give me a minute to get into place," says Lion.

He pushes over the lip of the cornice, sucks up his knees, and lands about eight feet below the ledge, carrying the speed into a power carve that deposits him on a high traverse. He slices across the face of the run and drops down a micro-chute between boulders. Emerging from the other end of the chute, Lion kicks his skis sideways into a little skitch-slide. This slows him down and lines him up for another sneaker line between rock walls. He slides between the stone and feels the terrain drop away. The added acceleration blasts him out the other side—way faster than expected.

Lion whips his skis sideways again, this time digging in his edges and sliding to a hockey stop on the top of a cliff, about thirty feet below the spot he was aiming for. He feels his pulse race.

Widowmaker, living up to its name.

Lion starts to sidestep back up the hill, but there's no way to reach his desired observation post. Instead, he spots a tiny clearing the size of a large dining room table, surrounded by boulders. There's a look-out perch at the edge of the clearing, where a low ramp allows him to slide atop a rocky outcropping.

The view should be perfect.

Lion sidesteps into place. He's eight feet above the ground, with a clear line of sight. He can see the whole of the chute, from the ridge down below to Lizzy up at the top.

Lifting his pole above his head, Lion wags it twice, giving her the go signal.

Lizzy backs away from the lip of the cornice, sliding onto a mellower apron of snow to her left, where she can enter the run without having to jump off anything, which is how Penelope would have had to enter. But that's where the similarities end.

Lizzy can really ride. She carves near perfect S-turns down the center of the chute. As she approaches the ridge, needing to ditch a little speed before the terrain drops away, Lizzy leans back, dragging one hand behind her, while lifting up the front end of her board, plowing flat side first through the snow. She nose-wheelies for about fifteen feet, rocks her weight forward, then spins a one-eighty off the ridge before disappearing from sight.

Nice turns, thinks Lion. But they were turns way above Penelope's skill level. If his on-again, off-again girlfriend skied this run, it was slowly, carefully, and most likely cursing up a storm all the way down.

He peeks over the edge of the boulder, at the eight-foot drop. Lion contemplates leaping, but then remembers how fast he shot down that micro-chute.

Looking for a different option, Lion glances left and notices something he didn't see before. Along the side of the table-sized patch of snow he traversed to get over here, there's a long, winding indentation, where something roughly six feet long and as big around as a man's fist slithered its way across the slope.

Snake track?

An angry hiss answers his question.

Lion whips toward the sound, finding himself three feet away from a very pissed-off snake. He recognizes the coloring. It's got the same grayish-brown beady-eyed head he'd seen floating in jars of formaldehyde in the research station. Only this head is attached to a serpentine body, reared back and ready to strike.

Lion leaps off the boulder. It's pure instinct. One moment he's standing atop his high perch. The next, he's taken flight, midair and *what the fuck?*

Out of the corner of his eye, he's pretty sure he sees the snake, sailing through the air after him. The animal appears to have flattened its body into a kind of thick aerodynamic ribbon. A quiet voice in his head tries to work the problem: Yes, you just leaped off a cliff. Yes, a snake just leaped after you. Yes, this is actually happening.

Lion lands on the downslope, absorbs the impact, and rockets forward. Pine trees whip by on both sides. Knife-slice left, ping-pong right, aiming for a clean sliver of snow.

Kicking his skis sideways, Lion schmears through the sliver, ditching enough speed to line up a final rock drop. The drop is bigger than anticipated and hurls him back into the belly of the main chute. He lands too far down the run and carrying too much speed. There's time to rail one hard turn—leaning his body far over the slope and dragging a hand in the powder to maintain his balance—before he sees the DANGER: CLIFF sign. It's directly in front of him, hanging from a rope positioned between two trees.

There's no way to stop.

Lion flattens himself backward, lying down over his skis. His shoulders drag across the snow as he fights to hold that position. The rope whizzes by his face, just inches from his chin. He pops back to his feet, but it's already too late.

The drop is directly beneath him. He's caught by the waterfall. Rocks on both sides and the cliff, coming up fast.

Lion has half a second to save his ass. He hops right so he can angle left off the cliff—the voice in his head reminding him that Lizzy said the landing was better in that direction.

Then he launches.

The drop itself is only eighteen feet, but with the extra speed, Lion realizes he's going to clear about forty before he hits the ground.

The extra air time is exactly what he needs.

He sucks up his knees, whirls his arms, and lets gravity do the rest. He feels his body drop back into alignment, spots his landing, and lands on his spot. Snow explodes in every direction. He absorbs the impact with a deep knee bend, his ass nearly smacking the snow, then blasts through the white out and onto the slope.

By the time Lion manages to come to a stop, he's three hundred feet below his landing and a hundred feet below Lizzy. His face is contorted into a crazy grin: terror, exhilaration, wild-eyed surprise.

"You okay?" calls Lizzy.

He doesn't answer. Instead, Lion leans over, puts both hands on his knees, and starts sucking oxygen.

She rides over and asks, "What happened?"

Lion stands, points up the hill, and moves his lips. His mouth opens, his mouth closes, but no sound comes out.

Finally he finds his voice. "Motherfucking snakes on the motherfucking mountain—that's what happened!"

The Devil's Dictionary

What do you mean, it leaped?" asks Lizzy.

They haven't moved. They're still standing in the clearing at the bottom of the run.

"The snake leaped after me," explains Lion.

"I don't understand."

"What part?"

"The snake leaped after you?"

"That's what I said."

"Snakes don't leap. Okay, that's not entirely true. There's a species of Indonesian tree snake that sort of flattens itself out like a ribbon and sails from tree to tree."

"That's what I saw."

"That's not possible. The snakes we've caught are a cross between inland taipans and black mambas. They both hunt on the ground. Neither are built to leap off trees or boulders."

"What if it's a new kind of snake?"

"Unlikely."

"Why?"

"How much do you know about genetic engineering?"

"Not enough, apparently."

"Remember the Human Genome Project?"

"From way back?" asks Lion. "Like, 2003—the first time we sequenced the entire human gene code?"

"Yeah. Sequencing—what that project relied upon—gives us the ability to read DNA. Around 2018, scientists went the next step and created the Genome Project-write. This time the goal was to build a DNA typewriter, something that could not just read DNA, but also write DNA. It's a machine that allows us to create new genetic codes—essentially to write life, from scratch."

"They built it, right?" asks Lion. "Like, four or five years ago?"

"They did. But it's basic. You still have to do most of the work by hand, or not by hand, but without too much AI assistance."

"Why does that matter?"

"Because we have the technology, barely, to boot up a new kind of snake. But to take something that's already complicated, a blend of mamba genes, taipan genes, and icefish genes, and add in all the tree snake genes that allow for flattening and flying—that's Devil's Dictionary kind of shit."

"What did you just say?"

"About the tree snake genes?"

"No, after that."

"The Devil's Dictionary?"

"Yes. Are you talking about the book by Ambrose Bierce?"

"What book?"

"*The Devil's Dictionary.*"

"It's not a book."

"It's a fake dictionary written by a journalist named Ambrose Bierce."

"No. The Devil's Dictionary I'm talking about is a techno-ghost story. Eco-terror for the anti-genetic-modification crowd. I heard about it in college, at Santa Cruz." Suddenly her eyes go wide. "That makes sense."

"What makes sense?"

"The Devil's Dictionary I know about is an AI-version of the DNA typewriter. It contains all the genomes of all the animals in the world, and just about all the genetic data that's ever been gathered. It's also got a voice-recognition interface. You just tell the AI you want a new species of animal—say, your black mamba meets inland taipan meets Indonesian tree snake—and the supercomputer spits out the correct genetic code, inserts it into a virus, slides the virus into a denucleated snake egg, and instant new species."

"Why is it called the Devil's Dictionary?"

"In certain interpretations of the Bible, God didn't speak the world into existence; God wrote the world into existence. The Book of Life is a real thing kind of idea. The opposite of the Book of Life is the Devil's Dictionary. Do you know what happens if you introduce a bunch of new, very aggressive exotic species into an ecosystem?"

"Sure," says Lion. "They kill everything. Soulé figured that out. Exotics are one of the fastest drivers of extinction."

"So an AI that can create life from scratch?"

"It could kill everything."

"That's why it's called the Devil's Dictionary."

Lion's brain tries to do the math.

The same warlord who has been pulling those Five Spikes and Buddy Holly strings; the same warlord who is kidnapping, torturing, and murdering em-trackers; the same warlord who is forcing Chinese women to kill themselves in order to finance a project called the Devil's Dictionary—so now that same warlord is trying to build an AI that can create life from scratch?

Lion could be right, he could be wrong, but either way, he definitely doesn't like that math.

HUMAN-MADE SNOW

Lion still wants to inspect the cliff—the one he skied right off.

Warlord or not, according to Alejandra, Penelope skied Widowmaker so she could get a look at that cliff. Lion needs to take a look as well.

"I'm gonna hike back up. I want to figure out why Penelope came here."

"I'm in," says Lizzy. "Except, you know, killer flying snakes."

"I know. I really shouldn't go up there without a trained professional by my side. If only I knew where to find a herpetologist."

"As a herpetologist, I think we should get our asses back to the lab. We've got protective gear and explorer robots."

"How long will that take?"

"If the robot's charged and loaded on the trailer, we could be back by the end of the day. If not, tomorrow."

"That's too long. Penelope's been missing for eleven days. That cliff is the only clue we have."

But, it dawns on him, there might be another clue.

During their holo-chat, Sir Richard said that Susan was the second person to get killed by snakes, not the first.

"That ski patroller who died," asks Lion, "where did they find the body?"

"Qing Shan. They found her in Killebrew Canyon."

"She was Chinese."

"Does that mean anything?"

Lion thinks for a second. Five Spikes and Buddy Holly glasses are Chinese. Zhong, the creepy Santa Cruz genetics professor that Penelope asked about, is Chinese. The Suicide Girls are Chinese. But there are more than eight billion people on the planet, and over twenty percent of them are Chinese.

This really could be a coincidence.

"It might," he says. "Where's Killebrew from here?"

Lizzy points toward the rocks where Lion first stood to observe her run. "Beyond those rocks is the tunnel wall. If you punched through, you'd hit the next ski run, then another wall, then the third tunnel, the unfinished run. On the other side of that is Killebrew Canyon."

Lion clicks out of his skis, takes his poles, and starts hiking up toward the cliff.

"Where are you going?" calls Lizzy.

Lion stops hiking and kicks the toe of his boot into the ground, sending a cloud of snow into the air. "The snow, it's man-made?"

"And woman-made," says Lizzy. "But yeah, besides the gender bias, it's human-made snow."

"Where do you keep the equipment?"

"Everywhere. Everything needed to maintain the Bypass is built into the terrain. There's temperature control units buried in the ground and the walls, and snowmaking guns tucked between rocks."

"Exactly," says Lion, pointing up the hill. "I don't think that's a cliff. I bet it's a snowmaking tunnel that connects to the other ski runs, and to PRML itself, on the Killebrew Canyon side—which is where that ski patroller's body was found."

He starts hiking again, angling toward a tall stack of boulders, anchored by a giant block of granite sticking vertically out of the earth. A second granite block leans against it. A third slab juts across the crevice between the two, its horizontal bulk blocking most of what might be the entrance to a small cave.

It's a little hard to tell from here because the shrubby branches of a young pine obscure the view.

Lion needs to get closer.

He creeps toward the base of the tree, cautiously double-checking for snakes. It's unusual for an em-tracker to fear animals, but tell that to his rising feeling of dread.

Reaching out a ski pole, Lion moves the branches aside, revealing a three-foot gap between the ground and the bottom of the boulder.

It's pitch-black inside.

Jamming his poles in the snow, Lion reaches into his jacket and pulls out the JOBZ. Switching the device into flashlight mode, he illuminates the hole.

But, as it turns out, he doesn't need the flashlight to find his next clue.

It's right there outside the entrance, tucked between the back of the pine and the bottom of the boulders, perfectly preserved in the snow: The imprint of a small ski boot.

Lion glances over at Lizzy. "How big is your foot?"

"What?"

"Your shoe size."

"Six—why?"

"There's a boot print in the snow," he says. "Penelope's also a six. Come stand over here."

Lizzy works her way to Lion, then sets her boot next to the imprint. "It's a match," she says. "So Penelope was here."

"It could have been Susan Jackson."

"Susan's petite. Maybe five-one. The print is too big. In fact . . ."— she glances to the side—"shine your light over there."

Lion does as she asks, and sees it, too.

Near the far left side of the cave, there's a second boot print, this one smaller than the first.

"That looks like Susan's print," says Lizzy.

Lion thinks for a second. "So Susan came this way before she died. Then a few weeks later, Penelope did the same. Or two people who happen to have the exact same boot sizes as Susan and Penelope came this way."

"I'm betting on the first." Lizzy slides her arms out of her backpack and drops it to the ground. "Pass me your light."

Lion hands her the JOBZ.

Lizzy ducks under the pine branches and plays the beam back and forth across the inside of the cave. "I don't see any eye shine. It's not a guarantee this place isn't a snake den. But . . ." She takes a step backward, whispering, "Back up. Slowly."

Lion's pulse rate spikes. He slides away from the hole, forgetting to exhale.

Lizzy ducks under the branches and then stops, still looking into the cave. "Wait," she calls, "false alarm."

"What?"

"Snowmaking guns." She points to her right. "There are three nozzles in the cave wall over here. They glimmered when I shined the light."

"Like snake eyes?"

"Uh-huh, but I think we're okay. And you're right: This tunnel has to connect to the underside of the Bypass. There's got to be a main water pipe to run those guns, and that has to connect to the biolab."

"Why the biolab?"

"Do you know how they make snow?"

"Pump water out of a gun, let the cold do the rest?"

"If you did that, you'd just get ice, not snow. Human-made snow is genetically engineered bacteria plus water. There's bacteria in clouds. Proteins on those bacteria bind to water molecules and form crystals—that's snow. But scientists figured out how to genetically engineer bacteria with more binding proteins. That's what gets shot out of a snow gun: water and genetically engineered bacteria. Our system connects to the biolab because Sir Richard—"

Lion finishes her sentence: "Sir Richard wants to build better bacteria."

Lizzy nods. "More proteins, bigger flakes, less water required to make the snow. We got another lecture. He said that sometimes we humans have a moral responsibility to improve nature."

"That sounds like something Professor Zhong would say."

"I wouldn't know," says Lizzy. "I never took his class." She drops to her knees and shines the JOBZ in front of her. "Yeah," she says, "I see pipes running and . . . fuck me with a tuba."

"What?"

"I think it's an abandoned snake den. There are, like, nine snakeskins on the floor. And something dead back there. I smell rotting flesh."

"You're sure it's abandoned?"

"No," she says, crawling backward out of the opening, "and I don't want to hang around and find out. I'm gonna have the lab send over the robot. There's a couple of techs who can operate it remotely."

"What are we going to do instead?"

"Can you reach into the main pocket of my pack, hand me the sampling jar, and pass me your ski pole?"

Lion grabs her pack and unzips the main compartment. It's less a jar and more of a squat barrel. He passes it under the rock. The pole follows.

Lizzy shoves the pole into the snow, unscrews the lid of the jar, and sets both lid and jar on the ground by her feet. She lifts up the pole again, extends it into the cave and fishes out a six-foot snakeskin. Trying not to break the skin, she lowers it into the jar, letting it coil along its natural curves.

"You can tell a lot from a snakeskin," she says, screwing the lid back on. "Once I get this thing into a sequencer, I can tell you if this is just inland taipan mixed with black mamba or if there are flying tree snake genes spliced into the code."

"How long will it take?"

"If we go straight back to the lab, maybe four hours."

"Then let's go straight back." An idea pops into his head. "Actually, let's not exactly go straight."

can we smoke in the truck?

It takes them forty minutes to ski out of the Bypass, down the mountain, and back to the parking lot. Lion climbs into Lizzy's truck, opens his backpack, and digs out a test tube of Ghost Trainwreck #69, courtesy of the dragon box. "Can I smoke in your truck?"

"Can *we* smoke in my truck?" replies Lizzy. "Yes, *we* can smoke in my truck."

"Do you mind if *we* don't talk? I need to think. I think *we* need to be stoned for me to think straight."

"I get that," says Lizzy, starting the vehicle, "but I've got to make a call first."

She drives out of the parking lot. Lion lights the joint, blowing the smoke out of the window between puffs.

Two drags later, he passes it over to her. Lizzy hits it and hands it back.

After another round, Lion's high enough to drift into em-tracker mode. The dread he felt while approaching that cave is at the center of his inquiry. Fear of snakes is innate human hardwiring, but that code is typically overwritten by the shift that turns an ordinary person into an em-tracker. Yet Lion definitely felt dread, and it was way too strong to be your standard ophidiophobia, even if the *ophis* in question are killer flying snakes.

Beside him, Lizzy slides on a pair of AR glasses and tells the voice-recognition system to phone the lab. The truck drifts dangerously close to the edge of the road.

"You sure you can use those things and drive?" says Lion.

"No one can use these things and drive," replies Lizzy. "But if there are snakes in the Bypass . . ."

Someone answers, and she dives into conversation. Lion stares out the window. Time passes. Lion drifts between ideas, and suddenly, the puzzle starts to snap together. The dread he felt wasn't individual. It was cultural. An AI that drives extinction by creating new life. It isn't fear of snakes. It's fear of what the snakes can bring. Total ecosystem collapse. The Devil's Dictionary.

Not good, thinks Lion.

Lizzy hangs up, takes off her AR glasses, and tosses them onto the center console. "The explorer bot is charged."

Lion keeps staring out the window.

"Lion?"

It takes an extra beat for her voice to register. "Yeah?"

"The explorer robot is fully charged. The techs are heading out now."

He yawns, then speaks: "That cave, the opening is pretty small."

"The robot was built to inspect nuclear disaster sites. It's designed to get into tiny crevices. Trust me, we'll see what the entire cave looks like."

"I want to know why it stunk like death."

"I want to know where those snakes came from in the first place."

"I think someone put them there. The cliff, the den, my guess, that's how the snakes got into the park."

"Why would someone release genetically modified snakes into PRML?"

"You said it yourself, ecosystem collapse. Those brown tree snakes that invaded Guam after World War II? It took less than twenty years for them to multiply into millions and crash the entire ecosystem. Plus, genetically modified creatures overrunning the world's first mega-linkage—that would totally destroy Sir Richard's reputation, cost him and his investors billions, and set back the environmental movement by a decade."

"Herpetology lore: Guam."

"Those killer flying tree snakes—this is intentional Guam," says

Lion. "For whatever reason, someone wants to destroy PRML and they're using a snake way more aggressive than a little brown tree snake to get it done."

"Killer flying snakes," says Lizzy. "It's a joke, right, like something out of a kid's comic."

"Japanese sci-fi from the 1950s."

"But why the Bypass?" asks Lizzy. "Why release the snakes in an underground tunnel? Why not just dump them into the park itself?"

"You answered that earlier as well."

"When?"

"When you said there were no cameras in the tunnels. They haven't been installed yet. But there are satellite overflights of PRML. Someone knew that. Like they knew that there were tunnels connecting everything together, so the snakes would get out of the Bypass and into the park."

"But to know about that tunnel and the missing cameras, you'd have to . . ." A worried look sweeps across Lizzy's face.

"Yeah," says Lion. "You'd have to work for Sir Richard."

THree OBVIOUS TarGeTs

Lizzy drops Lion at the Old School Inn. Her plan is to head to the lab, sequence the snakeskin, and text him as soon as the results come back. Lion's plan is a snack and a nap.

He grabs an Old School peanut butter and jelly sandwich from the Old School Deli, which is not old school at all. The deli is a glass case embedded in the back wall of the lobby, staffed by a voice-activated speaker attached to a sleek robotic grasping arm.

Lion takes his sandwich and heads toward his room. He has a vague memory of slotting key into lock. Maybe he ate his sandwich. Arguably, he fell into bed and slept for a few hours.

When Lion gets up, he stumbles to the coffeemaker and sets it to brew. Next, he texts Jenka, asking him to send over the architectural blueprints for the Bypass. A second later, Jenka texts back, wanting to meet for dinner, promising to send a car for Lion. Jenka also tells him that the blueprints should arrive momentarily. After agreeing to the meal, Lion tosses the JOBZ on the bed and heads into the bathroom to take a shower.

The Old School Inn has new-school water pressure, for which he is eternally grateful. The soap smells like pine needles.

Lion shaves, for the first time in days.

Exiting the shower, he gets dressed, pours himself a cup of coffee, grabs the JOBZ, and sits down on the bed.

Checking his texts, Lion finds a note from Lizzy telling him that there's a backlog of samples waiting to be run through the DNA sequencer, so their snakeskin test results won't be back until the next day. Meanwhile, the techs will have the robot in place to explore the tunnel by 8:30 A.M. If Lion wants to come by the lab early tomorrow morning, they can review the test results and check out the tunnel exploration at the same time.

He texts back a confirmation, then unearths the text from Jenka, with a link to the architectural blueprints. He clicks the link, finds a master blueprint menu for the Bypass, selects Widowmaker, then opens the plans.

Lion was right. A long snowmaking tunnel connects the cliff at the bottom of Widowmaker to the two additional underground ski runs and Killebrew Canyon. Almost a straight shot. The plans also show an emergency exit about twenty feet away from the door that opens into Killebrew. The exit leads to a staircase that rises directly to the surface. Could that staircase be how Penelope got out of the Bypass without anyone noticing?

Lion isn't sure, but he decides another cup of coffee is in order.

After it brews, he puts on his down puffy, then carries the cup and the JOBZ through a sliding glass door and onto a tiny porch.

The view is sunset skies, with darkness fast approaching.

Sitting on a rough wooden bench, Lion stares at the clouds. In the distance, an owl hoots and crickets answer. Then he remembers Penelope's note, still folded up inside his backpack.

He heads inside, grabs the note and comes back to the bench. Unfolding the paper, Lion stares at the whorl of Penelope's handwriting and those three short sentences.

Ask A about Zhong.

Not venom.

Something missing.

He did ask A about Zhong, which is how he learned about the Devil's Dictionary. "Not venom" still doesn't mean anything to him, unless Penelope was talking about snake venom, but that doesn't mean much. And "something missing" is what Zhong said was wrong with genetics. He called it God's mess, which we humans are morally obligated to clean up.

Lion also recalls what Sir Richard said about building better bacteria: That we humans are morally obligated to improve nature. Similar to Zhong's statement, but it's not like the notion of human superiority is anything new. It's there in the Bible, when God gives mankind dominion over the beasts. It's why we still tolerate everything from factory farming to puppy mills to animal testing. Back when Lion was a journalist covering the animal rights movement, he talked to plenty of scientists who spent their days experimenting on monkeys and mice. "It's for the greater good," they always said. What was Lorenzo's response? "Ain't nothing in the world more dangerous than the greater good."

Lion also knows that human superiority is exactly why the Humans First movement got started.

He nearly drops the note.

It's so obvious, he doesn't know why he didn't see it before.

If you really believed in human superiority, then you'd want to stamp out the empathy-for-all movement, which is exactly what the Humans First movement desires. And if that is the goal, then you'd have three obvious targets: mega-linkages, em-trackers, and Sietch Tabr.

Mega-linkages like PRML would have to go, both because they protect biodiversity and because they're the largest symbol of cross-species empathy currently on the planet. Em-trackers would also be high on that kill list, as they're the inspiration for all that cross-species empathy. Finally, you'd have to go after Sietch Tabr itself, which is the psychedelic that turned "Empathy for All" from a slogan into a feeling and from a feeling into a movement.

But it's hard to kill off a mind-altering substance—that much history has taught us. Cracking down on booze in the 1920s both increased our thirst for alcohol and birthed organized crime. The same thing happened with LSD in the 1960s, and MDMA in the 1990s. Instead, if you want to kill a psychedelic, you have to replace the drug with a better drug, a more exciting high, a superior secrets-of-the-universe reveal. LSD was cool until MDMA came along. MDMA was our drug of choice until DMT showed us a vaster cosmos. If you wanted to kill off Sietch Tabr, you'd have to override both the fun of the high and the feeling of cross-species empathy that it produces.

Lion flashes back to his first meeting with Kendra and Ibrahim, when he initially heard about Evo: a fantastic new drug that makes you trip evolution. Forget about cross-species empathy, Evo promises to show you the very force that created all those species in the first place.

Lion's suddenly sure, in the way that em-trackers are sure: A drug that makes you trip evolution, a drug like Evo, would be exactly the kind of mind-altering weapon you'd want to aim at a target like Sietch Tabr.

Evo, the assault on em-trackers, and the snakes in the Bypass that are jeopardizing the whole of PRML itself, they all point back to the same place—a mysterious shogun. Ichika's warlord. Does this also mean that that warlord is actually the head of some radical wing of the Humans First movement?

There are some pretty big gaps in his idea. It explains almost nothing about why Lion was tortured, or why the Bolex H-11 camera was used to record that torture. Nor does it tell him why Penelope disappeared. But one thing is for certain: The memory of Ichika's warlord brings up a memory of Ichika herself, and that brings up a deep loneliness.

Trying to shake off the feeling, Lion glances back at the note, this time turning his attention to the second page and the William James quotes with the missing letters.

Data bit finds data bit—and wait a minute.

He'd assumed that "something missing" referred to Zhong, because that's how he heard the story. He read Penelope's note, asked A about Zhong, and learned about "something missing," the error in God's genetic code. Immediately, he decided that was the meaning of Penelope's note.

Fundamental attribution error, a classic case.

But there's a simpler answer, one that is directly in front of him: The something missing are the letters from those William James quotes.

"Religion, in short, is a numenta chapter in the history of human egotism."

Numenta is actually *monumental,* so the "something missing" refers to the letters *mol.*

The next quote is, "A sense of humor is just common sense ancing." That final word should be *dancing,* so he adds a *d* to his list of missing letters.

They now spell *mold.*

Lion scans the rest of the quotes from James, writing down the missing letters. When he's done, he stares at what they spell.

Two words.

Now he understands what Penelope was trying to tell him; why she ditched her tracker and disappeared. He thinks about Jenka, about his mysterious Moldovan hacker past and his desire for revolution.

Does that past include a history with bioweapons?

Lion looks at his notebook again. The missing letters spell *Moldo-van neurotoxin*. That's what Penelope was trying to tell him about the snakes in the Bypass: their venom is not snake venom—it's a Moldovan neurotoxin.

The JOBZ buzzes with another text. Lion's ride has arrived. He puts the note back into his backpack and heads inside. It's time to go to dinner with Jenka—a Moldovan hacker with a mysterious past, a desire for revolution, and full knowledge of the tunnel system that leads in and out of the Bypass.

PART V

PRESENT TENSE, CRYSTAL BAY

Inappropriate Forms of Transportation

Walking out of the hotel, Lion sees a line of autonomous vehicles in the driveway, each hunting their passengers. A series of disembodied voices softly purr names.

"Sheldon Murphy, for two," says a dark sedan.

"Shabazz Ali, for four," says a Ford long bed.

Lion hears his name from somewhere down the driveway. He spins in that direction and spots an enormous black-and-gold Escalade heading toward him.

"Fucking Jenka," he says.

The Caddy is one of the newer electric models, but it's been retrofitted to mimic an old-school gas-guzzler, the kind favored by early rappers, complete with purple undercarriage effects, spinning gold rims, and bouncy hydraulic suspension, all topped off with a gold-plated grille that resembles the gaping jaws of a great white shark.

"Fucking Jenka," he says again.

Sending inappropriate forms of transportation to fetch Lion is Jenka's thing, like the white suits are Jenka's thing. Once he sent a pink stretch Hummer to pick Lion up from the San Francisco airport, knowing that the extra attention it attracted would drive him crazy.

Now Lion looks at the gold shark and just shakes his head.

The auto-door slides open and the thump of heavy bass erupts from the Escalade. The vehicle must have some kind of serious sound-proofing. Until the door slid open, he'd heard nothing. Now he hears the familiar sounds of that Yehuda Dread Ya-Mama's cover of "Two Dope Boyz (in a Cadillac)," the Yiddish remix—"Two Dope Goyz (in a Cadillac)."

"Stereo off," says Lion, climbing inside.

At least, he thinks, the Escalade doesn't have leather seats. Killing for stuff we don't need—it's just not Lion's vibe.

He's starting to wonder if having dinner with Jenka is his vibe.

Should he cancel?

Lion said yes because he was still worried about Penelope and before he knew about the Moldovan neurotoxin. But if Penelope ditched her tracker to get away from Jenka, is this dinner working against her needs? Is he walking into some kind of a trap? But if Penelope ditched her tracker and got away, then she might be okay and going to dinner with Jenka might be his only way of finding another clue.

And on and on.

Like a cruise ship leaving port, the Caddy glides out of the parking lot.

"Shalom Creole Yum," says a disembodied female voice. "Your destination is in Crystal Bay, forty-two minutes away."

"Shalom what?"

"Shalom Creole Yum has five stars on . . ."

"Never mind," says Lion.

"*Nevermind* is an album by the American grunge band . . ."

Not again, thinks Lion, but he tunes out the voice, leans back in his seat, and closes his eyes. The next thing he knows, the Escalade has rolled to a stop. The cessation of motion jars his eyes open.

"Shalom Creole Yum," says the disembodied voice. "You have arrived."

He must have fallen asleep

Rubbing his eyes, Lion glances out the door and sees Jenka standing in a parking lot, smoking a thin black cigarette and wearing his customary skinny white suit and no socks.

"Dope ride," says Jenka once the auto-door opens. "First class the only class."

"Nice socks," says Lion, stepping out of the truck.

Jenka crushes out his cigarette in an ashtray and leads Lion toward an old fishing shack made of rough, weathered wood. They walk up a flight of rickety steps and stop before a gray plank door.

"How was first adventure in Bypass?" asks Jenka.

"Interesting."

"Dah," says Jenka, "Interesting is what I have heard. I spoke to Lizzy. I think she is joking, at first. Killer flying snakes? I think, maybe, you take bad acid."

"Yeah," says Lion, "I know that feeling."

"Let us talk while we eat," says Jenka.

He knocks twice on the door, then peers above it, at an abandoned wasp's nest with a minicam tucked inside. There's a buzzing sound, followed by the thunk of a heavy dead bolt retracting.

The door opens.

Lion sees a tall Eastern European man cradling a sleek tactical shotgun. He recognizes the model. It's the same kind of shotgun that he'd seen in the Anti-Nagel colony, wielded by Ichika's hyena-faced guards.

Then he looks around the room. "This is Shalom Creole Yum?"

"Is private supper club," says Jenka, stepping inside. "Intersectional cuisine: Yiddish-Cajun fusion."

Lion sees a healthy crowd, primarily clusters of Hasidic men sitting amidst tall ceilings and four walls made from glass. The rear of the restaurant is a giant window looking onto the shimmer of Lake Tahoe. The other three walls belong to a floor-to-ceiling fish tank that wraps the entire room, revealing a brackish underwater landscape patrolled by an array of robo-catfish and the occasional holo-projection of a topless mermaid.

"Right this way," says a robo-mermaid hostess, this one wearing a bikini top.

Lion notices her mermaid tail hides a miniature tank tread. He looks around and realizes all the waitresses are robo-mermaids.

"The waitstaff is robotic?" asks Lion.

"Robots tell no tales," says Jenka.

They're seated in a small private room off the back corner of the dining room. It's an alcove of sorts, completely surrounded by the glass walls of the fish tank. A large robot catfish watches them take their seats. Almost as soon as Lion gets comfortable, a robo-mermaid appears to take their order.

"WhistlePig," says Lion, "neat."

"I'll have a vodka martini," says Jenka, "with a twist."

"Do you have a vodka preference?"

"Nothing Russian. Finnish is acceptable. Moldovan is preferable."

After the robo-mermaid glides away, Jenka says, "The Suicide Girls. I did some digging. Is not good news."

"Worse than killer flying snakes?"

"Dah. Is why I sent car. Is why we are at dinner at private club far from PRML. Is why, I now think, Penelope snuck out of Bypass."

"Did you figure out who the warlord is?"

"Worse than warlord."

"What's worse than a warlord?"

"Internet marketer."

"Pardon?"

"Turned self-help guru."

"What?"

"Chang Zee."

Lion blinks. "I come here on boat, now I own boat—that Chang Zee?"

"A long time ago, that Chang Zee worked for Sir Richard."

"'I am the singularity'—that guy worked for Sir Richard?"

"You know, of course, that before Sir Richard built Arctic, he started in online marketing, then internet advertising. Then he built research program for studying, I do not know word, how internet advertising impacts brain."

"Neuromarketing?"

"Dah. Chang Zee worked on neuromarketing project."

"That Zen-Christ Tantra buffoon, with the scarves and the jewelry, he worked for Sir Richard?"

"He was fired and project was canceled. Sir Richard shut down company, sold off parts, and formed Arctic. This was before my time, so I know little, but I know Chang Zee took project in direction Sir Richard was not willing to go."

"I didn't know there was a direction Sir Richard was not willing to go."

"That is point."

"Chang Zee is behind the Suicide Girls?"

"Dah," replies Jenka, "but is puzzle."

It's a puzzle, all right. If Zee is responsible for the Suicide Girls, then he's the warlord responsible for Kendra and Ibrahim's disappearance, Lion's torture, the destruction of the Anti-Nagel colony, and the killer flying snakes in the Bypass. But if Zee is behind all of this, then that Moldovan neurotoxin—Penelope's secret warning about Jenka—might not mean what Lion thinks it means.

In fact, is Jenka even involved?

"Lion?"

"Yeah?"

"Is puzzle, no?"

"Dah," says Lion. "Fucking dah."

LIE TO THE FISH

The robo-mermaid waitress brings their drinks, takes their food order, and leaves them alone. Lion sips his bourbon. Jenka points at the fish tank. "Do you recognize technology?"

"The robo-catfish?" asks Lion.

Jenka shakes his head. "Look at forest, not trees."

"The whole aquarium," says Lion, suddenly realizing. "It's a face scanner? Like the ones at airports?"

"Dah."

The last time Lion cleared U.S. customs, he had to walk through a face-scanning tunnel aquarium. The movement of the fish automatically attracts the human gaze. As people walk through the tunnel, their heads turn to watch the fish, and the facial recognition software gets more facial angles to recognize.

"Where are the cameras?" asks Lion.

"The catfish," explains Jenka. "Their eyes are cameras. But . . ."—nodding at a nearby table of Hasidic men in traditional garb—"my colleagues are not so trusting." He points at the topless mermaid holograms. "So there are backup cameras in nipples—is sneaky, no?"

"It's something, all right," says Lion.

"After I got your text," says Jenka, "I check doors to Bypass, tunnel beneath cliff, and stairway that connects to tunnel. The stairway is news to me. But I check—is there."

"I told you it was there," says Lion.

Jenka shrugs. "But I am not so trusting."

"Tell me about the stairway."

"It is emergency exit."

"Is there a record of who used it?"

"There is problem."

"What problem?"

"Tell me," says Jenka, absently fingering the rim of his martini glass, "you believe, I believe, snakes were snuck into Bypass via tunnel under cliff?"

"Yeah."

"In text, you ask about master architectural blueprint file?"

"I did."

"Is where problem encounters other problem."

Lion glances at the doorman holding the tactical shotgun, then at the silverware, then at Jenka. "Do you think I could shove the tines of my fork into your left eye before that doorman can get off a shot?"

"Ah," says Jenka. "In my mind, I ask similar question. It helps, no?"

"Tell me about the problem."

"The issue starts with code vulnerability. To comply with U.S. government ruling, all projects that receive tax credit under Soulé Act—which is PRML—must use open-source software."

"What code vulnerability?"

"Clickjacking," explains Jenka. "I know, is big word."

"When you click a 'like' button on social media," says Lion, "clickjacking is a bit of code that takes you someplace else. You're hijacked by the click—clickjacked. But how does that apply here?"

"Not bad," says Jenka. "But is exotic clickjacking, so not quite. I found clickjacking malware disguised as rootcode that activates countdown timer that function as zero-day hack. We have passed zero day. So now neural-net architecture of GX platform is completely infected. But perhaps I use too many big words?"

"I followed that," says Lion. "PRML got hacked. Someone's stealing information from the park."

"I do not think stealing. I think watching."

"Watching for what?"

"I found sniffer on system that control snowmaking."

"The snowmaking system?"

"As far as I can tell, they watch to see when equipment is turned on and off."

"Why?"

"I do not know."

"That's all they're watching?"

"Is second problem. They also watch doors to Bypass, the stairwell, and the digital access logs for master blueprint file."

"They're watching all the same things I asked about?" says Lion. "That's a weird coincidence."

"In Moldova," Jenka explains, "the parents of my parents have saying: 'Is not coincidence, is KGB.' So you know what I am saying."

"No," says Lion. "Not a clue."

Jenka sighs. "I know who use stairway. Whoever use stairway, I think, you think, they release snakes. But you have not told me the entire truth."

"About what?"

"Who is Two Tone?"

Lion flashes back to Defenestration, the last thing he heard before being knocked unconscious, Two Tone saying, "Smack a bitch up." But didn't the cops find Two Tone in a dumpster?

Lion says, "The only Two Tone I know is dead."

"Before then," explains Jenka, "Two Tone's company, Full Beef Security, installed security system in Bypass."

"Full Beef Security?" says Lion, trying to fit the pieces together. "Doesn't 'zero day' mean the code vulnerability was put there intentionally, when the system was installed, by whomever installed the system?"

"Dah. Two Tone installed zero-day hack."

"But if Two Tone is dead, who's watching the system?"

"Not just Two Tone. The two coders who helped him install system are also dead. But I check Full Beef Security. Still heartbeat. Is subcorp beneath Defenestration, Unlimited."

"Defenestration is a bar in North London."

"Is money-laundering operation in North London," corrects Jenka. "Bar is owned by shell that is owned by ghost corp: Zen-Christ Tantra Holdings."

"Zen-Christ Tantra?"

"Dah."

"Two Tone worked for Chang Zee."

Jenka nods. "And Zee worked for Sir Richard. And this is problem with problem with problem. The door to stairway is protected by animatronic handshake. Full Beef Security designed the system. But Two

Tone is dead, coders who work for Two Tone are dead. Yet someone is still watching snowmaking machines, Bypass doors, and stairway doors."

"You think it's Zee."

"Dah. But I do not think Zee used stairway to release snakes. This is real problem: The handshake for stairway door is not standard security. It requires secret handshake. And since Two Tone and his techs are RIP, there is only one person left who know secret shake."

"Who?"

"Sir Richard."

"You think Sir Richard is sabotaging his own mega-linkage?"

"I do not know what to think," says Jenka, "so we are here."

"Shalom Creole Yum?"

Jenka nods at the table of Hasidic men. "Sir Richard has few friends in this community. But I am Moldovan Jew, on my mother's side. And I do have friends. One of whom"—he nods toward the opening of the alcove—"owns this restaurant and has even more friends than me."

Lion glances up and sees a handsome Hasidic man with a thick beard and long sidelocks walk into the alcove. He's in his late fifties, wearing traditional garb: a wide-brimmed black hat, a long black overcoat, a white button-down, and a pair of silver-rimmed glasses low on his nose.

"Barry," says Jenka, greeting the man with a smile. "Lion Zorn, please meet Barry Rabinowitz, the owner of this fine establishment. He is my *almost* rabbi."

Crossing to stand behind Jenka, Barry does something Lion did not believe possible. With the fingers of his left hand, he penetrates the Brylcreem fortress of Jenka's all-white pompadour, messing up his hair, absently, as one would a small child.

"Jenka," says Barry, with a heavy Brooklyn accent, "it is good to see you." He looks at Lion. "And you must be the very famous em-tracker, Lion Zorn."

As Barry talks, two Hasidic men with tactical shotguns take up flanking positions at the edge of the alcove.

Lion looks at the shotguns. "Do you think the famous em-tracker is going to shoot the catfish?"

"Complicated times," says Barry. "And when I called you a famous em-tracker, I was not pulling your schmeckel. In my community, you have played a very important role."

"Is truth," says Jenka. "I tell them otherwise, but they do not listen."

"I didn't know I was an anything in your community."

"The Torah tells us we are all tangled together," explains Barry. "Noah did not just put people on the Ark, he put all of God's creatures. This is why, in the teaching of the Kabbalah, we are taught to conduct a Seder for the trees—a way of wishing them a happy new year and saying thank you. If we forget the trees, then neither the Jews nor anyone else will last very long. We humans breathe second. The trees breathe first. We inhale their exhales. That is the circle of life. Empathy for all, Lion Zorn. We are in your debt. You have reminded my people of something very important that we had forgotten."

Lion takes a sip of his drink.

Barry glances at the guards. "Mordechai, Joshua, why don't you head to the loading dock and make sure our friends . . ."—pointing toward Lion and Jenka—"have everything they need for tomorrow's adventure."

After they're gone, Lion asks, "Tomorrow's adventure?"

"You didn't tell him?" says Barry.

"Is reason we are here," explains Jenka. "Is time, I think, we have conversation with Sir Richard."

"He's meeting us here?" asks Lion. "I thought he was in Cambodia."

"Holo-chat," continues Jenka.

"And what, we're just going to ask him about Chang Zee, the snakes, and the secret handshake?"

"We can ask," responds Jenka, "but Sir Richard is good liar. Is useful talent, I think." He points at the aquarium. "But is hard to lie to fish."

"Sir Richard's gonna notice we're calling him from an aquarium," says Lion.

"That," explains Barry, "is the equipment that Joshua and Mordechai are unloading. We borrowed a holodeck projector from our friends at the Silver Legacy Casino. Jenka tells me that this alcove is about the same size as holo-chat room at PRML. We're going to make this room look like that room."

"So we confront Sir Richard and use the fish to read his face?" asks Lion.

"He will never know the difference," says Barry.

Lion thinks for a second, then remembers what Jenka said. "Jenka called you his *almost* rabbi."

"I was almost a rabbi," says Barry.

"Almost?"

"You know how it goes—God had other plans for me. Now I am an almost rabbi who owns a little club on the shores of Lake Tahoe."

"An almost rabbi who requires armed guards."

"Yeah," says Barry, "that too."

Jam Yo Hype

Barry pulls out a JOBZ from his pocket. He opens an app and clicks a couple of buttons. A pair of robo-catfish swim into position, directly across from Lion. They peg their eyes to his face, some kind of gaze-lock feature that most people might find unnerving. But Lion's an em-tracker. He likes catfish—even if they're robotic.

Jenka says, "You spoke to Alejandra—the Rilkean bartender."

Lion points at the catfish. "You think I'm going to lie?"

"I do not know," says Jenka. "Now I will know. What did you talk about?"

Lion takes another sip of bourbon. He definitely appears to be in the process of getting drunk. But that doesn't seem to be a reason not to tell Jenka and Barry about his conversation with Alejandra.

He walks them through the exchange: the mysterious Professor Zhong, the uproar caused by his book on genetic marketing, the story of the Devil's Dictionary, the cliff at the bottom of Widowmaker and what he and Lizzy discovered there, including the boot prints belonging to Penelope and Susan. The only thing he doesn't mention is Penelope's note about the Moldovan neurotoxin, wondering if he can fool the fish.

When Lion's finished, Barry glances down at his JOBZ. "Jam-yo-hype meter puts him around seventy-nine percent."

"Jam yo hype?" asks Jenka.

Lion snorts. "The language setting on the JOBZ, he's got it set on 'retro-urban.'"

"Retro-urban or not," says Barry, "seventy-nine percent is not completely truthful. So what aren't you telling us?"

"We will come back to that," interrupts Jenka. "How did Penelope get out of Bypass? The log shows entrance, but not exit. And how did Susan get in? We have no record of her at all, not entering or exiting. According to log, only Sir Richard use staircase."

"What about the door on the other side of the tunnel?" asks Lion. "The entrance into Killebrew Canyon, near where the ski patroller died—did you check the logs for the door?"

"Is good point. I did not check."

Barry pulls on his beard. "So, if Sir Richard used the stairway, then he released the snakes that killed Susan Jackson?"

"Susan and Sir Richard were close," says Jenka. "I do not see this happening."

Lion asks, "Did Susan work with Richard when Richard worked with Chang Zee? On the neuromarketing project?"

"I don't know," replies Jenka. "But we will ask him."

Lion thinks for a moment. "When Penelope ditched her tracker, it could have been to get away from Sir Richard."

"That is what I worry about," says Jenka.

Lion nods. If this is true, then the Moldovan neurotoxin—maybe it has nothing to do with Jenka. But before he can ask, Barry changes the subject. "The Devil's Dictionary. You think the flying snakes were created by an AI?"

"Lizzy," Lion explains, "the PRML geneticist, says we don't have the technology yet."

"Terrible things happen when you create life for the wrong reasons. It is a sin against God."

"We'll know more when the test results come back tomorrow," says Lion. "I'm meeting Lizzy in the morning. We're going to watch the explorer-robot inspect the cave."

"I link computers," says Jenka. "We watch from here."

"From here?"

"The meeting with Sir Richard is tomorrow morning," explains Barry. "It takes a while to set up a fake holo-chat room. We have cottages on the lake. It would be an honor to have you as our guest."

Lion makes a decision. "If I'm staying over," he says, turning to Jenka, "you said there was a metric ton of shit I didn't know about your past."

"Aha," says Barry, watching the jam-yo-hype meter on the JOBZ, "this is the thing you are not telling us."

Lion locks eyes with Jenka. "Does that metric ton happen to include weapons?"

"Weapons?"

"Arms dealing? Gunrunning? Perhaps bioweapons?"

Jenka's eyes widen. He glances at Barry. "Nobody knows."

"Nobody knows what?" asks Lion.

Barry gestures toward Lion. "He doesn't look like nobody."

"Who told you?" demands Jenka.

"Did the Anti-Nagels tell you?" asks Barry.

"Anti-Nagels?" says Lion. "I'm talking about a neurotoxin."

Barry looks puzzled. "Did you say neurotoxin?"

"What neurotoxin?" demands Jenka.

"What Anti-Nagels?" asks Lion.

Jenka looks at Barry. Barry looks at Jenka. Lion looks confused.

"Tell him," says Barry.

"Tell me what?"

Jenka sighs. "Since Splinter, Barry and I have little side venture."

"What kind of side venture?"

"For fair market value, we have been distributing armaments—for protection purposes only—to certain communities who might otherwise have difficulty obtaining such wares."

"You're arming . . ." says Lion, remembering all the fancy guns he saw at the Anti-Nagel colony. "Fuck, man, you're arming the poly-tribes?"

"Against Humans First," says Jenka.

"You're a hacker—where are the guns coming from?" Then Lion realizes and looks at Barry.

"In my business," says Barry, "one cannot be too careful."

"Your business?"

"Staying alive," says Barry.

"You disapprove?" asks Jenka. "I thought you might understand."

"Bioweapons," says Lion, shaking his head.

"I don't know anything about bioweapons," says Jenka. "This is not something I would deal. What are you talking about?"

"A certain Moldovan neurotoxin?"

Jenka doesn't react.

"You don't know what I'm talking about?"

"What are you talking about?"

Lion tells them about Penelope's note, the missing letters in the quotes from William James and how those letters spell the words *Moldovan neurotoxin*.

"Penelope was trying to tell us the snake venom that killed Susan and that ski patroller, it's not venom, it's a Moldovan neurotoxin."

Their food arrives. A troop of robo-mermaids whirls plates before them. Once they depart, the table descends into silence. Then Jenka looks at them in disgust and says, "Moldovan neurotoxin," as if he needs to spit.

Regular or Gangster?

The booze and food push Lion into a hazy space. Like being underwater. Like his brain is made from string. They talk about possible reasons Sir Richard and Chang Zee might be collaborating. They talk about possible meanings for the words *Moldovan neurotoxin*. Every time Lion says the phrase, Jenka winces, as if slapped in the face.

Barry asks about Lion's past.

"What about . . ."

Jenka throws down his napkin and jumps to his feet. "The rotten truth of this Moldovan neurotoxin," he snarls. "I will investigate."

"That's the spirit," says Barry. "And maybe take a look at this Professor Zhong while you're at it."

"His PhD thesis," says Lion. "What's that about? And does Zhong have any kind of relationship with Chang Zee?"

"Dah," says Jenka.

"The digital access logs," adds Lion, "for the gates into Killebrew Canyon, don't forget those."

"I am not stupid," mutters Jenka. He turns toward Barry. "Where did they park hoverbike? I left computer in saddle bag. I need computer to investigate."

"The upper garage," replies Barry. "But don't worry about it. I'll have Mordechai bring it to your cottage. It's number five. You want regular tonight, right? Not gangster?"

"Dah," says Jenka, "regular is fine." Then he glares at Lion. "But he is guest, so give him gangster."

Jenka stomps off.

Lion asks, "Regular or gangster?"

"We are a private club," says Barry, as if that explained it.

"For gangsters?"

Barry looks around the room, which is still half full of Hasidic men. "For lonely men with lonely jobs."

"I'm pretty drunk," says Lion. "So I might be missing something."

"It's not important," replies Barry with a cryptic smile. He stands up. "But you have had more than enough excitement for one day. Let's get you to your cottage."

They stroll out of the restaurant, across a back porch and down a flight of steps, heading toward a dirt path that drops down a steep hill. They follow the path down the hill, passing into a dense pine forest, the full moon illuminating tall trees all around them. Eventually they come out of the forest at a row of cottages on the shores of Lake Tahoe.

Lion hears the quiet lap of waves intermixed with the reedy whisper of insects.

Barry stares at him, thinking something through. "Gangster," he says eventually, "I think gangster."

"What?"

"Take the third cottage. The one with the pink shutters."

Barry pulls out his JOBZ, fiddles with the device, then look at Lion. "All set. The full effect. Have fun." Then he turns away, waves his hand once, and disappears into the night.

Bed, thinks Lion, must get to bed.

He trudges over to the cottage, climbs up the stairs and onto the porch, then heads inside.

Cute and small.

A living room with an overstuffed couch, a kitchen off to one side, with a large gift basket on the table, and the bedroom in back. Lion heads straight past the kitchen and into the bedroom and clicks on the light.

What the hell?

While the rest of the house looks like a seaside cottage, the bedroom is a different story. The furniture is elegant and modern, the lighting dim. But it's the bed that catches his attention, an oversized king, with shimmery black sheets and two women lying naked atop them, one Russian, the other Chinese.

Both are holograms.

The Russian hologram smiles and pats the bed beside her. The Chinese hologram points at the nightstand. Lion follows her finger and sees a pair of Hard Pump VR goggles, one of the newer models, complete with haptic penis sleeve and fetish-accessory kit.

"Gangster," says Lion, shaking his head.

Without bothering to get undressed, he climbs into bed, closes his eyes, and passes out. He wakes a few hours later, fully clothed and completely disoriented. Looking around, he sees writhing ghost bodies on either side of him.

He'd forgotten to shut off the holograms.

Lion finds the control on the nightstand, switches off the naked women, and wonders why he is awake.

Unsure of the answer, Lion gets out of bed and makes his way to the kitchen. He downs two glasses of water while examining the gift basket. Fresh fruit, chocolate, a selection of marijuana edibles and smokables, two bottles of wine, and a silver tin of anti-hangover tabs.

Lion picks up the tin of anti-hangover tabs.

These things never work, he thinks, but takes three anyway.

As he's washing them down, Lion realizes it was a question Jenka had asked him—something about his conversation with Ichika—that's what woke him up.

But all Jenka asked was what Lion and Ichika had talked about.

He replays his conversation with Ichika in his mind. She told him about the warlord and the Suicide Girls, and that the funds from the betting site were paying for two projects: the Devil's Dictionary and Pandora II. The Devil's Dictionary is the name of the AI that creates life from scratch. But Lion still doesn't know what Pandora II means—could that be what woke him?

Maybe.

Then it clicks. Right before the explosion, Ichika said, "The trail leads to New York."

So what's in New York? That's the question that pulled him from his slumber.

But he has no time to consider the answer, as Barry bursts into the cabin shouting, "The lion has roared, who will not fear?"

"What the hell?"

"Scripture," says Barry, looking around for the first time, noticing the darkness. "Were you asleep?"

"Sort of."

"Jenka said you'd be finished with the girls and smoking a joint. He said, well . . ."—shaking his head—"I will leave you, never mind."

"Tell me why you're here."

"The Moldovan neurotoxin," says Barry, pulling his JOBZ from his pocket. "You have to watch this video."

"Let's go sit on the porch," says Lion, grabbing a joint from the gift basket and heading for the door.

THE V-2 STRATEGY

"What am I watching?" asks Lion.

"Just look," says Barry, holding out the JOBZ so he can see the screen.

It shows a video of a teenage girl walking through an open-air market. She's maybe seventeen, with shoulder-length black hair and very blue eyes.

"That's the Green Market," explains Barry. "In Tiraspol."

"Tiraspol?"

"Moldova," says Barry. "Keep watching."

The girl crosses to the edge of the stalls, pauses to inspect a potato, then starts into the parking lot. She passes a line of autonomous taxis and an old black van and that's when it happens. Before she takes another step, a tranquilizer dart strikes her in the neck.

"No shit," says Lion.

"Keep watching."

The girl grabs the dart, starts to wobble, tries to steady herself, then drops like a stone. Before she hits the ground, the van's door flies open and a man in a black ski mask grabs the girl beneath the armpits and hauls her inside. The door shuts and the van backs out of the space. The windows are tinted, so the driver is invisible.

"That's it?" he asks.

"Keep watching."

After a few seconds of white noise, a second video starts to play. It shows a different angle of the same scene. There must have been a second camera facing the parking lot.

Lion sees the rear of the van pulling away, the license plate covered in mud. The driver stops at the end of a row of cars and a man in a ski mask carrying what looks like a guitar case steps out from between parked cars, opens the passenger door, and climbs inside.

Barry pauses the video. "Do you recognize anyone?"

Lion looks at the screen, studying the man. Then he sees it. Right at the edge of the ski mask, beside the eyeholes, the familiar edge of a pair of thick black plastic frames.

"Buddy Holly glasses," says Lion. "You think it's the same guy who darted me?"

"Jenka thought so."

"Who got kidnapped?"

"That's Maria Natalovich, daughter of Kristina Natalovich."

"Those names don't mean anything to me."

"I don't suppose they do. Maria's just a teenager. Smart kid, apparently, but this mishigas appears to be about Kristina, her mother. She's a Moldovan scientist, not very well known, but considered to be at the very top of her field."

"Which is?"

"She studied ichthyology and herpetology in Moscow, got a doctorate in applied genetic engineering from Oxford, then worked at a World Heritage Site in Sumatra, studying—"

Lion interrupts him. "Flying tree snakes."

"Now you're catching on," says Barry. "After Sumatra, Kristina took a job in Siberia, at Pleistocene Park."

"That woolly mammoth de-extinction effort?"

"Yes," says Barry. "Though I am not sure she had anything to do with the mammoths. According to Jenka, she mostly studied the thermoregulation capabilities of Siberian wildlife."

"Arctic beetle and icefish," says Lion. "She was studying the antifreeze proteins in their blood."

Barry nods.

"Sumatra," continues Lion, "is in Indonesia, where they have flying tree snakes and black mambas. Kristina built the snakes."

"Not by choice," explains Barry. "The video is four years old. That's when Maria was kidnapped. A week later, her mother went missing. Nobody, according to Jenka, has heard from either since."

"Where'd he get the video?"

"Jenka found it listed in a police evidence cold case archive. It was taken by two different CCTV cameras at the Green Market. The Moldovan cops discovered it right after Maria vanished, but the video was their only evidence. The van was stolen, the plates switched. Then Kristina vanished. She was divorced, and her husband—Maria's father—died in a mining accident years before this. No one was pushing the investigation. Case went cold. Eventually the police moved on. But that's not why I woke you."

"Why'd you wake me?"

"I recognize the strategy."

"What strategy?"

"This," he says, shaking the JOBZ. "During World War II, Hitler needed to build the V-2 rocket so his bombs could reach London. Of course, the very best scientists were all Jewish. No Jew would ever work for the Nazis. So Hitler kidnapped their children and held them in the concentration camps. As long as the scientists kept making weapons, their children were kept alive."

"Evil," says Lion. He stares at the screen. "Why are you sure it's the same strategy?"

"Jenka did a search. In addition to Kristina, over the past five years, three other top scientists and their children have gone missing. Two de-extinction specialists and an African ursinologist—but I don't know what that is."

"Someone who studies bears."

"That's why I woke you."

"The bears?"

"This kidnapping is a sin against God, like the Suicide Girls and the Devil's Dictionary."

Lion understands. "You think Zee is kidnapping scientists and forcing them to work for him?"

"Not just scientists. Do you remember the story you told at dinner? The regret you saw on Five Spikes's face right before he fired the rocket launcher."

"You think Zee kidnapped someone close to Five Spikes, so he would be forced to kidnap other people?"

"Yes. Maybe Buddy Holly as well."

"It explains a lot," says Lion, hitting the joint.

"That is why I woke you," says Barry. "Also, I wanted to ask you a different question."

"What?"

"Pass me that joint."

Lion hands it to him. Barry takes a deep drag, then exhales slowly. "Jenka said, before the Splinter, you worked as an em-tracker."

"Feels like a lifetime ago."

"Do you miss it?"

Two years in hiding; his friends, Kendra and Ibrahim, kidnapped or worse; his own torture by taxidermy; six long months chasing after

Five Spikes and Buddy Holly; his on-again, off-again girlfriend vanishing without a trace.

"I miss something," says Lion.

"When this is over," says Barry, "would you like a job?"

"Doing what?"

"Em-tracking, of course."

"Em-tracking what?"

"This or that," says Barry, with a smile. "This or that."

caffeinate before exit

WhistlePig and Ghost Trainwreck and strange dreams—that's what Lion recalls from the night before. Did he meet a pair of holo-hookers? Were Five Spikes and Buddy Holly forced to kidnap and torture him? These are the questions Lion confronts as he drags himself out of bed.

He staggers into the shower, gets out, gets dressed, and checks the JOBZ.

"Shit."

He slept through the robotic tunnel exploration. A two-hour-old text from Jenka tells him the whole thing already happened. "We have video," says the text. "We have more rotten truth."

That can't be good.

A second text sent an hour later tells him to come up to Shalom Creole Yum once he's awake. Lion debates: Caffeinate before exit?

He decides Barry will have coffee available.

Next he does a quick cottage double check. Living room, kitchen, bedroom. The Hard Pump VR headset sits on the nightstand. Naked women, merely a touchscreen away.

Lion ignores the headset, puts on his boots, jacket, and watch cap, and pushes out into the sunshine. He blinks at the light.

Looking around, Lion realizes Shalom Creole Yum has been built atop a cliff above a small cove. He's now at the cliff's bottom, where five micro-Victorian cottages stand on the edge of Lake Tahoe. There's no beach, but a long wooden dock stretches out into aquamarine water.

Beyond the beach, a garden path vanishes in the heavy shadows of an ancient forest. Not seeing other options, Lion decides that must be the trail he walked last night.

He starts hiking, banking inland and winding upward. His boots crunch the snow. In the breaks between pines, he spots ravens curling against the sky, black dots dancing to the music of wind.

A hundred feet later, the path opens onto a small snow-covered clearing, empty except for a gray wood bench. The ravens, he notices, are flying closer to the shore now, their black dots becoming commas, their commas becoming birds. In the distance, beyond the birds, Lion sees snowcapped mountains wrapped in a thick band of dark clouds.

There's a storm coming.

Lion stares at the clouds a moment longer, then follows the path back into the forest. Lodgepole pine and Douglas fir, their branches thick with snow, their barrel trunks rising high.

Hiking on, Lion reaches the side of another cliff, where a gap in the forest reveals the ravens again, swooping and frolicking, riding approaching storm winds like surfers on waves.

He feels a light tingle run down his spine.

Is he being watched?

Lion looks around the forest. Sentinel trees are always watching, but that's not the vibe he's picking up. He looks out at the ravens again and notices that one of the birds isn't swooping. Neither is it frolicking.

Instead, it's hovering—like a drone.

Like the raven-drone Lion saw yesterday while skiing—is it back for another round?

A second later, the drone swoops low over the lake, pulls up into a steep climb, and disappears into the clouds.

Did he imagine it?

Lion considers other options. The drone could be Buddy Holly, taking over Lion-tracking duties now that Five Spikes is dead. It might be Sir Richard, keeping tabs. Or maybe he's just hungover and paranoid and this is nothing more than a wildlife photographer hunting a close-up of ravens in flight.

Lion ducks back into the trees and peers at the sky through the branches, waiting to see if the drone returns.

Nothing happens.

Hungover and paranoid, he decides.

Starting toward the restaurant, he hikes upward for a few hundred feet, cuts around a tight switchback, and begins climbing again.

There are voices in the distance.

Cresting the hill, Lion pops out of the forest. The back porch of Shalom Creole Yum is directly in front of him. In its center, Jenka and Barry are drinking coffee at a small wooden table. Jenka wears his white snowsuit, unzipped to the waist, and a white T-shirt beneath. Barry wears a white button-down shirt, black trousers, black overcoat, and a black velvet yarmulke.

Lion glances at the sky, but the ravens are gone.

Barry spots him then, raises a hand, and waves him over. Lion crosses the lawn, climbs the steps, says good morning, and sits down on a wooden bench beside Jenka. Barry grabs a tall silver carafe and an empty mug from the table. He pours a cup of coffee and passes it to Lion.

"Thank God."

Taking a sip of coffee, Lion glances at the screen of an open laptop, sitting in front of Jenka. It shows a series of complicated chemical equations and long strings of DNA code.

"What is that?" he asks.

"Moldovan neurotoxin," responds Jenka, pointing at the laptop. "This is rotten truth."

Barry glances at the laptop. "That's not the rotten truth."

"You are saying I am liar?"

Barry points at the screen. "I'm saying you closed the rotten truth.

That's a different file. This is the one that shows what Lizzy discovered when she tested the snakeskin."

Jenka inspects the screen. "Dah. Barry is right. This is *Pseudomonas syringae.*"

"Amazing," says Lion, "that's exactly what I suspected. What the hell is *Pseudo* whatever?"

"Bacteria that grows on plants," responds Jenka. "But . . ."—pointing at the DNA code—"it has been altered. Is missing a part of key gene, so it forms ice-nucleating proteins."

"It's the snowmaking bacteria," says Lion, remembering his conversation from the day before. "Lizzy told me about it."

"More than that," says Barry.

"Is timing mechanism," explains Jenka. "Snakes are hatched, no, from eggs. The snakes, both original recipe that killed Susan Jackson and the newer flying version that try to kill you, their DNA has been changed. Inside egg, result is accelerated morphology. Embryos mature much faster than normal. Outside egg is other story. When outside of eggshell comes in contact with *Pseudomonas syringae,* snakes start to hatch."

"Why does that matter?"

"Lizzy thinks it's because the snakes don't live very long," explains Barry.

"If you want to use snakes as weapon," continues Jenka, "snakes must be alive, no? But this genetic code is still glitchy. Accelerates morphology, so embryos grow faster, but process doesn't stop at birth. The genes also accelerate decrepitude. Snakes live day, maybe two. Is what explorer robot discover in tunnel: hatched eggs and dead snakes. Many, many dead snakes."

Lion thinks for a moment. "That's why the tunnel smelled like death?"

"Dah."

"So, what, the snowmaking machines get turned on, the eggs hatch, and the snakes are released?"

"Like a gun, no?" says Jenka. "Just pull trigger and *boom.*"

ion drinks another cup of coffee and stares at the trees. Barry and Jenka discuss the details for the upcoming holo-chat with Sir Richard. Then Lion realizes the discussion has stopped and both men are looking at him.

"What?"

"Last night," says Jenka.

"When Barry woke me up?"

"You were sleeping?" asks Jenka, looking confused.

"I was unconscious."

"But you had gangster cottage—did you not meet Sasha and Xiu?"

Lion draws a blank, then remembers. "The holograms? They have names?"

"You did not try?" asks Jenka. "Are you not man?"

"They have more than names," explains Barry. "They're real people. Xiu is an industrial spy. In today's competitive market, her job demands proficiency in the sexual arts. And Sasha is the last of her kind. Trained in seduction by the KGB."

"She's a red sparrow?" asks Lion.

"All that wisdom," says Barry, "just for your benefit."

"How is that possible?"

"Whole brain connectome mapping," says Barry.

Lion thinks for a second. "The only whole brain connectome mapping I know about is ghost tech."

"What is whole brain connectome mapping?" asks Jenka.

"It's supposed to be a way to record all of the brain's network connections," explains Lion. "All the links between neurons. The theory is this will create a digital record of a life: memories, personalities, and . . ."—thinking about what Barry had just said about the training these women had received—"even skill sets."

Jenka gives him a look. "You know this how?"

"I heard a lecture at an em-tracking conference," explains Lion. "It's a combo tech, right? Infrared holography and portable magnetoencepha-something."

Barry nods. "They record straight off the retina. If you trigger an emotional response, these machines can follow it all the way back through the brain. They catalog every node of every network that activates and the connections between nodes. It's like a wiring diagram of a person's decision-making processes. If you had someone's connectome map, you'd know why they make the decisions they make. From a business perspective, it's a gold mine."

"Ghost tech," says Lion again. "It's years away."

"Sasha and Xiu—they're right there in your room."

"The Chinese," explains Jenka.

"Jenka's right," says Barry. "The Chinese military made a breakthrough. Don't ask me what, I have no idea. The version I have, well, let's just say that I shouldn't have the version I have. But, trust me, it definitely works."

"Sasha and Xiu," says Jenka. "I cannot believe you did not try."

Lion thinks about these women. Their entire sexual history is now available via Hard Pump VR. "Do memories constitute a form of intellectual property?" he asks. "If you record someone's connectome, who owns the recording? The person who lived the life? The neuroscientist who made the recording? Some multi-stakeholder split worked out by the courts?"

"Who owns a life?" says Barry. "That is a question for the Talmud."

"Wasn't long ago," says Jenka, "the question of who owns a life isn't question."

On the table beside him, Barry's JOBZ begins to vibrate. He glances at the screen, reaches into the breast pocket of his shirt, and pulls out a joint and a pack of matches. He strikes a match, lights the joint, and passes it to Lion.

"Hit this," says Barry.

Lion gives him a puzzled look.

"Trust me, I'm an almost rabbi, it will help."

"Help with what?"

Barry uses the joint to gesture at the text on the JOBZ. "We're ready to go. The holo-chat is set up."

"Is time to ask Sir Richard about snakes," adds Jenka.

"You sure this will work?" asks Lion. "The holo-chat replica? Sir Richard really won't be able to tell we're sitting in a restaurant?"

"He'll never know the difference," says Barry. "Now hit that shit. We need you at your em-tracking best."

"Why?" Then he gets it. "You want me to em-track Sir Richard." But he also realizes Barry has a point. Lion's a living, breathing jam-yo-hype meter. He sighs. "Pass me the damn joint."

As Barry hands it over, Jenka brings up another image on the lap-top, a spreadsheet filled with numbers. "I check handshake access log for doors," he says, pointing at the spreadsheet. "The other end of tunnel beneath the cliff, like you ask."

"The entrance into Killebrew Canyon?"

"Dah. According to log, door was not used by anyone but Sir Richard."

"You still believe he released the snakes?"

Jenka nods.

Something's gnawing at Lion, a memory, but he can't quite get there. Jenka starts to speak, but Lion holds up a finger for silence, takes an-other hit off the joint, and thinks some more.

"Products are for the dead," says Lion suddenly.

"What?"

"It's something Sir Richard said the first time we met. He asked if I knew what the Arctic Corporation actually did. I said, 'Guerrilla marketing and product development.' Sir Richard got pissed and gave a little speech: 'Products are for the dead. They're a relic of the last century, a nostalgia. Arctic doesn't develop products. Arctic may culti-vate them sometimes, but our business is change. Significant change.'"

"Dah," says Jenka, "I have heard this speech before. But what is bigger significant change than creating snakes? Sir Richard is playing God with DNA."

"I can't wrap my head around it," says Lion. "Empathy for all—that's always been the change Sir Richard wants. PRML is his legacy. Why destroy it before it's even built? And working with Chang Zee to make a Moldovan neurotoxin—that doesn't seem like—"

"Zee made Kristina make snakes," snaps Jenka, slamming the laptop closed.

"The V-2 strategy," says Lion. "Yeah, Barry told me."

"Chinese neurotoxin," snarls Jenka. "Not Moldovan."

"Whatever," says Lion.

Barry crosses himself.

"Did you just cross yourself?" asks Lion. "Aren't you an almost rabbi?"

Barry points at the now-closed laptop. "With this shit, we're gonna need all the help we can get."

ErGO

Barry wasn't exaggerating when he said Sir Richard would never notice the difference. The real holo-chat back at PRML, the fake Shalom Creole Yum version—as far as Lion can tell, they look identical. A white room, a wooden bench, and once the projectors are turned on, all traces of the face-reading aquarium vanish from sight.

"Let's get this party started," calls Lion. He has to raise his voice to be heard. Jenka and Barry are in the next room, fiddling with equipment.

Barry pokes his head around the corner. "What?"

"Dial up Sir Richard already," says Lion. "It's *go* time."

"T minus thirty seconds," snarls Jenka. "We *are* going."

Barry disappears around the corner. Lion sits down on the bench, fiddles with the zipper on his black Faction hoodie and takes a deep breath.

"T minus twenty seconds."

"Jam-yo-hype meter is on," calls Barry. "Relay projection working. Fish in position."

"T minus ten seconds."

Lion takes another breath.

Jenka says, "T minus five, four, three, two—Sir Richard."

The lights dim and a holo-version of the holo-version of R2-D2 waddles into the room. It's a replica of a replica, a perfect copy of the bullet-shaped robo-hologram used at PRML. The holo-bot stops mid-room, whistles and chirps, then projects a beam of light. A hologram of Sir Richard materializes inside the beam, about a foot tall, wearing jeans and a flannel shirt, his black mane poking out from beneath a white trucker's cap adorned with the NASA logo and the phrase *Let's get the hell out of here.*

"Hello, sport," says Sir Richard, as soon as the image steadies.

"Sire," says Lion, "I have news from the kingdom."

"Sire?"

"My liege. Your highness. Sultan of Swing. God of Rock."

Sir Richard looks at Lion.

"King of Kings, Lord of Lords. Chaka Khan, Chaka Khan, Chaka Khan, let me rock you, let me rock you, Chaka Khan."

"Are you high?"

Lion reaches into his hoodie, takes out a joint, and lights it up. "I'm so high I can talk to rain."

"Sir Richard is just fine," he says, glaring. Then, looking around, "Where's Jenka?"

"Caught up," says Lion. "We got the 911 asking for the 411 and his was outta here."

Not entirely bullshit, thinks Lion. Jenka *is* caught up. He's in the next room monitoring the lie detection software on the JOBZ and then porting the results onto a laptop positioned to Lion's left, fully visible from where he sits, but out of Sir Richard's line of sight.

The controls of the robo-catfish are Barry's job. He's sitting beside Jenka, making sure the cameras get good coverage of Sir Richard's facial expressions.

"Did you make any progress since yesterday?" asks Sir Richard. "Have you found Penelope?"

Barry, Jenka, and Lion had also discussed how to handle this question. Jenka thought they go right at him. "Ask hard question. Good cop, bad cop. Just, this time, no good cop."

Barry wanted to lead with the truth. "Thou shalt not steal, nor deal falsely, nor lie to one another."

Lion had disagreed with both. He thought the conversation should start with a little misdirection, just a touch of the weird. Follow the weird with a smooth ego stroke. "Tilt him," Lion explained, "then make him feel safe and happy and blabby. It's a dopamine thing. He'll open up."

"What dopamine thing?"

"Compliments light up the brain's reward centers," Lion continues. "Just like cocaine. Makes people talk too much. Then, in the midst of their blah-blah-blah, that's when you come hard. Ego tilt, ego stroke, then counterpunch. Or didn't you guys learn anything in em-tracking school?"

That ended the argument.

Now Lion catches Sir Richard's eye, holds his gaze, and abandons the weird. "I visited the Bypass," he says, coming in with the ego stroke. "Stunning to see it come to life. Blown away, man, I was blown away. Serious as a heart attack progress. You should be proud."

"The change is real," says Sir Richard, puffing up a little. "But there's a long way to go."

"Do you have a species count yet? I bet you've seen a rebound."

"Nature finds a way," says Sir Richard. "Isn't that always the lesson? Give her the space to thrive, she thrives."

Lion nods and says, "PRML was that space."

"The flora rebound was almost immediate," says Sir Richard, now starting to beam. "Plants are tough bastards. Fauna-wise, we've moved three species off the red list."

"Sir Richard," says Lion, "you're really showing me something here."

"The Sierra Nevada red fox, the Lahontan cutthroat trout, and the mountain beaver—they will all live to fight another day. Do you know the work of the philosopher Georg Wilhelm Friedrich Hegel? Hegel believed history is a dialectic, a living conversation about the nature of truth." Then Sir Richard switches to German, "*An-sich, Anderssein, An-und-für-sich.*" Then back to English: "In itself, out of itself, in and for itself. Or as we now know the idea: thesis, antithesis, synthesis."

Lion lets him ramble, every now and again sneaking glances at the laptop in the corner of the room. The jam-yo-hype lie-detection software requires a handful of truthfully answered questions to establish a baseline. Lion is waiting for a red dot to turn green, which is the signal that it's time to ask harder questions.

It's still red.

Pontificating without provocation, Sir Richard prattles on about how the swing to the left produced by Sietch Tabr is the thesis. This is followed by the antithesis, the swing to the right of the Humans First movement. Finally, the synthesis, the way forward, which Sir Richard appears to believe is his contribution, PRML itself. "Hegel teaches us that truth," says Sir Richard, "is to be found in neither the thesis nor the antithesis, but in an emergent synthesis that reconciles the two."

Finally the light changes color.

"Sport," says Lion, interrupting Sir Richard, "Full Beef Security, Two Tone's company, they installed the security system for the Bypass? The animatronic handshake doors?"

Billionaires aren't used to being interrupted, and Sir Richard is no different. He peers at Lion in silence.

"Two Tone?" says Sir Richard finally, drawing the syllables out in his annoyed British best. "I don't believe I know who that is."

Lion glances at the laptop. Jam-yo-hype meter reads 87 percent. Mostly, Sir Richard's telling the truth.

It clicks.

Lion says, "But you do know Full Beef Security."

Sir Richard peers at him again. "Yes, the firm came highly recommended."

"By whom?"

"One of my investors," says Sir Richard, an irked edge seeping into his voice.

"Susan Jackson?"

"How did you know?"

"Let's come back to that," says Lion. "How did you meet Susan?"

Lion sees it then, not a lie-detection signal, rather an em-tracking signal. A directional arrow into the future, almost like a giant sign hanging above Sir Richard's head. He understands exactly what he's looking at. "You dated her?"

"*Dated* is a strong word," says Sir Richard.

The JOBZ reads 94 percent accuracy.

"You slept with her," says Lion.

"It's a little more complicated. Why is my personal life relevant here? Why are you asking about my history with Susan?"

Lion shrugs. "It connects to what we found in the park."

"What did you find?"

"Snakes," he says casually. "We found a new kind of snake. Actually I found it, sort of the hard way."

"Yes," says Sir Richard. "I heard you are quite the skier."

"You talked to Lizzy?"

"Elizabeth. I spoke to her a few hours ago."

That's a surprise. Sir Richard rarely speaks to the help. He has people for that. Instead, Lion knew, Sir Richard prefers drop-ins. He calls it guerrilla management. Instead of a text or a phone call, Sir Richard likes to show up unexpectedly in his employees' lives. One moment you're heading to the store to pick up groceries. The next, Sir Richard has landed his custom-designed Bugatti Airliner II in the store's parking lot, and it's off to somewhere exotic for dinner and drinks.

"That's unusual," says Lion. "You talking to someone so far beneath your station."

"Fuck off, sport."

Lion sees it then, a subtle shift, something dark flashing across Sir Richard's eyes. Now, he thinks, hit him now. "If you slept with Susan Jackson," he says, "why kill her? Was the sex that bad?"

"Kill her?"

"I saw the access logs for the emergency exit."

Sir Richard gives him a blank stare. Lion's gut confirms. Just to make sure, he glances at the jam-yo-hype meter: 100 percent truth—Sir Richard really doesn't know what Lion's talking about.

"The emergency exit," clarifies Lion. "The one in and out of the Bypass."

Still nothing.

"The stairway that leads to the tunnel beneath the cliff on Widowmaker?"

"Ah," says Sir Richard, finally getting it. "Where the snakes are nesting. Yes, Elizabeth told me that as well."

"The tunnel is ground zero," says Lion. "It's where the snakes were released. It's the murder weapon."

"What is this about?"

"The animatronic handshakes. The system Two Tone installed."

"Yes."

"It records entrances and exits."

"The secret handshake," he says, his eyes popping wide. "Bloody hell. The access log, it shows that it was my handshake? The one I programmed in, the one no one else knows?"

"It says that you're the only one who used those doors."

"Ergo, I released the snakes."

"Ergo," says Lion.

"Bloody hell." Sir Richard takes off his trucker's hat and runs his fingers through his mane. "Susan Jackson. The snakes. Penelope. Bloody hell."

"What are you talking about?"

Sir Richard switches into command mode. "Find Jenka," he snaps. "Have him look into Penelope's employee vetting files, her old notes on Susan Jackson. And we need the time codes for the snowmaking equipment in the Bypass. We need both and we need them now."

"Sport," says Lion, "you didn't answer my question. What's going on?"

"Sport," says Sir Richard, "I'm afraid I'm at war."

war

"War?" snarls Jenka, abandoning his post and striding into the holo-chat. "What kind of war?"

"Hello, Jenka," says Sir Richard. "I appear to be at war with Chang Zee."

"The info-marketer self-help buffoon?" says Lion, playing dumb.

"He is not a buffoon."

"No?"

"A long time ago," says Sir Richard.

"Yeah," says Lion. "I heard about that. Skip to the good part."

"So you already know that Zee and I worked together on a project?"

"All I know is it was a neuromarketing project and Zee did something that freaked you out, so you shut it down."

"We were exploring new technologies," explains Sir Richard. "This was the second wave of neuromarketing. The first wave was bullshit—nothing worked as promised. But the second wave, we started to be able to get a picture of brain connectivity, network maps." He stops and waves his hand. "It doesn't matter. What does matter is that Susan Jackson worked for Zee. That's actually how we met. A few years before this, Zee had been a professor and Susan was his star graduate student. When he left academia and went into business, she went with him. Zee lived in China, even when we worked together, but he sent Susan to our offices in New York. She was the go-between."

"I thought Susan made her money in cultured beef."

"That was later," explains Sir Richard. "And I helped her start that company. That was our deal."

"What deal?"

"The neuromarketing project, right around the time I started thinking about shutting it down, I noticed information was going missing. At first I thought I was being spied upon, but then I realized it was sabotage. We were building an AI to help us analyze the neuro-data and someone was altering tiny bits of code. Not enough to break anything, but just enough that you could never use the system in the right way. The AI was coded to provide wrong answers. I ran an investigation. It was actually the first time I heard about Jenka. I couldn't hire him then, he was working on a different project, but he was one of the better grey hat hackers around."

"White hat," snarls Jenka.

"As you wish," says Sir Richard, with a slight smile.

"The sabotage," says Lion, trying to get back on track.

"It was Susan Jackson," explains Sir Richard. "She was the spy."

"She was spy?" says Jenka.

"What did you do when you found out?" asks Lion.

Sir Richard smiles. "I ran a covert operation of my own."

"That's when you slept with her."

Sir Richard gives him another look. "We spent some time together," he says. "Susan told me about her father's dying cultured meat company. She wanted to take over. She thought she could build it into a contender. So I made her an offer. If Susan agreed to switch sides and spy on Zee for me, then I agreed to make her dream come true."

"She was a double agent?"

"A long, long time ago, yes. But now, I wonder, maybe Susan switched sides again."

"Why?"

"It's something she said."

"What?"

"Zee is almost the exact opposite of you, Lion. You believe in empathy for all. Zee believes in human superiority. The perfectibility of man, the idea that we are morally obligated to improve both ourselves and creation. Pandora II—that's what he called it. His man-made perfect Eden."

"Pandora II," says Lion. "I've been trying to figure out what that meant."

"For years," continues Sir Richard, "I thought Susan went into cultured beef for environmental reasons. That's why I backed her. But lately she seemed to have a different agenda. She'd focused on genetically engineered super beef. Susan thought meat was a great protein-delivery system, but it had flaws. She wanted to change the amino acid structure, switch out the genes that cause cancer and heart disease, swap in genes that increase longevity. She thought her designer meat could double the human lifespan."

"I am not following," says Jenka. "What does this have to do with Susan switching sides?"

"I asked her about the super-beef project," Sir Richard says. "It was taking up a ton of her time. Her answer alarmed me. She said, 'Immortality—it's our destiny.'"

"What is point?" says Jenka.

"Immortality is about perfecting humankind," says Lion. "That's the point. That's why you think Susan's a triple agent."

"Not just that," explains Sir Richard. "A month ago, Susan told me she wanted to check out the Bypass. She's not a great skier, she can't snowboard, so she wanted to use the stairway. I taught her the handshake."

"Susan is snake-releasing bitch?" asks Jenka. "But she is dead, no?"

Sir Richard continues. "Lizzy told me about the snowmaking bacteria and how it triggers the snake eggs to hatch. But our whole snowmaking system has been screwed up for months. It keeps turning on and off by itself."

"Is zero-day hack," says Jenka.

"It's what?" asks Lion.

"That is what I discover late last night. Zero-day hack is for stealing information and control of snowmaking. That is why sniffer is there. But it is not sniffer. Is control system *disguised* as sniffer. Very sneaky."

"So," says Lion, "Zee killed Susan Jackson, his own triple agent? Why?"

"He's covering his tracks, sport."

"Why?"

"The same reason he's trying to destroy PRML," says Sir Richard.

"Which is?"

"Pandora II."

Lion's JOBZ buzzes. He ignores it. But it keeps buzzing. In a rhythm: dot-dot-dot, dash-dash-dash, dot-dot-dot.

It's Penelope's code, set up months ago.

What the hell?

"Excuse me," he says, pulling the JOBZ from his pocket.

He looks at the message.

It's a text from Penelope: "PRML under attack. Lizzy in danger. Get to her lab—now!"

A second later another text arrives.

"Get yer bloody arse in gear, ya wankstain. Lizzy! Lab! GO!"

PART VI

THIRTY MINUTES LATER, LAKE TAHOE

Stealth Flying Motorcycle Chase Scene, Take One

Hanging on by his fingers, Lion's a hundred feet off the deck, being towed through the sky behind Jenka's stealth flying motorcycle. Like three seconds ago, a hard left turn bounced him from the bike and into the air. He just seemed to float off the foot pegs and sail behind the seat, suddenly noticing nothing but empty space between him and the snow-covered mountains far below.

Realizing his predicament, Lion snapped out his right arm, grabbing for anything within reach. He missed Jenka's coat, missed the seat, but managed to catch hold of the bike's tail fin. His arm extended and his body stretched out until he was soaring in a straight line behind the bike, accidentally executing what fans of big-air motocross might recognize as a one-handed Superman.

In that instant, time started to creep, like someone had turned the speed-of-life tap down to a trickle. This gave Lion time to think about how he got here.

It's a puzzle, all right.

Thirty minutes ago, Lion had received Penelope's "Lizzy in danger" text—that's how it started. Twenty-five minutes ago, he and Jenka dashed out of the holo-chat room, sprinted through Shalom Creole Yum, and ran onto the restaurant's driveway. Twenty-three minutes ago, they bounded into Barry's upper garage, where Jenka's stealth flying motorcycle was parked.

It took five minutes for them to get their helmets on, audio links up, and the vehicle rolled out of the garage and onto the launch pad. Eighteen minutes ago, they jumped on the bike, with Jenka driving and Lion tucked in behind.

Jenka hit the power button on the dash, tilted the machine's rotors for vertical takeoff, and gunned the throttle. The bike shot straight up into the sky, banked right, and headed south.

Two minutes later they hit cruising altitude. They were a hundred feet above the treetops, heading southeast, following Highway 28 as it wraps the southern shore of Lake Tahoe.

Eight minutes ago, they left the lake in the rearview and began flying inland, over rugged, dense forest. That's also when the storm arrived, the sky darkening to the color of soot, the wind beginning to howl. Snow started to fall in thick flakes as big around as quarters.

Five minutes ago, visibility became a thing of the past and things got a little exciting. Jenka had been following the ridgeline down out of the mountains, flying close to the tops of the trees, using the canopy to block the wind. As they whipped around the nose of a grandfather pine, Lion thought he saw something in a break between the branches.

Just a splotch of black in an otherwise snowy sky.

A minute later, he saw it again.

Lion glanced over his right shoulder to get a better look.

Not a black splotch—a raven in flight.

He looked away, but then it dawned on him: Ravens don't usually fly at two hundred miles an hour.

Fifty seconds ago, Lion glanced behind them to get a clearer view.

That's when he realized: It wasn't a raven. It was a drone. It was the same raven-drone that had tailed him around the ski area, then shown up behind Shalom Creole Yum, and now, a third time, just a hundred feet off their flank.

Forty-five seconds ago, Lion said, "I think we have a tail."

Jenka punched a button on the dash, bringing up the rearview camera and a clear shot of the drone. Lion saw the lidar hump rising between the raven's shoulder blades and the chrome dome of an eye-in-the-sky lens protruding from its belly.

"Dah!" Jenka said, not twenty-five seconds ago.

Then he twisted the bike's handlebars, swooped left, and slowly dropped down into the trees.

Right, left, right. Douglas fir dodgeball at two hundred miles an hour.

Yanking back the handlebars, Jenka arced the bike upward at a dizzy angle. Their rotor blades grazed a Ponderosa, scattering pine needles, before blasting them back above the tree line and into the sky.

"Code red," shouted Jenka, his voice echoing through the speakers in Lion's helmet. "Do not fuck with the Moldovan."

"Please ask the Moldovan not to scream in my ear," Lion said, like twelve seconds ago.

"Stealth flying motorcycle chase scene, take one!" responded Jenka. "Hang on to your cojones!"

Unfortunately, between the shouting and Jenka's thick accent, the word *chase* sounded a lot like *cheese*. Ten seconds ago, Lion's brain was trying to decode "Stealth flying motorcycle cheese scene."

Nine seconds ago, he gave up and spun around to check on the drone.

Eight seconds ago, Jenka zigged the bike left, while Lion zagged his body right. Unfortunately, with Lion spun backward in the seat, the sudden motion of the bike loosened his grip.

Seven seconds ago, Lion's arm peeled from Jenka's waist and his feet lifted off the foot pegs.

Six seconds ago, Lion noticed the motorcycle, floating below him.

Five seconds ago, he crashed back into consciousness, snatched the bike's tail fin with his right hand, his body snapping horizontal behind the cycle, his one-handed Superman in full effect.

Four seconds ago, Lion screamed, "Jenka!" at the exact moment Jenka jerked the bike left again, making a desperate dodge around a lodgepole pine. The sudden counter-motion flung Lion in the opposite direction, his feet heading directly toward the left rear rotor, the whirling blades snapping at his limbs.

Three seconds ago, Lion twisted midair, nearly breaking his wrist. His hip smashed into the side of the engine, his boots missing the blades by inches. The impact kicked the vehicle into the snow-covered treetops, leaving a trail of white fractal explosions in their wake.

Two seconds ago, the bike caught a sugar pine, spun sideways, and twirled into a flat spin, with Lion still dangling one-handed off its rear.

A second later, there was an air horn blast followed by a booming male baritone: "Betta check yourself before ya wreck yourself." Then a pause. Then the same voice said, "Executing autonomous override."

The rotors shut off and the bike stalls midair. This flips them upright. Then the rotors tilt in different AI-determined directions, and fire up again. Immediately, the bike levels out of the flat spin, takes a few big bounces, and settles into a hover.

Lion whips his feet beneath him, missing the foot pegs, but flopping his chest onto the seat. Jenka releases the handlebars, spins around, and grabs Lion beneath his armpits, yanking him upright.

Time returns to normal.

"Thank you," says Lion, catching his breath, still quivering with adrenaline.

"Dah. Now you owe me two sex favors."

Jenka clicks a button on the side of the dash. Lion feels the foot pegs wrap around his boots, snugging his feet to the bike.

"Fucking hell," says Lion, "you're only remembering the sure-grip now?"

"We were in hurry," replies Jenka. "Where is tail?"

Lion looks around. "I think you lost it."

"Dah," says Jenka. "When I was younger, *Grand Theft Auto*, all day every day. This is not so different."

But they didn't lose anything.

A second later, the raven-drone rises into sight, its wings outstretched, its inky black feathers glistening in their headlights. The drone had been flying directly beneath them. Now it's hovering directly in front of them.

The raven's eyes light up red and start to blink.

Dot-dot-dot, dash-dash-dash, dot-dot-dot.

Did Lion just see that?

It happens again.

"That's Penelope's signal!" says Lion. "She's flying the drone."

"Penelope is tail?" asks Jenka. "So tail is not tail?"

The raven blinks again, the same pattern, then banks left, and starts to fly away.

"Follow the raven," says Lion.

"Dah," says Jenka. "Stealth flying motorcycle chase scene, take two."

SHOOT ANYTHING THAT ISN'T HUMAN

Jenka slaloms through the sky, trying to keep the raven in sight. The blizzard has gotten worse and is now blasting waves of white through their headlights. Vision is nearly impossible. Trees snap into view. Blue spruce dodge. Ponderosa pine weave.

A hundred yards ahead, they soar out of the forest, and the whole of the Carson Valley opens up beneath them. Lion looks down and sees the remains of Kingsbury Grade, the slender mountain pass that once connected the Carson Valley flats to the Sierra Nevada heights. Now the grade is hidden inside a tunnel, buried deep underground. Above it, there's a million metric tons of topsoil replanted with native shrubs and trees. What used to be a road for transporting humans has become a forest for meandering plants and animals. It's the eastern edge of PRML's migration corridor, now coated in a pristine layer of new snow.

Lizzy's lab is five miles down the valley.

The clouds hang low, thick and dark. Jenka's trying to keep the motorcycle in the thin band of visibility between the clouds above and the trees below. The winds are savage.

A heavy gust bounces them sideways, sending more curtains of white across their high beams. The raven vanishes in the squall. In its place, there's a flash of shiny burgundy, followed by twin headlights, as if there is another vehicle somehow directly in front of them.

"Look out!" shouts Lion.

Jenka yanks the handlebars left, flipping the bike on its side, skidding it sideways through the air. Lion's feet wrench against the suregrip pegs, but this time stay locked into place.

Spinning the wheel further, Jenka arcs them horizontal, so the bike is skipping backward as the outthrust of its rotors tries to slow them down.

They skid to a halt an inch away from the burgundy wall.

This close, the image resolves into the high-gloss exterior of a Lazzarini Hover Coupe, the retro-roadster model. It's been designed to resemble the Isotta Fraschini Tipo 8, an Italian automobile popular in the 1920s, with a squat central body supported by three giant rotors, one positioned off the tail of the vehicle, the other two flanking its nose. Behind the nose, there's an open-air cockpit protected by a slender, curving windscreen. Two passengers sit behind the screen, both wearing black jumpsuits and black helmets with black visors.

Lion and Jenka are still tilted sideways, with the underside of the flying motorcycle nearly kissing the coupe's front grille. Jenka swoops them horizontal, lifts up his visor, and starts screaming at the coupe's driver, first in Moldovan, next in Bulgarian, finally in Russian.

The driver flips up their visor and Lion hears a familiar voice. "Bite me, Jenka—ya drive like a numpty."

"Penelope?" shouts Lion.

"Follow me down," calls Penelope, snapping into business mode. "Three intruders. One already inside. Two coming in hot from the flanks. Tune your audio to channel nineteen."

Then Penelope snaps her visor down and peels her hover coupe into the sky. Jenka tucks in behind her, trying to stay close. They sail down the mountain in formation, the flying motorcycle drafting behind the larger vehicle, squalls of snow parting before them as they descend.

Just ahead, the outskirts of Genoa, Nevada, come into view. A few paved streets, a central square, a handful of stores.

Lion tracks uphill.

The lab is located a thousand feet above the town, at the end of a slender, winding road. They're now close enough that Lion can make out a trio of snowmobiles parked in a line and an empty clearing to their left. To their right, he sees the laboratory itself—the front porch, the main building, and storage room.

Everything looks quaint and snow-covered. There's no sign of an attack.

Jenka angles toward a parking spot beside the snowmobiles. Penelope and her hover coupe aren't going to fit. Instead, she aims the Lazzarini toward a break in the forest, as wide as a steamship, about a hundred yards behind the rear of the main building.

As soon as they land, Jenka fiddles with the dashboard screen, trying to find the right channel.

Finally he punches up nineteen.

Lion hears Penelope's Scottish accent coming through the speakers in his helmet. "Stay here," she says. "Shoot anything that isn't human."

"What?" asks Jenka.

"Not talking to you," says Penelope.

"Who is passenger?" demands Jenka. "Who are you talking to?"

"Later," says Penelope. "Now—Lion, Jenka, take the lab's front. I'll circle around back and make sure we're clear. Be careful. The radio is emergencies only. I'm not sure who's listening. And Lion—it's nice to see you again."

Jenka reaches into his coat and removes a black plastic square with a handle in the center. Grasping the handle, he punches a button with his thumb and flicks his wrist back and forth. There are two soft clicks as the auto-hingers unlock. Then the square unfolds into a sleek pistol grip and barrel—narrower at the back end, and widening out slightly, a little like a duck's bill, at the front. It's a PHASR pistol, capable of shooting an intense laser beam that induces temporarily blindness in anything with eyes.

"One question," says Jenka. "Who is attacking?"

"Not who," replies Penelope. "*What*."

"What is attacking?" says Jenka.

"The only animal that goes out of its way to hunt humans."

"Shit," says Lion.

"What is point of riddle?" asks Jenka. "Humans hunt humans."

"Polar bears," say Penelope and Lion simultaneously.

Hyper-carnivores

Lion watches nature documentaries. It's why he knows that polar bears are the largest land carnivore—technically "hyper-carnivores," because they eat only meat. Adult males grow to be eight feet long, weigh 1,700 pounds and run at forty miles per hour. Their bite force is 1,200 pounds per square inch, which ranks them number six on the list of strong-jawed creatures. But the bear Lion's staring at, the one shredding Lizzy's laboratory, looks even more hyper-carnivorous than anything he's seen on TV.

Still, Lion's pretty sure he's got this. Great relationships with animals are a built-in benefit of being an em-tracker.

The polar bear shatters a microscope into a thousand pieces.

Maybe he doesn't have this.

The rage is what worries him. In all mammals, anger brings out our primal instincts and blinds us to friendlier emotions. Until he knows for sure, Lion is keeping out of sight, kneeling on the front porch of the laboratory, tucked below the sill of the front window.

Jenka crouches about five feet away, also on the porch, hidden behind the lab's partially open front door, and temporarily off the bear's radar.

Lion knows—their luck won't last for long.

Polar bears have incredible senses of smell. They can sniff out a seal from twenty miles away. It's only this bear's rage and the fact that the wind is howling in the wrong direction that's keeping them safe.

Lion sneaks a peak through the window. He doesn't see Lizzy. The lab appears empty and destroyed. But the polar bear isn't focused on the lab anymore. He's reared up on his hind legs, growling and roaring, trying to beat down the door that leads into the storeroom.

"Door is flex-steel," hisses Jenka. "It will hold."

"Lizzy?" whispers Lion. "You think she's in the storeroom?"

Jenka nods.

Then Lion remembers what else is in the storeroom: the gun case, the tranquilizer darts, and the glass vials filled with enough knockout juice to incapacitate a herd of elephants.

Penelope said the radio was emergencies only. Do polar bears qualify as an emergency?

Fuck it, thinks Lion, tapping a button on the side of his helmet, turning his microphone on.

"Do you have visual contact?" he asks, trying to stay vague.

"Affirmative," comes Penelope's terse response.

"Where are you?"

"The rear of the lab, looking in the window of the storeroom."

"Break the glass," says Lion. "Have Lizzy pass out a tranquilizer rifle and ammo."

"Subject is down," says Penelope. "Head wound. Appears unconscious. I can see her breathing." A second later, Lion hears the sound of glass shattering. "I broke the window, I'm going in."

"What do you need from us?" asks Lion.

"Get over here. I'll toss you a gun and check on Lizzy. Cover my ass. There are two more bears heading this way."

"Copy that," says Lion, looking at Jenka.

"I will deal with this little problem," says Jenka, pointing his PHASR at the bear. "Go help Penelope. Try not to get dead."

The wind changes direction, carrying their scent into the lab. Up until that moment, the polar bear had been completely distracted by the prospect of a Lizzy-sized snack.

Not anymore.

Now it stops pounding, stops roaring, and turns around to catch sight of Lion. Their eyes lock. But something's wrong. There's no connection. No sense of animal-to-animal kumbaya.

Instead, Lion reacts out of instinct. He drops to his belly, landing with a thunk on the porch. Jenka jerks behind the open door, kicks it shut, then flicks a few fingers in Lion's direction, telling him to go.

Message received.

Belly-crawling across the porch until he's clear of the window, Lion stands up, takes one step toward the railing, and dives, tucking his shoulder mid-flight. He sails over the bannister and lands in a pile of soft snow, continues rolling and pops to his feet, sprinting toward the rear of the building.

Behind him, there's a giant crash of glass as the lab's front window is bear-punched out of existence.

Lion doesn't look back.

As he passes the side of the lab, there are more roars from somewhere off to his left. He pumps his arms to run faster.

A second later, the rear window comes into sight, broken glass littering the snow. A rifle sails out the window and lands butt-first in a drift. A case of tranquilizer darts follows it out, the words *Large Mammal Loads* visible on the side of the box.

There's only one problem.

Lion dashes to the window and looks inside. He can't see much of

Lizzy, just her legs sticking out from behind Penelope, who kneels beside her. Lion notices the curves of his on-again, off-again girlfriend. Her motorcycle helmet is off, her long red hair hanging down.

"I've never shot a rifle," Lion calls through the window.

"Bloody hell," says Penelope, standing up to face him. Then she breaks into a big smile. "Fancy a shag?"

"Absolutely," says Lion. "Before or after we deal with the bears?"

There's another roar from the front of the lab. Then a long silence. Finally Jenka screams: "Keep furry ass on ground!"

Jenka shouts something else, but Lion's distracted by a series of grunts and growls in the brush behind him.

Whipping around, he sees two more polar bears charge out of the woods. They stampede into the clearing, where the two snowmobiles and Jenka's flying motorcycle are parked. One bear stops beside the flying motorcycle, grabs the seat, and rips it off the machine, like plucking a grape. The other bear spots Lion across the yard. Their eyes meet and he feels that same lack of sensation. A chilly emptiness. Not a feeling, rather the absence of feeling. No connection. No kumbaya.

The wind kicks up, driving a wall of white between them.

Lion uses the snow as cover to whirl toward the window. Before he can leap through, Penelope appears on the other side, a heavy-duty tranquilizer pistol in her hand. She points the pistol toward the bears, looks at Lion, and says, "Em-track, ya gobshite."

"I can't," he responds. "The bears—there's too much anger or something—we've got no connection."

The wind dies. The bear catches sight of Lion and roars. This draws the other bear's attention. The animal had been tearing apart Jenka's flying motorcycle, but now pegs Lion with an angry glare.

Penelope aims the pistol and fires. There's a hard thud as the dart makes impact, followed by a grunt. She fires three more times, pumping two tranquilizer darts into each animal, hitting them twice, dead center in the chest.

Both bears should drop in seconds.

Neither drops.

The bear tearing apart the motorcycle barely notices. The other stares at the darts protruding from its rib cage, then swats at them with a paw, dislodging both with a single swipe.

"Why aren't they unconscious?" asks Penelope.

But there's no time for an answer.

One bear rears and roars, the other just roars. A second later, they're both hauling ass across the lawn, heading straight for Lion.

"Get in here," shouts Penelope.

Lion starts to climb through the window, but stops as he catches sight of Jenka, running into the yard, waving his arms and screaming in Moldovan.

Both bears look toward the noise.

Jenka drops into a shooter's stance, aims his PHASR, and before Lion can close his eyes or look away, fires at the animals. A flash of red light pulses out of the barrel, spreading across the yard like a light-house beam.

A searing pain rips through Lion's head. It's like getting stabbed in the brain with an icicle. His vision turns red, then white, then fades to black. He stumbles forward, his boot landing on the box of tranquil-izer darts. The box slips in the snow, shooting Lion's foot sideways and slamming him face-first into the snowdrift beside the rifle, his right hand bashing into the barrel. Realizing what he just hit, he wraps his fingers around the weapon, jumps to his feet, and shoulders the rifle. His sight is still splotchy, but Lion aims toward where he thinks the bears should be.

That's when he notices: silence.

No growling, no roaring.

Complete silence.

He aims the rifle left, he aims the rifle right.

Where the fuck are the bears?

S ettle down, cowboy," says Penelope.

The voice comes from Lion's right. Before he can spin in that direction, her fingers wrap around his wrist and lower his arm, pointing the rifle barrel toward the ground. He blinks again, but his vision is still splotchy. Penelope is a black stripe topped by a red flame.

"We're safe," she says.

Still gripping the rifle, Lion raises his free hand and rubs his eyes. When that doesn't help, he closes them and takes deep breaths.

Two minutes later, he can see again.

What he sees are the bears, about twenty feet away from him, wandering in aimless circles around the lawn. Jenka stands beyond them, holding the PHASR in his right hand, watching carefully. A second later, he drops the pistol to his side and walks over to one of the animals.

Grabbing hold of a big patch of shoulder fur, Jenka yanks it straight off the bear, revealing a control panel beneath.

Lion sees a touchscreen, with Cyrillic writing on the buttons.

Tossing aside the fur, Jenka reaches out and punches one of the buttons. The bear stops moving mid-stride, now frozen in place. Jenka walks over to the other animal and goes through a similar procedure.

"Robots?" asks Lion, when he's done.

"Dah, Russian robots."

"That's why there was no connection."

"Sorry about eyes," says Jenka, lifting up the PHASR. "This is what I learned from first bear. Laser scrambles lidar sensors, puts them in holding pattern."

Lion glances at the bears. "Where are the sensors?"

"Eyes and nose," says Jenka. "Very lifelike design."

"I'm going to check on Lizzy," says Penelope, starting toward the broken window.

"Front door is open," calls Jenka.

Penelope stops and redirects.

Lion walks over to one of the bears, rifle in tow. He uses the barrel to prod the animal. When nothing happens, he crouches down to inspect the touchscreen.

Jenka crosses to stand beside him.

"Why use robots?" asks Lion. "If you can make killer flying tree snakes, why not real bears?"

"Or more flying tree snakes."

"I don't get it," says Lion. "Robot animals aren't even exotic. Kids get them for Christmas."

"Toys do not have rage setting," says Jenka, pointing at the touchscreen.

"No," says Lion. "Still, this doesn't seem very Devil's Dictionary."

Jenka walks over to the bear and lifts up its arm, inspecting the pad of its paw. Then he inspects the other one. "Is sure-grip material," he says. "Well-worn."

"So this wasn't their first rodeo?"

"I have heard stories," says Jenka.

"Stories?"

"Rumors of secret prison camp in Siberia—where they use polar bears as guards."

Penelope pops her head out the window and calls to them, "Lizzy's asleep. It looks like she was trying to load one of the guns and tranquilized herself. There's a dart sticking out of her thigh. She must have hit her head on the ground when she fell. It bled a lot, she'll have a bump, but her breathing is steady and she's starting to come out of it. I put her in the cot. We should get a doctor to check on her, but . . ."

Lion doesn't hear the rest. Instead, he notices someone in a black motorcycle suit and black motorcycle helmet walking out of the trees and onto the lawn, stopping about fifteen feet away.

Penelope's passenger. With the bears, in the excitement, Lion had completely forgotten.

The passenger starts to take off the motorcycle helmet.

"Lion," says Penelope, in the same tone she reserves for delivering bad news.

But Lion doesn't acknowledge the tone or even look in her direction. Once the helmet comes off, he sees a familiar Chinese man wearing a familiar pair of Buddy Holly glasses.

"Lion and Jenka—please meet Ji Wan Li," says Penelope.

The man nods at Jenka, then looks at Lion. There's a flash of recognition when their eyes meet. It's the recognition that their eyes have met before, first in the Chinatown alley, next in the back room of Defenestration, and one last time, when Lion was tied to a bed.

Lion raises the tranquilizer rifle to his shoulder, pointing it directly at the man. "Ji Wan Li," he says. "Terrific to meet you."

He pulls the trigger. The dart smashes into Ji's chest with a wet thwack.

"Smack a bitch up," says Lion.

Turns out, he can shoot a rifle after all.

Then Ji collapses, just another dropped body. The place is littered with them.

call security

Apparently, Lizzy isn't the first person in the history of PRML to jab themselves with a tranquilizer dart. There's no need to call a doctor. Instead, Penelope finds a couple of syringes filled with wake-up serum in the bathroom med kit.

"It's basically low-grade speed," says Lizzy, postinjection, now sitting up on the cot. "I'm fine, but you might want to use it on your friend." She points at Ji Wan Li, unconscious, on the floor.

"Not until Penelope tells me what the fuck he's doing here," snarls Lion.

"He came to help," explains Penelope.

"Help how?" growls Lion.

"Help who?" snaps Jenka. "You turned off tracker and left Bypass, why? And where did you go?"

"Zip it!" shouts Lizzy.

Everybody looks at her.

"Lion, make a fresh pot of coffee. The machine's in the back corner of the lab. Penelope, sweep up the shattered glass on the porch so we can sit out there. Jenka, pick him up"—nodding at Ji—"and put him in the cot."

Lizzy stands up.

"And you are going where?" asks Jenka.

"To find my phone. Someone's got to call security." She glances at Lion. "Unless you're sure those are the last of the bears."

Lion looks at Jenka, Jenka looks at Penelope, Penelope looks at Lizzy. They all say: "Call security."

Dr. Neo Cortex

Penelope sweeps up the glass. Lizzy calls security. Satellites are mobilized. Overflights of PRML reveal no additional bears, but snowmobile patrols around the perimeter have been increased, and they're keeping a close watch on all the camera feeds.

Now Lion and Penelope face each other from opposite sides of the porch, sharing an uneasy silence. Jenka paces back and forth between them, smoking a thin black cigarette. The storm has abated, but the clouds remain, heavy and gray.

Inside the lab, they can hear Lizzy pouring mugs of coffee from the fresh pot that Lion brewed. Ji Wan Li is also back there. They decided not to shoot him up with speed, instead dumping him in the cot to sleep it off. Lion thought about killing him then. Maybe smothering him with a pillow. Quick and quiet.

Maybe not.

Maybe a battle-axe.

"Susan's a triple agent," says Penelope, breaking the silence. She's still wearing her black motorcycle suit, now unzipped to her waist, the cuffs pushed back to her elbows, revealing her arms, both sleeved in tattoos. "Susan worked for a guy named Chang Zee—"

"Dah," says Jenka, interrupting her. "This we know."

"What the fuck is Buddy Holly doing here?" demands Lion. "He also works for Zee."

"Dah," says Jenka again, "this we know."

Penelope starts to say something, but Lion talks right over her. "Zee kidnapped Ibrahim and Kendra. He tortured me. He dreamed up the Suicide Girls, slaughtered Ichika and who knows how many Anti-Nagels, killed Susan Jackson, his own triple agent, and, encore, sent killer flying snakes and psychotic polar bear robots to murder us, and—wait for it—destroy the planet's first mega-linkage."

"He is supervillain," says Jenka. "Like out of video game. Like Dr. Neo Cortex from the *Crash Bandicoot* of my youth. With the Evolvo-Ray."

Lion and Penelope look at him.

"What? Did you not play *Crash Bandicoot*? Dr. Cortex uses Evolvo-Ray to mutate animals and create evil super-army. Is same thing, no?"

Penelope says, "I'll answer Jenka's question first. I know Susan's a triple agent because I found her computer."

"I did not know it was missing," says Jenka.

"Stop," says Lion.

They both look at him.

"Start with Susan Jackson," he says. "That's where the story starts."

"It starts earlier," says Penelope. "When Susan was in graduate school."

"You know this how?" asks Jenka.

"When Sir Richard recruited Susan for Arctic," explains Penelope, "I vetted her. It was a deep background check." Then she turns her attention to Lion. "Did you get my message?"

"The William James cipher?"

"So you talked to Alejandra?"

"She told me you wanted to know if she had ever read Professor Zhong's PhD thesis, and that you went to inspect the cliff on Widowmaker. I checked out Widowmaker, but haven't gotten to the thesis yet."

"I checked it out," says Lizzy, walking onto the porch with a tray, five mugs of coffee, plus cream and sugar. The mugs are emblazoned with PRML's logo and the phrase *Empathy for All*.

"Zhong's the connection," explains Penelope. "That's where the story starts."

"What connection?" asks Jenka.

"I've become a slogan," says Lion, pointing at the *Empathy for All* logo on the mug.

"Is good slogan," says Jenka. Then, turning his attention back to Penelope, "What is connection?"

"Alejandra misheard me," continues Penelope. "I didn't ask about Zhong's PhD, I asked if she read any of the dissertations of Zhong's students. Susan Jackson was one of them. Zhong was her thesis advisor. That's the connection."

"So I read Zhong's PhD thesis for nothing?" says Lizzy.

"Susan's thesis," demands Jenka, "what is about?"

"Does one aspire to become a slogan?" asks Lion. "Is that a good thing?"

Penelope stands up, crosses the porch, sits down beside Lion, and takes his hand. "It's a fine thing, love. You should be very proud."

Lion drops her hand. "If you don't tell me why Buddy Holly is sleeping it off in the next room, I'm going chop him into bits with a battle-axe and feed his entrails to the ravens."

"We have battle-axe?" asks Jenka, looking around. "If there are more bears, might be useful."

"Do you really think it's a good thing that I'm a slogan?" asks Lion.

"Gentlemen," says Penelope, "we're on a clock."

"A clock?" asks Lizzy.

"We'll get there," says Penelope. "In fact, this is dumb. Lizzy, Jenka, zip it. Lion, tell me what you know. I'll fill in the details."

"Starting when?" asks Lion.

"Start in Los Angeles," says Penelope. "The last time we spoke, I had just sent you the JOBZ and was heading to PRML. You were in L.A. tracking the Bolex. Start then."

In the Grand Scope of Clue Discovery

Lion starts in Los Angeles.

He tells Penelope about his encounter with Five Spikes in the alley, his trip to Seattle, how Jenka saved his life, their arrival at PRML, the flying tree snakes, the secret stairway, the secret handshake, and Zee, the supervillain behind the attacks.

"You forgot zero-day hack," says Jenka. "How I discover hack controls snowmaking."

"I didn't forget," says Lion, "but, you know, compared to my uncovering of Chang Zee's involvement and the Devil's Dictionary, I'm just saying, in the grand scope of clue discovery—"

"Focus, Zorn," says Penelope.

Lion finishes the story. How he figured out the meaning of Moldovan neurotoxin, how he first assumed Penelope was talking about Jenka, then Sir Richard, and finally, Chang Zee.

"When I left you the note," she explains, "I thought it was Jenka, too. And that Sir Richard was involved. That's why I disappeared."

"No offense taken," says Jenka.

"That's what I figured," says Lion. "When did you find out it wasn't Jenka?"

"Not until I met Ji Wan Li," explains Penelope. "But that was later. Let me fill in the details."

"Start with when you first got to PRML," says Lion.

Penelope thinks for a second. "When I first got to PRML, Sir Richard briefed me. I asked him if anything else was weird, beside the snakes and the dead bodies. He sort of laughed and said, 'Other than that, Mrs. Lincoln, how was the theater?' Then he told me the snow-making was wonky. That the system kept turning on and off by itself. He didn't think much of it. Neither did I, not right away."

"What happened next?"

"I decided to backtrack Susan's movements. I checked out her house, her office. Everything looked normal, except I couldn't find her laptop. It bugged me. I got to know Susan when I vetted her. We weren't close, but we'd get drinks a few times a year. Every time, she brought her laptop. Once, we went dancing, she still brought her laptop. It went everywhere with her. So I had one of the techs run an IP check. It pinged from inside the Bypass, near the spot where they found her body. But I checked the logs. Two things were off. First, they found Susan wearing only one glove. She was skiing, got bitten by snakes, and what, the snakes carried away her glove? The second thing was that no one found her laptop, which is one reason why I went to check out Widowmaker."

"What is other reason?" asks Jenka.

Penelope points at Lizzy. "The toxicology report on the snake venom found in Susan's body. Lizzy ran the report, but I didn't know who to trust."

"You figured," says Lizzy, "I'm a geneticist with full access to the Bypass, maybe I made the snakes?"

Penelope nods. "I took your report to an outside source. Just to have it checked over. That's when I learned that the snake venom wasn't venom, but a Moldovan neurotoxin."

"Zee made snakes," snarls Jenka. "Is Chinese neurotoxin."

"He's a little sensitive," explains Lion.

"I figured that out, too," says Penelope. "A different source tracked the lab where the toxin came from, and this led to a Chinese company called Zen-Christ Tantra Holdings."

"Chang Zee's company," says Lion. "Same holding company that's at the end of the Suicide Girls' trail."

"Yes," says Penelope, "that led me to Zee. But remember, I had vetted Susan, so I already knew about him. Sir Richard said the project got canceled, but Sir Richard has lied before and . . ."—she looks at Jenka—"you're the only Moldovan I know. That's right when the tech called and told me Susan's laptop was somewhere on Widowmaker. I went into the park, stopped off at the End of Man, and . . ."—she taps Lion's thigh—"left you a note."

"Why Alejandra?" asks Lion.

"I met her right when I got to PRML," explains Penelope. "I needed a day off, so I went skiing. I ended up at the End of Man, having a drink, talking to Alejandra. She's a Rilkean, I'm a Rilkean, etcetera. Also, by then, I was worried about Jenka's and Sir Richard's involvement. I knew Lion would come looking, that he'd backtrack my movements. And since Alejandra was a Rilkean, I knew she'd keep her mouth shut. Then I went to Widowmaker. I was at the spot where they found Susan's body and noticed there were snowmaking nozzles sticking out of the cliff."

"You remembered what Sir Richard said," says Lion, "about the snowmaking being wonky."

"Yeah. So I went to take a closer look. That's when I found Susan's laptop. It was in the cave, beside the hatched snake eggs. I grabbed the laptop and went deeper into the cave. That's when I discovered unhatched snake eggs and the tunnel. I followed it to the door to the stairway."

"But how did you use door?" asks Jenka. "I check logs. Only Sir Richard use doors. And we know it was Susan using Sir Richard's handshake."

"Susan's other glove," explains Penelope. "She used it to wedge the stairway door open. That's how I got out of the Bypass."

"Where did you go?"

"I had Susan's laptop. I didn't know if I could trust Jenka or Sir

Richard or what the hell was going on. I ditched my phone, because I didn't want anyone to track me. Then I went to Reno, checked into a motel that took cash, and spent three days examining the laptop."

"What did you find?" asks Lion.

"Susan's PhD thesis, for starters."

"What's it about?" asks Lizzy.

"How much do you know about connectome mapping?" asks Penelope.

"Like Sasha and Xui," says Jenka. "From Hard Pump VR."

"Who are Sasha and Xui?" asks Penelope.

"Dah," says Jenka, looking at Lion, "is good question."

Lion ignores him. "What about connectome mapping?"

"Susan blended three ideas into one technological possibility. All had been around for a while, but she was the first, as far as I can tell, to stitch them together. The first was connectome mapping, specifically what's called the eye-brain connectome."

"Why is this useful?" asks Jenka.

"Bionic eyes," explains Lizzy. "If you want to optimize sight restoration technologies, the human-eye connectome is a great map to work from. Also, diseases like Alzheimer's have a retinal signature. So connectome mapping gives you a way to track the disease through the brain."

"What was Susan's other idea?" asks Jenka.

"She combined eye tracking and neurophysiology," explains Penelope. "Apparently, you can learn a lot about a person from their eyes."

"How?"

"I know this research," says Lizzy. "Most eye movement is spontaneous, but not accidental. The motion is governed by our goals and our fears. We look at stuff we want and at stuff that scares us. So if you combine eye movement with neurophysiological signals—"

"I am coder, not biologist," says Jenka. "What are neurophysiological signals?"

"EEG, heart rate, stuff like that," explains Lion. "But what does that combination get you?"

"It's what happens when you put all three techs together," explains Penelope. "Susan's PhD is about combining connectome mapping with eye tracking and neurophysiological data. She thought it would reveal a person's decision-tree matrix."

"Impressive," says Lizzy.

"What is big deal?" asks Jenka.

"The big deal is knowledge," continues Penelope. "Susan thought you could show a subject anything—a new product, an old toy, a photograph, whatever—and track not just their desire for or aversion to the thing, but every step in the neurobiological chain that led to that reaction."

"Zhong taught genetics," says Jenka. "Why would he advise on this thesis?"

"Not quite," says Lion, putting it all together. "Zhong's book was about using genetics for neuromarketing. If you had a person's connectome map and could follow their decision-tree matrix, you'd understand every step in the chain that led to their buying decisions." He turns to face Penelope. "That's it, isn't it?"

"You would know all that," she says, "but you would also know what kind of advertising campaign to run in order to change their minds. You could turn a decision not to buy into a decision to buy."

"It's the secret neuromarketing project," says Lion. "The one Sir Richard was working on with Susan and Zee. The one he shut down for ethical reasons."

"It was start of war," says Jenka.

Lion nods. "We need to speak to Sir Richard."

"Dah."

Lion thinks for a moment. "But how do we get from Zhong to Zee?" He looks at Lizzy. "You said you read Zhong's thesis—what's it about?"

"Creepshow genetics. Designing humans and animals to populate other planets. He figured people would soon be living in space colonies or on Mars, and that they'd need pets and livestock with them. He wanted to make super-animals to go along with his superhumans."

"Like Dr. Cortex with Evolvo-Ray," says Jenka. "I told you, is same thing."

"Worse. At the end of his thesis, Zhong argued for a new Eden. He wanted to use genetic engineering to perfect humanity and to perfect every other species humanity depends upon and then use these creations to populate other planets. He even had a name for his perfect new world, Pandora II."

"Zee's funding Zhong's project?" asks Jenka.

"And Susan was the go-between," explains Penelope. "She's the link from Zhong to Zee and from Zee to Sir Richard."

"Did you find anything else on the laptop?" asks Lion.

"I did," says Penelope.

"What?"

"She found me," says Ji Wan Li.

He's standing in the doorway, wearing the same black motorcycle jumpsuit as Penelope, unzipped to the waist, a black T-shirt visible beneath, and his Buddy Holly glasses.

"She found me," he says again.

WHO IS ZOO YOU GANG?

Ji Wan Li walks onto the porch and crosses to face Lion. "You are not a slogan."

Lion glares at him

"Chop me into bits with a battle-axe if you must," continues Ji, "but first know that you, Lion Zorn, have built a bridge between all species. Your effort is on par with the sacred work of Zhou Youguang."

"Who is Zoo You Gang?" snarls Jenka. "Is boy band?"

Ji starts to answer. Jenka cuts him off. "We talk on porch, you sleep in back room—how did you know about slogan?"

"Augmented hearing," says Ji, crossing to sit on the railing. "CRSPR-mods, implanted when I was in the military."

Casually, Jenka reaches his hand inside his jacket. It's the universal call sign: I'm getting my gun now.

"The real great leap forward?" asks Lion. "That Zhou Youguang?"

"Yes," says Ji, nodding solemnly. "That Zhou Youguang."

"Apology not accepted," says Jenka, removing the folded-up PHASR from inside his jacket. He flicks his wrist right, then left, snapping the barrel and pistol grip into place, then pointing the gun directly at Ji. "Do not move."

"Ya numpty," snaps Penelope. "Put that shite away."

"Not again," says Lion, raising an arm to shield his eyes.

"Not again," says Jenka. "I have switched PHASR setting. Now is set on kill."

"You mean," says Lion, "with the polar bears, you went for stun and not kill?"

Jenka nods. "I did not want to kill polar bears, not unless it was real emergency."

"The bears were charging at me, that wasn't a real emergency." Then Lion smiles. "Very cool of you."

"Dah, empathy for all. Is a good slogan."

Ji starts laughing.

"What is funny?" asks Jenka.

Ji points at the weapon. "That's a PHASR."

"Set to kill."

"Doubtful."

"You would like demonstration?"

Ji says, "The personnel halting and stimulation response rifle was developed by the U.S. Air Force Research Laboratory's Directed Energy Directorate. It uses a two-wavelength low-intensity laser, causing temporary blinding and disorientation, with its temporary effects being the only reason the U.S. was permitted to develop the gun, as signatories of the 1995 UN Protocol on Blinding Laser Weapons. You're holding the second-generation handheld model, the Stealth 9, with the Vortex SPARC 7 upgraded red dot sight, and quiver-correction intelligence built into the grip. But that generation PHASR does not have a kill setting."

"I will still blind you," says Jenka, "then stomp mudhole in ass."

Ji shakes his head. "Good luck with that. I'm former People's Liberation Army, South Blade, special ops, sniper. My eyes have been augmented. They shield out certain light frequencies, including those used by the PHASR. In my professional opinion, you'll have better luck with the battle-axe."

Jenka sighs, pushes a button on the PHASR, then snaps his wrists again, refolding the gun in a single motion. "Super-hearing, super-eyes, super-army of super-animals. I am saying, Zee is Dr. Neo Cortex."

Ji laughs again.

"Now what is funny?"

"Jet," says Ji. He looks at Lion. "I think, if I heard correctly, Jet is the man you know as Five Spikes."

"What about him?"

"Jet was a gamer. He also called Chang Zee, Dr. Neo Cortex. Not at first, but after . . ." Ji falls silent.

"After what?" asks Jenka.

Penelope says, "Zee kidnapped family members."

"Dah," says Jenka. "This we know. To force scientists to—"

"It didn't start with scientists," interrupts Penelope. She looks at Ji. "Tell them."

"Everything?"

Penelope nods, "Start with your father."

"Do not start with father," says Jenka. "I do not care about kind old man who carves you out of wood and gives you puppet strings."

"Enough," says Lion.

Everyone looks at him.

"I want to hear him out. Ji—what about your father?"

"My father is a scientist," explains Ji, "an evolutionary anthropologist working for the army. He isn't PLA, but whenever the military wants to build anything, they send his team to survey possible sites. My father figures out if there are fossils worth preserving or if the land is an ancient burial ground. My mother died during childbirth, so my father raised me. We moved from army base to army base. It's how I learned to shoot. I was good, almost Olympics good, but decided to join the military instead. This was how I met Chang Zee."

"Zee was in the army?" asks Lion.

"No. I met him because of what I learned in the military. I was South Blade, recon, similar to your Navy SEALs. My specialty was distance shooting and optics technology."

"You're a well-trained hired gun," says Lion. "So what?"

"I'm a filmmaker," says Ji, smiling. "Optics got me into the movies. Obsessed, really. Especially with some of the new neuro-tech. That is how I met Jet. He was ex-military, and also into movies and neuro-tech. We met at a conference on intracranial movie playback. I was a spectator. Jet was already a rising star with his own start-up. I quit the military to work with him. That's how I met Zee. He was our first client. He hired us to make movies."

"About?" asks Lion.

"Is not right question," says Jenka.

Lion looks at him.

"Question is not, tell me about your movies, Mr. Filmmaker. Why, Mr. Filmmaker, did you make Lion Zorn snuff film—that is right question."

Lion reaches into his pocket, pulls out a test tube containing one of the Ghost Trainwreck joints. He removes the stopper, slides out the spliff, fires it up, takes a drag, exhales, glances at Jenka, and says, "Shut up and let me work."

"I vote for mudhole."

Lion shakes his head and says, "We hear him out."

"Why?"

"Zhou Youguang," explains Lion.

"Who is Zoo You Gang?"

"They call him the Architect of the Bridge Between Languages," explains Lion. "Zhou Youguang invented Pinyin, the system that converts Chinese characters into the Roman alphabet. He educated China. Before he invented Pinyin, eighty-five percent of the country couldn't read. Today, literacy is higher than ninety-five percent. But that wasn't Ji's point."

"There is point?"

"Zhou Youguang is a hero to em-trackers," explains Lion, "that's Ji's point. More than anyone else in history, Zhou bridged the gap between East and West." Lion stretches out his hand, offering Ji the joint, "Doobage?"

"No thank you."

"Zee hired you to make movies about what?" asks Penelope.

"Evo-loo-shun," says Ji.

Lion blinks. It's Ji's pronunciation, those three syllables, just like Ramen in that Chinatown alley. *You want evo-loo-shun, you go ask Sharijee, Sharijee all the evo-loo-shun you can handle.*

"Evolution?" asks Lion. "As in Chuck Darwin, origin of species? Or the drug, Evo, that makes you trip evolution?"

"That's what I'm telling you," says Ji. "These were not ordinary movies."

sugar, you're Looking sweet

Wizard technology—that's Lion's first thought on hearing what Ji has to say.

Apparently, Jet figured out how to hijack the neuro-machinery behind dreams. All you need is Jet's nano-encapsulation tech to alter the brain's dream machinery and an internet connection to download the movie. What you get is Evo—a nasal spray that makes you have prerecorded dreams.

Ji explains further. "It's less about pumping the entire plot into your head, and more about pumping in sensory patterns that trigger familiar memories. That's what makes you dream along preexisting plot lines."

"So you don't trip evolution," says Lion, "you *dream* evolution—and it's a fake dream?"

"One of four fake dreams. That's all we shot. It's extremely slow filmmaking, more like the neurological version of hand-drawn animation. Then Jet discovered the money trail. Zee was funding our films with earnings from the Suicide Girls' betting site. We were just about to go to the cops—"

"About to go?" asks Lion.

Ji pulls out his phone and shows Lion the image on the screen. It looks like an old Abu Ghraib torture pic, the one with naked prisoners and snarling dogs, except instead of snarling dogs, Lion sees an old Chinese man and a young Chinese girl being threatened by polar bears.

So the stories Jenka heard—they're more than stories.

Ji says, "That is my father, and Jet's sister."

"That's why we're on a clock," says Lion. "Your father, Ji's sister—they're still alive." Then it dawns on him. "Does this mean Kendra and Ibrahim are alive, being held in a prison camp somewhere?"

"I don't know," says Ji. "They were kidnapped by a different team, for a different part of the research project, and taken who knows where. If they are alive, they're in New York. All the prisoners have been transferred to that facility. But it still might be too late—Zee's been cleaning house."

"It's not too late," says Penelope. "Our ride will be here any second."

"Our ride?" asks Jenka.

"You thought I only showed up to fight polar bears?"

"Final score: Jenka three; polar bears, zero. I do not see name Penelope on stat sheet."

Suddenly the sky starts to growl.

Lion looks up to see the gray clouds above the porch quiver, then cleave apart, split in half by the outthrust of the giant rotors attached to Sir Richard's custom-designed Bugatti Airliner II.

Looking like an art deco masterpiece from the 1930s, the Airliner descends into the clearing, whipping snow into a frenzy. Lion holds up a hand to shield his eyes. He removes it once the plane has settled, just in time to watch an auto-stairway unfold, the main hatch open, and a well-dressed Hasidic man appear in the doorway.

"New York, New York, big city of dreams," calls Barry. "All aboard."

A second later, two women appear beside Barry. They're identical twins, dark-skinned, each dressed like Black Power warriors from 1975, complete with Afros, army jackets, miniskirts, combat boots, and of course, actual machine guns. The woman on the right pegs Lion with a hard stare.

"Lion Zorn," she says, breaking into a wide smile. "Sugar, you're looking sweet. It is nice to see you."

An Army of Nerds

Kali and Shiva—aka the Black Power twins—are Rilkeans by belief and bodyguards by training. Kali is ex-Secret Service. Shiva is just pissed off. Both are coming to New York.

Lizzy can't make the trip. She needs to stay behind because the polar bear shredded her work and the snake eggs have to be swept from the tunnels. She's on cleanup duty for at least a week. Jenka stays behind because nobody knows what else Zee might send their way.

"Is temporary reassignment," he reassures them. "I will update security protocols, clean up snowmaking code, make guards carry bigger guns, then meet you in New York."

"The bears killed your bike," said Penelope, pointing at Jenka's now destroyed flying motorcycle. She tosses him a small black cylinder. "Take my hover coupe."

Then Lion, Ji, and Penelope head into the airliner.

The inside is just as art deco fancy as the outside: dark, glossy hardwood floors, oval windows running along the walls and ceiling, and sleek recliner seats, with arcing rosewood arms and auto-mold faux leather cushions.

Lion beelines for the closest seat, plops down, and sighs. Now that the adrenaline is wearing off, he can barely keep his eyes open.

"You sleep," says Penelope, walking past him. "I'll brief."

"Thank you," says Lion.

He grabs a blindfold and a pair of noise-canceling earbuds from the seat-back pocket. The buds look like miniature black roses. They expand to fill his ear and hum to life, blocking out the sounds of the world with a gentle forest rain. Slipping on the blindfold, Lion reclines the seat and falls asleep.

He wakes up four hours later, rubs his eyes, and wishes for a cup of coffee. A moment later, Ji appears beside him, holding a black art deco mug. Passing the mug to Lion, he says, "Americano, four shots, nothing else in it. Penelope told me."

"Appreciated."

Ji points at the empty recliner beside Lion. "May I join you?"

Lion raises his seat back, nods, and takes a sip of the coffee.

Ji sits. "I am truly sorry for what I did to you."

"You didn't have a choice."

"I had a choice," says Ji. "I made the wrong one."

"I missed the briefing, but I'm guessing your father's being held captive somewhere in New York, along with Jet's sister?"

"My father, Jet's sister, perhaps your friends Ibrahim and Kendra, most likely the missing scientists, and definitely Zee himself."

"Where exactly?"

"That's complicated. Ever ride the subway in New York?"

"Sure."

"You know how, every now and again, you flash by an abandoned subway stop or catch sight of a forgotten tunnel?"

"Uh-huh."

"There are miles and miles of abandoned track down there. New York has the largest underground tunnel system in the world. People say there's as much unused real estate as used real estate. It's all owned by the city. Or it was. Five years ago, they geo-mapped all the unused tunnels and put a blockchain layer beneath it."

"I heard about this," says Lion. "They turned the tunnels into parcels and sold them off."

"It was a climate change backup plan," continues Ji. "If sea levels swamped Manhattan and the surface became uninhabitable. That sort of thing."

"What does this have to do with Zee?"

"Two years ago, Zee had me in New York City. Lots of deal-making. Quietly, through dozens of shell companies, he bought up a considerable amount of underground property."

"What's he doing with it?"

"I don't know. I don't even know exactly where it is. On this deal, I was just a gofer, ferrying around information in encrypted packages. I couldn't access the data and wasn't allowed to visit the locations. But that's how Penelope found me. Zee and Susan Jackson were buying these tunnels together. That was one of the things Penelope found on Susan's computer, a paper trail. I thought I was keeping things pretty well hidden, but she figured it out."

"She does that," says Lion.

"I think Zee's running an underground prison camp and using the forced labor to create Pandora II, his perfect world. Or he's trying to."

"What do you mean trying?"

"Something went wrong. The robot polar bears. If Zee can create life from scratch—a real Devil's Dictionary—why make robots?"

"I asked the same question."

"I don't know the answer. Once Zee discovered that Jet and I knew what he was up to, he kidnapped my father and Jet's sister and cut us out of the loop. We went from filmmakers to forced labor. Your kidnapping, the experiments."

"The experiments—why was I tortured?"

"I'm still not sure. I was forced to kidnap em-trackers and make films with the Bolex H-11."

"The seventh Bolex," says Lion. "No one can tell me what it does."

"It records images off the back of the retina. My assignment was to provoke the most powerful emotional response possible in an em-tracker, which is why we used the Claridge's suite. Then record the results."

"But it was a fake room at the Claridge's."

"A hologram, of course, designed to resemble an earlier version of the hotel. Zee figured, if you went to the cops, they'd think you were crazy."

"It's why I never went to the cops."

"Nobody did, or maybe not until about six months ago."

"What changed?"

"People started turning up dead. Jet got set up. Two Tone was killed. Everyone who worked for Two Tone, missing. Sharijee—remember her?"

Lion nods.

"She's gone, maybe dead. A couple of the scientists who were forced to work on the snakes, they're also dead. Anybody left alive is in New York."

"How do you know?"

"The paper trail Penelope found. Susan was involved because Zee was out of cash. He's got everything in Pandora II. He's got no property left in China, sold off his island. If anyone is left alive, they've got to be in New York."

"So we're going to what—raid the tunnels?"

"Sir Richard sent Kali and Shiva." He nods at the women. "Barry's got training. I've got training. Penelope has training."

"Why not just go to the cops?"

"That is what I wanted to do. Penelope disagrees."

"Why?"

Penelope appears in the aisle. She's taken off her motorcycle suit and now wears jeans and a black tank top, a pair of librarian glasses, and her tattoos, plainly visible. "If we go to the cops," she says, pointing at Ji, "he goes to jail. Forever. Kidnapping, torture. Personally, I think he's been through enough. So, no cops, unless there's no other choice."

Lion looks around the plane. The Black Power twins, Ji with his Buddy Holly glasses, Penelope with her sexy librarian look, a Hasidic almost rabbi, and a very tired em-tracker.

"Super," says Lion. "This is the part where the army of nerds decides to fight Dr. Neo Cortex. I like our chances."

PART VII

TWO DAYS LATER: NEW YORK CITY

THE BLIP

Sunday is Z-Day. It's the day they plan on launching their assault on Chang Zee's underground fortress. Ji believes the weekend will provide lighter security, and Sunday is better than Saturday because that's when Zee likes to record his weekly *Zen-Christ Tantra World Beater* podcast. As he prefers to record alone, with only a producer in the studio, Sunday appears to offer their best chance of getting into Pandora II undetected.

Today is Saturday, midafternoon, and there's still plenty to do.

Lion, Penelope, Shiva, and Kali are in charge of "communications," which is why they're riding in the back of an oversized black SUV, threading through New York City traffic, heading to Masta Ice, an upscale jewelry store owned by Balthazar Jones. When Lion was in Los Angeles, it was Balthazar's cousin, Carlos Jones, who helped him backtrack the Bolex H-11. Now that he's in New York, Balthazar, who, beside making and selling jewelry, dabbles in high-end information and a kind of rarefied technical support, has agreed to provide them with wireless comms designed to work in underground caverns and an accurate map of the New York's tunnel system.

While Lion and Penelope are meeting with Balthazar, Ji's back at the hotel, working out the final logistical details, especially transport and medical attention for any prisoners they might find. Barry is also back at the hotel, gathering supplies and keeping a communication channel open to Sir Richard, who is still stuck in Cambodia, but demanded to be in the loop.

Jenka told Lion that Barry and Sir Richard had never met before, but Lion has been picking up different signals. Their sudden friendship bugged Jenka, too, and now it's really bugging Lion. The billionaire and the almost rabbi—there's something going on there. Exactly what that something might be, that's what he's been wondering while staring out the side window of their SUV.

Suddenly he's staring at the words *Masta Ice*.

They've arrived.

The SUV's doors glide open. Lion climbs out, and Kali, Shiva, and Penelope follow. They cross the sidewalk, push through the front door of Masta Ice, and find themselves in a gray concrete rectangle polished to a hyper-gloss. Spotlights illuminate jewelry display cases built from repurposed scientific equipment. Ruby pendants line the glass shelves of an ancient medicine cabinet, diamond-encrusted watches sit inside eighteenth-century entomological specimen jars, platinum rings adorn cork-stoppered test tubes being held upright by faded wooden racks.

"Lion Zorn!" booms a voice from his left.

Lion spins around to see a heavyset black man wearing an ornate jeweler's loupe over his left eye, a black silk do-rag, twin diamond studs piercing both cheeks, a red satin smoking jacket, and a living screen T-shirt displaying a rotating series of classic hip-hop cassette tapes from the late 1980s, EPMD's *Unfinished Business* now visible on his chest.

"Balthazar Jones," says Lion.

"Good to see you, my friend."

"Back at you. Did Carlos tell you I said hello?"

"He did indeed," replies Balthazar, lifting the loupe from his head, setting it on the counter, and crossing over to shake Lion's hand. Before that happens, Penelope cuts between them and wraps up Balthazar in a hug.

They go way back.

Afterward, Penelope introduces Kali and Shiva. Balthazar looks the women up and down, noting Afros, army jackets, and gun bulges by their sides.

"Sister," says Balthazar to Shiva, extending his hand.

"Brother," says Shiva, clasping it.

He repeats the process with Kali.

Then he gestures to their bulges and points to a sign beside the door, reading CHECK YO IRON, with an arrow pointing down to a square metal box that sits beneath it.

Shiva slides an old-school nine-millimeter out of her holster, walks over to the metal box, and asks, "What do I do?"

"Index finger on the scanner," replies Balthazar. "It codes to your print. Just drop your gun in the slot, then reverse the process to get it back when you leave."

Shiva sets her index finger on a square of shiny black plastic positioned in the center of the box. Lion sees the blue flash of a micro-laser, then hears a soft pop as the lid opens.

Shiva deposits her weapon. Kali does the same.

Once the guns have been stored, Balthazar turns to Penelope and says, "I've got everything you need."

He walks across the room, ducks behind the counter, and disappears through a doorway. Ten seconds later, he returns with an armful of old maps.

"I thought we were getting digital files," says Penelope.

"You are. I had them scanned for you. But I thought you might want to look at the real deal. These are New York subway maps, one from every decade since they started digging the tunnels."

"Why do you have them?"

"The blip," says Balthazar.

"What blip?" asks Kali.

"Most people only see a blip. They're on the subway and blip, there goes an abandoned stop, a forgotten line, a discarded station. But think about all the people who passed through that station. All of them with lives as thick as our own. That blip—it's a tiny slice of a tiny slice of a tiny slice of the past, yet it's millions of lives thick. Worlds inside of worlds inside of worlds, my friends. It just depends on how you slice it."

"Sugar," says Kali, "you look like a pond, but I can tell, you a lake."

"It's a hobby," replies Balthazar. "I like to remember forgotten New York."

He unrolls one of the maps on the counter.

Penelope gawks. "Yer oot yer face. Bloody thing looks like a maze."

"That's why I'm coming with you," says Balthazar.

Lion shakes his head. "Not a great idea."

"Six-two, 235," says Balthazar, patting his belly. "And I'm so mean I make medicine sick."

"Six-two, 235 wins the bar brawl," replies Lion, "but when it comes to squeezing through tunnels below New York? I predict a KO in round three."

Balthazar reaches below the counter, retrieving a dozen tiny earbuds. He dumps them onto a velvet display mat. They resemble the noise-canceling earbuds from the plane, tiny black roses, except with a micro-sparkle visible on the outer petal of the rose.

"Not like that," he says. "I'm a virtual tagalong." Balthazar points at the earbuds. "See that little sparkle?"

"I always like a little shimmy in my spyware," says Shiva.

"That's a deep core transceiver," says Balthazar. "These earbuds are used in gem mines. Their GPS works three hundred feet underground. The comms will go five hundred." He points to a vintage iMac sitting on a desk in the corner. "I'll guide you from here. Between me and the maps—well, something might kill you down there, but you'll know exactly where you are when you die."

Lion smiles. "In pharmacies all over the city, antibiotics are coming down with the flu. Right here, right now, medicine is getting sick."

"My friends," says Balthazar, "I'm just getting started."

Balthazar walks over to the iMac, clicks open a folder, and brings up an image. He twirls the screen around so everyone can see it. Lion recognizes the unpleasant sight of the Bolex H-11.

"Carlos asked me what this camera might be used for, so I got curious."

"Did you figure it out?"

"The thing about the Bolex H-11," explains Balthazar, gesturing toward the screen, "it records images off the back of the retina."

"We figured that out, too," says Lion. "But why does it matter?"

"The back of the retina is like a fingerprint. Everybody's is different." He points at Shiva and Kali. "Even identical twins don't have matching retinas. But scientists have known this for nearly a hundred years. Back in the 1970s, Bolex began experimenting with all kinds of novel optics—thermal cameras, underwater cameras, ultraviolet cameras. Recording off the back of the retina was just another geeky thing to do."

"Geeky?" asks Kali.

"Super-geeky: The camera projects an invisible beam of ultraviolet light. Retinal blood vessels absorb more of it than the rest of the eye. And it works—the camera, I mean—but there was no use for the tech back then."

"It became useful later?" asks Penelope.

"Later we learned that AIDS, malaria, chicken pox, some cancers, they all leave a signature in the eyes."

"So we use it for disease detection?"

"Yeah, but security was the killer app. Retinal scanners changed that game. Pretty much every three-letter agency in the world uses them to protect their locked rooms. But there's another use case that showed up even later, and that's what I think Zee is actually using the camera for."

"When did it show up?" asks Shiva.

Balthazar points at Lion. "After em-trackers came along."

"The eye-brain connectome," says Lion, suddenly putting it all together. "Zee's recording the retinas of em-trackers in peak emotional states. You're telling me he's trying to map our brains?"

"That's exactly what I think," says Balthazar.

"Why?" asks Penelope.

"Dunno," says Balthazar.

"I know," says Lion. "If you have a map of an em-tracker's connectome, you'd have a map of what creates our expanded sense of cultural empathy and, possibly, our future prediction capacity—or some version of it. Maybe it's Pandora II. If Zee wants to perfect human genetics, maybe he needs a map of an em-tracker's connectomes to get it done."

"So, what?" asks Penelope. "Zee wants to use em-trackers to upgrade the species?"

"Exactly," says Lion.

"Well, bugger me with a forklift," says Penelope.

"Yeah," says Lion, "exactly that, too."

FANCY THAT SHAG?

The SUV rolls up in front of their hotel. Kali climbs out first. Shiva, Penelope, and Lion bring up the rear.

"Welcome to the Joke," says the doorman.

The Joke is actually the name of their hotel. It's Sir Richard's latest folly, a sixteen-story remodel located on the banks of the Hudson, just north of the West Village. He bought the property a few years back and is currently in the process of renovating the lower floors. The upper floors have already been redone, including the penthouse, which has become ground zero for what Jenka insists on calling Operation Pandora.

Kali nods at the doorman, starts toward the hotel, but stops after a step to stretch out her shoulders. Must be one of those twin things.

Immediately Shiva begins to roll out her neck. A second later, they finish simultaneously and stroll into the Joke.

Penelope takes Lion's hand and follows them in.

The lobby is spacious and elegant, with black marble floors, tall ceilings, and a giant screen filling the rear wall. The screen currently shows a video of a priest, a rabbi, and a funeral director walking into a bar. The game, Lion knows, is to come up with a punch line to the joke. If you come up with a punch line to "a rabbi, a priest, and a funeral director walk into a bar" that's funny enough to crack up the desk clerk, you get half off your first night's stay.

The best joke of the week wins a free week.

As they walk across the lobby, the rabbi, priest, and funeral director disappear from the screen, replaced by the words *past, present, and future*.

Kali glances back at them. "The past, present, and future walk into a bar."

"It was tense," replies Penelope.

"Not bad, sister," says Kali before heading toward the elevators. Shiva walks beside her. Lion's about to follow, but Penelope tugs on his hand, pausing them beneath an ornate Victorian chandelier, the lightbulbs custom-designed to resemble famous comedians. Lenny Bruce and Lucille Ball are now directly overhead.

Penelope says, "Couple hours before dinner—fancy that shag?"

Before he can answer, there's a sizzling sound directly above them. The chandelier's lights dim, then brighten again. This is followed by a soft pop.

Lion yanks Penelope out of the way just as a rain of glass showers down.

Looking up, they see a John Belushi lightbulb has exploded.

An instant later, a pair of sweeper robots roll out from behind the check-in counter, zip across the lobby, and make fast work of the mess. A pale-skinned desk clerk trails the robots. He has that look on his face that pale-skinned desk clerks get when John Belushi lightbulbs explode in their lobbies.

"I am so sorry about that," says the clerk. "We've got a short in the system."

"I don't get it," says Penelope. "What's funny about John Belushi exploding?"

"Funny?"

"Bloody obvious—John Belushi blows up. Next you're going to tell me that Richard Pryor's head occasionally bursts into flame."

The clerk starts laughing.

A slot in the wall slides open and a humanoid robot, four feet tall with a white plastic body and big blue eyes, glides out, spins in their direction, and rolls over to them. The bot reaches into a chest pocket, extracts a golden ticket, hands it to Penelope, then retreats back into the wall.

"Turn it in when you check out," explains the clerk. "You'll get half off your first night."

She gives him a confused look.

"I'm on check-in duty. There are three face-reading cameras on me at all times. If the system detects even a touch of mirth . . ."—he points at the ticket—"this happens automatically." He becomes serious again. "Are you okay? Nobody got cut?"

"We're fine," says Penelope.

"I'm going to have to call maintenance again. This keeps happening. Dave Chappelle cracked up a few hours ago."

"Like you didn't see that one coming," says Penelope, squeezing Lion's hand and tugging him toward the elevator.

Lion makes it two steps before the JOBZ buzzes in his pocket. He stops walking, drops Penelope's hand, pulls out his anonymizer, checks the screen, shakes his head, then answers.

"Normally," he says, "I'd ask you how you got this number. The JOBZ is protected by nearly unbreakable code, so this shouldn't be possible."

"But you know better than that, sport."

"I do," says Lion.

"Are you talking to me?" asks Penelope.

Lion lowers the phone. "It's Sir Richard. I need to talk to him. I'll be up in a sec."

"Don't take too long," says Penelope, with a wink.

THE WRONG TOOL FOR THE RIGHT JOB

Sir Richard is pontificating without provocation again.

Lion lets him babble, crossing the lobby to an overstuffed chair in the corner. He sits down in time to see Penelope board the elevator, just catching a last glimpse of her long red hair before she disappears inside.

Turning his attention back to Sir Richard, Lion listens for a second, but decides he's not in the mood. "Tell me about Zee," he says. "How did the war start?"

There's a pause before Sir Richard responds. "*Buyology*," he says eventually.

"Buyology?"

"The book that introduced neuromarketing to the world. It was written by a Danish chap, Martin Lindstrom, back in the early 2000s."

"What about it?"

"The book changed the game. If you worked in advertising, neuromarketing was clearly the future. Any agency worth a damn, we all rushed into the space. But we all learned the same lesson the hard way: With brain imaging, those signals don't always mean what we think they mean. Most people rushed back out."

"But you stayed in?"

"I was interested in a different approach."

"Connectome mapping," says Lion. "I put it together."

Sir Richard laughs. "Very good, sport. Humor me, I'm curious, how did you put it together?"

While Lion was riding back from Masta Ice, he'd finally realized what was bugging him about Barry's sudden friendship with Sir Richard. It wasn't their multiple conversations. It was merely a tiny snippet of a single conversation. He'd overheard a second of chitchat, just passing by the penthouse's holo-chat suite on his way to the bathroom.

Barry said, "Sasha and Xiu."

"How are my girls?" Sir Richard immediately responded.

Lion didn't think much of it at the time, but on the drive back from Masta Ice, he started to wonder: If Sasha and Xiu are a technology stolen from the Chinese military, how could Sasha and Xiu possibly be Sir Richard's "girls"?

"Sasha and Xiu," says Lion. "They're not stolen from anyone."

"No."

"They're not Chinese defense tech."

"No."

"Arctic built them?"

"Actually, it was a KGB spin-off company that Arctic Pharmaceuticals bought a while back."

"Why would your pharma division invest in a holo-sex toy?"

"Sex is good medicine," explains Sir Richard. "I was wondering if VR might be a more effective delivery system for that medicine."

"But that's not where this started."

"No, you're right, it goes back further."

"When the first wave of neuromarketing fell apart: everyone else got out, you stayed in. Why?"

"Complexity science," explains Sir Richard. "Buying decisions, neurologically speaking, are complex decisions. That's what Lindstrom missed. That's why static pictures of the brain never told the whole story. Neuroimaging was the wrong tool for the right job."

"Connectome mapping is the right tool," says Lion.

"Right again. It's the first complexity-science-based approach to understanding the brain. I thought it might give me a way to map people's buying decisions."

"But this was, what?—ten years before the Human Connectome Project even got started. How did you manage to map anything?"

"We didn't, but the project was dead by then."

"Why?"

"Difference of opinion. I wanted to add an AI layer to traditional brain-mapping techniques, but Zee was fascinated by the visual system. Thirty percent of the cortex is devoted to vision. Nothing else in the brain gets that kind of real estate. He thought you could induce powerful experiences, then backtrack the reaction to that visual input as it ping-ponged through the brain."

"The eyes?"

"It's a smart choice. We have a leg up with the eyes. Retinal maps are genetic. So Zee thought if you could get a person's DNA, theoretically you could get a rough blueprint for their retinal map. At the time, the genetics weren't there. But gene sequencing, even back then, was doubling in power every five months. Zee thought that once the field caught up, if you had the eye-brain connectome in place, and you knew where and when a photon struck the retina—anyway, it was a primitive idea that didn't work."

"That doesn't sound ethical. It sounds technical. I heard you shut the project down for ethical reasons."

"Neuro-tech versus nanotech," says Sir Richard. "I wanted to map the brain. Zee wanted to miniaturize the technology that map brains. Then we got drunk one night and he mentioned that his real dream was to make a mapping device so small you could slip it into a pill."

"That sounds like spy tech."

"That's what I thought, too. So I did a deep background check on Zee. I expected defense contracts, the Chinese government, the Russians. Instead, I discovered that Zee changed his name."

"He's not Chang Zee?"

"He's Jerome Zhong, disgraced professor of genetics from the UC Santa Cruz."

Lion sits up straight. "Zhong is Zee?"

"Zee's not even Chinese. He's American. He was born in Shaker Heights, Ohio. Do you know the spot?"

"No."

"Ritzy. Robber-baron mansions."

"Chang Zee—'I come here on boat, now I own boat'—that guy grew up in a robber-baron mansion?"

"He also played lacrosse."

"If Zee wasn't in defense tech," asks Lion, "why the miniaturization? And why the ethical issues? Sneaky brain-mapping tech—no offense, but that sounds like Arctic's playbook."

"I resent what you're implying."

"But?"

"I also resemble what you're implying. Yet that wasn't my ethical concern. Zee was obsessed with the impact of disruptive innovation on advertising. Neuromarketing was a seriously disruptive innovation. But neuromarketing wasn't nearly as disruptive as another neural advancement that showed up around the same time."

"You're talking about em-trackers."

"Em-trackers feel how culture evolves. That's way more than you could ever learn from brain mapping."

"But if you had a map of an em-tracker's brain . . ."

"Exactly," says Sir Richard. "Em-trackers give you the end point in a long process—the direction that culture evolves. But Zee also wanted to know where the process began. He wanted the tech in pill form so he could give it to anyone, to regular consumers, so he could have a brain map of the birth of their buying decisions. If you know where people are starting from and you have a pretty good idea of where they're going to end up, making bank on the in-between is fairly straightforward."

"Money?"

"Zee was already thinking about perfecting the human species in graduate school. He wrote his thesis about it—which is why he knew it was going to be extremely expensive. That's why Zee got interested in neuromarketing."

"Why did he become a self-help guru?"

"More money. In the early twenty-first century, at the dawn of the social media age, being a self-help guru was the like owning the ATM. No one had the necessary defense mechanisms. Plus, it was a perfect way for Zee to convert people to his 'I am the Singularity' ideology."

"Zee isn't mapping the brains of em-trackers to upgrade the species. He's mapping our brains to pay for Pandora II."

"Exactly. Em-tracking is all about empathy, but Zee has no interest in empathy. He thinks we should use genetics to rise above the limitations of the human brain entirely, including our emotions and our innate divisiveness. If you do that, there's no need for empathy. But building his master race is expensive."

Then it clicks. "Evo," says Lion. "It's not a drug at all—is it?"

"No."

"It's a brain-mapping technology disguised as a drug. The reason you trip evolution is because . . . Fuck me, it's a honeypot. Jenka was right—it's a trap for em-trackers. Like the Suicide Girls. A fundraising scheme. I can't believe it—I was fucking tortured for venture capital."

"I did not know you were tortured."

Lion says nothing.

"You are okay?"

"I will be after tomorrow. I have a battle-axe with Zee's name on it."

"You have a battle-axe?"

"It's a metaphor," says Lion. "But there's still something I don't get: If all of this is to pay for Pandora II, why did Zee attack PRML?"

"Zee believes mega-linkages are backward-facing," says Sir Richard. "They're about conserving what was, about preserving the natural order. Zee wants a revolutionary new beginning. Burn the ships, destroy anything that doesn't lead in the direction of his future. But I think he started with PRML because he's especially angry with me."

"Because you canceled the project?"

"I didn't cancel the project. I canceled the version I was working on with Zee. And while we didn't part friends, the tech, his way, my way, it didn't matter. At the time, they were both nonstarters. But that's not the reason he's angry."

"Why?"

"The oldest reason."

"Money?"

"Older."

"Pride?"

"Older."

"You're talking about sex."

"Right a third time, sport."

"You slept with Zee's girlfriend. Wait a minute—Susan Jackson was Zee's girlfriend."

"In all fairness," explains Sir Richard, "she presented their relationship as an on-again, off-again thing."

"Yeah," says Lion, "I know that feeling. When Susan became a triple agent, did she and Zee get back together?"

"I thought that was it. And maybe that happened, but I think Susan became a convert. Maybe she always was one. Her thesis certainly pointed in that direction, but then she moved into cultured beef—which was all about protecting the environment."

"What happened?"

"I think her work with cultured beef taught her to improve upon nature. She made steak from stem cells, but it's healthier steak, fewer saturated fats, more good fats, improved protein delivery mechanics. I think Susan got carried away. She was optimizing flesh, so why not optimize the whole organism? I think it led her back to Zhong's original ideas, from graduate school."

"Susan put the snakes in the tunnel," says Lion.

"That's the only conclusion I can draw. In tracking her movements, I think she put three different kinds of snakes in the tunnel. The first batch didn't hatch at all, they just rotted. The second batch appears to have hatched early, and the ski patroller got killed. The third batch killed Susan and attacked you."

"So it was just a coincidence that the ski patroller who died was Chinese? It had nothing to do with Zee?"

"Judging from Susan's movements and phone records, the ski patroller's death shook her. Remember, everyone else was still trying to figure out how anyone could die from a snakebite in the winter in the Sierra Nevada mountains. Lizzy was in overdrive, and her research team as well. But after the ski patroller died, Susan went into overdrive as well. Why? It wasn't her problem. But she still made a flurry of phone calls. I think Susan knew something was wrong with the snakes but didn't know what. She went back into the tunnels to try to figure it out. What she also didn't know was that the snowmaking system was broken, that it could turn on accidentally."

Lion thinks for a moment. "So Susan went into the tunnels, was working on her computer, running tests, whatever, the snowmaking system turned on, the eggs hatched, and she got killed by her own weapon. That's . . . actually, that makes a lot of sense."

THE SHABBOS GOY

Lion walks into the elevator, still thinking about his conversation with Sir Richard. He's followed by two Hasidic boys, each in their middle teens, each toting a medium-sized suitcase, both wearing dark suits, white shirts, and wide-brimmed hats.

Lion pushes the button for the penthouse, still thinking about what Sir Richard said. He doesn't notice that neither of the boys push a button. When they exit the elevator together, turn the same direction down the hall, and find themselves clustered outside the penthouse door, finally they exchange glances.

"Are you the Shabbos goy?" asks one of the boys.

Before Lion can answer, Barry opens the door. "Shlomo and Uri," he says, "did you meet Lion?"

"They think I'm the Shabbos goy," explains Lion.

"The Torah forbids work on a Saturday," says Barry, stepping out of the way so they can enter. "Someone has to turn on the lights."

Lion walks inside the penthouse, followed by Shlomo and Uri, their suitcases in tow. From the other room, he hears Jenka's voice—apparently, he made good time in Penelope's hover-coupe—followed by Ji's voice, then Penelope's.

"Good news," says Barry. "Jenka made a breakthrough."

"A breakthrough?"

"Gentlemen," says Barry, "would you excuse us for a moment?"

He leads Lion to the other side of the living room.

Once they're outside earshot, Barry says, "Looks like we don't have to dodge trains and sneak in through Grand Central after all. There's a service elevator."

"Won't it be monitored?" asks Lion.

"Your old friend Two Tone installed the security system. It was Ji who hired him."

"How does that help?"

"This was after Ji started questioning Zee's agenda. He paid Two Tone to install a backdoor. Ji's got a security Bypass, Jenka found the elevator, Penelope's finalizing our route and . . ."—Barry points toward the boys—"Shlomo and Uri have arrived with our supplies."

Lion looks over, seeing suitcases filled with weapons open on the table. Shlomo catches his eye. "Latest and greatest," he says, pointing into the case, "and not available in stores."

"Pardon?"

Shlomo picks up a tactical shotgun. "LTX 9000—normally you have to be a UN peacekeeper to get one of these."

"Why do I want one?"

"I was told you didn't want to kill anyone," explains Shlomo. "The LTX fires beanbag rounds. Less lethal in all situations, but heavy stopping power." He sets down the shotgun and picks up a chrome pistol with a clear plastic snout. "Taser X29P, no longer a single-use weapon, now upgraded with quad-shot wireless heat-seeking rounds."

"Heat-seeking," says Barry, "that's new."

Shlomo undoes a flap on the second suitcase, revealing two PHASR pistols and two shotguns. He puts away the pistol, lifts out a PHASR shotgun, and passes it to Lion. "Check her out—she goes with your outfit."

Lion glances at himself in a mirror on the wall: black jeans, black sweatshirt, black laser-assault rifle. He's a balaclava away from being an absolute cliché.

"You look good," says Uri.

"Gangster," says Barry.

"I look like someone I don't know," says Lion.

"You look like someone I don't want to know," says Shlomo.

Handing the PHASR back to Shlomo, Lion walks over to Barry and keeps his voice low. "We've got a way into Pandora and routes to both the web-casting studio and the holding cells?"

"Yes."

"Ji said the guard situation will be light and Zee likes to record alone." He nods toward the weapons. "So is all this . . . really necessary?"

"Necessary? Are you meshugenah? This is Chang Zee we're talking about." Barry looks at Shlomo. "We'll take everything, and extra ammo. Put it on my account. And please tell your mother happy birthday and I'm sorry I missed the party. And please tell your father the Yankees still suck pork rinds."

"He won't like that," responds Uri. "He says the laws of kashrut cannot be applied to baseball. There is zero precedent in the Talmud, and nothing in any of the major commentaries."

"I'm going to take a nap," says Lion, pointing at the guns. "This needs to be someone else's life for a while."

GOD'S NOT HOME

The elevator that leads to Pandora II sits on a nondescript corner of Lower Manhattan, tucked between a Tesla-Verizon resale store and an anonymous office building, hidden behind a battered grate made from corrugated steel. Lion, Kali, Shiva, and Jenka stand ten feet away from the grate, ready for anything. Dressed in matching black jumpsuits, they all carry rough cloth tool bags and wear black combat boots: waterproof, heavy-treaded, steel-toed.

Barry's uniform is the only exception. Just in case anyone's watching, he wears his traditional garb: a long dark overcoat and a wide-brimmed hat.

Lion looks at Barry. "Ready?"

Barry nods, adjusts his hat, and walks over to a keypad on the wall beside the grate. He enters the sixteen-digit code that Ji taught him. The grate rises upward automatically, revealing an elevator on the other side.

After uttering a soft prayer, Barry pushes the call button three times, pauses for a four count, then hits it twice more.

A second later, a husky woman's voice says, "I push my fingers into my eyes."

"It's the only thing that slowly stops the ache," replies Barry.

"Is White Stripes lyric?" asks Jenka.

"Slipknot," says Lion. "Figures that's the security code Two Tone installed."

"What is Slipknot?"

"Metal."

"Metal what?"

"Pre-poly-tribe neoclassical heavy not-quite death metal."

"I ask again—what is Slipknot?"

A second later the elevator dings and the doors open, revealing an empty car. Barry glances at Shiva, who glances at Kali, who glances at Jenka, who glances at Lion. Lion slides his fingers inside the rings of his newly purchased death punch, this one with the Taser upgrade, looks at Jenka, and says, "A seven nation army couldn't hold me back."

"See," says Jenka, "is catchy. There is nothing wrong with White Stripes."

They all climb aboard.

The elevator is innocuous: four walls of ancient faux wood paneling and a drab gray floor.

The doors creak shut.

As soon as they're closed, Barry tosses his hat in the corner and slides off his overcoat, revealing a matching black jumpsuit underneath. The others crouch down, unzip their tool bags, and remove an assortment of weapons.

Jenka stands up with his folded PHASR pistol and one of the PHASR rifles. He snaps the pistol open, then straps the rifle across his back. Barry has a matching PHASR pistol in a side holster and an old chrome-plated Desert Eagle in his right hand. Kali and Shiva pack two pistols each, one of the nine-millimeter variety, the other a PHASR. The nines are in hand, the PHASRs are folded-up squares hanging from their utility belts. Everyone also carries a small backpack with water, food, night-vision goggles, and emergency medical supplies. Jenka added a hacker's tool kit to his gear, but with Two Tone's master passwords, they're hoping they won't need it.

If everything has gone according to plan, their little party makes up waves two and three of what Jenka now insists on calling Operation Pandora: Assault on Fortress Zee.

Penelope and Ji were the first wave.

Two hours ago, they boarded this same elevator, executed this same code, and launched the assault.

Unfortunately, according to what Balthazar told them before they left the hotel, there's some kind of heavy-duty sonic shielding down below. Since Penelope and Ji entered Pandora II about two hours ago, while Balthazar can see their GPS trackers moving—so he knows they're alive—he hasn't heard a peep.

The elevator descends slowly. Barry said this was intentional, something about fooling ground-penetrating satellite radar.

"The NSA?" Lion asks. "You were serious? They built this elevator?"

"Post 9/11," explains Barry. "The NSA decided to build secret installations hundreds of feet below every major city. A handful got built. If you're ever in L.A., that tourist mall next to Grauman's Chinese Theatre. It's two stories high with no basement. But get into the elevator, push the buttons in the right sequence, smile for the camera, and the elevator goes down, like fifty floors down, and lets you out in an underground bunker—though it looks more like a high-tech Holiday Inn."

"These bunkers are under every major city?" asks Kali.

"No," says Barry. "But the elevators are. The funding dried up. They completed a half-dozen bunkers, but about two dozen elevators. I heard the NSA was trying to sell some off. I guess Zee found a way to buy one."

The car stops, coming to rest with a polite ding.

"Ear mics on," says Barry.

In unison, they lift up their hands and double-tap the small black roses in their ears.

The doors part. The elevator's single bulb casts a pale glow about ten feet in front of them. Lion sees a nearly pitch-black abandoned railway tunnel, the walls coated with some kind of flame-retardant foam that looks like rust-colored cotton candy.

"Flashlights and night vision," says Barry.

Shiva and Kali slide on night-vision glasses. These are silver aviator shades, like cops wore in the 1970s, but with full thermal capabilities and image enhancement up to a thousand yards. The goal was to get glasses for the whole team, but there was a screwup at a truck stop in Buffalo and they only ended up with four pairs. Ji and Penelope took the first two, Kali and Shiva the others. Still, if a mouse moves in the darkness a quarter of a mile away, the Black Power twins will know.

The twins slip out of the car. Kali fans right, Shiva left. Jenka follows, PHASR at the ready. He also wears night-vision goggles, only his look like traditional ski goggles—a mirrored red lens that covers half of his face. Between the red lens and the goggle's strap pushing his bleached white pompadour nearly vertical, Jenka looks, Lion decides, like an overworked time-machine repairman—not an actual traveler, merely the guy who checks the tires and changes the temporal displacement module.

Barry and Lion bring up the rear. Barry has stowed his PHASR pistol but carries a flashlight and his Desert Eagle. Lion wears the death punch on his left hand. On his right, he tugs on a black neoprene glow glove with high-wattage knuckle lights and three settings: flashlight, infrared, and cannon. Flashlight is a thousand watts' worth of glow. Infrared fires a pulse beam that temporarily illuminates anything within a hundred feet. Cannon blasts 50,000 lumens of hot white, the equivalent of a stadium spotlight array and completely blinding.

But it's much ado about nothing.

Kali and Shiva trade hand signals. Shiva turns toward Jenka and whispers, "All clear."

"Stay silent, kids," says Balthazar into their ear mics. "There's an acoustic sensor in the wall about a hundred feet north. You'll come to a hard right turn. Go slow, no talking. I'll guide you in. And welcome to Pandora."

Lion clicks the trigger on his glow glove, turning on the flashlight. He sees a long narrow corridor, the walls also coated in rust-colored flame-retardant spray foam.

They move slowly and quietly.

A hundred feet ahead, the spray foam gives way to the walls of an old subway tunnel: packed dirt, steel girders, and old track. Dank and dingy. They pass graffiti from another century.

Someone named Lady Pink was down here. As was Blaze.

Up ahead, Shiva lifts up a closed fist. The group halts in unison. They've reached that hard right turn.

"Coast was clear earlier," says Balthazar, "but I'd be creeping and peeping, if you know what I mean."

Lion kills his glow glove. Barry snaps off the flashlight.

Like a church at midnight, darkness swallows them with its lonely reminder: God's not home.

LIKE GIANT FLOATING MOONS

Shiva steps around the corner, her gun in a two-handed combat grip, thumb over thumb, barrel pointing into the darkness. Kali crouches and extends her weapon, covering her sister.

Lion stays behind the wall but pokes his head around the corner. His eyes have begun to adjust to the gloom. Even with his glow glove off, he can make out rust-colored cotton candy on the walls. It's another spray-foam-coated tunnel, slightly smaller than the first.

Jenka steps past Lion and walks into the opening, removes a tablet computer from his pack, attaches a small plug-in sensor, like a tiny silver lightbulb, and hits a button.

A blue light runs over the bulb's surface, revealing a rotating lens inside.

A second later, Jenka touches a hand to his ear, confirming Balthazar's concern: Someone's listening. Then he taps a forefinger below his left eye and shakes his head no—meaning there are no cameras down here—then points down the passageway and nods yes, giving Kali and Shiva the signal to proceed.

They start down the tunnel.

"There's a door four hundred feet ahead, on your left," says Balthazar, "but this is where the shielding starts. I'm gonna lose you after two hundred feet. It's GPS only from this point on. You'll get haptic buzzes in your ears. One short buzz means stop. Two straight. Three left. Four right. And one long buzz—turn around and run like hell."

"We cover this already," whispers Jenka.

"Just trying to be careful," replies Balthazar.

They trudge onward. Nothing happens for one hundred feet. Nothing happens for two hundred feet. At three hundred feet, Kali holds up a closed fist and everyone freezes.

She glances at Lion, taps her right finger to her right eye, then taps her right fist twice. Lion nods, switches the setting on his glow glove from flashlight to infrared and extends his fist down the tunnel. He punches the thumb trigger. A pulse of orange light shoots down the corridor.

Did he see that?

Lion hits the trigger again, sending out a second pulse.

Eighty feet ahead, temporarily outlined in fuzzy orange, a full-size jackrabbit stands in the middle of the tunnel.

As soon as the second pulse hits, the rabbit looks at Lion.

Kali also looks at Lion, but hers is a different kind of question, one only an em-tracker can answer. Proof of life: Is the rabbit real or robotic?

Lion raises his fists stomach-high, knuckles facing together. He gives her the double thumbs-up, then lifts his thumbs toward his chest—the sign language sign for "alive."

She gives him a third look. He understands this one as well. It's the obvious follow-up: What's a rabbit doing five hundred feet underground?

Lion doesn't know that answer. He looks back at Kali and shakes his head. The universal answer: "Not good."

They keep moving.

Three hundred feet ahead, their ear mics buzz once, stopping them in front of a patch of darkness chiseled from the rust-colored spray foam. It's a nearly invisible black metal door.

Now it's Lion's turn.

Ji spread around the security codes, so no one had to remember too much. Barry got the numbers for the exterior door and the voice prompts for the elevator. But this interior door, which apparently leads to something called Plumbing IV, is protected by an animatronic handshake, similar to the ones guarding PRML, except far more complicated.

Modeled on a design by former NBA player Russell Westbrook, the shake involves a couple dozen handslaps, lap slaps, heart thumps, God points, a chorus of dabs, and a complicated bro-down knuckle-tap sequence that ends with Lion having to chest-bump the center of the door.

But it works.

They hear the hiss of an air lock unsealing, and the door slides open.

At a glance, Plumbing IV is as advertised: a snaking maze of white and green pipes, heavy ductwork, and gray concrete. Clear plastic tubes full of LED lighting run along the ceiling, revealing a garden of forking paths. Computer server racks blink in the distance, and closer in, there are squat round tanks of liquid nitrogen.

The door's on a timer.

They slip through quickly, hearing a muted hiss as the air lock re-seals behind them.

Jenka creeps a few feet forward, lifts up his tablet computer and the bulb sensor, and runs another scan.

Then he walks fifty feet ahead of them and does it again.

"Ji was right," says Jenka once he returns. "Nothing down here. No sensors."

"Outside the door," asks Lion, "in the corridor, why use an acoustic sensor? Why not a camera?"

"I learn in war," says Jenka. "For wilderness combat, to distinguish animal from human, acoustic sensor and machine learning algorithms can tell jackrabbit from whatever."

"From whatever?"

"Dah. Polar bears. Flying tree snakes. Whatever."

"But why outside and not inside?"

Before anyone can answer, their ears buzz twice. Two longs. The signal for Assault on Fortress Zee, Phase Three.

"Time to split up," says Barry.

"Catch you boys on the flip side," says Shiva.

"Stay safe, sugars," says Kali.

Lion watches the twins walk away, the silhouette of their Afros disappearing into the fading light of the tunnel, like giant floating moons.

That's Life

With Kali and Shiva gone, Jenka takes point, walking into the maze of pipes ahead of them. Lion and Barry trail behind. The only sound is a faint machine hum and Barry's breathing, from somewhere to Lion's left.

They hike down forking corridors, their ear mics buzzing directions. Around another corner, the computer servers, nitrogen tanks, and white pipes vanish. Now it's just green pipes, concrete floors, and the yellow stripe of LED lights extending ahead of them like freeway lines.

"This place is huge," whispers Barry.

They head straight, then left, then right, then down a diagonal splinter tunnel still under construction. Through a gap in the wall, Lion sees an old subway track. The rails ripped out, the scrap metal sold off.

A hundred feet farther, the glow glove illuminates unfinished mosaics of dirty white tile and the remains of a sink jutting out of a wall. It's an old subway bathroom, not yet completed, or left this way intentionally, a reminder of who knows what.

Up ahead, Lion hears Jenka's voice. "Son of bitch."

"What?" calls Barry, walking faster.

Lion gets there first, reaching a break in the pipes and glancing inside. Jenka stands a few feet away, on a raised observation deck made from railroad ties, facing an enormous glass window.

"Is not real," says Jenka, staring through the window.

"Holy crap," adds Lion.

The window reveals a vast desert. A long undulating plain of sagebrush, piñon trees, cacti, rocks, dirt, and sand extending far into the distance. There are mountains beyond the desert and a wide blue sky above them.

"I think it's real," says Lion, stepping onto the viewing platform. "Though I can't believe it's possible."

"Is screen. Or holo-projection."

"Em-tracker, remember? I'm genetically designed to recognize life." Lion points at the desert scene on the other side of the window. "That's life." He raises his finger to the mountains. "That's where life ends. The sky, the mountains, that's a hologram. I think it's the same kind that Sir Richard uses at PRML. But the land between there and here, that's actual soil, dirt, plants. It's the real deal. I'm pretty sure we're looking at the world's first fully completed underground mega-linkage."

"Well," says Barry, coming up to stand beside Lion, "that would explain the jackrabbit."

"Doesn't explain how it got out," says Jenka. "That was air-locked door."

"Doesn't explain the other thing, either," adds Lion.

"What other thing?" asks Jenka.

"Why a rabbit? It seems like a pretty strange choice for a super-villain. And we know it's hard to create life. The snakes died after a couple of days. The polar bears were robots. So why did Zee go to all that trouble for a rabbit?"

"Maybe Zee got the rabbit from a pet shop," says Barry. "Or maybe he's breeding real rabbits down here."

"That's what I was thinking," says Lion.

"What is point?" asks Jenka.

"Back when I was a reporter on the animal rights beat, I tagged along on a couple of raids of testing labs. Some of those labs had rabbits."

"Dah, animal testing. Is sick fucking world."

"Or . . ." says Lion.

"Or?"

"A few of the labs I visited, the rabbits weren't being used for testing. They were food. They were being fed to animals—well, animals much bigger than rabbits."

"But robot polar bears do not eat anything," says Barry, wandering off to their left.

"So what is Zee feeding with rabbits?" asks Jenka.

"That's my point."

"There's a door over here," calls Barry. "My ear buzzed. I don't know if it's where the rabbit got out, but, according to Balthazar, it's where we go in."

"Is like old joke," says Jenka, "A rabbi, an em-tracker, and a Moldovan walk into a mega-linkage."

"What's the punch line?" asks Lion.

"That *is* punch line."

GHOST DOG

Lion, Jenka, and Barry find the entranceway, then hike cautiously into the mega-linkage, coming to a stop in a slender arroyo, beside the gnarled branches of a piñon pine.

"When I was a kid," says Lion, glancing around, "I spent a summer in Abiquiu, New Mexico."

"Where the painter Georgia O'Keeffe used to live?" asks Barry.

"Exactly. There was this big cinder cone volcano there. Pedernal Peak. O'Keeffe called it her private mountain. 'It belongs to me,' she said. 'God told me if I painted it enough, I could have it.'"

"What is point?" asks Jenka.

Lion nods at the desert. "Same terrain."

"This is supposed to be New Mexico?" asks Barry.

Lion points at a flat-topped mountain in the distance. "I think that's the Pedernal."

"How big is it?"

"The Pedernal? Ten thousand feet."

"Not the mountain," says Barry, lifting his hand into the air and twirling his forefinger in a circle. "This place."

"Good question."

The room seems to stretch three hundred feet across at its widest spot, but there are choke points where the mega-linkage narrows to as little as thirty feet.

But its length is another story.

The terrain undulates right and left, up and down, following an internal logic all its own. It appears to stretch on for miles. Lion assumes this is holo-magic at work, but it doesn't alter the strangeness of finding himself standing in a desert beneath downtown Manhattan.

There's a rattle in the bushes to their left. Barry and Jenka whirl around, guns ready.

"Jackrabbit," says Lion, gesturing to his right. "Beneath that juniper."

Barry lowers his weapon.

"Another rabbit?" asks Jenka, still wary.

"More than one," says Lion, pointing in the other direction. "They're everywhere."

As if on cue, two jackrabbits hop past them, stopping to nibble grass beside a staghorn cholla cactus.

"Does that mean that whatever is eating rabbits is everywhere, too?" asks Jenka.

"I don't think so."

"How do you know?"

"Barry," says Lion, pointing at the rabbits, "can you walk over there?"

Barry gives Lion a puzzled look, but strides over to the bunnies. Both animals perk up their ears, but neither runs away.

"They're not afraid of you," says Lion.

"Maybe there are no predators here," says Barry.

"Still strange. Rabbits are a prey species."

"Under right conditions," says Jenka, "everything is prey species."

"True. But in prey species, fear of predation is supposed to be innate." Lion points at the rabbits. "Instinct alone should have made them hightail it out of here."

"Is this an em-tracker thing?" asks Barry. "Is that the reason they're not running away?"

"I'm a ghost dog," says Lion.

"A what?"

"Bird fetishist, fish petter, ghost dog. It means I speak dog, not rabbit."

Their ears buzz: one short, two long. Balthazar telling them to head straight ahead and step on it.

Wordlessly they set off.

Jenka takes point, leading them away from the rabbits, out of the arroyo and up a long, low rise. They crest the hill, passing a small series of sandstone cliffs, the rock stained pink and orange.

A quarter mile later, Lion realizes that it's more than a hologram projecting the illusion of vastness. Barry was absolutely right—this place is huge.

A quarter mile after that, Barry disappears around a Pinyon tree, then emerges from the other side. Jenka picks his way past a prickly-pear cactus. Suddenly, midstep, Lion freezes.

"What is it?" hisses Jenka.

Lion squats down and reaches his glow glove under a bush. He comes back with big chunk of sun-bleached scat.

"We are stopping because you found shit?" asks Jenka.

"It's too big for rabbit shit," says Lion.

He snaps the piece in half, revealing small red berries pressed between the dried cakes. "Maybe it's coyote scat. But it's little big for a coyote."

"Unless they're really big coyotes," says Barry.

"So is mystery scat?" asks Jenka.

"There's no hair in here," says Lion, studying the remains. "Whatever it is, it doesn't eat rabbit."

Jenka looks around. "Would coyotes attack humans?"

"Rare," says Lion. "Occasionally kids, old people, or someone seriously wounded. Unless . . ."

"Unless?"

Lion tosses the scat onto the ground, wiping his glove on his jumpsuit. "Unless they're really hungry."

Their ears buzz again—three short buzzes, three long buzzes, and two short buzzes.

"Did you feel that?" asks Lion.

"Dah."

"Three short, three long, two short?"

"Dah. It's the signal. Ji and Penelope found the prisoners."

"At least everyone's still alive," says Barry.

Lion hopes Barry's right. He's been thinking about Kendra and Ibrahim all morning. He even found himself telling Barry about Ibrahim's preppy Muslim vibe—his tartan turban, his lime-green penny loafers, all the little details that Lion never expected to miss.

There's another buzz in their ears.

"Let's move," says Barry.

They file down the middle of the mega-linkage, following a thin animal track as it rises up another hill. The temperature is in the low sixties. Warm for this far underground, but cold for the desert landscape the mega-linkage appears to be trying to duplicate. Lion grabs his water bottle from his pack and stops to take a sip. Jenka peels off to his left, disappearing behind a blue spruce. He reappears on the other side, a furrow on his brow.

"I found door," calls Jenka. "It does not appear that Barry is correct."

"Correct about what?"

"It does not appear that everyone is still alive."

DOUBLE TAP

Kristina Natalovich," says Jenka.

"The scientist who made the neurotoxin?" asks Barry. "It's a little hard to tell."

"Dah. Without her, I do not think we find door."

They're standing on the other side of the blue spruce, where an open door is secreted behind the branches, almost completely hidden from view. As further camouflage, the door has a full-color photo of a matching blue spruce secured to its outer surface. With the holo-sky in the background, you'd never know it was there. Even from ten feet away, it looks like just another indistinguishable swatch of desert.

Kristina is the only reason Jenka found the door.

Her body lays in the entrance, wedging it open. She's wearing a white lab coat over a simple gray dress, little makeup, and a bullet hole in the middle of her forehead. There's another hole in the middle of her chest. The coat and the dress are stained with blood, as is the floor beside her head.

Lion stares.

"Double tap," says Barry.

Forcing his eyes away from the body, Lion tries to determine what's on the other side of the door.

The room is dark, but it looks like some kind of research lab.

He points his glow glove through the opening and clicks the thumb trigger. The beam reveals a medium-sized workspace, tall metallic shelves against the far wall, workbenches and scientific equipment everywhere else. There's a mass spectrometer in the corner that looks like a prehistoric copy machine, beside an autoclave that resembles a microwave oven and a Quatro-Tech TC-5 DNA Editor and Analyzer shaped like a Quatro-Tech TC-5 DNA Editor and Analyzer.

"What the . . ."

Lion hops over Kristina's body and strides into the lab, crossing directly to a metal counter against the far wall. Reaching below it, he comes back holding an old movie camera. "It's the Bolex H-11," he says. "I think . . ."

But Lion never finishes that sentence.

Instead, his eyes pop wide. He nearly drops the camera, but somehow manages to set it down on the counter. His hands do all the work; his eyes haven't moved. They're still pegged behind the door, where a wall-sized projection screen displays the results of a science experiment.

"Are those . . ." asks Jenka, stepping into the room and following Lion's gaze.

"Slices of brain under a microscope," says Lion.

"From fMRI scan, no?"

"No. They're human connectome maps. I've only ever seen them from mouse brains before."

"Is hard to do?"

"Well, you have to kill the animal and dissect their brains to make them."

"Lion," says Jenka, "I am so sorry."

"Sorry about what?" asks Barry, stepping into the room.

Then he mutters in Yiddish and places a hand on Lion's shoulder.

The screen shows four different slices of the human brain, two vertical sections, two horizontal, all stained bright purple, with neuronal connections dyed fluorescent green. The slides have been labeled with a name and date. The four slides they're staring read: "Evo: 7–15; Ibrahim Ali."

"That is same Ibrahim?" asks Jenka.

Lion nods.

"You did not mention last name."

"It's Ali. The dates are right. This was done not long after Ibrahim and Kendra disappeared."

"The images are being projected from here," says Barry, pointing at a microscope cabled to a laptop.

"So this is what?" asks Jenka, pointing at the brain slices. "Beside sickness?"

Lion isn't sure. He's having a hard time thinking right now. He's having a hard time standing right now.

Barry walks over to the laptop. The screen is dark, but a key tap brings it to life. It shows a directory of some kind.

Grabbing a nearby stool, he sits down to read.

Jenka walks over to the metal bookshelves, peering beyond them. "There's a hallway back here."

It takes Lion a moment to realize Jenka is talking to him. "What?"

"Hallway," says Jenka again, pointing between the shelves.

Lion follows his finger, seeing a closed door with a small window in the center revealing a skinny corridor beyond.

"You guys check it out," says Barry. "I want to poke around here for a little bit."

"What is it?" asks Jenka.

"I think it's Kristina's laptop. Right before she got shot, as far as I can tell, she was looking at Evo research."

"There are more experiments like this?" Jenka asks, nodding toward the brain slices.

Barry glances at a line of names running down the right side of the screen. "A lot more."

"What happened in here?" asks Lion, pointing at Kristina. "Why is Zee's chief scientist dead?"

"Oy vey," exclaims Barry. He's staring at the column of names. He moves the cursor, punches a key, and opens a file.

"What?" asks Lion, walking over to take a closer look.

Barry hits another key.

Four more brain slices appear on the laptop's screen. They look very similar to the slices of brain being projected on the wall, but instead of Ibrahim's name in the bottom right corner, Lion sees Kendra's name.

"Zee killed them both," says Barry.

Something very heavy sits on Lion's chest.

He turns away from the screen, blinks tears out of his eyes, takes a deep breath, steps past Jenka, slides around the shelf, and starts toward the closed door. After opening it, he looks back at his friends, and says . . .

But there's nothing to say.

Are THOSe cats?

The hallway that Jenka discovered is dimly lit, fifteen feet long and painted hospital white. Beside the entranceway, there are four doors, two on each side, also painted hospital white, each with a black handle made from auto-mold plastic in its center. Grip the handle, and the plastic reforms in your hand, revealing a hidden trigger. Pulling the trigger unseals an air lock, and the door slides open. Then you're in.

Jenka and Lion are still out.

They're standing just outside the first door on the left, which is the second door they opened. The first was the first door on the right. Behind it was a destroyed laboratory: demolished microscopes, a laptop with its screen punched out, an industrial glass sterilizer that took a double-barrel blast to the belly.

The room smelled rank. Lion tracked the odor, finding two flying tree snakes crushed beneath a shattered autoclave.

They shut that door in a hurry.

The second doorway reveals a dark corridor lined floor to ceiling with industrial shelving. Glass-fronted drawers take up every inch of shelf space. There must be thousands.

"Is storeroom?" asks Jenka.

"Maybe," says Lion.

"Why is storeroom whispering?"

Lion hears it, too—like rushing water running over jagged rocks, or a hundred people breathing heavily at once. The sound is too uneven to be the hum of a machine, too loud to be the ventilation system.

Then it dawns on him. "Snakes," says Lion.

He hits the trigger on the glow glove and shines the knuckle lights into the drawer closest to them. There's a coiled black fire hose pressed against the glass. When the light hits the cage, the hose slithers and writhes, revealing rows of hexagonal scales that glimmer like tiny stars.

"Black mamba," says Lion.

He shines his glove on the next three drawers, seeing the same black writhe.

"Is breeding farm?" asks Jenka.

A second later, at the far end of the corridor, a giant metal box rolls into view. It's the size of a dishwasher, with four arms, one extending from each of its upper corners. At the end of each arm, there's a metallic grasping claw with fingertips made from black foam.

The box rolls down the corridor, heading directly toward them. It stops fifteen feet away, and the two arms on the left side of the platform whirl into motion. One arm grasps the metal handle on the front of a drawer and tugs it backward. The second arm hovers above the open drawer, then lowers the claw inside. It retracts a black mamba, squirming in its grasp.

Unclasping the metal handle, the first arm rises upward and telescopes outward. Once the claw dangles above the center of the open drawer, the arm stops moving and starts descending. The claw's metallic fingers stretch outward, disappear inside the container, then re-emerge seconds later, wrapped around a snake egg.

With a smooth arcing motion, the arm rotates inward, positioning the claw directly above the box. The lid retracts, revealing the hot orange glow of heat lamps on the inside. The claw descends, lowering the egg into the box, then retracts again, fingers empty.

The robot repeats this process four more times, until five snake eggs have been deposited inside the box. Then the snake is returned to the drawer, the drawer is closed, and the robot rolls five feet closer to them, tugs open another drawer and starts over.

Lion despises seeing animals in cages. He hates the thought that this is some kind of science experiment. He thinks about releasing the snakes, but black mambas loose in the subway system would definitely not improve human-animal relations in New York.

Feeling sick about it, Lion shuts the door, walks down the hall, and grasps the next handle. The air lock unseals and the door slides open, revealing another dark hallway lined with glass-fronted shelves.

Lion hears snakes but smells death.

Shining his glow glove down the corridor, he peers through the glass of the drawers to his right, seeing a slither of shiny green.

"Killer flying tree snakes?" asks Jenka.

"Do you smell that?"

"Dah."

Lion aims his knuckles into the darkness, illuminating the back half of the hall. It's been ransacked: drawers tugged open, strewn in haphazard piles, glass shattered into shards. Smashed snake eggs are everywhere, their shells in hundreds of pieces on the floor, dried yolk streaking the walls.

"If drawers are open," says Jenka, "where are snakes?"

Toggling his glove to infrared, Lion re-aims down the hall and hits the trigger. A wave of light travels the corridor. For the first twenty feet, the glass on every drawer glows soft orange.

"More tree snakes," says Lion.

But the rear of the corridor stays dark and lifeless, save for a tiny slither at the far end of the hall, really nothing more than an orange undulation, like the crack of a neon whip, twisting across the floor, then vanishing from sight.

Lion jumps out of the room, yanking Jenka along for the ride. He slams the door shut, not exhaling until the air lock reseals.

They exchange glances.

Lion changes the setting on his glow glove to cannon.

"Be careful," says Jenka, tapping a finger to the red lens of his goggles. "You do not have protective eyewear."

Lion nods, walks up to the last door, and grabs the knob. Once he hears the air lock unseal, cautiously, he slides it open.

Inside is a well-lit hallway, a hundred feet long and ten wide. One side is taken up by more metal shelves filled with square white boxes. A silver metal counter runs down the other side, with research stations every few feet. Each station has a chair, a computer, a microscope, and a pair of viewing binoculars attached to a flexible tripod. Above the counter, there's an enormous mirror, two feet high and running the entire length of the corridor.

Lion walks a few feet into the room and points his glove at the mirror, but before he can hit the trigger, it starts to change colors. The silver dissolves into black, which turns to smoke and evaporates into clear glass. It's now a normal window, revealing a barnyard scene.

"Rabbits?" asks Jenka.

"Baby rabbits," says Lion.

The window reveals hundreds of baby jackrabbits inside a grass-lined pen, thirty feet deep and as long as the room itself. Heat lamps that resemble miniature spotlights provide warmth, casting bunny shadows across the back wall.

Yet something feels off.

Lion scans the pen, trying to find the source of his unease. Then he realizes that it's not the rabbits, it's a shadow projected on the wall behind the rabbits. At a glance, it looks like five bunny heads in a line. The first two have long narrow ears, the next three have short round ears, like tiny dinner plates.

Whatever is making those dinner plate shadows is definitely not a rabbit.

Still standing in the doorway, Lion tracks forward from the back wall to a heat lamp, then forward from there. Noting the expression on Lion's face, Jenka follows his gaze, then asks, "Are those cats?"

Lion takes a tentative step into the room, inspecting the shelves to his left, looking for anything slithering between the white boxes.

Satisfied the room is snake free, Lion strides over to one of the research stations, pushes the desk chair aside, and leans over the counter to stare out the window.

Jenka walks over to stand beside him.

"Cats?" asks Jenka again.

"Not cats."

"Dogs."

"Not dogs," says Lion. "Unbelievable. They're hyenas."

Directly in front of them, three spotted hyena cubs stand in the middle of a sea of rabbits. Two are swatting each other with paws the size of soup spoons; the third is licking the rabbit beside it, grooming the fur on its neck.

Looking around the pen, Lion now sees hyena cubs interspersed between bunnies, nearly everywhere. Most are spotted hyenas, like someone grafted a dog's head to a leopard's body, but a few are striped, like a zebra's coat on a fox's body.

"Don't hyenas eat rabbits for lunch?" asks Jenka.

"Not at this buffet."

"They are not real."

Lion shakes his head. "They're not robots. They're real."

"So what is Zee doing?"

"I have no idea."

A second later, they hear Barry calling for them, his voice an urgent whisper.

Jenka strides toward the door, his PHASR pistol gripped tight. Lion follows him out. They find Barry about fifteen feet away, crouched in the doorway to the laboratory, hidden from view by the metal shelf, which, Lion now notices, is filled with more large white boxes.

"We've got company," hisses Barry, keeping his voice low.

"How many?" Jenka whispers back.

"Many," says Barry, pointing through the lab and into the mega-linkage, "and not human."

A second later, Lion catches up to them. He moves one of the white boxes out of the way to get a better view, realizing it's filled with rabbit food, mostly dried vegetables, according to the ingredients listed on the side.

But he's not paying attention to the ingredients.

Instead, he's staring out the lab's open door, past Kristina's body and about twenty feet into the mega-linkage, where a full-size spotted hyena stands staring back at him. Two more hyenas perch beside this one, their mottled coats blending into the desert landscape.

"Robots?" whispers Jenka.

"No," says Lion, keeping his voice low. "They're real, too. Those are hyenas."

"Did you see another way out back there?" whispers Barry.

"No."

Jenka looks at Lion. "You will em-track our way out of this?"

"I don't know."

"Are you not ghost dog?"

"Hyenas aren't dogs," says Lion, his voice still hushed. "They're canine, feline, and a bunch of other stuff."

"Is right time for genetic lesson?"

Barry interrupts them. "We need another way out."

"There might be a door on the far side of the rabbit pen," Lion says quietly.

"I will check," murmurs Jenka, disappearing into the hall.

"Look out for snakes," Lion whisper-calls after him.

Barry gestures past the boxes. "Before I ran to get you, I checked the mega-linkage—there are more hyenas."

Lion raises an eyebrow.

"A lot more."

Lion stands up and walks around to the front of the bookshelf, takes a breath, and glances back at Barry. "Stay here."

"What are you going to do?"

"I've never met a hyena before."

"So?"

"So I thought I'd go to go introduce myself."

Then Lion walks into the mega-linkage.

THE SHARIJEE MENU

Lion walks toward the hyenas, thinking: Easy, brother, like Sunday morning.

The first animal tilts its head to watch. She's an adult female, standing waist-high and five feet long, like a dust-colored Rottweiler on steroids.

Lion stops walking about ten feet away, crouches down, and averts his gaze. Eye contact is a sign of aggression. Instead, he keeps his eyes pegged on the ground, extends a hand and holds still.

The hyena takes a step closer and sniffs the air.

Lion draws in a slow breath, trying to dial in the signal. The animal takes another step, then glances back at its friends and grunts softly.

Not good, thinks Lion.

Hyenas live in clans that number into the eighties. They have complicated dominance hierarchies and strict rule enforcement. Despite their scavenger reputation, they're smart, social animals and skilled pack hunters, more than capable of using vocal signals to coordinate behavior and take down big game. This is also why, when the largest hyena steps closer to Lion, the other two slip quietly around his flank.

And not just his flank.

Lion hears grunting behind him.

Slowly turning his head, he sees three more hyenas standing about twenty feet away. Two are spotted adults, one a striped teenager. They're perched atop a cliff, watching him with considerable interest.

The hyena closest to Lion moves in closer, her jaws nearly touching his right ear.

"Hey there," he says, his voice friendly.

She leans in closer, barely pressing her nose against his neck.

Moving very slowly, Lion returns the gesture, reaching out a hand to lightly scratch her beneath the chin.

She freezes, then yips twice, and pulls back from his neck.

From his left, two more hyenas approach, stopping about five feet away.

Are they waiting for a signal?

Lion knows that coyotes will sometimes seduce their prey with kindness before coming in for the kill. Is the same true for hyenas?

He glances around, realizing the animals now have him surrounded.

Lifting his gaze to the cliff, Lion sees that the three hyenas perched up there have all raised their hackles.

Not good, he thinks again.

When animals raise their hackles, it's both an attempt to make themselves appear larger and a clear signal of bad intentions. The three on that outcropping—yeah, thinks Lion, message received.

He glances back at the hyena closest to him, then sights Jenka in his peripheral vision, edging into the room. Jenka's traded his PHASR pistol for the PHASR rifle and is aiming at the hyena closest to Lion.

Lion catches Jenka's gaze, shakes his head, and decides to make a move. He reaches out and gives the animal another scratch under the jaw, then runs his hand from chin to belly and belly to leg, gently taking hold of the hyena's foot and tugging it toward him. This is dog talk, a canid gesture of playful dominance, meant to break the ice and help establish Lion's place in the clan.

Will it work with hyenas?

He isn't sure. But he's outnumbered and needs fast pack acceptance by a ranking member.

The hyena gives him a look.

Lion wonders if he's made a terrible mistake.

But then she grins and lets him slide out her paw, allowing herself to be pulled down until her chest rests on the ground and her haunches are up in the air. Then she yips again, rolls onto her back, and exposes her belly.

Lion gives her a two-handed scratch. The other two hyenas close the gap between them. One stops to sniff his leg. The other digs its head into the ground near his feet, flops over, and rolls around in the dirt.

"They are like dogs," says Jenka from his left.

Lion's eyes pop when he realizes that both Barry and Jenka have walked back into the mega-linkage and are now ten feet away, on the other side of the spruce.

"Stop walking," he says, keeping his voice friendly. "Crouch down and look away. Do it now, do it slowly. Take off your goggles and glasses, both of you, they need to see your eyes. Do it now."

Barry and Jenka freeze, realizing their error.

But before either can move, three hyenas trot out of the bush and head directly for them, curious expressions on their faces. One stops to sniff Barry. The other two press their snouts into Jenka's legs.

Jenka leans over, rubs one on the head, and glances at Lion. "Em-tracking," he says, "not so hard."

"Are they habituated to humans?" asks Barry.

"No," says Lion, pointing at the three hyenas on the cliff—all with their hackles still raised. "That's wariness. I'm pretty sure they've never been around people."

"Then what?" asks Barry, now scratching a spotted hyena behind the ears.

"I think they've been genetically modified," says Lion.

"Modified how?" asks Jenka.

Lion stands up and glances around. He finds what he's hunting about fifty feet away, then points in that direction. "I don't think they're carnivores anymore."

Jenka and Barry spin around to look.

"Son of bitch," says Jenka.

There's a long trough lining the wall of the mega-linkage. It appears to be filled with the same food that was in the large white boxes: an array of dried vegetables and something brown and crumbly, maybe some kind of artificial protein. It must be delicious. Three adult hyenas and five full-size jackrabbits stand side by side at the trough, peacefully sharing a meal.

"It is a blessing," says Barry.

Lion says nothing. He can't stop staring.

A moment later, the section of holo-screen above the food trough quivers, then starts to bow. Lion blinks, thinking there must be a glitch in the hologram. An instant after that, the entire wall explodes inward, blasting chunks of concrete in every direction. Dust and debris fill the air. A ragged seven-foot hole appears above the food trough, flames licking its edges, like skinny candles visible through the dense haze.

Two human bodies sail through the hole, passing through Lion's line of sight like a comet, before crashing into the shrubbery. Their impact kicks up another dust cloud and makes seeing anything else just about impossible.

But Lion can hear just fine. And he hears the wet thunk of punches landing.

Then the dust starts to clear. A woman pops to her feet in front of him. Some kind of poly-tribe apparition. Balinese bone structure, Lebanese skin tone, wearing a short black dress and a familiar platinum blond wig.

A moment later, a large Polynesian man in a dark blue uniform jumps up beside her. The woman clucks her tongue, shakes her head, then snaps out her right fist. She smashes the man in the nose, sending him straight back to the ground in another cloud of dust.

"Bondage," says the woman, straightening her dress and looking over at Lion, "is not on the Sharijee menu."

Before anyone else can move, the mega-linkage erupts into chaos. Animals leap into flight. Rabbits bound across the desert in waves. The hyena that Lion befriended jumps to her feet, knocks him sideways, and disappears into the brush. Another sails past his head, just a flash of fur in a cloud of dust.

Suddenly there's a rising tide of hoots, grunts, and growls. It's a giggle chorus—the alarm call that hyenas make when attacked.

None of these animals, Lion realizes, have been exposed to violence before.

And the show's not over.

An instant later, two men career through the hole in the wall. They're both big, maybe Polynesian, with tribal tattoos and dark blue uniforms. One clutches a stun baton. The other wields advanced alien technology, like a French horn turned into a space gun.

To Lion's left, Barry and Jenka sprint into sight, heading toward their new attackers, weapons drawn. Barry fires his Desert Eagle into the ceiling. It's a warning shot that booms like a cymbal crash.

Tracking the noise, Space Gun spins toward Barry, trips over a rock, and tomahawks down the slope, smashing into a thicket of desert sage not far from Lion.

Stun Baton is the more agile of the pair. He hears the shot and dives forward, clearing ten feet of hillside, then tucking, rolling, and popping upright with Sharijee in striking range.

Before Lion can shout a warning, a rifle cracks and a tranquilizer dart strikes Stun Baton in the neck. He grabs the dart, yanks it out, looks at it, looks at Lion, then crumbles to the ground.

Whirling in the other direction, Lion hunts for the dart's shooter. He finds nothing but dust clouds and flames, then notices Ji, crouched in the dirt beside the hole, sighting down the scope of a tranquilizer rifle.

Ji's aiming at something right behind Lion.

Twirling back around, Lion finds Space Gun back on his feet and aiming his weapon at him. The man's not Polynesian, maybe Mongolian, with a wispy goatee, silver hoop earrings, and a scowl so menacing it looks rehearsed.

A curious question pops into Lion's mind: What does a gun shaped like a French horn actually shoot?

He never does find out.

Sharijee strides into view, about eight feet to his right and four feet from his attacker. Closing the gap with two quick steps, she snaps her foot out like a Thai kickboxer, striking the man in the inner thigh and smashing his sciatic nerve. The longest and widest nerve in the body, a direct hit induces stabbing pain and temporary paralysis of the leg. Sharijee uses this frozen moment to finish the job, following her kick with an uppercut to the jaw.

The man twirls to the ground like a wounded ballerina, clutching his thigh. The space gun skitters into the bushes.

Sharijee glances at Lion. "I've always wanted to be a dentist."

"What?"

"Don't get me wrong," she continues, shaking a pebble out of her shoe. "I like the glamour of my current occupation; but what's nicer than a nice smile? It says 'hello' in every language."

Gunfire blasts from the other side of the hole.

Sharijee and Lion look over to see Kali and Shiva sail through the opening, nines in hand. Mid-flight, Kali twists her body to aim back through the hole, firing twice.

As her sister fires backward, Shiva rotates sideways and fires forward. The bullet screams by Lion's ear. As he whips his head around to figure out who Shiva was shooting at, Lion feels a forearm wrap around his neck, closing off his windpipe.

He's yanked backward, feet kicking the air, attempting to find purchase. Grabbing for the arm, Lion tries to loosen the attacker's grip on his throat.

When that fails, he tries again.

And again.

Running out of oxygen and running out of options, Lion confronts another curious thought: the death punch. He feels the flex-steel rings wrapping the fingers of his hand.

Lion snaps left, hooking his fist around his body, trying to strike his attacker in the ribs.

His first attempt is a miss.

The second punch catches his attacker square. The electrified pistons smash outward, cracking ballistic steel into bone as the Taser shock sends fifty thousand volts of don't-fuck-with-me coursing through his flesh.

Contortions wrack the man's body, breaking the choke hold.

Ripping the arm away, Lion rolls free and kicks backward, smashing his boot heel into the man's chest and bouncing him over the lip of a steep arroyo.

Lion flops onto his hands and knees, coughing violently. His chest heaves for air. There's a ragged cut on his left arm, and his neck is starting to swell. But there's no time to lick these wounds as the pop-pop-pop of an automatic weapon erupts over his head.

Lion dives behind a boulder. To his right, cymbals crash—Barry firing his Desert Eagle once again.

Peeking over the rocks, Lion notices Penelope in the distance, leading a ragged line of ten people across a faraway ridge.

The prisoners?

There's an old Chinese man that could be Ji's father, a teenage girl that could be Maria Natalovich, and Penelope, his on-again, off-again girlfriend, urging them onward.

A moment later, Lion understands why.

A heavyset white woman barrels through the hole. She looks like an enforcer for a roller derby squad, a punk fever dream crossed with German special forces proficiency. She wears the same blue uniform as the other guards, but her sleeves are rolled up in thick cuffs, revealing heavily tattooed flesh below. Her shirt is unbuttoned, tied in a waist-knot above a wife-beater tank top; her hair is short, spiky, and dyed white; her meaty hands, with TANK GIRL tattooed across the knuckles, wrap around a thick black tube that she wields like a baseball bat.

But it's not a baseball bat.

It's a rocket launcher—exactly like the one that Five Spikes used to destroy the space colony.

Tank Girl gets four steps into the mega-linkage and spots Ji, crouched to her left.

"Behind you!" screams Lion.

But before Ji can spin around to look, the woman swings the rocket launcher at his head. The tube strikes him below the ear with a hard thwack.

Ji sprawls unconscious into the dirt.

Tank Girl completes the swing, whipping the weapon up to her shoulder. Taking a second to locate Penelope and the prisoners, she sights down the range finder and prepares to fire.

"Fuck this," says Lion.

He lifts up his right fist and points his glow glove toward the woman. Squeezing his eyes shut, he punches the trigger.

Four white stars supernova across his knuckles—it's like someone blew up the sun.

Somehow the woman still manages to get off a shot.

There's a supersonic whoosh and a gigantic explosion. Rocks, dirt, shrubs, and screams fill the air. Chunks of concrete wall rain down. Lion covers his head, feeling pebbles pelt his back. The prism lens of a holo-projector smashes into the sand to his left, still smoking.

When he uncovers his head, Lion's ears are ringing and there are billowing clouds of color everywhere he looks. Then his vision starts to clear and the clouds condense into shapes, the shapes into scenery.

Tank Girl's shot went wide—that's the first thing Lion notices.

Penelope and the prisoners are still on the ridge, clutching their eyes.

About fifty feet beyond them, on the far side of the room, there's another burning hole. Crumbling concrete, jutting rebar, and on the other side of the opening, the brilliant green canopy of a tropical jungle.

"Thou shalt not move a goddamn muscle," shouts Barry.

Lion whirls around to see something out of a Hasidic Western. With yarmulke askew, beard coated in dirt and blood streaking his cheek, Barry stands between a pair of cacti, wearing mirrored shades and pointing his Desert Eagle at the woman who fired the rocket launcher.

Jenka stands behind him, protected from the blast by his goggles, his PHASR aimed at a pair of blinded attackers.

Kali and Shiva stand farther right. Kali looks like she's been shot in the leg. Shiva just looks pissed. Both have their nines aimed at the remaining guards.

And that's when Lion notices those same three hyenas, the ones with hackles raised and bad intentions. They're still perched on the cliff, standing dead-still on that bluff, high above the chaos. Every other animal has vanished from sight, but these three are still there, still focused on the mayhem below.

And Lion realizes: They like what they see.

GOBSHITE

G obshite," says Penelope. "Fucking gobshite."

Kali's shot in the thigh.

Shiva holds her up.

Sharijee ripped off the bottom of her dress and fashioned the fabric into a tourniquet, which she's now tightening into place on Kali's leg.

Kali winces but stays silent.

Penelope is about twenty feet away from them, armed and dangerous. Her left eye is black and swollen. Her right eye is watchful. The escaped prisoners stand beside her.

In the other direction, Ji is beyond repair. The side of his head is completely caved in. Probably dead before he hit the ground, and now a bloody, crumpled heap. The old Chinese man crouches beside him, sobbing quietly.

"Gobshite," says Penelope again. "Fucking gobshite."

Thanks to Jenka and Barry, all of their assaulters have duct tape wrapped around their mouths and feet, and hands bound behind their backs, synched in place with zip-tie cuffs. The woman who fired the rocket launcher squirms against her bonds. The men remain still and silent.

Lion gets his first good look at the hole in the far side of the mega-linkage.

The jungle isn't a holo-illusion.

He sees a tall wall of massive green tropical trees, giant ferns, with vines hanging down. A pair of rainbow eucalyptus trees stands in the center of the opening, their bark streaked with oily reds, blues, and purples. Beyond them, Lion can make out the spiked fruit of a durian tree, like yellow porcupines dangling from branches.

But something feels off. Lion's life-detection machinery is sending out a signal.

Then it clicks. He'd expected stillness. He tracks motion. There's something alive in that jungle.

He jogs across the desert, scrambling up a series of stacked boulders to get a better view. With the added height, Lion realizes the lush green tropical paradise is more like a Hollywood movie set of a lush green tropical paradise. It ends about thirty feet behind the durian tree, the foliage replaced by a dirty warehouse: concrete floors, drilling equipment strewn around, and an old pickup with potted plants on its bed. Beyond the truck, tall iron girders support a not-yet-completed back wall, half plastered, a large hole in the center, and an old subway tunnel visible beyond.

Then Lion sees more movement: a green slither on a vine. A familiar green slither.

"Killer flying tree snakes!" he shouts, pointing at the hole.

Everybody turns in that direction, just in time to see the snake leap off the vine, flatten itself into a foil, and sail into the mega-linkage.

"Snakes," says Sharijee, "are not on the Sharijee menu."

"Bloody hell," snarls Penelope.

"Let's move," says Shiva.

Penelope nods in agreement, tells Jenka and Barry to be careful, and kisses Lion goodbye. She takes point, PHASR ready, leading the prisoners into the desert, heading in the direction of the door that leads into Plumbing IV. Shiva and Sharijee walk behind her, supporting Kali between them. Trailing them are the ten rescued prisoners: the old man, Ji's father, escorted by a teenage girl, Maria Natalovich, three frightened teenage boys, and five older science types, three women, two men, all of whom look skinny and disoriented.

"We are this way," says Jenka, even before Penelope and company are out of sight. He points toward the laboratory. "There is door in back of rabbit pen that leads to maintenance corridor. According to Balthazar, entrance to podcast studio is at other end."

"When did you talk to Balthazar?" asks Lion. His earbud hasn't buzzed since they got into the mega-linkage. More shielding, he'd assumed.

"Beyond pen, there is signal."

"Zee's going to know we're coming," says Lion.

"We only have to distract them long enough for Penelope to make it to the elevator," says Barry.

"Might not be problem," says Jenka. "Two days ago, I examine Zee's supply orders. Ji gave me codes. I find order for noise-canceling wall panels. Very high-end. Made for professional podcasters."

"The recording studio is soundproofed?" asks Lion.

"Dah."

"You think Zee is still delivering his Sunday address?"

"Is real possibility."

Barry takes three steps forward, bends down, and grabs Tank Girl's rocket launcher off the ground. Wrapping the strap across his chest, he slides the rocket launcher onto his back and says, "Let's go find out."

Lion points at the tied-up prisoners. "What about them?"

"They are science experiment," says Jenka.

"What experiment?" asks Barry.

"Is burning question," replies Jenka. "Do killer flying tree snakes like taste of Mongolian beef?"

THE DANGERS OF LARGE CETACEANS

The maintenance corridor is a winding passageway that follows the outer edge of the mega-linkage. It looks like Plumbing IV, just without the plumbing: concrete floors, bare walls covered with drop cloths, and flickering overhead lights, like there's a short somewhere.

"Where are guards?" asks Jenka.

"Sunday," says Lion. "Ji said the place would be deserted."

Barry scans the corridor. "This is too deserted."

They trod on for another hundred feet, before the hallway turns left. Here the passageway narrows and the drop cloths are gone, revealing light gray walls so glossy smooth they look hand-polished. With the matching color of the concrete floors, the walls give Lion the feeling that he's passing through the gullet of some great gray beast, a "Jonah and the whale" situation, a story whose moral . . .

"What's the moral of Jonah and the whale?" asks Lion.

"Biblically," says Barry, "it's about the futility of trying to run away from destiny. The modern version adds in free will. Destiny becomes purpose. It's what the psychologist Abraham Maslow meant when he said, 'Whatever one can be, one must be.'"

Jenka shakes his head. "Is not story about dangers of large cetaceans?"

"I wanted a mission, and for my sins they gave me one," says Lion, quoting his friend Lorenzo quoting the movie *Apocalypse Now.*

"Exactly," says Barry.

Lion glances up and down the corridor. "Yup," he says, "I know that feeling."

very action hero

At the end of that corridor, they find a pair of closed doors, a black auto-mold handle in the center of each. Barry aims high. Jenka aims low. Lion grips the handle on the first door and whips it open.

Inside, there's a rectangular room with tools hanging from a pegboard on the far wall. Two large metal tables stand in the center. One table is bare; the other holds a robot polar bear. It's lying on its back, belly flayed open, revealing an array of circuit boards attached to artificial muscles.

"Is not Santa's workshop," says Jenka.

"Fucking dah," says Lion.

Shutting that door, they open the next one.

It's another jungle, bigger than the first, yet completely unfinished. Just a few rows of transplanted trees, tall ferns, and a large ventilation duct blowing hot air into the room. Behind the duct, the jungle ends in a dirt-floored warehouse housing only a parked boring machine, a giant white tube with an enormous drill bit at the end, similar to the one Lion saw back at PRML.

"I don't like it," says Jenka.

"Copy that," says Barry.

They continue down the hall. About twenty feet ahead, there's a hard right turn and the corridor disappears from sight.

"Around corner," says Jenka, tapping his earbud, "comms should work again."

They turn the corner. This hallway is larger than the first, maybe fifteen feet wide and a hundred feet long. The walls are smooth and gray; the floor is polished concrete.

Thirty feet down, Lion spots a dozen red lockers against one wall. Across from the lockers, on the other side of the hallway, three antique barbershop chairs stand in a line. They have red leather seats and chrome metal sides.

None are occupied.

Balthazar's voice crackles in their ears. "Satellite One, do you copy? This is the Mothership Connection. Repeat: This is the Mothership Connection."

But no one answers him.

Twenty feet beyond the barbershop chairs, they all see the reason this part of the mega-linkage is deserted.

After all, who needs guards when you have a robot polar bear?

The polar bear is sitting on his back haunches, facing away from them and peering down at something in his lap. But the sound of their footsteps catches his attention.

Slowly the bear turns his head to look at them.

"I have seen this movie before," whispers Jenka. He lifts up his PHASR pistol and prepares to fire.

"Wait," hisses Lion.

Before they left the mega-linkage, just in case he needed to use his glow glove again, Lion borrowed Kali's mirrored aviator shades. As quietly as he can, he slips them on.

"Is good look," whispers Jenka. "Very action hero."

Then Jenka fires.

The red beam of the PHASR blasts down the hall and smacks the bear in the face.

Nothing else happens.

The bear doesn't roar, doesn't freeze, and doesn't wander in aimless circles—which is what happened at PRML, the last time Jenka shot a bear.

"I don't think we've seen this movie before," whispers Lion.

"Must be upgrade," mutters Jenka, backing up. "Like Ji's eyes. Shielded against PHASR."

Just then a baby jackrabbit hops into view. It must have been sitting in the bear's lap, hidden behind his bulk. Now it plops onto the floor, wobbles slightly, tries to stomp its foot, and falls over with a whimper.

"You stunned a bunny?" asks Barry.

The bear reaches out a paw, laying it softly on the rabbit's side. Once, twice, on the third stroke, the whimper subsides.

Now the bear spins around to look squarely at Jenka, growls twice, and pops to his feet.

Barry unclips the rocket launcher's chest strap, lifts the tube to his shoulder, flips open the rangefinder, and sights down the scope.

"Wait," whispers Lion.

The bear is no longer looking at them. It's turned its head slightly to peer down an adjacent hallway.

Barry stands ready to fire.

Jenka stands ready to run.

Lion's picking up a different signal. He hears a thousand raindrops pelting a hollow pipe.

"What is that?" asks Jenka.

"Rain?" asks Barry.

"Not rain," says Lion. "Footsteps."

Just then the bear sits down on its haunches and lowers its chest to the ground, staring down that adjacent hallway. A baby rabbit hops into view, and a second one follows. They're three feet from the bear's nose, whiskers twitching. A third rabbit pops into sight, then a fourth, then a dozen.

Lion realizes that Jenka was the last one through the baby rabbit pen. "You released the rabbits?"

"I leave door open," says Jenka. "Stay. Go. Is free country."

Lion smiles.

Jenka shrugs. "No one should live in cage."

Gently the bear tries to tap one of the bunnies atop its head. The rabbit hops sideways, then jumps back to its original spot. Slowly extending its paw, the bear pushes the rabbit in the chest. It's just a tiny tap. The rabbit slides backward, stomps its paw on the ground, then jumps onto the back of the bear's paw.

"They are playing?" asks Jenka.

"Uh-huh," says Lion.

"Is robot, no?"

"Not right now it's not."

A moment later, they hear more rain. The sound grows louder, turning into a furious storm. Dozens of rabbits spill into the corridor in liquid waves of fur.

The bear looks right, looks left, then rolls onto his back, letting the rabbits swarm across his belly.

"It's now or never," says Lion.

Sliding his feet against the floor so he doesn't accidentally trample a rabbit, Lion starts down the hallway. Jenka and Barry mimic his gait. They glide past the barber chairs, now swarming with rabbits, and approach the bear. He's still on his back.

Lion and the bear exchange glances.

Then he glides down the hall, Jenka and Barry behind him, and all around them, a sea of baby rabbits.

LUNACY

Around the next corner, they find a medium-sized corridor ending in a black handshake door. Balthazar's voice crackles in their ear mics. "It's the same dap as last time."

Lion goes to work. He takes off his glow glove and executes the same complicated handshake required by the previous door. Knuckle tap, fist bump, dab to the left, dab to the right—Jenka keeps glancing behind them, making sure the bear is still focused on the bunnies.

Chest bump, back slide, and finally the door opens.

Barry aims high, Jenka aims low.

But there's nothing to shoot.

They see the empty lobby of an old movie palace. Walls papered in crushed blue velvet, ceiling inlaid with ornate gold flake, a twelve-candle Victorian chandelier dangling from the center. On one side of the room, a mahogany staircase descends to a lower level. On the other, a pair of thick, soundproofred saloon-style doors lead into the theater itself.

Lion slips inside the lobby, trailed by Jenka and Barry. Behind them, the door closes automatically.

Glancing back at Jenka, Lion points in the other direction, above the theater doors, at the red glow of an ON AIR sign.

Jenka nods, drops to one knee, and aims his PHASR about three feet below the sign.

Lion and Barry cross the room.

Barry sets up a few feet from the door, aiming his Desert Eagle head high.

Crouching down, Lion places his palm against the door, glances at his companions, then cracks it open. He sees a dark narrow corridor that leads to the upper deck of the movie palace.

Nodding at Jenka and Barry, Lion starts inside.

A few feet later, the movie screen comes into view. It shows a still image of the full moon against a pitch-black night sky.

Behind him, he hears Jenka and Barry creep into the theater.

Lion slides forward, keeping his back against a black velvet curtain that covers the left wall. To his right, there's a small balcony, like an oversized opera box. Ten rows of empty theater seats. But it's what's positioned among the seats that has Lion's attention.

A dozen cardboard cutouts have been carefully arranged throughout the upper deck of the theater. They're life-size black-and-white photographs of famed self-help gurus and major historical figures. They look like old movie props, or something you might see in a wax museum. There's an English triptych against a far wall: Margaret Thatcher, Winston Churchill, and Aleister Crowley. A few rows away, Confucius stands between Tony Robbins and Jack Canfield. Genghis Khan, Dale Carnegie, and Ronald Reagan have the back of the balcony. And the front row must be murderers' row: Mao, Stalin, Hitler, and Napoleon Hill.

Chang Zee's voice booms through the theater. "The full moon," says Zee, "it makes us crazy. Riots, looting, murder, werewolves—we have all heard the stories. But ask around, ask the right people, they're more than stories."

Lion turns toward the lobby but realizes Jenka and Barry are standing right behind him.

Jenka raises an eyebrow.

Barry shrugs.

"If you talk to cops," continues Zee, "the ER docs, the fire department, even the lonely old ladies who stare out their windows, they all see the same thing. The full moon brings it out. Lunacy, depravity, insanity, rape, murder, mayhem—the very worst our species has to offer."

On the screen, the full moon vanishes and Zee's face suddenly fills the theater. He's wearing a flowy white button-down, blue jeans, tribal jewelry, and a purple cashmere scarf. His hair is black, shaved on the sides, rising sideways from his forehead like a partially completed freeway ramp.

"But lunacy is a fairy tale," says Zee. "The full moon doesn't make us mad. Scientists have done studies. Violence does not go up during full moons. Arson, rape, murder, depravity of every variety—none of these things increase one iota. The only thing that increases during a full moon is illumination. We're not more insane than normal during full moons. We're this insane all the time. In the light of the full moon, we can see better. We simply notice more of our insanity."

Lion makes it to the edge of the balcony. He takes in the rest of the theater for the first time. Zee is standing at the front of the main stage. From the image on the screen, the camera must be set up in the middle rows of the first floor, in the center of the theater.

In person and on screen, Zee pauses to adjust his scarf, then stares back into the camera and continues: "Our species is an imperfect specimen, a flawed creature, perhaps, if you will, God's error. And the closer we look, the more illumination the moon provides."

Lion's left foot slips on something—a folded-up piece of paper.

He bends to pick it up, his handing breaking a nearly invisible laser beam. An instant later, an alarm starts to sound—a trio of piercing whoops, immediately followed by another trio.

Lion spins toward the door, but before he can take a step, a panel in the wall slides open and a machine gun mounted on a robot arm swings outward, its barrel pointed directly at the three of them.

A different panel near the rear of the theater's upper deck and very close to Ronald Reagan's head does the same. There's now a second machine gun aimed in their direction, pinning them down completely.

"Goddamn it," shouts Zee.

He stomps to the front of the stage, pounds his shoe on a foot pedal and keeps shouting: "Alex! Goddamn it to hell, Alex. The fucking alarm, again with the fucking alarm. I told you to get that polar bear under control, I will not tolerate these interruptions to my flow. . . ."

Suddenly Zee looks up into the balcony and spots Lion, Jenka, and Barry. He redirects his shout: "Who. The fuck. Are you?"

Dr. Neo Cortex, I Presume?

The lights snap on.

Lion sees the entire theater for the first time. The screen extends into a dimly lit backstage area, empty except for a stack of cardboard cutouts lying on their sides. More cutouts stand in the theater itself, evenly spaced between the seats. He can make out Deepak Chopra, Eckhart Tolle, and Pol Pot in the fourth row. Walt Disney and P. T. Barnum stand together in the fifth. Finally, the stage itself: a black box jutting out in front of the screen.

Stage left is empty.

Stage right is Chang Zee, standing beside a small table holding a glass of water and a toy gun—a hot pink revolver plastered with Hello Kitty stickers.

Jenka creeps up to the balcony. The robo-gun tracks him as he moves. He takes off his backpack, drops it by his feet, glances at the stage, slides his goggles onto his forehead, and says, "Dr. Neo Cortex, I presume."

"Shut up!" screams Zee. "Shut up! Shut. The fuck. Up. Who the fuck are you? I know who the fuck you are. Jenka, the dread Moldovan hacker. Very scary. And your sidekick, the famous em-tracker to the stars, Lion Zorn. La-di-da. Empathy for all? Empathy for pussies."

Jenka glances at Lion. "I think he knows who we are."

Grabbing the pink revolver, Zee shoots Deepak Chopra between the eyes, the cutout flying backward into the wall. Apparently not a toy gun.

"Empathy," snorts Zee, shooting Eckhart Tolle in the gut. "That's your solution?"

Jenka stretches down his left arm to unzip the main compartment of his backpack.

Zee notices and aims the gun at his forehead.

"Excuse me," says Lion, attempting to distract him. "But what the hell are you talking about?"

Zee lowers his gun and starts speaking in a voice so calm and soft it doesn't seem to belong to the same person. "We can't get out of our own way."

"What?" asks Lion.

"We can't get out of our own way," repeats Zee, this time speaking a little louder. "What haven't we tried? We tried religion, charity, compassion, empathy, empathy for all." He glances at Jenka. "You even tried to force Sietch Tabr on the masses. A lot of good that did. Humans First. Love your species. Humans first? Why? Why should humans ever be first? What madness is that?"

"The Suicide Girls," says Lion. "What madness was that?"

"Culling the weak," says Zee. "Those women were brainwashed by a fable. Like any god cares if you fuck. Rabbits fuck. Cows fuck.

Nearly everything fucks. But only humans care. Why? Because we're scared of the dark and we're scared of death. So we made up a story so we can sleep at night. These women kill themselves because of a fable about a fantasy about a god who cares that they fuck. Bye-bye. Thank you for erasing your stupidity from the gene pool."

"Keep him talking," whispers Jenka, slowly working his tablet computer out of his pack.

"Buddy," says Lion, "you are definitely a couple jalapeños shy of a taco. You know that, right?"

"Yes," says Zee. "Pathological narcissism with a heavy dose of on the spectrum and—ask anyone—advanced sociopathy. You think I'm a monster. I think you're right."

Barry slides up to the railing, a few feet away from Lion. He peers down at Zee, his Desert Eagle hidden behind his back.

Zee fires a bullet over Barry's head, then calmly looks back at Lion.

"But I ask you this: *Homo sapiens* has been around for 500,000 years, modern humans for 200,000, civilized humans for 15,000. In that time, we have colonized every continent, created language, poetry, art, science, technology, and Lady Gaga. We are the most dominant species in the history of the planet and yet, we permit a man like me to exist. How is that even possible? Why do we tolerate violence here in the twenty-first century? Why do we accept our own insane brutality as if it were an inescapable conclusion? You think I'm a monster, Lion Zorn, so why are you willing to live in a society that is willing to tolerate the likes of me?"

Jenka works his tablet up to the railing and whispers, "Keep him talking."

Barry nods slightly and starts to ask Zee a question. Before he can get two words out, Zee shouts, "Shut the fuck up!" and shoots him in the shoulder.

The bullet whirls Barry to the ground, his Desert Eagle dropping onto the floor near his feet. He groans and sits up, resting his back against the balcony, applying pressure to the wound, his jumpsuit stained with blood.

Lion says nothing.

Jenka taps away at his tablet.

"Better," says Zee. "Now, do you know why you tolerate me? It's a two-billion-year-old problem. Carnivore, from the Latin, *caro*, meaning 'flesh,' and *vorare*, meaning 'to devour.' An evolutionary novelty: a creature who exists solely on the flesh of others. With the psychology to match: aggression, domination, violence—traits buried so deep in our genes that not even the mighty sword of culture can sever that tie." He looks at Lion and smiles. "Did you like my snakes?"

"You hyper-optimized for aggression," says Lion, "but it didn't work. You overtaxed their biology. Accelerated decrepitude. Your snakes have a three-day lifespan."

"Yes," says Zee. "There have been setbacks. But that is how science goes. Yet there has been progress, too. Did you like my hyenas?"

"You bred down aggression," says Lion. "Again, what's the big deal?"

"So why do they live longer?" asks Zee. "Did you wonder? Clearly my snake foray was a failure." Whirling to his right, Zee shoots a third-row Einstein cutout in the face. "So yes, I severed certain relationships and recruited different talent."

"You killed Kristina. Didn't she build the snakes?"

Zee nods. "I run an agile company. We move fast and break things. What's the other option? Like Sir Richard and his vanity project—the Pacific Rim Mega-Linkage—will ever get it done. Turn back the clock. Preserve nature. This is nature we're talking about, red in tooth and claw. Like that'll work. Laughable. Do you know that the oldest brain with the same anatomical structure as the human brain belongs to the tiger salamander? Our brains evolved from the brains of tiger salamanders. Do you know why they call it a tiger salamander? Because it's the tiger of the amphibian world. The original hyper-carnivores. They'll kill everything and anything. Deadly efficient. That's us—our common ancestry, our genetic history, that's who we are and why we are who we are. Preserve nature? Why bother when you can upgrade it completely. But you didn't answer my question: Why do the hyenas live longer?"

"I give up."

"Because I wound the clock all the way back. I changed their genetic history. Instead of trying to get a carnivore to not act like a carnivore, I removed the possibility completely." Then he gazes sympathetically at Lion. "What, you thought my hyenas were nice to you because you're an em-tracker? They're nice because they don't know any better. And because I had the balls to upgrade the prehistoric technology stuck in their heads, they will never know any fucking better."

Lion flashes on the three hyenas standing on the cliff, the ones who were fascinated by the carnage, the ones with bad intentions. He wonders if they still don't know any fucking better.

A few seconds later he has his answer.

At first he registers only a tingle near his spine—his life recognition machinery recognizing something . . .

But what exactly?

Lion scans the stage. He doesn't see anything. Then he glances into the wings and finds a familiar face.

It's his hyena friend, now crouched behind the cutouts, glaring at Zee.

The animal's jaw is open and Lion notices her canine teeth are missing. Instead of sharp points, Lion sees the flat grinders prominent in herbivores. Zee wasn't lying—the hyena he's looking at is no longer a carnivore.

Motion in the wings catches his attention.

Lion sees three more hyenas, also familiar. They're the three from the cliff, the ones who liked the mayhem, the ones with the bad intentions. They're now moving into flanking positions, evenly spaced around Zee.

To his right, Barry seems to have gotten his Desert Eagle back in hand. He's looking at Jenka, waiting for some kind of signal. Jenka darts his eyes toward the robo-guns, then back at the tablet. His left finger hovers above the keyboard. He looks back at the guns, looks at the keys, and shakes his head no.

Then it clicks. Jenka has Zee's access codes. He's hacked the system and found a way to shut off the robo-guns. Now Lion understands the plan. Jenka's gonna turn off the guns, Barry's gonna shoot Zee in the face.

"No need," says Lion, nodding toward the hyenas in the wings. "Hit it, drop, and go."

"Shut the fuck up!" shouts Zee.

"Bruddah," says Lion, glancing back at Zee, "I wasn't talking to you."

Punching a button on his keyboard, Jenka deactivates the robo-guns. Before Zee gets a shot off, Lion and Jenka dive to the floor.

Bullets whiz over their heads.

Lion tucks, rolls, and sprints toward the door.

Jenka stops to help Barry, crouching low, staying out of sight and hopefully out of range of Zee's gun.

Zee shouts something else, but they can't hear his words. There's a thunder in the distance, a low growl, growing louder. As they burst through the theater's doors and into the lobby, the growl becomes a dark laughter, a fast whoop, the sound hyenas make before they attack. But the doors are completely soundproofed, so they swing back into place and choke off Zee's screams.

Lion glances over at Jenka. "Thanks, man. I had to get out of there. That dude was just droning on."

so dang cute

They leave Zee to the hyenas, backtracking past the empty barber chairs, finding the polar bear and baby rabbits nowhere in sight. They wind their way through glossy gray corridors, the mostly empty rabbit pen, and the four-doored hallway housing the robo-snake farms.

Lion pauses then, thinking about releasing the snakes, hating the idea of leaving them in cages. But he knows their plan is to get back to the hotel and call in the cops. Lion also knows a handful of people in the reptile rescue community—he can definitely put in that call as well.

They leave the hallway and arrive back in the laboratory beside the mega-linkage, where the blue spruce remains visible through the still-open door. Lion walks into the room, stepping around the metal bookshelf and stopping in the lab itself. He notices the empty projection screen again, the one that used to show slices of Ibrahim's brain.

Did the laptop get disconnected?

Lion shines his glow glove toward the workstation, but all he sees is a single FireWire cable sitting on the counter. Looking at Jenka, he says, "Did you take the laptop?"

"What laptop?"

"With the Evo research," says Lion. He points to the now-empty spot on the counter. "It was right there."

"No."

Lion spins in the other direction. "Barry?"

But the lab is empty.

"Have you seen Barry?" asks Lion

"He was right behind me," says Jenka, looking around.

Walking past the bookshelf, Lion pokes his head down the four-doored corridor. It's also empty.

"Did he go into the mega-linkage?" asks Lion, coming back into the lab.

Jenka shrugs and heads through the open door and into the desert. Lion follows him out. They pass the blue spruce and stop about thirty feet later, near the small rise where Lion and Sharijee made their stand.

But the mega-linkage is deserted.

Jenka says, "Where's Barry?"

Lion doesn't answer. He's not paying attention to Jenka anymore.

He's staring about ten feet to their left, where a solitary rabbit ear lies in a small pool of blood. The outer edge of the ear is ragged, like it had been torn from the rest of the rabbit's body by teeth not quite built for the job.

"We have to . . ." says Jenka.

"Carnivores," says Lion, pointing at the ear.

"What?"

"Zee changed the hyenas' nature, but we changed their nurture. That's a rabbit kill." He shakes his head sadly. "The fight we had in here exposed the hyenas to violence. We taught them how to be carnivores."

They hear footsteps behind them and whirl around to find Barry jogging into the mega-linkage, holding his shoulder and slightly out of breath.

"Sorry," he says. "I got caught up. There were two hyena cubs playing with a couple of baby rabbits—so dang cute—I just had to stop and watch."

BLOOD FOR MILES

They set off across the mega-linkage, keeping an eye out for snakes, armed guards, and sociopathic self-help gurus.

But there are no snakes. No guards. No gurus. Other than their quiet footfalls and Barry's labored breathing, there's not even much noise.

They shuffle through the landscape, lost in their own thoughts, putting this mighty underground desert in their rearview mirror and making it back to Plumbing IV without incident. The black handshake door has been disabled, the hand snapped at the wrist, now dangling at an awkward angle.

The door is wide open.

They exchange looks, slip through, and keep going.

With Lion's glow glove for illumination, they wind their way through a maze of dim corridors, passing long white pipes and oversized metallic ducts, arriving back at the elevator without any trouble.

Barry glances up at a camera and quotes Slipknot.

Nothing happens.

He tries again.

Still nothing.

Spinning toward the wall, Barry starts punching numbers into a keypad, but stops halfway through the code when he hears a polite ding. The elevator has arrived on its own.

The doors open; the car is empty.

Jenka shrugs, steps inside, and pushes the button for the street level. Lion and Barry follow.

As they rise, in the mirrored reflection visible on the metal panel that surrounds the elevator's buttons, Lion notices Barry has tucked his Desert Eagle out of sight. Jenka, meanwhile, has folded up his PHASR pistol and broken the rifle into parts, one a nondescript black pipe, the other a futuristic toilet plunger. Lion takes the hint, slips off his glow glove, and shoves it into his backpack.

But he holds on to the death punch—just in case.

Afterward, Lion glances back at the metal panel and notices Barry checking out his own reflection, trying to clean clumps of dirt out of his beard and brush dust from his clothes. Then Barry notices Lion watching him. He looks away quickly, trying for nonchalant.

Something about Barry's expression—was that guilt?

Lion forgets his question the moment the car stops and the doors open. They're greeted by a small horde of journalists, all armed with cameras and microphones, all surprised to find anyone in the elevator.

"Reporters?" asks Jenka.

"Marlin Perkins," says the man standing in front of Lion. "*New York Times.*"

"Excuse us," says Barry, trying to push through the throng.

No one moves.

One of the reporters starts to ask Barry a question, but before he can finish, Lion glances at Jenka and says, "You get the hyper-plunger, the turbo-suck vac, and the portable generator. I'll grab the rest of the tools." Then he spins toward Barry. "Rabbi, I am so sorry we had to pull you out of temple—we'll get the clog fixed and get out of your way." Lion glances at the reporters. "Big mess down in Plumbing IV."

"You're wearing a death punch," says Marlin, pointing at his left hand.

"Snakes in the subway," he says. "Just trying to be careful."

Jenka claps his hands twice. "Men at work. Make a hole."

The reporters step out of the way. Jenka, Barry, and Lion pass between them. On the other side of the scrum, Lion sees a dozen news drones hovering nearby, and a trio of autonomous broadcast vans parked down the block.

They head in the opposite direction.

Sirens start to wail as they reach the corner. Lion glances back and sees five police cars followed by three animal control vans speeding onto the street and toward the elevator.

"More reporters?" asks Barry.

"Plus cops and animal control," says Lion. "How'd they even know about the mega-linkage?"

"Carnivores," says Jenka. "They smell blood for miles."

Ain't Nothing Free

The story broke later that evening. The headlines were as expected: MAYHEM IN MEGA-LINKAGE BELOW MANHATTAN. KILLER SNAKES LOOSE IN SUBWAY. SELF-HELP GURU'S SECRET LAIR.

Before that happened, they'd split up.

Sir Richard made some calls. Then Kali and Shiva accompanied Sharijee and the rest of the escaped prisoners to a private flying car port in outer Brooklyn and on to a private hospital in Upstate New York, both far from nosy reporters. Balthazar sent a doctor over to the hotel to care for Barry, then took a much-needed vacation someplace tropical. Jenka, Lion, and Penelope joined Barry at the hotel, deciding to ride out the storm while hidden away in their penthouse suite.

They slept for a day. The next morning, Jenka commandeered the dining room table, setting up five computers and three screens. Since then he has been monitoring the feeds—police channels, news networks, social media, even dark web chat rooms—watching the fallout and deploying his considerable hacking skills to ensure their names stay out of the fuss.

Balthazar's doctor came and went. The bullet that caught Barry in his shoulder went straight through the muscle. It'll hurt like hell for a while and mobility might be an issue down the line, but Barry swallowed a couple of painkillers, washed them down with a couple shots of tequila, and had been on the holo-chat with Sir Richard since yesterday.

Earlier today, Lion was on his way to grab an apple out of the fridge when he overheard Barry and Sir Richard blathering about wire transfers, digital property rights, and seed capital priming before technological deployment of the blah-blah-blah.

Lion didn't think much of it. He left the fridge and went back to the master bedroom, where Penelope was waiting for him. All afternoon, they'd been hard at work, trying to hold down the king-size bed—some kind of problem with gravity, if they don't lie tangled in the center of the sheets—well, never mind, the physics are complicated.

Around dusk, Lion finally gets a few moments alone.

Penelope had gone out to pick up Chinese for dinner, needing to stretch her legs and get some fresh air. Before she left, Lion asked her a quick question about Sir Richard's finances.

"Everything he's got is invested in PRML," she said, giving him a look.

"Just trying to work something out. No biggie."

She gave him another look, then headed out the door.

Now Lion scans the room, spotting his backpack in a corner. He gets out of bed and crosses to the pack, digging out the dragon box and finding one final Ghost Trainwreck joint inside. Then Lion remembers the piece of paper he'd found in the theater. He'd shoved it into his pocket when Zee appeared.

Does he still have it?

He grabs his pants and finds the note. Unfolding the paper, he sees an advertisement for Pandora II. Literally, just the words *Pandora II* bolded across the top of the page and a few paragraphs of text. The text appears to be a quote from an author named Richard Manning.

Special as we humans are, we get no exemptions from the rules. All animals eat plants or eat animals that eat plants. This is the food chain, and pulling it is the unique ability of plants to turn sunlight into stored energy in the form of carbohydrates, the basic fuel for all animals. . . .

Scientists have a name for the total amount of plant mass created by Earth in a given year, the total budget for life. They call it the planet's "primary productivity." There have been two efforts to figure out how that productivity is spent, one by a group from Stanford University, the other an independent accounting by biologist Stuart Pimm. Both conclude that we humans, a single species among millions, consume 40 percent of the Earth's primary productivity, 40 percent of all there is. This simple number may explain why the current extinction rate is 1,000 times that which existed before human dominion of the planet. We [8] billion have simply stolen the food, the rich among us more than others.

Below these paragraphs are five more words printed in bold: *Pandora II—Because We Owe Them.*

Lion stares at the paper for a long time, then folds it up and slides it back into his pocket. He double-checks his other pocket to make sure he has the test tube with the Ghost Trainwreck joint, then leaves the bedroom, walks down the hall, and pokes his head into the holo-chat suite.

Barry glances over.

"Safety meeting on the bedroom balcony," says Lion, wiggling the test tube in his fingers. "Ghost Trainwreck #69." Then he notices Sir Richard on the holo-chat and smiles. "Hello, sport."

"Barry filled me in," says Sir Richard. "He told me about Zee's speech."

"Yeah," replies Lion, "I know."

"Zee wasn't wrong," continues Sir Richard. "It disturbs me to say this. Certainly, his methods were unsound, but his position on the human race and our propensity toward violence and mayhem—"

"I know," says Lion, cutting him off. "The friendly hyenas, the friendly robot polar bear, a functional mega-linkage—Zee was uncomfortably right about a lot of things."

"I wasn't finished. Zee was also a psychopathic killing machine who deserved to be fed to the hyenas."

"There is that," says Lion.

"It's never black-and-white," adds Barry.

"It never is," says Lion, glaring at Sir Richard. "Which is why I'm gonna go smoke this spliff and stare at the night sky. You folks take care. Em-tracker, out."

He leaves Barry and Sir Richard and heads onto the balcony. The cold air feels refreshing. Lion fires up the joint and checks out the view. He can see the black ribbon of the Hudson, and on the other side, another city, a million lights, like a blanket woven from fireflies.

Barry joins him three minutes later.

"Rabbi," says Lion, passing him the joint, "I need your counsel."

"What troubles you, my son?"

"A couple of things."

"Like?"

"Like what's the Jewish position on vanity?"

"Vanity?"

"Personal appearance, ego, that sort of thing."

Barry thinks for a moment, hits the joint, and thinks some more. "Why do you ask?"

"In the elevator, you were brushing dirt out of your beard and cleaning up your appearance."

"We were about to be back on the street."

"We were," says Lion. "Where there were a lot of reporters, a lot of cops, and a lot of animal control people all suddenly there—long before we had planned on calling them."

"God," says Barry. "He works in mysterious ways."

"And you vanished for a minute," says Lion. "Back before we got to the mega-linkage. That was also mysterious."

"You mean when I saw those baby rabbits playing with the hyena cubs?"

"Of course," says Lion. "Of course, the cubs. I also noticed you went missing in the part of Pandora where the comms worked. I'll bet that my JOBZ, with its satellite hookup, could have made a call from down there. You have a JOBZ, too, Barry, right? *The New York Times*—do you happen to know their number?"

"Why would I know that?"

"Forget that," says Lion. "Different question. What are the chances that sometime over the next few days, I'm going to hear about Sir Richard and a coalition of, say, environmentally-minded Jews purchasing the property rights to Pandora II?"

"That's a lot of underground real estate," says Barry. "It would be extremely expensive."

"Zee's been disgraced," says Lion. "Whoever called the reporters made sure of that. So his shareholders are gonna fire-sale everything and get the fuck out of Oz."

Barry puffs the joint, then passes it back. "What tipped you off?" he says eventually.

"Your sudden friendship with Sir Richard bothered Jenka, so it bothered me. In the elevator, you were cleaning yourself up and going for nonchalant, but you looked guilty. So why would you feel guilty about brushing dirt from your beard? Then I overheard you and Sir Richard talking wire transfers and digital property rights and my brain put it together. When does the story break?"

"Later this week," says Barry. "We'll leak it quietly. Sir Richard, who already has experience managing a mega-linkage, and a coalition of—let's call them—concerned citizens, have swooped in to save the day, etcetera."

"You also stole the laptop with the Evo research."

Barry stays silent.

"Sir Richard's sunk every penny he's got into PRML," continues Lion. "Rich as he is, even with whatever you bring to the table, Pandora's a metric fuck-ton of New York real estate. Gonna be pricey. That's why you stole the Evo research. A whole brain connectome map made from the brains of real em-trackers? The ability to track products into the future? You were right—it's a gold mine. And I'll bet you my lunch money, Sir Richard's already got a team of data nerds trying to turn it into real dollars."

"Keep your lunch money," says Barry.

"How long have you guys been planning this?"

"Sir Richard brought me in a week ago. How long has he been planning this? You'd have to ask him. But a mega-linkage under Manhattan. A place for plants and animals to have room to roam. An honest to G-dash-D American example of a better ecological future. Doesn't take an almost rabbi to know—these are not bad things."

"No," says Lion.

"Anyway," replies Barry, "I wouldn't know anything about it."

"I guess you wouldn't."

"But you're right, that Evo research, you could make some cold coin."

"Yup," agrees Lion. "Icy."

"Ain't nothing free in this world," says Barry. "That's what the Good Book teaches us."

"That's what the Good Book teaches us?"

"Nothing for free, Lion Zorn. Nothing. Not even empathy for all."

ACKNOWLEDGMENTS

Some deep gratitude is in order. My terrific wife, Joy Nicholson, and all my amazing furry friends at Rancho de Chihuahua—that's the real origin story of empathy-for-all. Thank you so much. I love you all. I always will.

I also need to thank a pair of fantastic editors: Michael Wharton and Peter Wolverton. Michael has worked with me for over twenty-five years, editing almost everything I've written. Once again, he was a tireless beast on this book. I truly appreciate all the heavy lifting, my friend, I couldn't have done it without you. I also need to thank another incredibly talented editor, Peter Wolverton, at St. Martin's, without whose guidance, wordcraft, and faith in my fiction skills, this novel would simply not exist. My agent, Paul Bresnick—this is the tenth book we've done together and wow, thanks for another amazing journey. Also, everybody at St. Martin's: you championed my fiction and have been wonderful to work with along the way! Thank you all.

Additionally, my dear friend, Vika Viktoria, alongside my amazing parents, Harvey and Norma Kotler, were all kind enough to give this book a few tough reads and to provide me with truly excellent notes—a deep thanks to all of you. An extra debt of gratitude is owed to my friend Chip Hopper—Chip really worked hard on this one, under impossible deadlines, and with considerable good cheer. Chip's insights and writing wisdom were invaluable, and very much appreciated!

Another deep thanks is owed to Dr. Andrew Hessel (who runs the Human Genome-Write Project that's referenced in this book). You're a good friend, and you've been exceptionally patient over the years while answering my endless array of synthetic biology questions. So many of the core ideas in this book would never have emerged without all those wonderful conversations.

Thank you to Dr. Michael Mannino, who is another close friend and a brilliant neuroscientist who helped me imagine a future for whole brain connectome mapping and the technologies that might be involved. It was also Michael Mannino who first told me about a talk given by legendary neuroscientist Walter Freeman, where he discusses the tiger salamander's brain and its unusual place in our shared evolutionary history.

I also need to thank my great friend and business partner, Rian Doris, who spent many long hours talking about the ideas in this book with me while managing to keep the Flow Research Collective thriving after I disappeared into the world of fiction—very much appreciated.

Thanks is also owed to Ryan Wickes. When I wasn't writing this book, I was trying to forget about writing this book by chasing Ryan through the mountains at ridiculously high speeds—which is what truly kept me sane along the way!

Antony Randall, Gabrielle Hull, Robert Suarez, and the rest of the Planet Home crew: Thank you for helping to carry the environmental ideas in this book into the world! The WhistlePig in this book—yeah, that one's Antony's fault. Appreciate the expensive bar tabs, my friend.

Another big debt is owed to my dear friend and occasional writing partner, Peter Diamandis, who has helped shape so much of my vision of the future—I see so much farther because of you, and deeply appreciate it!

I'd also like to thank the amazing science writer David Quammen. It was his outstanding book *The Song of the Dodo* that first introduced me to the writings of Michael Soulé and the concept of mega-linkages. If you're interested in any of the core ecological ideas in this novel,

David's book is a truly fantastic (and fun) place to start diving deeper. I also want to thank everyone at the Wildlands Network who worked so very hard to keep the idea of mega-linkages alive, and to help move the notion from the concept phase into actual protected ecoscapes on the ground.

Keep up the good fight—every species on Earth is pulling for you.